KAREN ROBARDS

THE MOSCOW
DECEPTION

HODDER

First published in Great Britain in 2018 by Hodder & Stoughton
An Hachette UK company

This paperback edition published in 2018

2

A CIP catalogue record for this title is available from the British Library

B format ISBN 9781473647411
eBook ISBN 9781473647381

Typeset in Bembo Std

Printed and bound in Great Britain by Clays Ltd, Elcograf S.p.A.

Hodder & Stoughton policy is to use papers that are natural, renewable
and recyclable products and made from wood grown in sustainable forests.
The logging and manufacturing processes are expected to conform
to the environmental regulations of the country of origin.

Hodder & Stoughton Ltd
Carmelite House
50 Victoria Embankment
London EC4Y 0DZ

www.hodder.co.uk

To Jack, Christopher and Peter,
who are why I get up in the morning.
With lots and lots of love.

THE MOSCOW
DECEPTION

1

You never see the bullet that takes you down.

Somebody Bianca St. Ives was pretty sure knew what he was talking about had once said that. It was the thought she couldn't get out of her head.

They were hunting her. Pulling out all the stops. Searching the globe. Along with what was arguably worse—searching the internet.

Sooner or later, they were going to find her.

They were stone-cold professionals. Seeker-finders. Assassins. Locating people and killing them was their job. And they were good at it. The best in the world.

Someday—most likely someday soon—a shot would be fired. Unless she was very, very lucky, she would die.

The thing was, Bianca wasn't a big believer in luck.

She was a big believer in preemptive strikes.

Which was why, at 7:58 p.m. on a cold, rainy Thursday in November, she was in Great Falls, Virginia, a swanky bedroom community not too many miles from DC, staring down the scope of a sniper rifle at a man's shadowy figure as she prepared to blow his brains out.

Here's looking at you, kid.

Cloaked by darkness, she lay flat on her stomach beneath the branches of a towering, too-fragrant blue spruce, settling the stock of the .300 Winchester Magnum bolt-action rifle into a more comfortable position against her shoulder. A tree root protruding through the muddy ground provided a natural support for the rifle's barrel, taking most of the weight of the weapon so that she didn't have to worry about muscle fatigue setting in in her arms. She was dressed all in black, from the military-issue balaclava that covered her head and most of her face to her gloves and combat boots. Her jacket and wristwatch were at least waterproof, which was a good thing considering the steady drizzle. The rest of her was already damp. And cold. The temperature was in the midthirties.

If shivering counted as exercise, she was the workout queen.

Through the Win Mag's magnifying scope, she carefully zeroed in on her target. When he was in DC, he was a creature of habit, and he habitually arrived home at 8:00 p.m. Right now he was in the backseat of the big black car rolling up the oak-lined driveway of a two-story, ten-thousand-square-foot brick mansion at twelve o'clock to her position on a small, wooded rise in the enormous front lawn of the property across the street. The mansion where he lived came equipped with multiple layers of protection, including motion-activated security lighting, real-time monitoring via surveillance cameras and a rotating quota of armed guards complete with large dogs patrolling the five-acre property.

The dogs, the guards and the surveillance cameras were all new additions, dating from approximately one week previously, shortly after the time the man in the backseat of the car had returned from his latest "advisory" trip to Europe. So was the bulletproof, bombproof car and the personal-protection officer sitting up front beside the driver.

Expecting trouble much? Bianca silently asked her target.

Was she the trouble he was expecting? She'd done her best to make him think she was dead. He was either a careful man, or he wasn't convinced of her death, or he had more enemies out there.

She was going with all three. But Reason Number Two was the biggie. It was why she was lying beneath the tree.

Over the last few days, her spiderweb of connections on the dark web had started whispering of an all-out man (woman?) hunt raging across Europe. People she knew of and people she knew had been swept up, brought in, questioned. Disappeared.

Who were they hunting? No one seemed to be sure. But the entire shadowy community of criminals and their connections, of which she was a part, was taking precautions. They were running, hiding, scuttling away like startled crabs into their hidey-holes until the coast was clear.

Bianca had a bad feeling that the heat wouldn't die down until the target of the hunt was found and neutralized.

She had an even worse feeling that said target was her.

Only she wasn't the scuttling-away type. She was the deal-with-your-problems type.

In the words of some long-ago Mafia boss, *If you want to kill a dog, you don't cut off the tail, you cut off the head.*

The man in the car was the head.

So here she was, getting ready to cut it off.

She had to give him credit for taking precautions. But they weren't going to be enough.

Sometimes you eat the bear, and sometimes the bear eats you: words to live by. Bianca knew what side of that equation she intended to be on.

Fixed in her crosshairs was Alexander Groton, recently retired head of the Defense Advanced Research Projects Agency—DARPA—and current sub rosa "consultant" for the CIA. He was talking on the phone. She could just see his dark shape through the rear windshield as the car passed beneath the security lights, which blinked on one after the other and shone in through the tinted glass.

The last—and only—time they'd met face-to-face, he'd been holding a rifle on her, threatening her life. Because, among other reasons, he'd wanted her to come to work for him and the CIA, and she'd turned him down. Then she'd hurled herself off a cliff and fallen to her death.

Or not.

So she'd already done the flight thing. Now she was in fight mode: calm and centered, her emotions turned off, every sense she possessed focused on what she was there to do.

The morality of it, the ethics, the unnerving glimmer of a possibility that she might be opening herself up to some really bad karma or a long stint in a scary-hot place—she'd considered all that.

Killing him was the only way to keep herself and everyone she cared about safe. He was one of a handful of people who knew that she existed. He'd seen her, spoken to her, could physically identify her. She was as sure as it was possible to be that he was the one who'd set the hunt for her in motion. What he didn't know about her—yet—was her identity as Bianca St. Ives and anything about the life that went with it. With the vast resources he had at his disposal, she was very much afraid that it was only a matter of time until he found that out. And then the hunters would close in.

The only way she was ever going to get away from him was if she died.

Or killed him instead.

Through the obscuring glass, she watched the denser darkness that was Groton as he turned his head. He was directly behind the driver.

Her right index finger quivered with the effort it took to keep it away from the trigger. Her heart rate increased just enough to be noticeable. That, plus the shivering, was not good.

When you're on the job, block out everything except the job: it was one of the rules.

She did. Her heart rate came down. The shivering stopped. She really wanted to get this over with, but—

Her index finger relaxed.

Not. Quite. Yet.

Like the rest of the car, the rear windshield was bulletproof, although she could always send the bullet drilling through the metal flashing around the window, which was the protective cladding's weakest spot. Still, the angle wasn't the best. With the driver located directly in front of the target and a body-guard on board as well, there was a real potential for collateral damage.

Bottom line, she didn't have the shot she wanted. She would get only one chance at this. She meant to get it right.

Her life depended on it.

The balaclava had a flap specifically designed to accommodate a listening device, and the earwig she'd chosen to wear with it was state-of-the-art audio surveillance. She touched the button on her earwig, switching on its receiver. Primo spyware, it could wirelessly pick up sounds—including conversations—within a range of fifteen hundred yards with no need for a mic.

"...afraid I'm going to have to bow out of next Tuesday's lunch," Groton said into the phone.

Bianca made a small grimace of satisfaction as she recognized his voice with no possibility of mistake. She was using the earwig specifically to avoid such unfortunate occurrences as collateral damage, or just plain shooting the wrong man. It performed as expected, picking up Groton's voice as clearly as if she were right there in the car with him, rather than a thousand yards away burrowed into a carpet of soggy-cold pine needles with the wind shaking the branches overhead so that they creaked and groaned and the rain landing with a steady tap-tap all around. The house that belonged to the yard she was in—another oversize brick mansion—had lights on in three downstairs windows. She'd already ascertained that an elderly couple lived there alone. The lights came from their kitchen, where they had just finished their evening meal, and living room, where they were currently ensconced watching TV. They would be turned off at precisely nine o'clock when the couple headed upstairs to bed.

"I'm heading back to Oslo tomorrow."

Back to Oslo, hmm? Bianca had firsthand, personal knowledge that Groton was lying. She didn't know where he was planning to go, but she did know that he had just come from the near vicinity of Heiligenblut, Austria. At, what she'd discovered, after being kidnapped and taken there, was a CIA-controlled black site. Which was where, not quite two weeks ago now, Groton had tried to recruit and then, when she'd refused to work for him and his murderous cabal of covert operatives, kill her. Because, as it turned out, she was not the daughter of a world-class thief and con man with an eight-figure price on his head who had graced most-wanted lists all over the world for decades as she had been raised to believe. Instead, she was a genetically enhanced test-tube baby, the product of a highly classified Department of Defense experiment designed to create so-called super soldiers for the military. That experiment had gone horribly wrong and led to the murders of forty-seven of the forty-eight infants that had resulted, along with their gestational mothers.

She was the only survivor of what had been known as the Nomad Project.

She was Nomad 44.

Jump back, Harry Potter. Just call her the girl who lived.

Yeah, she was having trouble getting her head around it, too.

That was the other reason Groton and his minions wanted to kill her. The main reason. The facts were that the Nomad Project was unethical, illegal, unknown to Congress and had resulted in the murders of dozens of American citizens by government-sanctioned killers. The careers and possibly the freedom and even the lives of those who'd been in charge of the program were on the line if knowledge of its existence should ever get out. That was reason enough for them to want to wipe her and every trace of the program that had created her off the face of the earth.

Which she was 99.9 percent certain was what they were currently going all-out to do.

Big surprise, being the target of a CIA-sanctioned fatwa wasn't her idea of a rousing good time.

That whole super-soldier thing? Not her fault. Also, not who she was.

She liked clothes. She liked shoes. She liked makeup. She liked guys. In other words, she was a perfectly normal twenty-six-year-old, five-foot-six-inch, slender blonde with a pretty face and enough sex appeal to occasionally turn it to her advantage.

Who'd been trained in martial arts by skilled sensei, weapons and explosives by special-ops retirees, pickpocketing, theft and the art of the con by the top pros in the game—

Okay, so maybe Barbie's got a brand-new bag. It's not like she was the Terminator or anything.

She was basically just your average girl. Your average girl with an unconventional past. Your average girl with certain mad skills. That included the ability to kill a man with a sniper rifle in rainy, windy, less-than-optimal conditions at a distance of a thousand yards.

Boo-yah and all that.

The thing was, she wasn't really the kill-somebody-in-cold-blood type. She wasn't even the kill-somebody type.

She was, however, the didn't-want-to-be-killed-herself-or-captured-and-turned-into-a-murderous-lab-experiment type, so given the choices, here she was.

Kill or be killed: it was the oldest rule of all.

She knew which side of that equation she meant to be on, too.

"I'll call you when I get back and we'll set something up," Groton said into the phone. "Say hello to Molly for me." Disconnecting, he added to someone in the car, "Did you tell the pilot that it's wheels up at 9:00 a.m. tomorrow?"

"Yes, sir," came the reply. It was hard to be sure, but Bianca thought the speaker was the driver.

The car was now almost even with the house, which for all its grandeur did not have an attached garage. The vehicles were kept in a former carriage house out back that had been converted into a four-bay garage. Ordinarily, Groton would have parked in the reconfigured garage and walked into the house through a back door. Also ordinarily, Groton drove himself, and his security consisted of any personal weapons he might possess and a standard security alarm on the house.

Bianca got it: desperate times call for desperate measures. Right there with you, sir.

Under these particular desperate measures, Groton's car would stop sixty-two feet short of the garage. He would be hustled out of the car and into his house through a side door under the close protection of his bodyguard.

From the car door to the house door was a distance of approximately seventeen feet, including three ascending steps that led to a small stoop. The time required for Groton to cover that distance was twenty-one seconds. She'd timed it, just like she'd measured the distances involved and calculated the best angle for her shot, during her two dry runs.

The period of optimal exposure would be when Groton was on the steps, which weren't wide enough for two men to climb side by side.

That was her window.

She wasn't going to miss.

The light beside the side door of Groton's house came on, illuminating the area where he would exit the car.

A mistake on the part of whoever had flipped that switch,

Bianca thought, but not one that was going to make a difference. She would have taken—and would have made—the shot regardless of the lighting.

Groton said, "My wife will be coming with us in the morning, by the way. After you drop me at my plane, you're to take her to Dulles. She has a flight to Arizona."

"Yes, sir," the driver said. "You to Andrews, Mrs. Groton to Dulles."

"That's right."

Looking through the scope, Bianca honed in on the spot where she expected to pick up her target even as she registered that the wife was being taken out of the way. A good tactical move on Groton's part: it reduced his vulnerability, which family members always expanded.

Too bad that by morning the horse would already have left the barn.

The car pulled to a stop so that the rear driver's-side door was in near-perfect alignment with the door through which Groton would enter the house. The front passenger door opened. The bodyguard, a tall, fortyish man with a buzzed head and a small goatee, got out and came around the front of the car. He was holding an open umbrella with a solid, dark canopy in deference to the shimmery fall of rain. The bodyguard was a pro: it was there in his walk, in his body language, in the way his overcoat and suit jacket were left open to allow easy access to the weapon in his shoulder holster. Without missing a step, he visually scanned the surroundings for possible threats. Unfortunately for him and Groton, it was too dark and she was too far away for him to spot her.

Showtime. Bianca had trained with some of the best military snipers in the world. They favored the BRASS method of assuring precise shot placement. The acronym stood for breathe, relax, aim, stop/slack, squeeze. She instinctively began the sequence.

Breathe in.

Many snipers were taught to hold their breath when taking a shot. Bianca's instructors felt that this caused the body to struggle internally as it fought for air and thus interfered with optimal accuracy. Instead, she began to regulate her breathing so that when the time came she would be pulling the trigger in the two- to three-second interval between inhaling and exhaling.

Breathe out.

The house door opened and was held open by someone inside whom Bianca couldn't see.

"Let's go, sir," the bodyguard said as he opened the rear driver's-side door. Groton stepped out. He was a tall man, rangy in the dark overcoat he wore over his suit, moving easily despite his seventy-three years. Sheltering Groton with the umbrella in a way that blocked the top half of his head from Bianca's view, closing the car door with a backward sweep of his arm, the bodyguard stayed half a step behind him.

The umbrella was unexpected. She would have to make adjustments. Bianca caught herself holding her breath as she concentrated on finding her shot despite its presence.

Relax. Breathe in.

Groton and the bodyguard strode toward the house.

Bianca was still cold and wet, but she was no longer aware of either. The shivering had stopped. Her heartbeat was strong and steady. Her arm and neck muscles were loose, supple. Her trigger finger was relaxed. She briefly glanced into the nearby darkness to take the strain off her eyes, then squinted back down the scope.

Her senses sharpened, focused, while around her everything else seemed to slow down. The spicy fragrance of the wet spruce intensified. The patter of the falling rain became a drumbeat. The steady drizzle separated into individual, beautifully rendered teardrops. She became supremely conscious of the direction and strength of the gusting wind, of the play of light and shadow over the target area, of the distortion created by uncertain lighting and distance.

"Where's Mrs. Groton?" Groton called to whoever was holding open the house door.

"In the living room, sir." It was a woman's voice. A maid? Bianca couldn't be sure.

Still shielded by the umbrella, Groton reached the steps.

Breathe out. Aim.

Bianca aligned the target in the crosshairs. A body shot usually yielded the highest percentage of success, but a head shot was absolutely, positively lethal, and she couldn't afford anything less. A miss would be disastrous. If she had to shoot through the umbrella, she would. The silky fabric wouldn't deflect the bullet by so much as a hairbreadth.

Groton put a foot on the bottom step. The bodyguard was still behind him. As her target began to climb, the umbrella tilted back out of the way.

Groton's craggy features and thick gray hair were exposed. Yes. Bianca refined her aim, refusing to be distracted by the rain that caught in his hair and shone like diamonds in the light.

Stop/slack.

Her index finger touched the trigger at last, the lightest of contact to ensure that there was no slack in it. She felt its carefully calibrated resistance throughout her body. The only thing that was required now was for her finger to retract and the weapon would fire.

Groton was on the middle step.

Breathe in.

She had an unimpeded shot. All she had to do was pull the trigger.

Squee—

Thud. She was surprised by a sound that made her think

of a fist punching flesh. It came through her earwig and was actually the sound of a bullet finding its target, she discovered a split second later as blood exploded in a red geyser from the center of Groton's chest. The maid screamed. Grabbing for his weapon, the bodyguard lunged forward with an inarticulate cry. Groton's body dropped like a stone, then tumbled down the steps.

Bianca's heart leaped. Her finger dropped away from the trigger. Stunned, she lay unmoving, her eye still glued to the scope.

Groton had been shot.

But she hadn't pulled the trigger, hadn't fired her weapon, hadn't taken him out.

Which meant—

There was another shooter on the ground.

2

Panic wasn't something Bianca did.

Good thing, because her instinctive reaction felt a lot like panic.

Her heart slammed. Her breath caught. She was instantly wired from head to toe as an explosion of adrenaline hit her body systems.

Use it. Channel it. Make those physiological responses work for you.

Across the road, panic was the name of the game. The bodyguard dropped to a knee beside Groton, who was crumpled on his side at the bottom of the steps hemorrhaging blood, then leaped to his feet with weapon in hand to sweep defensive arcs in the direction from which the shot had come. The maid, a plump woman in a black uniform, flew down the steps. The driver burst out of the car. The security guards ran toward the scene, dogs on leashes running with them and barking wildly.

"Mr. Groton!"

"Call 911!"

"Let the dogs go!"

"Pick him up! Get him in the car!"

"—shouldn't move him!"

"Don't you understand what's happening? There's a live shooter out there! The car's armored! Get him in the fucking car!"

The dogs, released, ran around barking. The security guards

each grabbed one of Groton's limbs and carried him in an awkward running shuffle toward the back door of the car, which the driver ran ahead to open. The maid followed, lamenting loudly. Another woman appeared at the top of the steps. She was tall, thin, dark-haired, and wearing dark slacks and a light blue blouse.

"Alex! My God, what's happened? Alex!" She ran down the stairs and along the trail of blood toward the car.

The maid turned back toward her. "Oh, Mrs. Groton—"

Tearing her gaze away from the scene, Bianca snatched out the earwig, pocketed it, rolled to her feet and grabbed the rifle case, which she slung by its strap over her shoulder. The adrenaline burst resolved itself into laser-like focus, rapid, precise thinking, smooth, controlled movements—and an elevated pulse rate that pounded in her ears.

Could anybody say *holy freaking disaster*?

Oh, she could.

Ducking low to avoid the dripping branches, the heavy rifle at the ready, her every sense alert, she emerged from the shelter of the tree to warily scan her surroundings through the veil of rain that distorted everything. Rain soaked through her mask so that it felt clammy and cold against her skin, but she dared not remove it. She bent forward again in an attempt to protect her weapon. Across the road, the car that was once again carrying Groton backed at speed down the driveway. In the distance she could hear the high-pitched wail of approaching sirens.

Go, go, go.

It wouldn't be long before the area was cordoned off and the roads were blocked. The local police were just the first wave. The FBI would be on the scene soon, along with no telling what other alphabet agencies. Law enforcement would blanket the neighborhood. Helicopters would zoom overhead. Alexander Groton was an important man: every resource at the federal government's disposal would be brought in to aid in the search for the shooter.

Who, as it turned out in a surprise development, wasn't her.

It didn't matter. If she was arrested, no one would believe she was innocent. Even if they eventually did, she was still Nomad 44. Someone somewhere knew that, or would figure it out. Once she was in custody they would have her exactly where they wanted her. In all likelihood her survival would be measured in hours rather than days. She needed to get gone.

Except for the rectangles of light that spilled from the downstairs windows over part of a stone walkway and a section of low hedge, the two-plus-acre front lawn was as dark as the inside of a cave. That was good in that it helped conceal her and bad in that it helped conceal anyone else who might be in the vicinity, which was the part that made her want to jump out of her skin. Shadows lay everywhere. Small trees and topiaries and a damned garden statue all looked terrifyingly human at first glance. The sound of the rain was loud enough to mask any nearby movement.

Judging by the angle of the shot that had felled Groton, a shooter with a high-powered rifle was approximately sixty yards to her left, down by the road at the far western corner of the very property she was fleeing. Or at least, that's where he'd been when he'd taken the shot. By now he could be anywhere.

Like right in front of her. Or behind her. Or beside her. Or overhead, as in, in a tree or on a roof.

For all she knew, he had night-vision equipment and could see her. Had his weapon trained on her right that very moment.

Her skin crawled with the knowledge that a shot could come winging her way at any second.

You never see the bullet that takes you down…

The only thing to do was exactly what she was doing:

get the hell out of Dodge. Which she hoped and prayed the shooter was focused on doing, as well. After all, he couldn't be waiting around to take a shot at her, because he couldn't have known that she was going to be there, because nobody had known that she was going to be there, so taking her out couldn't have been part of his agenda.

All she had to worry about was him not being the type to say no to a happy accident if he stumbled across one.

Which getting the chance to take out Nomad 44 might be, if he was there as part of an effort to clean up the last messy remnants of the Nomad Project.

Back in that secret government gulag in Austria, she'd been given to understand that only a handful of people knew that Nomad 44 had ever existed. At least one—now two—of those were dead.

But that was then, this was now. She had no idea who might at this point be looking for her, gunning for her. A government assassin? A contract killer? A whole army of them? For all she knew, her picture and the various false identities they had for her might have been added to an international hit list.

If there was a price on her head, nobody looking to claim it would be too particular about why.

They didn't have to know that she was Nomad 44. They just had to know that someone was willing to pay the big bucks to whoever succeeded in killing her.

Bianca shivered and immediately attributed the reaction to the cold and the rain. Like panic, fear wasn't something she did.

Fear will get you killed faster than any bullet: it was one of her father's axioms. Wait, no, it was one of Mason Thayer's axioms. Turns out the man she'd always thought was her father, Richard St. Ives, was neither her father nor Richard St. Ives. Instead, he was a former CIA assassin named Mason Thayer who'd been sent to kill her and her gestational mother when her gestational mother had run away with her as an infant before whoever was in charge of terminating the Nomad Project had gotten around to killing them. Instead of doing what he'd been sent to do, Thayer had fallen in love with her mother, Issa, and hidden the two of them. When her mother was killed by another CIA assassin, Thayer fled with the surviving child (her) and changed their identities to Richard St. Ives and his daughter, Bianca. All of which Bianca had discovered at the same time as she'd made the acquaintance of Alexander Groton, which was the same time she'd found out that every government official who knew of her existence wanted her dead. Preferably yesterday.

Still, it was just as likely that Groton had been shot for a reason that had nothing to do with her.

Wasn't it?

There was no way to be sure. But the timing, she was afraid, spoke volumes.

And it wasn't saying anything good.

Staying low to the ground, her every nerve ending attuned to the possibility of danger, Bianca fled across the acres of well-kept lawn toward the woods at the northern edge of the property. The smell of the rain, the sound of it, the way it obscured her vision, put her nerves on edge because it interfered with the normal functioning of her senses. Such obstacles as a birdbath and a garden swing and a couple of benches loomed up out of the darkness without warning, making her heart bump even as she identified and skirted them. Her gaze swept her surroundings in a continuous back-and-forth motion. Her finger stayed poised above the Win Mag's trigger. In the direction she was heading, the ground was uneven and sloped away from the house. Her feet kept sliding on the wet grass. She tripped over a discarded hose and got slapped in the face by a branch and blundered into a flower bed, and blamed it all on the idea that the rain was affecting her depth perception. But no matter how much she tried to deny it, the truth was that she was rattled. Seriously rattled. As in, totally freaked out.

Deep in her bones, she was convinced that Groton's shooting had everything to do with the Nomad Project, which meant that it had everything to do with her. It also meant that the hunt for her was suddenly a whole lot closer to home than she'd thought.

To her enormous relief she encountered no one, and no other shots were fired.

As she slipped into the pitch blackness that was the woods, she spared a regretful thought for the tiny flashlight that she didn't now dare use, because using it would be the equivalent of painting a target on her back for anyone who might be close by. Once again, being obsessive about preparation was paying off—she'd memorized the route back to the dirt bike that she'd specially modified to accommodate tonight's need for stealth down to the exact number of steps it would take to get there. Looking out through the trees as she slipped beneath them, she saw half a dozen cop cars converging on the property across the road. Stroboscopic lights revolved in violent explosions of blue. The sirens' screams tore through the night.

In the house belonging to the old couple, more lights came on. They had clearly heard the sirens. Or maybe investigators were already knocking on their front door to question them about anything out of the ordinary they might have seen or heard.

Which would be nothing, at least nothing that related to her. She'd been careful as always, and the rain, which was coming down in buckets now, should obliterate even the smallest chance for them to have seen or heard anything, as well as any minute amounts of trace evidence that might have been left behind.

Every dark cloud...

Anyway, if the investigators were worth their salt, the bulk of the forensics would be concentrated sixty yards from where she'd lain beneath the tree to take the shot that she'd never gotten off.

Where the actual shooter had been.

The shooter whose next target might well be Bianca St. Ives.

A little more than eight hours later, Bianca pulled into the gated underground parking lot beneath the eight-story building in which she lived, in a top-floor three-bedroom condo, just outside Savannah's historic district. As the gate closed behind her silver Acura and she drove toward one of her two designated parking spots, she allowed herself to sag a little with relief.

At least the solid concrete walls meant she didn't have to worry any longer about getting shot by a sniper.

It was after 4:00 a.m. Her journey from Great Falls had involved the dirt bike, a stolen pickup and a lot of back roads until she'd retrieved her own car from where she'd left it in a one-time tobacco barn just outside of Fayetteville that she owned and had converted into a specially designed storage unit. Then, and only then, had she felt confident enough to hit the expressway. The journey had also involved an un-nerving degree of paranoia as she'd wondered if she'd been spotted, if she was being followed, if she was being targeted. She'd employed every trick she'd ever learned about throwing tails. She'd imagined every possible scenario, from a sniper's bullet blasting through her windshield to a team of opera-tives attempting to waylay her car and take her captive. That nothing like that had happened was good.

Didn't mean that it still couldn't. That it wouldn't.

Even now, at the end of her journey, she was wired and slightly wet and a whole lot worried. Along with keeping an eye out for anyone who might try to do her harm, she'd spent the drive speculating about the identity of the shooter. The most obvious candidate was her not-father, Mason Thayer, whose motivation for getting rid of Groton was at least as strong as hers. He had the advantage of having been a professional assassin along with the resources to get the job done and the ability to kill without remorse. She would have instantly fingered him as the gunman except for the fact that he'd been severely wounded on the same day that she'd escaped from Groton. That made it almost impossible for him to have fired that shot. She thought *almost*, because experience had taught her to never totally dismiss anything where he was concerned, and he had escaped, via helicopter. Once she eliminated him, however, the other possibilities were legion. She couldn't even begin to guess at all of them. By the time she got home, she was so fuzzy-headed from stress and exhaustion that she was no longer able to even try.

The only thing she wanted to do was take a hot shower, pull on some dry pajamas, crawl into bed and put the events of this nightmare of a night on hold until morning.

Under the circumstances she might have opted for a swig of NyQuil first just to settle her mind enough for sleep, but she had to be at work at 8:00 a.m. Yes, she was the boss, but she was never late, and the last thing she wanted to do was raise any questions in the minds of those who knew her about what she'd been up to the previous night to make her most uncharacteristically sleep in.

She imagined that by sunrise every newspaper, TV channel and internet source in the world would carry news of Groton's murder.

No connection here, folks.

Unless he'd somehow managed to follow her despite her

best efforts, the shooter couldn't know where she lived. He couldn't know of her life in Savannah or her identity as Bianca St. Ives.

If he did, she'd already be dead.

Unless she was somehow ranked below Groton on his hit list.

The possibility sent a chill down her spine.

It's not paranoia if they're really after you.

The lighting in the parking garage was dim and spectral. As she drove down the row of cars closest to the wall, it flickered a little, probably because of a sputtering fluorescent fixture. Under the circumstances, the effect was unnerving. A wary glance around told her that—duh, it was after 4:00 a.m.—the structure was deserted. The thought that someone—an assassin, a kidnapper—could be hiding among the parked cars made her tense up, had her hands tightening around the wheel.

Most of the spaces were filled. The space next to her empty one, which was her second space, was occupied by Evie's blue Volvo. Evie was Evangeline Talmadge, her best friend dating all the way back from their shared school days at the Swiss boarding school Le Rosey. They were as close as sisters, but it was a fundamentally unequal relationship. Bianca knew everything about Evie, her hopes, dreams, fears, family, all her secrets. Evie thought she knew everything about Bianca, but the Bianca she knew was her friend from Rosey, the maid of honor at her wedding, her buddy and shoulder to cry on and confidante. She did not know Bianca the international criminal, the fugitive, the super soldier. Evie had no idea *that* Bianca even existed, and Bianca never meant for her to find out.

Five months pregnant and in the process of divorcing her cheating dirtball of a husband, Evie was currently staying with Bianca. She was also working for Bianca's company, Guardian Consulting, the security firm Bianca had founded when she'd been setting up a bolt-hole to go to ground in between pulling thefts or cons or other illegal but lucrative jobs with her not-father. Earlier, Bianca had told Evie that she had a meeting with a client tonight that might run way late, but if Evie happened to be awake she would be worried—and curious. And Evie was never one to keep her worry, or her curiosity, to herself. Fortunately, pregnancy made Evie the human equivalent of a Snorlax, so Bianca was pretty confident that she didn't have to worry about Evie being awake and waiting for her.

Anyway, if she made it inside alive and in one piece, concocting a believable lie for an awake Evie would be a small price to pay.

Something—a sound, a movement spotted out of the corner of her eye—made Bianca sit bolt upright and look over her shoulder, with a suddenly accelerated pulse rate, just as she started to turn into her spot.

Quincy Pack burst into view, running down the aisle she'd just driven through toward her car, his arms and legs pumping a mile a minute, his eyes as round as hockey pucks, his mouth moving nonstop as words spilled from them that she couldn't quite hear.

Recognizing him, Bianca relaxed a little. Her foot eased up off the brake—she hadn't even realized that she'd hit it—and she continued to pull in. Quincy was the eleven-year-old son of the building's live-in super, Angela Pack. He was undersized for his age and wiry, with buzzed black hair and a thin face that was all sharp bones and big dark eyes. Tonight he was dressed in jeans and a gray hoodie, she saw when he reached her trunk and pounded on it and waved his arms at her like that was what he needed to do to flag her down. This would be in complete disregard of the fact that she was easing into a narrow spot with cars on either side of her and a concrete wall in front of her.

In other words, much as she might like to, she wasn't going anywhere.

Bianca frowned. If there wasn't an axiom saying that no one ever got good news at four in the morning, there should be. It belonged right up there with, *no good deed goes unpunished.*

Quincy now knew she was getting home at 4:00 a.m. He would see that she was most uncharacteristically (for Bianca St. Ives) dressed in a black turtleneck, black cargo pants and black combat boots, and that her shoulder length blond hair was pulled back into a tight bun. She cast a quick glance around the interior of the car. He might notice the empty foam coffee cup from the truck stop in South Carolina in the cup-holder between the seats. It had Dum Spiro Spero, the South Carolina state motto, scrawled across a map of that state. He might notice that she was damp around the edges, although it hadn't rained in Savannah for the last two weeks. He might notice that her coat, which was in the back seat, was water-proof and rain-spotted and too heavy for Savannah's current temperature. He might—

He was a kid. Kids didn't notice those things.

Kids were also usually asleep at this hour.

Crushing the telltale coffee cup with one hand, she shoved it into the small storage bin between the seats and closed the lid on it.

"Miz Guardian! You gotta help me!" Quincy had reached her door and was pulling on the handle even before Bianca turned the ignition off. He called her that because of the magnetic signs advertising Guardian Consulting that she usually kept affixed to the Acura's doors, because tax deductions were a wonderful thing. At the moment, however, the signs were in the trunk, along with the Win Mag and other assorted stuff she wanted to keep out of sight. "Quick! It's an emergency!"

Bianca might have been truly alarmed, if Quincy's last emergency hadn't involved a stolen Nintendo 2DS.

"Shouldn't you be in bed? Don't you have school tomorrow?" If Bianca sounded grumpy as she pushed the door open and got out to survey him with a frown, that would be because grumpy was how she felt. She'd helped Quincy out by recovering the game system a few weeks back, no big deal. Tonight, though, she really wasn't up to taking on the neighborhood bully on the kid's behalf. *I got ninety-nine problems but you ain't one*, was the response to his urgency that flitted through her head.

"Snake and his gang took Francisca! And Sage went after them! He's got my mom's gun!"

"What?" It was the gun part that grabbed Bianca's attention. Sage was Quincy's brother. At seventeen, he was the oldest of the three Pack boys, the middle one of whom was fifteen-year-old Trevor. Snake, aka Shawn Torres, was the previously mentioned eighteen-year-old, NFL-linebacker-size neighborhood bully she'd liberated the stolen Nintendo from. Bianca had no idea who Francisca was. She was really hoping that it wasn't going to be necessary for her to find out. "Your brother's got your mother's gun? Did you tell her?"

He shook his head violently. "She's not here. She's been working a couple of nights a week at some old folks' home because we need the extra money. Look, what you did before—that beat-down you laid on Snake—it was awesome. Word's all over the street that he got smacked around by some kind of ninja *pussy*, and the guys have been ragging on him like you wouldn't believe. That's because of *you*. You're *the pussy*. I won't tell nobody, but I know it was you. Please, you gotta help me save Sage. Snake and those guys are packing. They see Sage has a gun, they'll blow him away!"

"You've got to be—" Bianca broke off, because it was obvious from Quincy's agitation—he was dancing from foot to foot and practically hyperventilating—that he wasn't kidding, that he was, in fact, dead serious. Ordinarily she would have had a major problem with being called a pussy, but tonight it was pretty far down her list of things to give a damn about.

Besides, in this case she could kind of see where it might be coming from: when she'd retrieved the Nintendo from Snake, it had required a certain degree of forceful persuasion on her part to get him to cooperate—and at the time, to conceal her true identity, she'd been wearing a Hello Kitty costume. Obviously there'd been a witness, and in the garbled, telephone-game way of gossip everywhere at some point the ninja Kitty might well have become a ninja pussy. *Sigh.* Bottom line, what was the responsible thing to do here? "Okay. If your brother has a gun, we've got to call your mother. And we've got to call the police. And by the way, if you want to live a long and happy life, you should never, ever refer to a girl as a pussy. We don't like it."

"Sorry." He shot her a half-penitent, half-scared look.

As Bianca reached into her pocket for her phone, she remembered she hadn't taken it with her on her mission to murder Groton because cell phones were trackable and traceable. Also, a trackable and traceable cell phone left in a location where you were not provided something in the way of a cyber alibi. (As in, *I was home watching TV the whole time. You can check my phone. See?*) She did have a burner phone, acquired especially for the occasion in case of emergency because she believed in being prepared, but the last thing she intended to do was call Mrs. Pack and give her the bad news on it. Mrs. Pack would know who she was. Mrs. Pack would remember the call. The question of why she had called on a burner phone might never come up—but then again, it might. *Don't screw up the details*: it wasn't one of the rules, but it was important enough that it should be.

Grimacing, she held out her hand. "Give me your phone. We're going to call the police first, then your mother."

"No!" Alarm replaced Quincy's penitent expression. "We

can't call my mom because she didn't pay the cell phone bill and our service got cut off, so I don't even have my phone on me anyway. Besides, what could she do? She'll just get herself shot. And we can't call the police because—" Quincy hesitated. Bianca braced for the new shaft of bad news that she could feel was getting ready to come whizzing her way. "Francisca's illegal and Sage was selling weed and her and her family will get deported and Sage'll go to jail." He blurted that last part out in one long, run-on burst of words.

"Christ on a cracker." Bianca felt that stronger words were called for, but swearing in front of a kid just seemed wrong. Mentally, however, she gave herself full rein. Some people's bad days consisted of things like traffic tickets and burned dinners. Hers tended to be populated with assassins gone wild and stupid kids with guns. "Do you know where Sage is?"

"He was heading over to the Bloods' house because that's where Snake and them were taking Francisca." He crossed and uncrossed his arms, bounced up and down on his toes. "Will you help me?"

The smart thing to do here would be to walk away. After everything that had gone down tonight, she had too much at risk, too much to lose—like her life—if she got involved in something that attracted the notice of the wrong people.

Job Number One: stay the hell away from trouble until you can get things figured out.

His eyes begged her. "Please?"

She said, "You know where the Bloods' house is?"

Quincy nodded vigorously. "Yeah. Eastside. Over on—"

What was it Forrest Gump had said? Right, *stupid is as stupid does.*

So buy her a box of chocolates and call her Forrest.

She was about to do something really stupid.

She knew the Packs' circumstances. They were hard up for money and devoid of anything resembling power or influence. If things went south for them, they had nowhere to turn. Only this big-eyed kid had just turned to her.

"You can tell me on the way," Bianca interrupted. Opening her car door, she jerked a thumb at the passenger side. "Get in."

3

"You rock!"

Quincy fist-pumped, ran around the car and jumped in. By then Bianca was back in the driver's seat and had the car started up again.

She rocked, all right. As in, she had rocks in the head.

"Smells like a wet dog in here." His nose wrinkled as he looked around.

That would be me. Thanks for noticing.

"Put your seat belt on." She backed out. "So where's the Bloods' house?"

He put his seat belt on. "It's over on Bay Street, right by Hitch Village."

"Oh, goody."

Hitch Village was a public housing development in one of the most crime-ridden parts of town. It had been torn down in 2010 and rebuilt, but the new development was just as crime-ridden as the old one. The primary difference was that now all that crime was happening around upgraded kitchens and bathrooms.

"How long ago did Sage leave?" Bianca reached the street, looked both ways—one car farther down the street, but it was heading away from them, which meant that it probably didn't pose a threat—and pulled out. The combination of the soft glow of the historically correct, reproduction gaslights on the corners of the tree-lined square out front and the security lighting for the condo buildings and storefronts and restaurants that lined the street kept the encroaching darkness at bay. A sweeping glance found a homeless guy asleep on a bench in the square. No one else in sight, and the homeless guy didn't move as the Acura drove past, so she was pretty sure he wasn't an assassin in disguise. Farther away, the twenty-story Stillwell Towers and the slightly shorter Westin Savannah anchored the downtown skyline. The lit-up buildings were bright against the moonless night sky.

"Right before you got home. He was with Francisca in front of her house when those guys drove up and pulled her into their car. He had to run all the way back here and get his car and the gun before he could go after them. I tried to go with him, jumped in the car and everything, but he pushed me out. I was out there on the sidewalk when I saw you drive past." Quincy wrapped his arms around himself as if he were cold. Outside, it was a chilly 46 degrees, but the car was warm. Damp as she was and cold as most of the drive home had been, Bianca had had the heat cranked the whole way back to Savannah and it was still blowing strong, so she was guessing that cold wasn't what ailed Quincy. Nerves, more like. Hey, she could relate.

"Lucky." Bianca tried hard to keep her voice irony-free.

"Yeah, that's what I thought. Miz Guardian, no offense, but you drive like a girl. We got to catch up to Sage before he gets to Snake."

"You mean, like a *smart* girl? Because if I drive too fast, we'll get pulled over." Which wouldn't be so terrible, except for the whole calling-attention-to-herself thing. To say nothing of the a-traffic-ticket-is-a-searchable-record-that-she-was-out-and-about-at-4:00-a.m thing. Oh, yeah, and there was the little matter of the Win Mag and other tools of her sometimes trade in the trunk if a cop got particularly curious. They were concealed, but not impossible to find.

As if to underline the point, one of Savannah's finest rolled through a cross street in front of them. Bianca, who actually was driving too fast but not, she judged, fast enough to get stopped, had to fight the urge to hit the brakes, which was always a bad idea, because if you did that when they were looking, cops automatically assumed you had something to hide. Quincy tracked the patrol car with obvious alarm.

He said, "You maybe don't want to drive too fast."

"Oh, you think?"

The Acura bumped through the intersection without incident. They were deep in the east side now, heading toward the Savannah River. A few people—mostly hookers and drug dealers—hung out on street corners. Bars and pizza parlors and delis and hair salons, locked down for what was left of the night, crowded close to the sidewalks. Trash, graffiti and potholes became the norm. The buildings grew more rundown, and the vehicles parked in front of them grew older with every passing block.

If anyone was following them, he deserved the Tail of the Year Award. She hadn't spotted him, and she was good at things like that.

"So your brother's selling weed. Did he rip Snake and his friends off? Is that what this is about?" she asked.

Quincy shook his head. "They're mad 'cause he was selling in Bloods territory. Snake and them, they're Bloods. Only Bloods are allowed to sell weed on the east side, they say."

With its stately mansions and park-like squares and streets lined with Spanish-moss-festooned live oaks, Savannah was one of the most beautiful cities Bianca had ever seen. When she'd first started visiting, many years ago, she'd fallen under its spell. But since then she'd learned that beneath the history and the charm lay an ugly streak. Crime was a problem. Gangs—including the Bloods on the east side and the Crips on the west—were a part of that.

"Sage is a Crip?" she asked. It was darker now as they

reached Bay Street, which ran parallel to the river. Working streetlights were few and far between. A barge churned past, its lights catching on the boats tied up at the wharves farther along the shore. The river itself was as black as ink, so black that it was hard to tell where it ended and the sky began. Weeds grew waist-high along the rickety-looking chain-link fence that separated the street from a pair of graffiti-adorned, abandoned warehouses that stood close to the river. On the other side of the street were a few small houses and a row of identical two-story apartment buildings. The houses were dark. The apartment buildings had a couple of dim security lights on poles in their parking lots, which were overflowing because any number of people might live in a single unit. The next day must be trash day, because heaped-high cans were sitting out all up and down the street.

"Hang a right," Quincy directed, then as she obeyed answered her question. "He's not in a gang. He was just selling some weed on his own to make a little cash. Now Snake says he's got to give him all the money, and all the weed he has left, and tell him who sold him the weed, and maybe he'll let Francisca go. Only Sage can't tell them who his dealer is or the dude will kill him himself."

"Selling weed is wrong." Bianca's tone was stern. She was pretty sure that this was what people who dealt with kids would call a teachable moment, and she didn't for one second want Quincy to think that she was down with what his brother had done even if she was prepared to save that brother's ass. Just for good measure, and in case she hadn't been clear, she added, "Smoking it is wrong, too. You need to stay away from weed. From all drugs."

"I know." Quincy's quick agreement was gratifying. Could she trust it? Who knew? Not for the first time in her life, Bianca was glad she didn't have kids. "This isn't me, it's Sage. I'm smarter than that."

"Good." Her response felt anticlimactic. Giving up on the teachable moment concept, she followed up with the question she'd hoped it wasn't going to be necessary to ask. "Who's Francisca?"

"Sage's girlfriend."

"You said she was here illegally?"

Quincy nodded. "She came here from Mexico when she was ten with her mom and sister. Her mom works for a day care center. Her sister's a year younger than me."

"How old is Francisca?"

"Sixteen. She's real pretty." Quincy shot Bianca a look. "You think Snake and them'll hurt her?"

"I hope not." From her previous encounter with Snake, who'd called her a crazy bitch and ordered her to get out of his face before she'd surprised the hell out of him by putting him on the ground, Bianca wasn't so sure.

"There's Sage's car!" Quincy leaned forward, gripping the dashboard and pointing out into the darkness blanketing the street. "Look! And there's Sage!"

Sage's car, a junker Chevy Malibu, was haphazardly shoe-horned into a half-space in front of a fire hydrant, its back end jutting out of the line of vehicles parked along the street. Sage himself was pounding down the sidewalk past the last of the apartment buildings toward a section of shoebox-size one-story houses in tiny, weed-choked lots.

Brandishing a gun.

"Sage! Stop!" Quincy yelled to his brother. Since he yelled before he got the window rolled down, the shout's impact was mostly limited to inside the car.

Wincing at the sudden explosion of sound practically in her ear, Bianca said, "Shh! You want to let the whole street know he's here?"

Then she did Quincy one better: she stomped the gas so that the Acura shot past Sage, jerked the wheel as car and kid reached the driveway of the first house almost simultaneously, barreled in front of him and slammed on the brakes.

Thump. Sage hit the side of the car and bounced off. He windmilled backward before crashing onto the sidewalk on his ass.

"Sage!" Quincy had the window down now. "It's me!"

"Stay inside the car and *keep quiet*," Bianca barked at him as she slammed the car into park and jumped out. Forget not getting out in the open: she was going to do what she needed to do. Anyway, if somebody was following her around meaning to shoot her, it would have happened by now. She was almost sure. Sage took one look at her as she ran around the hood toward him and went scrambling after the gun, which had bounced from his grasp and lay some six feet away in the ankle-high grass.

"Oh, no. Not happening." Bianca pounced on the gun just as Sage dived for it. It was close, but she came up with it.

"Give it back! It's mine." He grabbed at the weapon as she snatched it out of his reach. It was an old Colt .45 revolver, she saw at a glance. Revolvers in general and this model in particular were about as accurate as an elephant shooting spitballs. Which was to say, it *might* hit the broadside of a barn. Or it might not.

"You mean, it's your mom's." She shoved it into her waistband at the small of her back. The twin beams of the Acura's headlights speared up through the open carport attached to the house at the top of the yard they were in. All the windows were dark. Bianca devoutly hoped that the residents were sound sleepers. "Believe me, it's the last thing you need."

"Who the hell are you?" Sage sprang to his feet. Facing her, he went into a half crouch with what appeared to be the clear intention of tackling her for the gun. Like Quincy, he was wearing jeans and a hoodie, although his hoodie was black. Also like Quincy, he was skinny with a face that was all bony angles and dark eyes topped with buzzed black hair. Unlike

Quincy, he was five-eight or so, and what meat there was on his bones looked like solid muscle. His expression said he'd sized her up, realized he was bigger than she was and was confident in his ability to physically wrest the gun away from her.

Nice that he was confident. Too bad that confidence was sadly misplaced.

"Somebody who's trying to keep you from getting your idiot self killed," Bianca said, at the same time as Quincy, now hanging head and shoulders out of the window, stage-whispered urgently, "It's Miz Guardian. From the building. She's gonna help us! She's *the pussy*!"

Bianca did a mental face-palm.

"What?" Sage's head swiveled toward Quincy, who nodded with so much enthusiasm that he almost fell out of the window. Sage gave her a quick once-over, his expression skeptical.

"No fucking way."

"Way, I swear," Quincy said.

"Get in the car," Bianca said to Sage. She wasn't quite talking through her teeth, but it was close. She was tired, she was on edge and she was not in the mood to put up with crap. Or with being saddled with a handle like *the pussy*. "*Now.* Or else I call the cops *and* your mother and call it a day."

"Bloods got my girl," Sage protested.

"She knows," Quincy said.

"You told her?" The look Sage shot his little brother boded ill for his future well-being. "What'd you tell her?"

"Everything," Bianca said before Quincy could reply. "And that would be because he's the smart Pack brother. You're in luck: I'm going to get your girlfriend back for you. Now get in the car before I decide I've got better things to do with my night."

"Give me back my gun and I'll get her myself," Sage said.

"You don't want to get in the car? Fine. No skin off my

teeth. But I'm making the phone calls. And I'm keeping the gun." Bianca started to walk back toward the driver's door.

"You can't keep it." He followed her.

"Watch me."

She sensed rather than saw him leap toward her. His obvious intent was to jerk the gun free of its place in her waistband. She whirled before he could reach her, caught his wrist while he was still in midair, gave a twist and sent him cartwheeling through space.

He landed on his back in the grass with a thud and a pained *oomph*, then lay there blinking bemusedly up at the night sky.

Quincy winced. "Oh man. I *told* you she's *the puss*—"

He faltered under the force of Bianca's basilisk stare.

"I mean g-g-guardian," Quincy finished, wide-eyed. "*Miz* Guardian."

"There you go," Bianca said approvingly. To Sage she said, "You want my help, get in the car. You don't, I'd be thinking up a good story for your mom and the cops."

She walked around the hood and got back behind the wheel. The gun dug into her spine. Removing the revolver, she tucked it into the pocket on her door where it would be out of sight—and reach—of a hotheaded kid.

"Sage, come on," Quincy urged as Bianca shifted into reverse.

"This is some bullshit," Sage replied, but a moment later he slid into the backseat.

"Good call." Bianca looked at him through the rearview mirror as the car rolled down the drive.

The look he gave her back was the opposite of warm and fuzzy.

Quincy said, "See? She can handle herself. And Snake."

"With a gun, anybody can handle anybody," Sage said.

"Guns are for show, brains are for pros," Bianca said as the Acura backed out into the street.

"What's that mean?"

"It means using a gun's dumb. Guns get people killed. People like you and your girlfriend." She shifted gears and drove in the direction Sage had been running. "Also, guns attract attention. You go in there and start shooting, they're going to shoot back. The cops are going to come. If your girlfriend's still in there and still alive at that point, which she probably won't be, the cops will rescue her, but they'll also take her into custody and find out that she's illegal, which is what you don't want to have happen. If you're still alive at that point, which you probably won't be, and still on the premises, they'll arrest you. If you run, they might not arrest you then, but they'll be looking for you. You'll be on their radar, which you don't want to be, especially if you're selling weed, which, by the way, is going to get you busted sooner or later. And if Snake or any of the other guys you shoot at in there are still alive, they'll be looking for you, too. Believe me, there's no good way this ends if you go in there with a gun."

"How you think you're gonna get Francisca out then? Them guys that got her are strapped up," Sage said.

That meant heavily armed, Bianca knew.

"In a situation like this, you use your brain. First, you set your goals. Your goals are, you want your girlfriend out safely and you want Snake and his buddies to leave you and her alone in the future. So you ask yourself, how do I accomplish that? Then you make a plan."

"So what's the plan?"

Bianca shrugged.

Sage scoffed. "You don't have one."

"She has one," Quincy said. "Don't you?"

Actually, no. But she would come up with one. Easy peasy. Probably.

"Like I said, Quincy's the smart one," she said. *Always tell the truth unless you can't*: it was one of the rules.

Quincy grinned. Sage made an inarticulate sound of disgust,

then said, "You know what? I don't have time for this shit. They told me I had one hour to bring them the dope I have left and the money I made selling it and the name of the guy who sold it to me. They said if I didn't show, nobody'd ever see Francisca again. But I already spent the money, and I can't give them the name of my dealer 'cause he'll kill me and my whole family if I do, and even if I gave them everything they asked for I don't trust them to keep their promise to let her go. So give me back my gun and let me do what I gotta do. I—"

"Hold it," Bianca interrupted. "How much time is left before the hour they gave you is up?"

"About fifteen minutes. Look, if I can get the drop on them I might can get Francisca—"

Bianca stopped listening. She was too busy casing the area. Maybe two dozen houses were crammed together in a space that should have held half that number before another row of apartment buildings took over. The sickly glow of a porch light at one house and a couple of lighted windows at another provided the only illumination. Cars were parked bumper-to-bumper all along the street. The headlights caught the gleaming eyes of a cat slinking toward a trio of garbage cans at the curb. Except for that, nothing stirred. It was, Bianca thought, a safe bet that most of the people inside the houses were asleep. It was an equally safe bet than any assassin that might be out looking for her wouldn't be looking here.

She felt some of the tension knotting her muscles ease.

Sage was still talking. She interrupted again: time to cut to the chase. "Which house is your girlfriend in?"

"That one there." Sage pointed to the one with the lighted windows, which made sense, because it was the only one that showed any indication that someone was awake inside. The one-story house was identical to all the others except for the maroon color of the vinyl siding. A small concrete slab leading to the front door served as a porch. Light shone through closed curtains covering the big, fifties-era plate-glass window that marked the living room. Light also showed through a second window, a small double-hung at the far end of the house closest to the apartment building next door. That window was covered by a pull-down shade and appeared to belong to a bedroom. The house was at the very end of the row, which was a good thing as far as ease of access was concerned.

Sage said, "See that Impala? That's Snake's car." He pressed his face close to the window as they approached, looking out at the house. A newer-model Impala was parked in the driveway behind a battered-looking ice-cream truck, of all things. A moment later his tone changed, went high-pitched with incredulity. "Hey! You just gonna drive on *past*?"

That was said, obviously, as Bianca drove on past.

"Sit tight." Just to be on the safe side she depressed the button that locked all the doors. The last thing she needed was for Sage to decide that now was the moment to try to be a hero, leap from the car and make some big commotion that would alert everyone in the vicinity, to say nothing of Snake and his gang, to their presence. "First thing to do is get the lay of the land."

"You locked my door!"

Equally indignant, Quincy said, "She locked mine, too!"

"Live with it," Bianca told them, and ignored the resultant curse from the backseat as she focused on the oddity of the ice-cream truck. "The Bloods are selling ice cream now?"

Sage snorted. "Yeah. Soft serve. Along with weed, hashish, blow, percs, whatever you want. That thing's a rolling drug store. I guarantee you it's kitted up, probably got machinery and everything."

Bianca understood that to mean that it probably had all kinds of drug paraphernalia and equipment inside.

"Oh, yeah?" She momentarily entertained the idea of stealing the truck and trading it back for Francisca. There were problems with that solution, however: (1) arranging and making the trade would take time, and time was not on their side; (2) Snake et al would know who did it, meaning she would draw unwanted notice to herself; and (3) it did nothing to get the thugs who'd kidnapped a sixteen-year-old girl off the street. Still, that truck might be something she could use—

"So you gonna do something or what?" Sage demanded, looking back as the house receded behind them.

"Depends. How many were in the car with Snake?" Bianca pulled into the parking lot of the apartment building next door, turned around and emerged onto the street again, heading back the way they had come. The good news was, in a neighborhood like this any security cameras that had ever been installed anywhere in the vicinity would have been destroyed long since, so nobody was taking her picture. The bad news was, short of Armageddon, the police weren't rushing down here. And if the plan that was beginning to take shape in her mind was going to work, she was going to need the police.

After all, she was just one lonely super soldier. And, keeping the now-urgent need to maintain a low profile in mind, she really didn't want people laying Snake et al's takedown at her door.

Sage said, "Two."

"Two plus Snake?"

"Yeah. Probably more in the house. That's their trap house. A lot of people coming and going most of the time. You can bet they don't leave it empty."

A trap house was one that nobody really lived in; it was primarily used to sell and store large quantities of drugs. Armed guards could be expected to be present.

Her night just kept getting more and more fun.

Sage finished up with a suspicious, "What'd you mean, *depends*?"

Bianca scrutinized the house as they passed it again. "On you doing what I tell you."

4

"What you tell—" Sage broke off to address a more immediate concern. "You're not stopping this time *either*? Francisca's in there, remember? I got—"

A glance in her rearview mirror told Bianca that he was looking at the dashboard clock.

"—twelve minutes to get her out," he said.

"I hear you."

"So *do* something." Sage rolled onto his knees on the back seat to stare out the rear windshield as the house was left behind once again.

"She's going to," Quincy said, defending her. He looked at Bianca. "Right?"

Sage's car was coming up on the left.

Bianca said, "Yes, I am, but both of you have to do something for me first."

"What?" Sage whipped around to scowl at her as Bianca braked beside his car.

"Go home," she said.

"What?"

"You don't want the Bloods to think you had anything to do with what's about to go down. Plus, I can't do what I need to do if I'm worried about you two getting caught in the middle of it. Either you go home, right now, or I take you home and call the police and let them deal with rescuing your girlfriend. Your choice."

"No!"

Quincy turned around in his seat to look at his brother. "We gotta do what she says."

"You stay out of this! What'd you go running to her for anyway? How'd you even know who she is?"

"I'm the reason she beat up Snake in the first place. She was helping *me*. You know if you go back there by yourself Snake and them are gonna kill you, right? Mom'll *cry*. And—I don't want you to get killed."

Bianca looked back to catch Sage's reaction to Quincy's words. Despite the glare he was directing at his little brother, she thought she could read a hint of uncertainty in the tension at the corners of his eyes and the thinning of his lips.

"I'll get your girlfriend out of there in one piece, I promise," she told Sage, her tone gentler than it had been until that moment. Call her a sucker for the whole sibling-bond thing, but their interaction touched her. "All you're doing here is eating up time. Go home, wait for me in the parking garage, and I'll bring her to you in twenty minutes tops. Okay?"

Sage looked at her with clear indecision.

"Ticktock," Bianca said.

Quincy said, "Sage, please let's go home. *Please*."

Bianca said, "You can trust me."

Sage's eyes held hers. He let out a breath. "*Shit*. Okay."

Quincy fist-pumped. "Yes!"

"You can just shut up," Sage told him. "This is all your fault."

"It is not! I'm saving the day!"

"You better hope so, you little—"

Bianca unlocked the doors. Sage and Quincy got out.

Quincy said something to Sage that Bianca missed. Sage punched him in the shoulder.

Ah, brotherly love.

"Straight home," Bianca ordered, rolling down a window.

"Twenty minutes," Sage retorted over his shoulder.

Bianca waited while the two got in Sage's car. Quincy gave her a little wave as the Malibu drove away.

According to the dashboard clock, ten minutes of Quincy's hour remained. She could make that work.

Now she had a plan.

She drove back to the trap house, pulled into the parking lot of the apartment building next door, parked as close to the house as possible, got out and opened the trunk. She'd already disabled both the interior light and the trunk light in honor of the night's earlier mission, so she didn't have to worry about them coming on and attracting attention, not that, as far as she could tell, there was anybody around whose attention she needed to not attract. Conversely, the disabling of the trunk light meant that she had only the dim halogen set in a distant corner of the parking lot to aid her in finding what she needed. Good thing she was organized: she knew exactly where everything was without really having to see it.

A place for everything and everything in its place: more words to live by.

Depressing the latch that unlocked the false bottom she'd had installed in the trunk by an under-the-radar body shop she occasionally worked with, she shifted the Guardian Consulting signs aside, lifted the carpet-covered floor and peered down at what lay beneath.

The Win Mag was secured in a special side unit. She wouldn't be needing it, or the gun she'd taken off Quincy. She wasn't bulletproof, she could get shot just like anybody else, but minus a stray sniper or two she wasn't worried: she had no intention of letting that happen. And since she had no intention of shooting the moronic teenage thugs in the house either, a gun would just get in her way.

What she took from the trunk was the balaclava, gloves, earwig and a custom tool kit, which was kept in a canvas messenger bag. She added a length of rope to the bag and was good to go. The only other thing she needed—a large rock or other heavy weight—she was going to have to scavenge.

Suiting up as she crossed the strip of overgrown grass that separated the parking lot from the house, leaping the trash-filled ditch that ran down the middle of it, Bianca was thankful for the darkness. Clad all in black, with the balaclava and gloves covering her blond hair and pale skin and the tool kit slung over her shoulder, she was just one more shadow among many. She *knew* a sniper couldn't have her in his sights because he couldn't have gotten here before her and thus wouldn't have had time to set up. And he couldn't have gotten here before her because no one could have known she would be here, because she hadn't known herself. And she was almost 100 percent positive that she hadn't been followed. Therefore, the creepy-crawly feeling at the back of her neck could only be the product of her own edginess.

So get over it.

This late at night, the whirring of the insect population accounted for most of the noise. A series of faint metallic clanks on top of that had her looking swiftly toward the sounds, but only the clumsiest assassin on earth would make that much noise so she attributed the clatter to the cat and the trash cans. The dank smell of the river mixed with the rotting-meat smell of what Bianca hoped was trash. She wrinkled her nose.

She pressed the button on the earwig. Through it, she could hear a girl—she assumed it was Francisca—sobbing even before she reached the lit-up double-hung window on the side of the house.

"—*hoy nuestro pan de cada dia. Perdona*—" The girl's voice was soft and punctuated with sobs. During the few seconds that it took Bianca to translate, realize that the girl was praying in Spanish and the prayer was the Padre Nuestro, or Lord's Prayer, she ascertained that the window belonged to a bedroom, as she had suspected, and was indeed covered by a pulled-down roller shade. The lock was an ordinary sash lock. From elsewhere in the house she could hear muffled shouts. The voices were male.

Bianca frowned as she listened.

"—*nuestras ofensas*—" Francisca murmured.

More male shouts: "—got my head blown off!"

"You shoulda lobbed the grenade!"

What?

"Give me the damned controller!"

Oh, a video game.

Placing a gloved hand on the wall for support, Bianca edged through the waist-high, half-dead azalea hedge that ran the length of the wall and peered through the narrow gap between the frayed edge of the shade and the window frame.

"—*perdonamo a los que nos*—" Francisca prayed. Shouts continued from wherever the video game action was happening, but now that she knew what that was all about, Bianca tuned them out.

What she saw was a Pepto Bismol–pink wall with maybe half a dozen half-full and tied-up black trash bags piled against it and a corner of a mattress—no bed frame, no box spring, just a mattress plunked down on the stained hardwood floor. The mattress was covered with a pink-and-green floral fitted sheet. To the right of the mattress, a pair of oversize feet in red high-topped sneakers and long, thick legs in black sweatpants stuck out into the room from what she had to assume was a chair in the corner. The feet and legs clearly belonged to a male. Bianca couldn't see his face—but, resting across his lap, she could see his Marlin .22 rifle. Otherwise known in military and law-enforcement circles as a mouse (as opposed to an elephant) gun. She didn't know about the others, but this particular member of the junior punk version of the Juarez Cartel wasn't packing the heavy artillery tonight.

"—*caer en tentacion*—"

From the direction and proximity of the girl's voice, Bianca was certain that Francisca was lying or sitting on the mattress.

"Hey, Snake, how much longer we gonna wait?" The sudden yell from red high-top dude in the corner was loud enough to drown Francisca out and make Bianca jump as it blasted through her earwig.

"Pip-squeak got eight more minutes," came the answering yell, which originated from wherever the video game marathon was happening, i.e., somewhere else in the house. Snake: Bianca recognized his voice.

"You hear that, bitch?" red high-top dude said to Francisca. "Eight minutes, and then I'm gonna give you something to *cry* about."

"*—libranos del mal.*" Francisca finished her prayer in a shaking voice and started over again. "*Padre nuestro—*"

Step one: locate the girl.

Check.

The sounds from the bedroom faded as Bianca moved on around the front of the house.

Three double-hung windows—one lit up behind a shade, belonging to the bedroom Francisca was in; one the same size and dark, another bedroom; one smaller and dark, probably a bathroom—later, Bianca strode past the closed front door. The slab porch connected to a pebbled concrete walkway that led to the driveway, and she followed it. She was just registering the house number—112, in bronze metal numbers affixed to the siding beside the door—when she spotted a concrete block that had been upended in the middle of the front yard to hold a birdbath. The concrete block could work as the weight she needed. She made note of it for later use.

"Watch out for that guy!"

"Where?"

"On the roof!"

Forget the earwig: the sounds of the video game and the

players' voices were loud enough to be heard without it even before she stepped up to the plateglass window and peeped through a gap in the curtains, so she hit the button to turn the thing off. The TV hung on the outside wall. On it a virtual soldier was firing an M16 at a target Bianca couldn't see. On the shelf of a pass-through window that led to what she presumed was the kitchen, stacks of folded foils announced the presence of crack for sale. If Sage had it right, various other drugs were kept in the house as well, but the small aluminum foil packets were all that were within her line of sight.

From her vantage point she could see only parts of the four males present: a blue-jean clad leg, a pair of stubby-fingered hands feverishly working a controller, an arm with a full tat sleeve, and the back of a head in a red baseball cap, which was on the same level as the rest because the guy was sitting on the floor. They were gathered around the TV playing their evil little hearts out. She could hear four distinct voices, including Snake's.

Step two: find out where the bad guys are.

Check.

Since the conversation in the living room consisted of exchanges like, "Get him!", "He's over there!", "Shoot him!" and "Blow him up!" amid the frantic sounds of the game, Bianca dismissed it as worthless except for its sheer volume— *the better to drown you out, my dear*—as she got on with what she needed to do.

Picking up the pace, she jogged around to the back of the house and located the only other door, which opened out of the kitchen. The kitchen curtains were drawn and the room was dark, but the light spilling through the pass-through from the living room and a gap in the curtains covering the window in the kitchen door combined to allow her to see mounds of baggies piled high on the counter. She couldn't tell what the baggies contained, but she could tell that they held something and was willing to bet that that something was an illegal substance. The empty kitchen also served to reinforce her conviction that the only people in the house were the four in the living room and Francisca and red high-top dude in the back bedroom.

It took her less than thirty seconds to remove the doorknob from the door.

If anyone tried to exit the house through the kitchen, the inner doorknob would come off in that person's hand. It wouldn't keep the junior punk cartel inside the house forever, but it should keep them inside long enough.

Picturing the blank look on Snake's face if the would-be escapee happened to be him made her smile. She was still smiling—and pulling on surgical gloves from her tool kit over her leather ones—as she ran back around to the front of the house.

Now she really had to hustle: a glance at her watch told her that there were a little more than six minutes left.

Step three: cut off a twelve-foot section of rope.

Bianca scooted under the Impala, grimacing as the rough surface of the driveway dug through her turtleneck to gouge her back. She located the fuel line. Using an awl from the tool kit, she punched a hole in it. Gas began to trickle out, dribbling down onto the asphalt and filling the area beneath the chassis with its acrid smell—and its fumes. She dredged the rope in the gas before tying one end around the punctured pipe. That done, she shimmied out from under the car, taking care to avoid the growing puddle. Once she was on her feet again, she laid the gasoline-damp rope flat along the driveway, then removed the gas-tainted surgical gloves and stuffed them into a Ziploc bag in her tool kit.

Then she grabbed the concrete block from the center of the yard and lugged it over to the ice-cream truck. A curtained serving window set into the truck's side was framed by a painting of a grinning clown holding a chocolate cone with sprinkles, and the words *I scream, you scream, we all scream for ice cream.*

More like, *I scream, you scream, the police come, you get arrested.*

Time remaining: three minutes, forty-one seconds.

Through the driver's window she saw that there was no key in the truck's ignition and the vehicle had manual locks. She also saw the wire to a car alarm. It ran along the edge of the window, which, of course, was rolled up.

The junior punk cartel was probably making too much noise with their video game to hear the alarm if it went off, but she didn't want to chance it.

It took less than a minute to insert a slim jim in between the weather stripping and the door frame, use it to rip out the alarm wire and then hook the notch in the end of the bar around the lock's rod mechanism. She dragged the slim jim forward, heard a click and the door unlocked.

Opening the door, she heaved the concrete block onto the floor inside. It landed with a heavy thud that shook the truck. A quick sweep of a flashlight around the back of the vehicle revealed a digital scale, digital caliper, a number of spice grinders, stacked bundles of rolling papers and bulk cans of pure caffeine powder. Clear plastic canisters served as vases for about four dozen limp-looking red roses. They were the kind of roses that were sometimes available for individual purchase in drug or convenience stores. Bianca was momentarily baffled by their presence—until she took a closer look, saw that each stem was thrust into its own test-tube-like glass vial, and realized that the roses weren't what was being sold. Customers purchased the vials, which were used as cheap crack pipes and were sold with roses in them to disguise their true purpose. All of it was drug paraphernalia—the caffeine powder could be used to cut heroin—and it was right out there in the open on the shelves, alongside ice cream scoops and syrups and sprinkles. There wasn't time to look inside the cabinets, but there was enough in plain sight to attract any cop's attention.

Plus, once the door was opened the smell of weed was unmistakable.

Just to be sure, Bianca hopped in and yanked the curtain off the serving window. That way no one—read cop with a flashlight peering through the window—could miss what the ice-cream truck was really selling.

You are going down, she silently promised the gang in the house.

Jumping out of the truck, she hurried back toward the loose end of the rope. Pulling the burner phone—*once again, preparation pays off, although in a slightly unexpected way*—from her pocket, she dialed 911 as she went.

"Nine-one-one. What's your emergency?" a female operator answered.

"Help! Send the cops! Lots of 'em! There's guys in this here house sellin' drugs and there was this huge explosion, and— oh, the address?" Bianca rattled off the address, using her best breathless and terrified teenage-girl-from-Georgia's-meanstreets voice. At the same time, she pulled a cigarette lighter from her tool kit. Flicking her Bic, she bent to the end of the rope and set what was essentially a twelve-foot-long wick alight. As the flame caught, flaring bright because of the gas on the rope, she let her voice verge on the hysterical. "There's an ice-cream truck they've been selling dope out of and it's— oh, no, here they come, they all got guns and—help! *Hurry!*"

She ran back toward the ice-cream truck as she disconnected, racing the fire that was eating hungrily through the rope. Jumping inside the truck, she grabbed the drill from her tool kit, shoved it into the keyhole, turned it on and destroyed every lock pin the bit could reach with one quick *whir*. Yanking the drill free, she thrust a screwdriver into the keyhole in its place and turned it just like she would have done if it had been the key.

The engine started on the first try.

Success.

The rumbling engine was loud, but at that point it didn't matter if the group in the house heard: in a matter of seconds they were going to *know* something bad was going down. Stomping the gas, she spun the ice-cream truck out into the front yard and watched out of the corner of her eye as a fringe of dancing orange flames surged along the rope. A few more feet, and the flames would reach the pool of gas, and the fumes, beneath the Impala.

Hanging a one-eighty, she aimed the truck at the house, steering with one hand and using the other to drag the concrete block onto the gas pedal so the vehicle would keep charging on without her.

Boom!

The Impala blew up just as she leaped from the truck. The force of the explosion sent the car shooting skyward like a goosed bullfrog. Flames shot out everywhere. The front yard was bathed in a sudden burst of orange light and strafed by exploding car pieces. The blast made the ground shake, rang in Bianca's ears, filled the air with a tsunami of heat and a nasty burning smell. One thing was for sure: the cops weren't going to have a problem finding the house.

Meanwhile, the ice-cream truck hurtled forward, rattling over the grass, bouncing over the walkway—

Hitting the ground, rolling to mitigate the force of the impact to shoulder and hip, Bianca watched the blazing Impala crash back down to earth, now a fireball on four wheels. The house's front door started to open—

Bam! The front wall of the house caved as the ice-cream truck slammed into it, crashing through at an angle that took out the front door and the plate-glass window and stopped up the house like a cork flying into, rather than out of, a champagne bottle.

A lot of yelling erupted inside the house. One of the junior punk cartel out-and-out screamed.

Probably the guy opening the door.

The truck came to rest with a shudder, half in and half out of the house, totally plugging up the hole it had created and making any exit from the front impossible. Chunks of vinyl siding, drywall dust and shards of glass hit the ground along with Impala parts. A smoking (literally) side-view mirror landed at Bianca's feet.

Step four: unleash Armageddon.

Check.

With sixty-two seconds to go.

Bianca would've given herself a big ole "atta girl," but she was too busy racing toward the window of the bedroom where Francisca was being held.

Shouts, sirens, the crackling roar of the burning car and the fainter sounds of opening doors and running feet (neighbors? 'Cause nobody was getting out of that house this fast) followed her, along with the tinkling strains of "Pop Goes the Weasel."

It took Bianca a moment to realize that the crash had set off the ice-cream truck's Pied Piper-ish music.

She rounded the corner of the house at a dead run: the clock was ticking down.

She didn't know what the junior punk cartel had planned for Francisca when time was up. She did know she didn't want to find out.

5

Bianca shoved through the hedge, reached the window, hit the on button on her earwig and looked in. As she'd expected, red high-top guy was gone. He'd almost certainly bolted to join his friends. After all, it wasn't every day that an ice-cream truck rammed the living room of the house you were in.

"—*madre de Dios, ruega pro nosotros pecadores ahora*—"

Francisca was still in there, praying and weeping.

"—the hell happened?" It was a bull-like bellow from the living room.

"Damn truck hit me! In the house! My arm's broke!"

"What'd you have in your fucking *car*?"

"Nothing! Some beer!"

"It blew the fuck up!"

"Not my fault!"

"Truck's in the fucking living room!"

"Would you look at my *arm*?"

"Shit, you hear that? It's the cops!"

"Of all the—"

"Let's get out of here!"

"Grab the dope! Stuff it down your damned pants if you have to!"

"—my arm!"

"Would you *shut up*? Nobody gives a shit about your arm!"

Those shouts from the junior punk cartel reached Bianca even as she turned off the earwig, grabbed the awl and punched through the window just above the lock.

The escalating wails of the approaching sirens, the cheery melody of "Pop Goes the Weasel," the snap-crackle-pop of the burning car, plus the commotion inside the house, added up to so much noise that even she could barely hear that one small pane of glass shatter.

In a flash her hand was through the broken pane and she was unlocking the window. Seconds later, she was inside. Speed was of the essence. The junior punk cartel could remember their captive at any second. Plus, the cops were coming.

Francisca lay curled in a fetal position on the mattress. She was petite, dressed in jeans and sneakers and a purple satin bomber jacket, with what seemed to be yards of glossy black hair tangled around her. Zip ties secured her wrists and ankles. Her eyes were tightly shut and her lips were moving: "—*de nuestra muerte*—"

Bianca kept her voice low. "Francisca!"

The girl's lips stilled. Shaking the hair out of her face, Francisca looked up, her eyes full of fear. As she focused on Bianca, who was leaning over her, her eyes widened even more. "*Orale.* Are you, like, Batgirl or something?"

Bianca was momentarily taken aback. Then she remembered the balaclava.

Too bad she hadn't thought to accessorize with a cape.

"No. *Shh.*" Bianca grabbed her hands—they were soft and ice cold—and cut the zip tie. "I'm here to get you out. Sage sent me."

"Sage?" Francisca sat up, rubbing her wrists and blinking away tears as Bianca sliced through the tie binding her ankles. As Quincy had said, she was a pretty girl, with big brown eyes now swollen from crying and plump red lips. Her round cheeks were damp and flushed. "Oh, I knew he wouldn't leave me to *los bastardos!*"

"Are you hurt? Can you walk?"

"Nobody hurt me—yet. They were going to—"

"Tell me later. Come on."

In the background, the shouts from the junior punk cartel continued unabated as, from the sound of it, they stampeded into the kitchen.

"Move it! Go!"

"Damn pants are falling off! This shit's heavy!"

"You got to get me to a doctor. My *arm*—"

"What about the bitch?"

"I forgot about her. Go get her."

"*You* go get her. I'm outta here."

"What the fuck are you doing? Open the damned door already!"

"I can't! It broke!"

"What broke?"

"The door!"

"*What?*"

"The doorknob came off! Look!"

Bianca had no time to enjoy the dumbfounded note in the basso profundo voice of the guy who'd apparently tried to be first out the door, no time to picture an oversize punk staring blankly down at the doorknob in his hand.

She was too busy hauling Francisca, who seemed to be having trouble walking, to her feet, pushing her toward the window, helping her out, getting out herself.

"What's happening? Did the house blow up? Is it on fire?" Francisca whispered, panic lacing her voice, as Bianca dropped down beside her. The girl crouched, trembling, in the bushes. Her eyes darted all around. Bianca could understand her confusion. The night was alive now with sound and color. Screaming sirens and screeching tires and shouts from arriving cops or neighbors, or maybe both, overlaid the steady roar of the fire. Incongruously cheerful, "Pop Goes the Weasel" kept on keeping on. The orange of the blaze flickered through the bright blue flash of the lights on arriving patrol cars. The smell from the burning car was strong.

"What's that music?" Francisca sounded even more frightened.

"Never mind." Bianca wasn't up to explaining "Pop Goes the Weasel." "See that car over there?" She pointed to the Acura. "We need to run for it."

"I don't think I can. My feet are asleep."

"You have to. We have to."

Grabbing Francisca's arm, Bianca half pulled, half carried her toward the Acura. They'd no sooner gotten inside the car than a pair of cops raced around the corner of the house, flashlights in hand, shining them over the side of the house and the hedge and the ground.

"Oh, no." Francisca looked petrified. "If the *pinche Hura* get me, I'll be deported. So will my mom and—"

"Shh! Duck!" Bianca pushed the girl's head below the level of the dashboard and followed suit.

Careful as always, she'd closed the bedroom window after exiting. Apparently missing the smashed pane, the cops didn't stop, but ran on around back.

Bianca took advantage of their absence to start the car and *go*, heading around the back of the nearest apartment building. If the Acura was seen leaving, it would be better if it looked like it was coming from somewhere not so close to Ground Zero.

Francisca sat up and looked toward the house. "Are they after *me*?" Her voice shook. Clearly she was every bit as afraid of the cops as she was of the Bloods.

"No. They don't even know you exist. They're here for the drugs, and the pushers."

"Good. *Los bastardos* deserve it." Francisca sniffled, then eyed her warily. "Who *are* you?"

Fair enough. The girl had just been kidnapped, after all.

Trust issues were to be expected. And then there was that balaclava.

"A friend of Sage's."

Francisca didn't look reassured. "Where is he?"

"I'm taking you to him."

Much as Bianca disliked letting anyone get a look at her under these types of conditions—when she'd just done her thing, so to speak—and especially disliked it given the current harrowing circumstances, she had to admit that driving around in a black cloth helmet that revealed only her eyes and mouth looked suspicious, to say nothing of weird. She could see why Francisca was having doubts. Cops seeing her like that would have more than doubts: what they'd have would be probable cause.

Which would be bad.

Besides, there was no way of keeping Francisca from finding out who she was. Sage and Quincy would spill everything they knew the minute the three were reunited, she was sure. Fortunately, Sage and Quincy actually knew very little about what had gone down. None of the three of them had directly witnessed the exploding car, or the ice-cream truck being driven into the house. All Sage and Quincy knew was that Bianca had promised to rescue Francisca. All Francisca knew was that Bianca had broken a window, climbed through it, cut her free and gotten her out. As for the rest, anything could have caused the truck crash and exploding car. It wasn't necessarily her. Since no one knew for sure, a hundred different stories would probably spring up. Bianca thought—hoped—she could limit any potential gossip or social media posts—that linked her to any of it by impressing on all three kids the importance of keeping their mouths shut. She would do that by pointing out how much trouble they would be in with the Bloods, the cops and their parents if any word of what had really happened tonight leaked out.

In her experience, self-interest was a supereffective motivational tool.

She popped out the earwig and pulled off the balaclava and tossed both in the backseat.

"Oh." Francisca sounded disappointed at discovering that Bianca was a perfectly normal-looking human being.

"If we should pass a police car, just sit there," Bianca warned. "Don't duck or try to hide your face or anything."

Francisca nodded. Bianca turned on the headlights as they rounded the building because leaving them off would attract more attention than having them on if anyone should happen to notice the moving car. As she drove decorously toward the exit, both she and Francisca looked toward the trap house.

A giant bonfire still engulfed the scorched black skeleton that remained of the Impala. At least half a dozen silhouetted figures raced around it; Bianca couldn't tell what they were doing. Four patrol cars, rack lights flashing, filled the street in front of the house. Their sirens were turned off now. "Pop Goes the Weasel" had been shut down, as well. Two cops shone flashlights through the portion of the ice-cream truck's serving window that wasn't embedded in the house. Their body language made it obvious that they were excited about what they saw. As Bianca watched, the junior punk cartel marched into view. Four cops escorted them toward the patrol cars. Except for the punk bringing up the rear who was holding his arm, their hands were cuffed behind their backs. The one in the lead seemed to be wearing boxer shorts. Remembering the conversation (shouts) she'd overheard, Bianca wondered if he'd been the one to stuff what she had to assume were the foils down his pants. If so, it obviously hadn't worked out so well for him.

Snake was third in line, his hulk-like size making him impossible to mistake even at that distance. His head was down and his shoulders slumped. Every step he took embodied dejection.

"Are they going to jail?" Francisca sounded like she hardly dared to hope.

"Looks like it," Bianca said. "Probably for a long enough time that you won't have to worry about them anymore."

"*Gracias a Dios.*" Francisca's tone was devout.

There was only one way into and out of the parking lot. The combined entrance-exit was closer to the trap house than Bianca would have liked, but the only alternative—hide in the car until a better moment to escape presented itself—was riskier than leaving. A curious cop could decide to check out the parking lot and spot them inside the car, or someone could make a note of her license plate, or the street could get cordoned off. All kinds of things could go wrong. Plus, the sun would start to rise in a little over an hour.

But—they were the only car moving in the parking lot. Some nimble-brained officer could easily see them and make the connection with what was going on at the trap house. If that happened, if they were stopped and questioned, Bianca reluctantly rejected making a run for it in favor of bluffing it out. She could say—what? She was busy concocting what she hoped would be a believable story when two fire trucks raced into view, turning a corner and barreling down the street toward the blazing Impala. The clamor of their sirens and the pulsating vibrancy of their lights could have been custom-made to serve as a distraction.

Fortune favors the bold. Also, apparently, the felonious and fleeing.

Bianca pulled out into the street, heading away from the scene. In a matter of minutes she reached a cross street, turned west and left the excitement behind.

Step five: save the girl.

Check.

As they drove through the sleeping city, Francisca talked nonstop, telling her everything that had happened from the moment Snake and the others had pulled her into his car, along with all her thoughts and feelings related to it. Bianca registered just about every third word. Her attention was increasingly focused on her surroundings. Funnily enough—or not—the closer she got to home the less safe she felt.

Whoever had taken down Groton was still out there.

If he or whoever had sent him was looking for her, if they found her, while she was entering or exiting her building would be the perfect time to stage an attack.

Take a sniper, for instance. Once he knew where she lived, all a sniper had to do was lie in wait.

The thought made Bianca's stomach tighten. Her pulse quickened until she could hear it drumming in her ears.

The ten-minute drive home felt twice as long, because she spent it keeping a wary eye out for tails and possible ambush sites and, oh, yeah, speeding vehicles that might potentially ram hers in an effort to make her dead or unconscious so she could be grabbed, because that particular gambit had been used on her before. Every minute or so found her glancing nervously into her rearview mirror, checking upper-level dark windows for a glint that might warn of a rifle, scanning rooftops for movement or a shape that didn't fit. All while she murmured "mmm-hmm" and "really?" at suitable intervals as Francisca chattered on.

Bianca didn't realize how tense she was until she'd made it into the parking garage of her building and was surrounded by solid concrete walls. No one had shot at her. No one had tried to kidnap her.

Didn't mean she was safe.

Tired as she was, she was totally juiced on adrenaline.

She did a visual scan of every vehicle, every pillar, every shadow in that parking garage.

Nothing that shouldn't be there.

Quincy and Sage were sitting in Sage's car. They came running as she pulled into her space and parked. Francisca scrambled out of the car and fell into Sage's arms.

As Bianca got out of the car, she saw that Sage and Francisca were locked in True Love's Kiss. The sight did not fill Bianca's heart with twinkly stars and dancing unicorns. Instead it made her grimace.

"You da man, Miz Guardian," Quincy greeted her, beaming.

Sage looked up from his lip-lock to say, "Yeah, I owe you. Big-time."

"I owe you, too. Thank you," Francisca chimed in, looking around.

"You want to pay me back, stay out of trouble." Bianca pocketed Mrs. Pack's revolver before retrieving her own belongings from the backseat. The Win Mag she would carry up later, when there were no witnesses around.

"How'd you do it? They give you any trouble, Snake and them?" Sage asked. His arm was around Francisca's shoulders now. She had both her arms wrapped around his waist.

All right, so maybe they looked kind of cute together.

"They were distracted by a car accident, so I was able to get Francisca out a window without running into them," Bianca said. "It was actually pretty tame. She can tell you all about it."

Francisca shuddered. "It was not tame at all."

She started to tell Sage her version of events.

"You didn't have to ninja them?" Quincy asked Bianca, clearly disappointed.

"Nope. Shouldn't you go to bed? Don't you have school in about three hours?"

He shrugged. "I can sleep at my desk."

Go, local school system.

"What time does your mother get home?"

"Seven." He looked at her anxiously. "You're not going to tell her, are you?"

"I'm thinking about it." Even though she probably should—she was reasonably certain it was the adult, responsible thing to do—Bianca already knew that she wasn't going to tell Angela Pack about the night's events. If she broke the kids' trust and told on them, the next time they ran into trouble they might not turn to an adult, and given their track record they might very well get themselves killed trying to handle on their own whatever mayhem they managed to stir up. Not that they were her responsibility, and not that she meant to make a habit of getting them out of trouble, but still.

Breaking into Francisca's chatter, she gave the happy couple, and Quincy, the spiel she'd prepared about keeping the night's events to themselves. They promised. She was as sure as it was possible to be that they understood and would do as she told them.

Self-interest was a wonderful thing.

Three can keep a secret, if two of them are dead. That was Benjamin Franklin, by way of her not-father, talking in her head. Since she wasn't about to kill this trio of kids, she ignored it. All she could do was hope that in this instance at least the pair of them were wrong.

"Hey, what about my gun?" Sage called after her as she headed for the elevator.

Bianca threw her answer over her shoulder. "It's your mom's gun. You want it, you get her to ask me for it. Good night."

"Ah, *hell.* That's not—"

Fair, was her guess as to how that protest ended, but she didn't stay to hear it. Reaching the elevator, she stepped inside, punched the button for the eighth floor—and stepped out again. The elevator went up. She took the stairs.

For the first time ever since she'd come to live in Savannah, she was in full-on self-preservation mode. Instinct and training had kicked in. It was unlikely that there was an assassin up there watching the floor numbers as the elevator rose, waiting for her to reach eight and step out, but using the stairs instead was an elementary precaution. Elevators were a death trap: if an enemy knew you were in one, all they had to do was wait for the doors to open and you were toast.

Emerging cautiously out into the eighth-floor hallway, Bianca was relieved to see that it was empty. Still, she felt the weight of unease settle around her like a blanket. She didn't expect to be attacked inside her building. She'd chosen the building with its restricted access, thick walls and absence of security cameras, and her condo with its strategic location in the eighth-floor corner that came with multiple sight lines and avenues of escape, with her specific protection needs in mind. She'd subsequently modified her condo and the approach to it to make the logistics of an attack difficult. But difficult didn't mean impossible, and so she kept a wary eye out, evaluating the quiet, softly lit hallway for any sign of intrusion. Her stomach tightened and her heart rate increased with every step she took. That didn't abate even as she reached her own (steel reinforced beneath its traditional-looking six-panel oak facade) front door, unlocked the pick-proof, drill-proof and kicking-in proof dead bolt, and stepped inside.

Evie had left a light on for her in the foyer. The soft eggshells and creams and taupes in which the apartment was done, the dark shine of the hardwood floors, the barely there scent of lemon furniture polish, was comfortably familiar.

For years now, this place had been home. Her bolt-hole. Her safe haven.

It didn't feel safe anymore.

6

In Lyon, France, not far from the banks of the Rhône, the headquarters of Interpol didn't attract much in the way of notice. Tucked away on Arrondissement 6E amid the bustling environs of France's second largest metropolitan area, it was surrounded by trees and a green lawn and an asphalt parking area complete with a rack for the red-fendered bicycles-for-rent that were the area's newest rage in transportation. The building itself was blocky, square, glass-fronted, pleasant enough but nondescript. Even the logo above the main entrance, a globe surrounded by olive branches beneath plain block letters spelling out INTERPOL, was ordinary and uninteresting.

In that way, the building was misleading, Colin Rogan thought as, late for his meeting, he strode through the marble-floored lobby. It was the beating heart of the organization, a bustling hive with hundreds of employees, many of whom worked around-the-clock collating the most sensitive pieces of information on the most wanted, and dangerous, individuals alive. Its heavily encrypted databases tracked criminals around the world, linking crimes and perpetrators, establishing patterns, creating a highly effective virtual trail for law enforcement to follow without the barriers posed by politics or national borders. Its collections of fingerprints and DNA samples, facial photos, criminal and method of operation—

MO—histories, most wanted lists and known aliases, were the most extensive in existence. By means of a program known as I-24/7, investigators in any member country could contact Interpol at any time and request assistance and/or access those databases. It was a one-stop shop in the world of international criminal investigations.

As a former MI6 agent and current tracking dog, among other things, Rogan did not feel particularly honored to be a part of it. He'd been freelancing since separating from Her Majesty's Secret Service some four years previously. Present self-bestowed code name: spy-for-hire. He once had been part of that sliver of the Secret Intelligence Service—SIS—that no one was willing to admit existed. Known as the Increment, they were tasked with the spy agencies' most clandestine black ops missions. The ones that would be illegal if some high-level bloke with the prime minister's ear hadn't gotten them secretly declared legal under certain highly specific conditions (like being ordered by the prime minister). The ones that would be disavowed by the British government if word of them ever got out. He'd gotten fed up with risking his ass for things he didn't believe in while taking shit from politicians, and when the last highly classified mission had left a sour taste in his mouth, he'd gotten out. He and another disaffected spy had formed their own company, Cambridge Solutions, and he'd been going merrily about the business of making a (hella good) living when Laurent Durand had called with an urgent request for his help in finding Mason Thayer, former CIA operative, current international bad guy. Rogan owed Durand. They went way back. When he'd been a wet-behind-the-ears rookie spy, Durand had put his own career on the line to give him some highly classified information that had ended up saving his life. Durand needed his help, and he was there.

Once he'd been briefed on exactly what kind of international bad guy Thayer was, and how big a threat his activities posed to the world as they knew it, he wasn't just on board for Durand. He was on board because finding Thayer was both stratospherically above Top Secret in classification, which meant gossipy official channels were out, and mission critical.

When he'd gotten the call that morning from one of Durand's assistants about the urgent need to present himself at headquarters without delay, he'd been in Paris. It was not quite 5:00 a.m., he'd just gone to sleep for what had felt like the first time in days, and despite the vital nature of the mission he'd expressed the thought that if he'd wanted to come like a lapdog whenever he was called he would have stayed with MI6.

Then he'd been told about Groton.

He'd hopped on the A6 and endured the grind of the toll road, with its heavy traffic and endless parade of tourists who got in the EZ pass line without an EZ pass, thus clogging up the whole system, to Lyon. All told, he'd been on the road for almost six hours, with at most two hours' sleep in the preceding thirty. His last meal had been the previous day's grabbed-on-the-run fast-food dinner.

He was not, therefore, in the sunniest of tempers as he walked into Durand's office.

"You heard that Alexander Groton was shot?"

As the administrative assistant who'd admitted him closed the door behind him, Rogan was greeted with that curt question by Durand himself. Durand was a one-time *gendarme* with forty-plus years of experience in criminal investigations, twenty-five of which had been spent with Interpol. Now head of the Organized and Emerging Crime Programme, which focused on international criminal networks, multinational organized crime and illicit markets, Durand was in his mid-sixties, burly, with thinning dark hair, narrow dark eyes below bushy gray brows, heavy features, and swarthy skin left scarred by a long-ago bout of acne. His gray suit was rumpled. What looked like a coffee stain marred the end of his yellow tie.

He was seated behind his desk when Rogan entered. The desk was large, metal with a wood veneer top, cluttered, and it appeared he'd been in the middle of perusing a folder that was open in front of him when interrupted. Behind him, a framed photo of a cabin cruiser on what Rogan thought must be the Seine took pride of place over a credenza. A woman and a boy waved from the deck of the boat. Family? Probably. Rogan had no idea what Durand's personal circumstances were. He'd never needed to know.

Durand didn't stand up or offer to shake hands as Rogan approached. Instead, he ran his eyes over Rogan's leanly muscled, six-foot-three-inch frame, took in his well-tailored navy suit, white shirt and blue-striped tie, then condemned with a glance and a twitch of his brows the length of Rogan's wavy black hair. Brushed back from his face after a hurried shower and shave, it curled against his shirt collar in back because he'd been too busy working to find the world-class criminal Durand had brought him on board to find to get a haircut.

Durand's eyes met Rogan's, which Rogan knew were bloodshot and shadowed from lack of sleep and thus possibly not the most confidence inspiring, and narrowed. Then Durand cast a significant look at the man standing to his left. Dressed in a black suit, that man had his back to the room and his hands clasped behind his back as he looked out one of the long, narrow windows at the leaden gray sky outside.

From the look of the clouds, rain was imminent.

"Yes," Rogan replied. There was a clear warning in Durand's gaze. Rogan kept his expression impassive as the unknown man turned.

"We're interested in the whereabouts of Mason Thayer," the second man said. He looked to be a few years older than

Rogan's own age of thirty-two. At a guess, Rogan would say thirty-six or -seven. A hair over six feet tall, a 180 or so pounds, muscular and fit. Reddish hair cut military style. Blue eyes, pale skin, blunt features. "Mr. Durand says that you've had the latest sighting of him."

"And you are?" Rogan asked. The abruptness, the accent— American. If Rogan had to guess, he was going with CIA.

"Forgive me, I should have introduced you." Durand rose at last and came out from behind his desk. His expression was now pleasant, his manner one of professional courtesy. "Steven Hanes, Colin Rogan. Special Agent Hanes is with the CIA."

Called it. Rogan shook hands.

"You got here fast," Rogan observed. The shooting of Groton had occurred approximately fifteen hours before. He did a quick calculation: sevenish hours to fly across the pond from the US East Coast, and then—

"I was in Zurich," Hanes said.

Under four hundred miles, less than an hour by air, four and a half hours by train or car. Assuming he was telling the truth about where he was coming from. In Rogan's experience, everybody lied. The CIA simply made a policy of it.

"Ah," Durand said. "Beautiful city, Zurich."

Hanes looked impatient. "We have reason to believe that Thayer might be a person of interest in Groton's murder. Groton had contact with Thayer less than two weeks ago. Our information is that you were present at the time. How is that?"

Durand's gaze flicked to Rogan, and he gave a slight nod, directing Rogan to answer. The previous look Durand had given him had provided all the subtext Rogan needed: carefully.

"I tracked Thayer to Granite." Granite was the code name for the CIA's black site in Heiligenblut, Austria. "Groton was there when I arrived."

"Along with Thayer?"

"Yes."

"You had contact with both of them?"

Rogan remembered that there had been eyewitnesses: security guards, building staff, soldiers, a six-strong contingent of armed muscle that he presumed, from their actions, had been Groton's personal team. "I had contact with Groton. I saw Thayer. I had no contact with him."

"What happened?"

"I walked into a firefight. Apparently your people kidnapped Thayer's wife and daughter in an attempt to lure Thayer to Granite. It worked. Only Thayer managed to fight his way out. I got there just as he escaped via helicopter with his family. He appeared to be severely wounded."

"Do you have any idea where he was going?"

"No."

"When you say his family, you are referring to—?"

"His wife and daughter. Did I mention that the daughter is seven years old? A little girl whom your people kidnapped."

With a gesture, Hanes dismissed that as an unimportant detail. "Did you observe any contact between Groton and Thayer?"

"Other than Groton shooting at him? No."

"You said that Thayer appeared to be severely wounded. How severely?"

"Severely enough that I question whether he can be considered a viable suspect in Groton's murder."

"Did you see Thayer's wounds closely enough to be able to vouch for how severe they were?"

"No. My judgment's based on how he reacted to them, what I could tell of their location and the amount of blood he was losing."

"What was the nature of your contact with Groton?"

This was where Rogan had to be careful. Not to avoid revealing sensitive information that Durand didn't want revealed, because that was easy enough. To avoid revealing sensitive information that Rogan considered personal and private and for his use alone. While at the same time remembering that there were eyewitnesses to the events he was recounting, which meant that he needed to stick very close to the truth.

Rogan said, "After observing Groton taking part in the unsuccessful gun battle with Thayer, I joined him in pursuit of Thayer's fleeing associate, a woman. I was one of a group of seven or eight, I believe, including Groton. We were on snowmobiles, as was she. She ultimately was cornered, and after a brief conversation with Groton drove off a cliff rather than surrender. He tried to stop her by shooting at her. I fired a warning shot in Groton's direction when he did that, because the woman was no good to us dead. But as I said, she drove off a cliff, so she ended up dead anyway. Groton left Granite almost immediately afterward, as did I."

"This woman." There was something in Hanes's expression as he said the words—a barely perceptible sharpening of his eyes, a sudden tension in his jaw—that told Rogan that his interest in the subject was acute. Rogan's interest in Hanes's interest was suddenly acute, as well. "You said Groton had a conversation with her. What was it about?"

"I wasn't able to overhear it." Which was the truth. The roar of the snowmobiles' engines had been loud, and until the very last minute, Rogan had been wearing a helmet.

Hanes's face tightened with dissatisfaction at the answer. "Do you know the woman's name?"

Sylvia. Only that, of course, was not her real name. Which Rogan didn't know, so this answer also would be the truth. "No."

He continued to watch Hanes closely, without, he hoped, giving any indication that that was what he was doing.

"Can you describe her?"

"Not with any degree of accuracy. I didn't get a good look

at her." Not then. On their two previous encounters, however, he'd seen her extremely well: a beautiful blonde with a taste for sexy underwear—and a talent for even sexier kisses. Watching her plummet to her death had been more of a shock to his system than he was prepared to admit. Given her boss's history, though, Rogan wasn't by any means sure that she was actually dead. It annoyed him to realize how much he hoped she was not. "She was bundled up in a heavy coat and hat, and the light was fading." He took a stab in the dark. "I would imagine that there's surveillance footage of her from cameras in and around your facility. As well as footage of Thayer."

"All surveillance footage from that day is missing."

If Hanes was speaking the truth, that told Rogan a lot: whatever Groton's business had been with Thayer—and Sylvia—Groton or some other operative with enough clout to order it done had wanted no photographic evidence of it. The CIA's previous official reason for its interest in Thayer—that he was one of theirs who'd faked his own death and then turned criminal, thus besmirching the Agency, and now, its suspicion of his involvement in Groton's killing—might, in Rogan's opinion, support the degree of zealousness with which they had been and were pursuing him.

But given that Sylvia was no more than Thayer's unimportant associate and no one was suggesting that she had been involved in Groton's death, the CIA's interest in her should have been minimal.

Hanes's was not.

Rogan could see it in the other man's eyes.

And if Hanes *wasn't* telling the truth about the surveillance footage, that said something, too. At a minimum, that the CIA had an agenda that it wasn't willing to share.

Either way, something was up.

Rogan continued to probe. "Eyewitnesses, then."

Hanes shrugged. "You know how reliable eyewitnesses are."

Yes, he did: not reliable at all. It was the first time that Rogan had ever considered it a plus.

Durand had been listening to this exchange with an attentive expression. Now he addressed Hanes, asking, "How can we help you?"

Hanes said, "My job is to determine if Thayer killed Groton, and the first step in doing that is to find Thayer." He looked at Rogan. "I understand that you've been searching for Thayer, as well. I'd like you to share with me what you've learned, and to provide me with real-time updates of the progress of your search as it continues."

Would you now? Rogan met his gaze full-on, and said, "Thayer's managed to elude me thus far, so apparently nothing I've learned is of much value."

Hanes's lips tightened.

Durand said, "You can count on Interpol's full cooperation, of course. We have already put out a Red Notice on Thayer, and we will follow up aggressively. You will be kept informed. Now, if you would like to move into one of our conference rooms, I will have our staff pull all the information we have on Thayer and bring it to you." He walked to his office door and opened it, gesturing to Hanes that he should follow. Sticking his head out, he spoke to someone in the reception area. Rogan assumed it was the middle-aged man behind the desk he'd passed coming in. "Bender, take Special Agent Hanes to the Mitterrand Conference Room and get him—" he looked questioningly at Hanes "—coffee?"

"Yes, thank you."

"You have merely to tell Bender how you take it."

Hanes nodded his thanks and walked out the door.

When Hanes was gone, Durand turned back to Rogan. Deep creases in the older man's forehead and around his mouth told Rogan how troubled he was.

"We have received credible information that the Americans

are tearing up half the cities in the world searching for something. I think it is Thayer. We must get to him first." His eyes bored into Rogan's. His urgency was palpable. *"Find him."*

Rogan nodded. And silently added *find her* to the directive.

Three minutes later, he strode out of the building into a cold rain.

7

Friday morning woke up beautiful. Crisp but sunny. Cerulean sky. Clouds like fluffy white bunny tails. Birds chirping. Tugboats tooting. The ornate white fountain in Forsythe Square burbling merrily as it shot water high into the air. Silver-gray tendrils of the Spanish moss that hung from every live oak in town (and there were hundreds of them) swaying in the breeze. The river busy with everything from kayaks to barges. The streets home to a mix of early-morning runners, holdovers from the previous night's revels who were straggling toward home, and delivery people of all descriptions, including Nora-on-the-bicycle who dropped off the *Savannah Morning News* for those in the building who subscribed.

Bianca was not in the mood to appreciate any of it. Fortunately, since what she'd managed to squeeze in was basically an hour-long power nap, she functioned fine on little sleep. She'd always thought that was just a lucky quirk in her metabolism, but now she wondered if it had something to do with the whole super-soldier thing. Which in turn led her to wonder what, exactly, were the "genetic modifications" that had been done to the test-tube embryo that was her. John Kemp, the now-dead CIA assassin who'd kidnapped her and brought her to the attention of Alexander Groton, thus setting this whole race-against-death thing in motion, had spoken of enhanced strength, intelligence and stamina. He'd also said something about athleticism, fighting ability and—was it a gift for languages? Yes, it was. The list of cut-and-paste "improvements" that had been made to her zygote—to *her*—was, he'd told her, long.

She could almost feel the scar on the underside of her jaw tingling. It was two-inches long, fish-hook shaped—and it was all that remained of the tattooed-on number 44 that had once marked her as a product of the Nomad Project.

A *product*. A thing. Groton had said, "We made you."

The idea of it horrified her. So she did her best not to think about it. After all, she'd lived in this body for over twenty-six years and had found nothing to complain about concerning it so far.

In fact, it was a super-duper body. Only, that had been the point, right? A super-duper body for a super soldier.

Fine. Next time she had a couple of hours to spare she'd schedule an official freak out. Right now, she needed to go to work.

Bianca showered, washed her hair, blew it dry and pulled it back into a low ponytail at her nape, applied the minimum of makeup and got dressed. It helped that her closet was arranged by item, color and style, with coordinating pieces grouped together. That meant that she could pair a white blouse and black skirt with a gray jacket and the appropriate shoes, bag and jewelry without having to think about it. The reason for the skirt was, as always, that she meant to be prepared: this time for trouble.

The sheer black stockings she wore with the skirt were held up by a garter belt. The garter belt had been specially made for her by SiuSiu Tseng, a tailor in Macau who crafted cheap custom-made clothes for tourists as well as, for a select list of highly confidential clients, what SiuSiu called spy clothes, although clothes for criminals was closer to the truth. Bianca's garter belts bristled with well-disguised tools, including a screw driver, lockpick, hacksaw–pry bar and stun gun, all wand-thin, made of strong-as-steel polymers, and miniaturized to fit in the straps that clung to her thighs. The stocking clips at the ends of the slender straps concealed a button-size flashlight, a locator beacon (to be used only in the case of extreme emergency because, of course, when it was turned on, duh, it could be located), and two hundred feet of dental-floss-thin, 250-pound rated cord that spooled out from a hook (the clip itself, which was designed to serve as an anchor). The cord allowed her to drop or rappel down as much as nineteen stories if necessary. The fourth clip contained a tiny switchblade with a wicked, lethal blade.

And, yes, she knew how to use it.

The flimsy garments were lined with a substance that kept the concealed tools from being spotted on X-ray, and prevented them from being felt in the course of a pat down. Their sexiness was designed to serve as a distraction if (male) security encountered them. And security details almost always included at least some males.

She'd often thought that the garter belts should come complete with an illustrative photo and a warning label: *men—this is your brain on lingerie.*

Whatever, they were field-tested and did the trick.

She had a nice selection of garter belts. The last time she'd had an up-close-and-personal encounter with someone who wanted to kill her, she hadn't been wearing one. She didn't mean to be caught off guard again. For the foreseeable future, she intended to be one with them.

Passing on her usual morning workout and run—she was under too much of a time crunch and, anyway, taking part in the game of spot-the-sniper the run would entail would, she felt sure, rob it of its chill-out benefits—she extracted the Win Mag from the Acura. She took it up to the apartment in its custom-made case that made it look like she was carrying a guitar and stowed it in the walk-in-closet-size vault hidden behind a wall in the pantry that contained, among other things, a nice selection of weapons and a grab-and-go bag packed with essentials, including cash and a number of false IDs, because life, as the saying goes, is uncertain. She dropped Angela Pack's revolver in there, too, where it would stay unless and until the woman (not Sage) came asking for it. Then she drove straight to work, grabbed a giant black coffee from the Starbucks on the corner and headed up to the fifteenth floor, where Guardian Consulting, her legit, young but growing security company was located.

Taking a chance that an assassin wouldn't be waiting for her in the hallway of a commercial office building with a security guard downstairs and tenants beginning to arrive, she rode the elevator. Climbing up fifteen floors was more of a concession to what in the bright light of day she really, really hoped was paranoia than she felt prepared to make right then.

Anyway, the centerpiece of the dangly silver pendant with which she had completed her outfit was a throwing star. Encased in its Lucite setting, it made an attractive piece of jewelry. But if she needed to use it, all she had to do was pop and pitch.

The lights were off, the air-conditioning emitted its usual low hum, and the sleekly modern suite of offices with its gray walls and black leather, stainless-steel and glass furniture was exactly as it should have been: no sign of a lurking assailant anywhere. Evie's desk beneath the big silver Guardian Consulting sign that took up almost the entire long wall of the reception area was empty, Bianca saw as she entered. She hoped it stayed that way for a while: poor-little-rich-girl Evie's zeal to excel in this, her first paid job, meant that she came in early a lot. Bianca had had no idea if today would be one of those days. Although they were temporary roommates and worked at the same place, they drove to work separately and frequently didn't even see each other in the morning before arriving at the office.

On this morning in particular, Bianca really didn't want to see Evie for a while.

Evie knew her well enough to know when something was wrong, and Bianca didn't feel up to making up believable lies before she'd even finished her coffee.

The doors to Doc's and Hay's offices were closed. Bianca didn't think either of them would be in yet—it was 7:29, and work did not officially start until 8:00—but she didn't stop to find out.

She needed a short time alone with her coffee and a highly encrypted computer before the regular business of the day began. As Guardian Consulting's head of cybersecurity, Doc—Miles Davis Zeigler, a twenty-five-year-old computer genius who'd gone to prison for hacking into the Department of Defense computer system, been released after three years and immediately thereafter started to work for her not-father as part of the team he'd put together to pull off a two-hundred-million-dollar robbery in Bahrain that had gone spectacularly wrong, which in turn had led to Bianca bringing him back to Savannah with her—had made their system unhackable and everything they did on it untraceable.

That was her kind of system. Especially since tugging on the wrong string in the interconnected tangle of the web might set off an alarm in some watch-dog system somewhere that would alert the wrong person to her interest—and her presence.

She neither turned on the light nor opened the curtains. Closing her door, she went straight to her desk, sat down, turned on her computer, drank her coffee, and searched every news outlet and gossip site and government feed she knew of for information on the shooting of Alexander Groton.

The only thing of interest she found was a brief reference

to an unrelated but major drug bust involving the Bloods on Savannah's east side the previous night.

Hah.

At least she could chalk that up as one problem solved.

It wasn't until she heard Evie's cheery, "I've got muffins!" and Hay's interested reply of "Blueberry?" through her closed door that she realized that she was no longer alone in the office, that it was now 8:05 and that she'd spent over half an hour fruitlessly searching the internet while finding nothing pertaining to Groton. It was then that the truth hit her: she'd found nothing because there was nothing to find.

Groton's death wasn't being reported anywhere.

Bianca's first thought—*maybe he isn't dead*—was immediately countered by her memory of that gusher of blood erupting from his chest.

And even if he wasn't dead, there should be some report of his being shot.

Maybe it was too early. Maybe the news wasn't yet widely known. His wife's Facebook page sported a recipe for apple-and-walnut stuffing from yesterday. His children—he had two grown sons—had no recent posts.

The Department of Defense news feed contained nothing but links to hearings and scheduled appearances and live events.

There was nothing on the DARPA site, nothing on the Director of National Intelligence site, nothing on the Great Falls, Virginia, police logs.

Not even a record of a callout last night to anywhere in the vicinity of Groton's house.

There should have been a record of a callout. She'd been there. She'd seen the cop cars arrive.

A knock on her door interrupted her thoughts.

Bianca looked up and said, "Yes?"

Evie stepped into the room. Five-three and currently the

approximate shape of a Butterball turkey, she had a round, pretty face with big brown eyes, a small, upturned nose and a wide, well-shaped mouth. Her coffee-brown hair fell in a riot of natural curls to her shoulders; today a deep pink satin band held it back from her face. Her skin was milky pale except for the roses in her cheeks, which Bianca assumed could be attributed to a judicious application of blush. She wore a hand-knit cardigan in the same rosy pink as her cheeks over a deeper pink trapeze dress that exactly matched the headband. Her shoes were navy flats. Evie hated wearing flats, but pregnancy plus heels made her ankles swell.

Everything she was wearing cost the earth, and looked it. That's because Evie was rich. Or, at least, Evie had been rich. Right at the moment, not so much.

The only child of a real-estate magnate and Savannah's leading socialite, Evie was by birth one of the Deep South's A-listers. As was the custom among the old money crowd that was her natural milieu, she'd been formally presented to Society at the age of eighteen and subsequently named Savannah's Debutante of the Year, to her mother Rosalie's immense pride. She had further fulfilled her destiny by marrying another scion of Savannah wealth, William Wentworth Thornton IV, otherwise known as Fourth, and getting pregnant.

After that, unfortunately, it had all gone to hell. Fourth had cheated, Evie had found out, and she was in the process of divorcing him in the teeth of strenuous objections from Fourth and both sets of parents. In an effort to make Evie reconsider, Fourth had drained her bank account and stopped her credit cards, and her extremely wealthy family had cut her off financially.

So Evie, who'd never previously worked a day in her life for pay, had given the entire bunch the figurative bird and gotten a job, with Bianca and Guardian Consulting. To her own surprise, and even a little bit to Bianca's, she was proving to be excellent at it.

"Is there a reason you're sitting here in the dark?" Evie surveyed her with a frown.

Bianca thought about saying that she had a headache, but Evie knew she never got headaches and would question that. She thought about saying that she'd been napping, but she rarely napped and never at the office and anyway the glowing computer screen—which now showed only her email inbox—bore silent witness to the fact that she'd been doing *something*, because if left alone it went into sleep mode.

The real reason she hadn't turned on a light or opened the curtains—that she hadn't wanted to tip off any potential assassin on the street below to her presence in her office—was obviously not something she could share.

"My hands were full," she said. "I had to come over to the desk to set some things down, and while I was here I turned on the computer, and then I decided to check something out and—here I am."

That explanation was apparently believable enough, because Evie didn't question it. Instead she asked, "How did last night's meeting go?"

Bianca experienced a frisson of remembered disaster. "Fine."

Evie walked around Bianca's desk and started opening the curtains covering the floor-to-ceiling expanse of glass that composed the entire fourth wall. The large corner room was immediately flooded with sunlight.

To the tune of rattling curtain rings Evie said, "You do remember that you've got that meeting at Cymba International at nine, right?"

Bianca groaned, and dropped her head in her hands.

"Shoot me," she said.

"It's a big contract." Evie finished with the curtains. From her desk Bianca could see a huge container ship chugging through the muddy green waters of the Savannah River, and, on the other side of the river, Hutchinson Island. "You should be thanking me."

"I take that back," Bianca said, looking up as, on the way back out of the room, Evie paused beside her desk. "Shoot you."

"Networking is how the world works. I introduced you to Les Harper, he mentioned you to his father, who owns Cymba, and Guardian Consulting gets invited to make a presentation to take over Cymba's computer security. There's nothing wrong with that."

"Right," Bianca said. "No pressure whatsoever on me to sleep with Les."

Les Harper was a friend of Fourth's. Right before Evie's marriage went down in flames, Evie had tried to fix Bianca up with him by inviting them both to her beautifully restored mansion in the historic district for dinner. The thing was, Bianca had been expecting a dinner party, not a cozy four-some, because Evie hadn't told her it was a fix-up.

Les, on the other hand, had been in the know from the beginning and had considered the two of them on a date. To say it had gotten awkward was an understatement. Les had been calling weekly ever since, trying to get Bianca to go out with him on a second date.

Bianca still blamed Evie for making him think there'd been a first date.

"It's a five-year contract worth a million a year," Evie said. "Look at it this way—if you do end up sleeping with Les, you'll be taking one for the team. In fact, if it comes right down to it, you can always close your eyes and think of Guardian Consulting."

"Evie? Don't make me fire you."

"This is a great opportunity, and you know it. Les might not even be there. If he is, it won't hurt you to be nice. Or to smile. And for God's sake take that elastic band out of your hair." Evie grabbed the coated elastic that was holding Bianca's hair in its low ponytail and yanked it off.

"Ouch!" Bianca's straight, shoulder-length hair fell forward in a cool slide. Glaring, she instinctively tucked it behind her ears.

Dropping the elastic into the pocket of her cardigan, Evie headed back out into the reception area, saying over her shoulder, "Sexy singles do not wear ponytails. Ten-year-olds do."

Bianca jumped up and followed her. "You know what? Forget firing you. I'm going to strangle you."

Evie kept walking, but wagged a finger at her. "Ah-ah. Violence is not the answer."

"So what's up?" Holding a muffin in one hand and a coffee cup in the other, Hay emerged from the small kitchen on the far side of the reception room. They both stopped where they were to look at him. Hay was Haywood Long, Bianca's second in command. Ex-military and a former cop, he'd been in charge of the day-to-day operation of the company when she was away since she'd hired him not long after Guardian Consulting's inception four years earlier. He also oversaw all but the highest level jobs when she was present. Six-one with short fair hair that had been blond when he was a kid, he had bright blue eyes and the muscular, almost stocky build of the high school football star he had once been. He was twenty-nine, single, and his all-American good looks meant that he had plenty of women interested in him. Bianca had known him almost as long as she'd known Evie, and she considered him one of her best friends. He was down-to-earth, level-headed and she trusted him, if not completely then enough.

The thing was, she didn't trust anyone completely, because she couldn't. Hay, for example, had absolutely no idea about her secret life as a world-class thief, etcetera, much less the whole super-soldier thing and the nightmare that went along with it. With Hay, it was a case of what you see is what you get, and he thought she was like that, too. But she wasn't, and she could never be, and that created what was for her an insurmountable barrier between them. If he sometimes made noises like he wanted to be more than a friend to her, she overlooked them. She liked him far too much to spoil their relationship by letting it take a turn toward the romantic. Besides, he was great at his job, and that was more important to her than any transient hookup.

"Evie's doing her matchmaking thing again," Bianca told him.

Hay immediately frowned at Evie. "Stop. This is a sickness," he said. He looked back at Bianca. "She asked Grace Cappy if she was going to that damned historic thing tonight, and when Grace said she wasn't because she didn't have a date, she told her that I didn't have a date, either. So Grace called me. She *asked* me. What could I say? Nothing, that's what, because she caught me by surprise and I couldn't think of a damned thing. So now I'm *taking* her."

Bianca hooted. "You know that presentation I'm going to make to Cymba International this morning? That's Les Harper's father's company. You know Les is going to be there. You know he's going to ask me to lunch. Or dinner. Or something. Probably something." She frowned accusingly at Evie. "She knows it, too. Look at her face. She's *evil.*"

"Grace Cappy is nice, unlike some women you've dated recently," Evie said, defending herself to Hay. "I did you a favor. You'll see."

Hay said, "You're talking about Susan, aren't you?" He looked at Bianca. "She's talking about Susan."

"To be fair, we never did like Susan," Bianca told him.

"What? You never said anything!"

Evie said, "That's because we're polite."

Hay snorted. "Since when?"

Evie was already looking at Bianca. "And I'm glad to take

credit for this meeting with Cymba International. In fact, if we get the contract I want a bonus."

"In your dreams," Bianca said. "I could have gotten the meeting on my own. And I wouldn't have to play dodge-the-date with Les Harper."

"You play dodge-the-date with everybody," Evie retorted.

"You want me to go with you, run interference?" Hay asked Bianca. If she feared that a male client might get too friendly to be dealt with politely, she would often take Hay with her to their meeting. Just the fact that she had brought another male along seemed to discourage most of them from getting too touchy-feely.

Bianca shook her head. "Doc's going with me. He's the best equipped to explain all the technical aspects of what we can do for them. Anyway, aren't you supposed to be overseeing security for the Savannah Food and Wine Festival today?"

"Yeah. I was just on my way out the door." He bit into his muffin. "As soon as I finish this."

"Great." Bianca looked at Evie. "If Monica Prickett with Prickett Construction calls, set up an appointment for me to meet with them sometime early next week, would you please?"

Evie nodded, and sent a significant glance toward the clock on the wall. "It takes twenty minutes to get to Cymba's offices in traffic."

Bianca didn't even bother to sigh. Bottom line, given that her bank accounts were sadly depleted thanks to her not-father's conscripting of her money to help fund the failed job in Bahrain, Guardian Consulting needed the payday Cymba International could potentially provide. To say nothing of the prestige of landing a major new client.

Assuming that Guardian Consulting would continue to exist.

If she was being targeted, if she was being hunted, her best bet might be to shut down the company, put the condo on the market and *go*.

As in, run for her life.

The thought was unutterably depressing.

So don't think about it. For now, just keep putting one foot in front of the other.

Bianca said, "I'm on my way. Let me grab Doc."

Evie and Hay went about their business as Bianca knocked on Doc's closed door.

"You ready to go?" she asked when she opened the door in response to his muffled grunt, which she took as a *come in*.

Doc was sitting behind his desk, scowling at his computer. At five-ten and somewhere north of three hundred pounds, he dwarfed the small, ergonomic chair he insisted on using despite all her offers to get him another one more suited to his size and the restless movements he made when he was working, the combination of which she was convinced were going to pitch him onto the floor at any given moment. She registered that, per instructions, he was wearing a white dress shirt and subdued tie, and that his shoulder-length mane of frizzy black curls was pulled back. A closer glance at his gray-and-black-striped tie revealed that it was dotted with tiny, bright green rabbits, and his pulled-back hair was twisted into a man-bun at the back of his head. Green bunnies and man-buns weren't quite the norm in Savannah business circles, but Doc was from the Bronx, and there was no making him over into something he wasn't, like, say, a Savannah businessman. Attempting to do so would be like sticking a fancy tail on a pigeon and trying to convince onlookers that what they were seeing was a peacock.

Doc looked up at her—she got the impression that he had to make an effort to tear his gaze away from whatever was on the screen in front of him—and she saw that his pale, chubby-cheeked face was set in uncharacteristically grim lines.

She repeated her question, he nodded in reply, and then said, "Uh, boss, you wanna come over here a minute and take a look at this?"

Bianca felt her stomach drop. She knew that tone.

It meant that whatever he was getting ready to show her, she wasn't going to like.

She braced for her already very bad day to take a sharp turn for the worse, and stepped inside his office.

8

"What is it?" Bianca asked.

For a few minutes there, while she'd joked around with Evie and Hay, she had, Bianca realized, felt like herself again, like the person she'd been before she'd gotten kidnapped and transported to that damned black site in Austria and discovered that everything she thought she knew about her life was a lie. In the short walk from the door she closed behind her to where she stopped, standing behind Doc's chair, she felt the warmth, the fun, the sense of belonging and friendship she'd been experiencing dissipate like mist in the sun, to be replaced by the now all-too-familiar sensation of having an iron fist gripping her by the throat. She hated the feeling, hated what caused it. If she could have changed things so that she didn't know what she was, or could have willed the whole thing away, she would have done it. With every particle of psychic mojo she possessed, she wished for her life to go back to normal. For *her* to go back to normal.

I didn't ask for any of this.

Too bad, so sad. Suck it up, buttercup.

"See that?" Doc tapped his computer screen with a stubby forefinger.

He didn't need to. Bianca was already looking at what was on the screen. She felt like the breath had just been knocked out of her.

It was a picture, a photograph from a newspaper. She'd seen it before. It had made her dizzy and sick then.

She refused to let it make her dizzy and sick now.

Bianca looked at the image of her mother—her *gestational* mother—and slammed the door on the tsunami of feelings that rushed her.

Keep emotion out of it: that was one of the rules.

The pretty, petite young woman in the picture had long black hair that was being ruffled by the wind. She was sitting alone at a picnic table biting into an enormous sandwich beneath a banner announcing The World's Biggest Fish Fry. The town was Port Washington, Wisconsin, and Bianca knew now that the woman's real name was Anissa Jones.

In the caption beneath the photo, she was identified by the newspaper as Sarah McAlister.

The accompanying article reported her murder, supposedly at the hands of her husband, Sean, who had supposedly also killed their daughter, Elizabeth, before committing suicide.

The only true thing in that article was that the woman had been murdered.

She, Bianca, had been the daughter, Elizabeth McAlister: *Beth*.

Her not-father, Mason, had been Sean McAlister.

One of many fake identities that he'd assumed over the course of his life.

It was all a long time ago, she'd been four years old, and she had only fuzzy memories of any of it.

Of her mother.

She was not, not, not going to get upset.

"Back when we first found this picture, I put an alert on the names Sean, Sarah and Elizabeth McAlister," Doc said. "So I'd get a notification if any kind of search was run on any of the three of them. This morning I got a notification. Somebody's looking for Elizabeth McAlister, and they downloaded this photo."

Oh, God. Her heart lurched. The timing was too pat. The

internet search for Beth McAlister—for *her*—had to be connected to Groton's death.

It hit Bianca with all the force of a baseball bat to the head: the only reason she hadn't been gunned down like Groton was because they hadn't found her yet.

There was now no doubt about it: they were looking.

The knowledge chilled her to the bone.

"Boss?" Doc twisted around to glance up at her. "You okay?"

"Yes." Bianca didn't pretend that the news didn't bother her. Her grip on the back of Doc's chair had her nails digging crescents into the black aerated foam of the seat back, and she had a feeling that her face was a study in *oh, shit*.

Didn't matter. Doc knew the truth about her. Not all of it, but some of it. More than almost anyone else. He did not know that she was the genetically enhanced product of what was basically a DARPA science experiment. He likewise didn't know that she was *not* the daughter of Richard St. Ives/multiple other identities/Mason Thayer. He did know about that part of her life that had been spent as the daughter of a world-class thief. He knew that she'd robbed people, institutions, etcetera, for a large percentage of her living. He knew about Elizabeth and Sarah and Sean McAlister, and that she had once been Beth McAlister. He knew that the man he thought was her father had once been, among other identities, Sean McAlister, Richard St. Ives and Mason Thayer, his apparent true name, under which he had worked as an assassin for the CIA. What Doc might have inferred from all of that, she couldn't really say.

What *she* knew was that she trusted Doc, and needed him. Without his help she would now be fighting blind in a cyberworld that did its hunting through search engines and data mining programs and algorithms and a whole host of other things she didn't even want to know existed.

"Anything on the Nomad Project?" she asked. Since her return from Austria, she'd had Doc rooting around in the back alleys of the Department of Defense computer systems for any information he could glean on the program that had created her. So far, he hadn't come across so much as a mention of it.

"Nada," he said, confirming. "You ever gonna tell me what that's about?"

"One of these days," she said, knowing she wouldn't. "Maybe."

Doc didn't press. Secrets he understood. "If it makes you feel any better, as soon as I got this, I searched for links between the McAlister identities and Bianca St. Ives. I couldn't find any. And if I couldn't find any, nobody else can either, you know what I mean?"

Despite everything, his faith in himself almost made her smile. As far as Doc was concerned, he was one of the best computer hackers on the planet. And from everything she'd seen, he was right.

"Thank God we're on the same side," she said, and meant it.

"Go team," he agreed.

"If they got to this picture, they know that Mason Thayer was once Sean McAlister," she said, feeling her heart clutch again as she walked herself through a situation that was devolving into wheels within wheels within wheels. The enemies that she knew of who'd known of her Beth McAlister identity—that would be Groton and Kemp—were now dead. (At least, she was 99.9 percent sure Groton was dead. Until she had confirmation, she was keeping open a tiny sliver of doubt.) But whoever had downloaded that picture was now also following that trail, and she had no idea what else they might know, or dig up. "This tells them that Sean McAlister had a daughter, Beth. If they find out about his Richard St. Ives identity, they might try checking to see if Richard St. Ives has a daughter." The thought sent a tremor along her nerve endings. "Can you see—can you search and find out if any of those names can be linked to Richard St. Ives?"

He nodded and started typing.

Bianca held her breath and watched the screen.

"Richard St. Ives comes up," Doc said. "Actually, forty-seven of them come up—a dentist, an international business consultant, a hardware store owner, a truck driver, a ski instructor. Just about everything you can think of except a big-time thief. There's a whole bunch of biographical stuff about each one. The important thing is, none of them show a connection to Mason Thayer or Sean McAlister —or Bianca St. Ives. I'm not saying that none of them are him. I'm just saying that there's no traceable connection—no birth dates, no previous addresses, no employment history, etcetera linking them—which for our purposes is the same thing."

"Thank God." Bianca breathed a little easier. Her not-father had been a pro at constructing false identities.

"What about a picture?" She was thinking of facial recognition software.

Doc clicked something and nodded at the screen. "Right there."

Bianca looked. None of the forty-seven faces looking back at her from the neat rows that filled the screen bore any resemblance to her not-father.

"He's covered his tracks," Bianca said. Of course he had. Like her, he rarely left anything to chance. "Would you do that for my name—for Bianca St. Ives?"

Doc did. There were thirty-six Bianca St. Ives, and twenty-eight Bianca Stives. In the US alone.

When the neat rows of pictures of Bianca St. Ives/Stives filled the screen, one of them was her. It came from the eight (that's right, eight) business licenses she'd been required to obtain before opening Guardian Consulting.

That was one too many pictures for Bianca's peace of mind,

but given the fact that she existed as a business owner in the modern world of Google and search engines, what could you do?

Your best to make sure you don't look like you, that's what.

For her business licenses, driver's license and other official photos, she had worn a dark blond wig in a cut that was inches longer on one side than the other. The asymmetrical bob concealed her temples, ears and the sides of her face. It was styled with long, piece-y bangs that hung down over her forehead and had a section covering her nose bridge area, which was a key facial landmark and identifying feature. A prosthetic nose tip added scant millimeters to her nose, but it was enough to alter that biometric marker without changing her appearance very much to the naked eye. The computer expects to encounter symmetry, so she had made up each side of her face differently, subtly creating different peaks and valleys and altering the shape of her eyes and mouth.

What she had to worry about was facial recognition software: measurements being read by machines. Computers routinely scanned millions of photos, comparing the approximately eighty nodal points that made up a recognizable image with the image they were programmed to locate. Every human face had individual, distinguishable landmarks. The key to defeating facial recognition technology was to alter those landmarks. Fooling a standard surveillance camera was easy enough: in most cases a big grin would do the trick. If she wanted to get more sophisticated, they had hoodies with antisurveillance technology built in and Carnegie Mellon had developed some nifty tortoiseshell glasses that were printed with a pattern that was perceived by a computer as the facial details of another person.

In other words, if she was wearing those glasses, the computer would scan her image and see, say, Taylor Swift.

But big grins weren't allowed on most ID photos. Neither

were hoodies, or funky, image-altering glasses. And probably having a computer spot Taylor Swift in a batch of Savannah, Georgia, business licenses would be counterproductive
in terms of deflecting attention.

"That's you." Doc pointed to her picture. He glanced up
at her. "On a really bad hair day?"

"The point was to defeat facial recognition software."

"That might work." The fact that he didn't sound sold
wasn't reassuring. "Something bad going down?"

"Maybe," Bianca said. The need for silence had been
drummed into her literally from birth—*Keep your cards close
to your vest* was one of the rules—but the hard, cold truth was
that if she was going to survive this she needed help. Doc
was the best hope she had for keeping the computer blood-
hounds at bay.

"Yes," she amended. She wasn't going to tell him everything, but she was going to tell him enough so that he could
do his cyberwizard thing. The whole test-tube, genetically
enhanced super-soldier deal—that he didn't need to know.
That nobody needed to know. It unsettled her to discover
that she was deeply uncomfortable with what she apparently
was. She was ashamed of it, horrified by it, afraid that if anybody found out she would be viewed as a freak or a monster
or—or a *thing*.

To say nothing of the fact that *what she was* was the reason
whoever was after her wanted her dead.

If he knew the truth, Doc would be in deadly danger, too.

Oh, God, was just being around her putting him in danger? What about Evie and Hay?

The thought made her insides twist.

"Boss?" Doc prompted.

"I think someone is out to kill me," she said. "The same people who are after my—" she almost said not-father "—Mason

Thayer. I think they're looking for me, and among other things they're using the internet to try to find me."

A tap on the door interrupted.

"Bee?" It was Evie, reminding her of the time. "You're cutting it close."

Deep breath.

"I'm just going," Bianca called back. Evie's voice, the reminder of her obligations as Bianca St. Ives, president and CEO of Guardian Consulting, steadied her. Somewhere, a shadow posse of assassins might be hunting her like hounds after a fox.

She still had to make payroll. And pay the rent. And eat.

Unless and until she decided to cut and run.

Which was starting to look like a choice she might have to make.

"Come on," she said to Doc. "We have a presentation to get through. We can talk on the way."

The presentation went well. Afterward, Les Harper walked them down to the lobby of the Cymba International building. Les was around thirty, of average height and weight, medium brown hair in a banker's cut, medium blue eyes framed by wire-rimmed glasses, regular features. Attractive without being handsome. He possessed an upper-crust lineage, an Ivy League education, a pile of family money, a pleasant personality and at least two nice suits, the one he'd worn to Evie's that night for dinner and the one he was wearing now. Unfortunately, Bianca was not even remotely attracted to him. Also, right now she had other things on her mind than dating.

Like staying alive.

"I'll have more free time after the holidays," Bianca told him as he saw her off. A moment before he'd asked her to dinner, anytime she was available. She'd turned him down, she hoped gently. "We're just so busy right now."

"I understand." Les released her hand, which he'd held on to after they'd finished their goodbye handshake. "The holidays are a busy time for all of us. Well, maybe you can save me a dance tonight at the Preservation League party."

"I will," Bianca promised. With an inner sigh she registered that he was planning to attend. Not that she was really surprised. All the Society types, all the big money business people, all the movers and shakers in Savannah would be there.

"Who are you going with?" His forehead wrinkled in inquiry. His tone said that he'd known but forgotten. He hadn't, because she hadn't told him.

"Evie," Bianca said. Doc had gone ahead to retrieve the car from the parking lot at Les's suggestion. *He's getting me out of the way so he can ask you out*, Doc had warned in an undertone before leaving. Doc now pulled his red Prius around in front of the brass-framed revolving doors and stopped, obviously waiting for Bianca to come out. She spotted him with relief. "There's Doc. I should go. I hope you'll give serious consideration to our proposal."

"You can be sure of it. Dr. Ziegler is a little—unique, but he certainly does seem to know what he's talking about. We'll discuss it internally, and let you know."

"Thank you." Bianca left him with a smile. Trying to explain to him—again—that Doc was not actually *Doctor* Ziegler seemed like a waste of energy. And to be honest, anything that helped the cause...

"I'll see you later," he called after her.

Bianca responded with a wave as she pushed out through the door and headed for the car. Sunlight glinted off the windshields of the vehicles parked in rows just beyond the *porte cochere* where the Prius waited. The cool breeze carried a hint of car exhaust. Traffic was especially heavy because of all the tourists in town for the Food and Wine Festival. Considering everything—Les, the ridiculous costume she was going to have to wear, *potential killers on her trail*—she was tempted to skip the Preservation League function, the official name of which was the Historic Savannah Auction and Gala. Only the thought of Evie having to face her soon-to-be ex-husband, her disapproving mother, her angry in-laws and the entire gossipy Savannah social register alone kept her from backing out.

But she wanted to.

"So did he?" Doc shifted into drive as she slid in beside him. He was asking whether Les had asked her out, she knew. They were in his car instead of hers because Bianca was now officially playing defense and she felt that there was far less likelihood of an attacker following Doc's car than her own.

She wasn't going to answer that: kiss-and-tell wasn't her style.

"None of your business." She cast an assessing look around as they pulled out onto Broughton Street. A red tour bus was in front of them. Through its windows Bianca could see the passengers craning their necks to take in the sights being described by their guide, who was standing up in the front of the bus with a microphone. The black sedan directly behind the Prius was worrisome at first glance, but the white-haired woman behind the wheel was not. The wide brick sidewalks were packed with pedestrians, tables at the outdoor cafés were filling up, and students from the Savannah College of Art and Design (she could tell because their black T-shirts had SCAD printed in white on the back) were setting up displays of giant, wildly painted papier-mâché flowers at the intersections.

As far as she could tell, no assassins in the lot.

"He did." Doc was clearly pleased at having been right. "You know, you going out with him would probably go a long way toward helping us get that contract."

"You sound like Evie." She glanced over at a horse-drawn carriage as they passed it. The white carriage horse was clip-clopping along next to the curb. The driver was a wizened little man in a top hat and tails. The tourists in the back looked like a honeymoon couple: no assassins there, either. The problem was, among so many people it would be surprising if she *did* spot an assassin. Like Groton, she was most likely to discover that a killer was nearby when a bullet drilled through her head. "I refuse to be pimped out. Besides, I think we've got the contract in the bag anyway. You did a great job explaining what their weak points are and how we can fix them. Really impressive."

"Thanks." He sounded almost bashful. Bianca was reminded that this—the legitimate business side of hacking, the corporate arena, his real-world job at Guardian Consulting—was all new to him. He might consider himself to be the best at what he did, but he was used to being on the wrong side of the law and to hiding rather than showing off his skills. He wasn't quite comfortable being Guardian Consulting's head of cybersecurity yet.

Baby steps.

She smiled at him. "How about I take you to lunch? As long as we eat fast. And keep an eye out for death squads."

Doc rolled his eyes in her direction. "Not funny."

The thing was, she wasn't kidding. The other thing was, he knew it.

On the drive over, she'd fed him her cover story about the source of the danger she thought she might be in, framing it as an offshoot of the international seek-and-destroy mission that had been launched as a result of the Bahrain debacle.

"Oh, crap, does that mean they're after me too?" he'd replied, because of course he'd also been in on the job in Bahrain. He'd seemed to take heart from Bianca's reassurance that nobody had even known he'd been there.

He had further reassured himself with, "I have standing alerts set up on myself. Nothing's come up, so I think I'm good."

The situation was made slightly more complicated because she also hadn't acquainted him with the fact that her not-father, the mastermind behind the Bahrain job who'd supposedly perished in it, was not, in fact, dead.

Oh, what a tangled web and all that.

But the need-to-know principle was something she'd been brought up with, and in this case Doc didn't. She was keeping quiet out of loyalty to the man who had raised her, out of training, out of caution.

She trusted Doc. She really, truly did. But—

People can't tell what they don't know.

Ordinarily Bianca would have suggested that they grab food at the City Market, or at one of the tents set up all over town in conjunction with the Food and Wine Festival, but the idea of walking around in the open gave her the willies. Instead, they ate inside, at a back table in Huey's Southern Café. Doc, who was in the process of falling in love with (most) Southern food, ordered the low country boil, a spicy crab, shrimp and smoked sausage dish, while Bianca had her usual grilled chicken and salad.

Then, because it was close by and the longing looks Doc cast at it practically begged her, they ducked into River Street Sweets where he got a bag of his favorite pralines and she got a single licorice Twizzler.

The two of them were alone in the elevator on the way back up to the office when, between munches, Doc said, "I've been thinking—are there any pictures of you as Beth McAlister out there anywhere? Like in any newspaper or anything that could be searchable online?"

Bianca's pulse was already beating faster than it should have been because of the risk that went along with entering the building. The good news was, a hit man had to locate her before he could lie in wait, which she was almost—*almost* being the operative word here—sure hadn't happened. The bad news was, the niggling uncertainty had made her ditch her half-eaten Twizzler before they'd even entered the building.

Sticky fingers and throwing stars were a bad mix.

Bianca said, "I don't see how there could be. Why?"

"Because whoever pulled that picture now has that name, and they're going to be looking for a photo to go along with it. And if they get a photo of Beth McAlister..." Doc didn't finish. He didn't have to.

If they got a photo of Beth McAlister, they'd run it through every search engine and computer system they had access to, which was basically every search engine and computer system in the world. Since the face of Beth McAlister could potentially be linked to a multitude of names, including Bianca St. Ives, there was no telling what might turn up.

"I was only four years old." Bianca was thinking aloud. "We were in hiding. I can't imagine there'd be any pictures at all."

"You know, I could fix any photos of you that are online. Switch 'em out for something similar, but that couldn't possibly ring the bell in the biometric data searches because it isn't you. What are we talking about here, driver's license and—"

The elevator dinged as it reached the fifteenth floor and stopped. Bianca instantly tensed as every instinct she possessed screamed, *battle stations.*

9

The elevator door rolled open. Bianca focused on the space in front of them—

Clear.

With Doc still talking, they stepped out. She darted a quick, comprehensive look over the terrazzo-floored, white-walled hallway, including the nine-foot ceiling: it was surprising how few people ever looked up, and how often an attacker took advantage of that.

Nothing.

Guardian Consulting's suite of offices occupied one-half of the fifteenth floor. The offices of the floor's other tenant, Hoover Investment Group, took up the other half. Hoover's door was closed.

As she and Doc walked toward their own black-painted office door with its silver-lettered Guardian Consulting sign, Bianca made a mental note of the hallway's vulnerabilities: four windows, two of which had direct sight lines from a nearby building and thus could provide an opportunity for a sniper. Two restrooms, a men's and a women's, either of which could conceal an assailant. Like the door to her own offices and the Hoover Investment Group offices, the doors to the restrooms were solid and closed.

Anybody could lurk behind those doors.

Damn it. What was she supposed to do, nail them shut?

Doc had quit talking and was waiting for a reply. Bianca had heard every word even as she assessed the area for threats, because she excelled at Criminal Multitasking 101: looking normal and surviving at the same time.

She said, "Any time I had to have a picture taken, I took care to make sure that facial recognition software wasn't ever going to be able to get a hit on it. You saw that with the photo that came up."

"I think I should still change the pictures," Doc said. "Just in case."

"Actually, that's smart. I agree. Candid shots, too. They're what I'm most worried about. Things like Facebook, Snapchat, pictures I don't even know are out there," she said as they walked into the office. She didn't realize how tense she'd been until the door closed behind them and her shoulder and neck muscles unknotted.

What did it say about her life when the fact that she hadn't been murdered on the way in to work made her want to emulate Quincy's fist pump?

"How'd it go?" Evie asked. In the act of carrying a tray loaded with what appeared to be tall glasses of iced tea out of the kitchen, she paused to look them over as they entered.

"Really well," Bianca responded. "I think we're going to get the contract."

"Yay, bonus," Evie responded with a grin. "Let's make it ten percent. Was Les...?"

"You do not want to go there." Bianca fixed Evie with a gimlet gaze. "Trust me."

Evie laughed and turned an inquiring look on Doc.

Shaking his head, he held up both hands as if to say he wanted no part of the conversation. The River Street Sweets bag dangled from one hand. Glancing at it, he appeared to find inspiration.

"Praline?" he asked Evie, swinging the bag back and forth as if to tempt her with it.

"You can't bribe me," Evie replied.

"Next time try Oreos," Bianca said to Doc. "Or ice cream."

"That's just low." Evie tossed her head. "Fine. Don't tell me what happened. I'll hear all about it from Les anyway." As Bianca narrowed her eyes threateningly Evie added, "Your two o'clock's here. Pete Carmel of Carmel Construction. He's got four of his site supervisors with him. That was a little much for the size of your office, so I went ahead and put them in the conference room. I'll just take this to them."

"Tell them I'll be right there."

Evie nodded and headed for the conference room with her tray. Bianca moved toward her office. She needed to drop off her purse and get her iPad, which she meant to use to illustrate the methods Guardian Consulting would employ to keep her client's construction sites, which had been experiencing a rash of thefts and vandalism, secure.

Then she thought of something and turned back to Doc, who was likewise heading for his office.

"Yearbooks," she said. "Institut Le Rosey. Sarah Lawrence College. I don't know if they're online or not, but—"

"I'll check," Doc said.

"Can composite sketches be used with facial recognition software?" She was thinking of an associate of Laurent Durand's who knew she worked with her not-father, although said associate didn't know the precise nature of her relationship with Mason or anything about the whole super-soldier thing. (She didn't think; at this point, who knew?) He also didn't know her name was Bianca St. Ives, although he knew the name he called her by—Sylvia—wasn't real. Which was fair: she didn't know his real name, either. She knew him as Mickey. He was some kind of cop/law enforcement/agent/whatever. Anyway, he'd seen her up close and personal. Actually, extremely up close and personal: as in, he'd kissed her twice. Not that there was any kind of "romance" going on.

Both times were because of operational necessity. First hers, then his.

Jackass.

Despite the fact that the last time she'd seen him he'd been firing a shot at Grogan, who'd been taking a shot at her.

The point being, he could describe her well enough to get an accurate composite sketch going. Which left her with two questions: was he part of this? And if he was, could facial recognition software use a composite sketch to find a photo of her that could be identified as Bianca St. Ives?

"Depends on the quality and accuracy of the sketch," Doc said. "If we change all the searchable photos of you, we shouldn't have to worry about it."

"Okay. Good to know. Go for it."

Doc gave her a thumbs-up as Evie emerged from the conference room carrying the now-empty tray. She glanced at Doc, then lifted questioning eyebrows at Bianca. Silent message: *what are you doing standing around? You're messing up the schedule.*

Evie—who'd have thunk it?—was big on keeping to the schedule.

"I'm going," Bianca said, and strode off toward her office.

Behind her, she heard Evie say to Doc, "Your costume's in your office, by the way."

"My costume?" Doc sounded both surprised and wary. "You mean for that historic thing? I'm not going."

Evie said, "You are now. We need somebody to take charge of tracking the bids who can actually work a computer. That's you. And since Hay's date has her own ticket, we now have an extra and you're going to use it."

Evie was the event co-chair, so she made those types of arrangements. Evie also, Bianca knew, had felt bad about leaving Doc out when she, Hay and Bianca were all going. Since the event had been sold out for nearly a year, there hadn't been a lot she could do about it until now. Conscripting Doc to work was Evie's way of making sure he was part of things.

Next thing Doc knew, Evie would be matchmaking for him.

Now that was something Bianca could root for. And laugh at.

Doc said, "I can't. I—I've got plans." There was no mistaking the note of rising panic in his voice.

Evie said, "We need you."

Bianca walked on into her office, which meant she missed the rest of the exchange. Not that it mattered: she was as sure as she was that the sun would rise in the morning that Evie would emerge victorious. When she walked back into the reception area a moment later, iPad in hand, Doc had retreated as far as the doorway of his office.

He was still protesting. "I'm from New York. I'm a Yankee. If I show up, the Savannah historic people will probably stone me."

"Just don't put sugar in your grits and you'll be fine," Evie said.

"They're having—" Doc began, only to be interrupted as the phone on Evie's desk started to ring. Walking past him, Evie answered it with a crisp, "Guardian Consulting. May I help you?" even as he finished with "—grits?"

The word was full of loathing.

In the Venn diagram of Southern foods Doc had tried, grits ranked on the far side of the hate circle.

Busy talking on the phone, Evie replied with a nod. Doc groaned.

"Life's a bitch," Bianca commiserated as she walked past him.

Then she opened the door to the conference room, shook hands with Pete Carmel and the supervisors—okay, that sounded like the name of a boy band; not a thought she needed to be having right then—and got down to business.

★ ★ ★

After seeing the group from Carmel Construction off, Bianca had no more appointments for the rest of day. It was a little after 4:00 p.m., and if she went home she would have time for another power nap before she had to get dressed. Evie was busy at her computer, Doc's door was closed and Hay wasn't back yet. Bianca went into her office, meaning to gather her belongings and leave. First, though, she took a moment to recheck all the sites she'd visited earlier in search of information on Groton's murder.

Still nothing. Not a mention. Not anywhere.

Bianca's mouth went dry.

The best explanation she could come up with for that was an information blackout, a cover-up that was being orchestrated at the highest levels of what almost had to be the US intelligence services.

Why? To avoid spooking other, related targets.

It was the answer that made the most sense.

She knew about what had happened to Groton only because she'd been there. Otherwise she would have had no idea that a sniper had taken him out.

Given that Beth McAlister was the object of a computer search, Bianca felt that it was a near certainty that Groton's death was connected to the Nomad Project. That meant related targets would be anyone else who was involved with it. To her knowledge, that was her, her not-father—and who else?

She had no clue.

So what to do?

Think a problem through before you make a move: it was one of the rules.

First things first: she should probably have Doc search for information on Groton's shooting. Maybe he could find something where she could not.

Gathering up her things, she headed for his office.

When she stepped out into the reception area, Evie was seated behind her desk with her head buried in her hands.

As soon as she heard Bianca's approach Evie straightened, squared her shoulders and pasted a smile on her face. The phone started to ring, and she reached for it.

"Hold it right there," Bianca said before Evie could pick up the phone. As the call went to voice mail, she stopped in front of Evie's desk and looked down at her with a severe expression. "Let's have it. What's up?"

Evie grimaced. Her lips quivered. She pressed them tightly together and closed her eyes. A single tear trickled out to roll down her cheek. Bianca would have been upset at that evidence of Evie's distress except that, lately, Evie tended to cry over everything from TV commercials to growing grass.

Bianca said, "Evie?"

Evie opened her eyes, swiped the tear away, and said, "I just got a call from my lawyer. Fourth's filed a petition for joint custody of the b-baby."

Her voice shook on the last word.

Bianca's chest constricted at the look on Evie's face. The ongoing divorce was the hardest thing her friend had ever gone through—and Bianca had a bad feeling that once the baby was born things between Evie and her slimeball ex were going to get worse.

Then it occurred to her that she might not be around to see any of it, and the tightness in her chest turned into an actual physical ache.

A problem for later.

She said, "All right. Deep breath. You're pregnant. There's no way he can get any kind of custody while you're pregnant, unless he thinks he can find a judge to order you to spend every other weekend with him so that he can talk to your belly. You have months to work this out."

Evie's hands, which had curled into fists on her desk, relaxed. Her face lost its tragic expression.

"You're right. Thank God. I have time."

"Besides, you know Fourth. Do you really think he's going to want to deal with a crying, puking baby that needs rocking and feeding and gets its diaper changed every couple of hours?"

Evie blinked. Her lips slowly stretched into a smile. "When you put it like that, I don't think I want to deal with it, either."

"Yeah, well, you're stuck. Listen, we're done for the day. Why don't you go on home?"

Evie nodded. "I think I will."

"See you in a bit, then," Bianca said, and went on into Doc's office.

She told him what she needed and waited while he ran a search. Standing behind his chair while he did his thing, she entertained herself by looking at the black-and-white prints on the walls. Doc was a major conspiracy theorist. He surrounded himself with a selection of framed images ranging from JFK in the motorcade moments before he was shot to Neil Armstrong taking the first step on the moon to Jimmy Hoffa walking into the restaurant from which he'd supposedly disappeared. In his spare time, Doc liked to work on delving into alternative explanations behind those world-famous events.

The *real* truth, he was convinced, was still out there.

Doc turned up nothing on Groton's death.

Bianca's uneasiness grew. Two things she knew for sure: whoever had run that search on Beth McAlister had not given up. And the sniper who'd taken out Groton had not vanished into thin air.

"I'm heading home," she told Doc, doing her best to mask her disquiet after he gave her the news. He was still sitting at his desk as she turned to go. Her gaze slid to what had to be the costume Evie had been talking about: a vintage white frock coat and trousers hanging from a handle on Doc's file cabinet. A black string tie dangled down the front of it. *Shades of Colonel Sanders.* "I'll see you at the gala later."

"Think Evie'd notice if I don't show?"

"Count on it."

"You could—" Doc broke off abruptly as something flickered on his computer screen. His head swiveled as he glanced at it, and then his whole body swiveled along with the chair so that he was once again facing his computer. He stared at the screen. His eyes widened. His face went from flushed to dead white in a matter of seconds.

"What?" Bianca asked.

He looked at her. His mouth opened, closed, opened again. His eyes were as round as quarters as they met hers.

"It's bad." His voice was a croak.

Alarmed, Bianca stepped closer to look past him at the screen.

All at once she couldn't breathe. She felt as if someone had just punched her in the gut.

Her face looked back at her. Her face as Jennifer Ashley, with the red wig and prosthetic overbite. That picture filled up half the screen. Beside it, filling up the other half of the screen, was her face as—her.

Bianca went weak at the knees. She had to grab on to the back of Doc's chair for support.

In the picture her hair was scraped tightly back. Her lips were thinner than she knew her own to be, her cheeks fuller, her eyes darker blue, her hair darker blond. But those were small differences, and the face was clearly recognizable as hers.

For a moment the screen, the desk, Doc himself, seemed to shimmer. Bianca willed away the shock, forced herself to focus.

She'd seen that picture before. In Austria, on a wall at the black site where she'd been held.

The picture wasn't of her, exactly. It was a computer-generated image of Nomad 44. Age progressed from an actual photo of her as an infant that had been taken not long after she'd been born.

Before her mother—her *gestational* mother—had escaped the coming slaughter by running away with her.

In the version of the picture that she'd seen in Austria, the number 44 had been tattooed on the underside of her jaw right where her scar was now.

Bianca found herself touching the scar before she realized what she was doing. It felt puckered and hard beneath her fingertips.

The tattoo, and the scar, were both missing from the photo. Bianca took that to mean that whoever had posted this photo didn't want the world at large to know about the Nomad Project.

Above the side-by-side pictures was a number written large enough to stretch across the screen: $1,000,000.

Below them was a brief, not entirely accurate physical description, and a warning, in all caps: SUBJECT'S INTACT CORPSE MUST BE PROVIDED BEFORE PAYMENT WILL BE PROCESSED.

Apparently they were taking no chances of paying out for a faked death. She had an instant vision of being felled by a sniper and then having a whole army of minions scurry in like ants to carry off her body.

Oh, God, she even knew why—they couldn't afford to have an autopsy conducted by any source outside their tight little circle. An autopsy might uncover what she was. Her blood, her cells, her tissue—any of that might bear signs of the *thing* they'd created.

Hyperventilating wasn't an option, so she didn't. Instead she took a deep breath, and read on.

Underneath the description, it said: multiple identities, including Jennifer Ashley and Elizabeth (Beth) McAlister.

Not Bianca St. Ives.

Okay, there *was something to be thankful for.*

"Where did this come from?" Talking felt weird, like her lips were numb.

Doc said, "I— Remember how I get a notification on anything concerning Elizabeth McAlister? This just now popped up. It's a—" He broke off, swallowing. Beads of sweat dotted his forehead.

Bianca knew how he felt.

"I know what it is." Her voice *sounded* normal. Of course it did. All her life she'd been trained to keep her cool.

Never show weakness: it was one of the rules.

Not even when you find yourself featured on an international hit list. *Come one, come all! Step right up, kill this woman and get one million dollars!*

10

Whoever had posted that had put every bounty hunter, hit man and assassin in the world on her trail: a cast of murderous thousands.

Bianca felt cold all over.

Doc said, "That second picture. It's you but—different." He squinted at the screen.

"Not different enough," she said, then added, "Who put this out?"

Doc hunched over his keyboard, typed something, then looked back up at her as what, to her, was an undecipherable string of computer code scrolled across the screen.

"It's posted on a bulletin board on the dark web. The money's guaranteed by Darjeeling Brothers."

Bianca's blood congealed. "The Exterminators."

Doc blinked at her. "What?"

"That's what they're called." She took a breath. *Keep it together.* "It's kind of an insider joke. You want someone dead, you call the exterminators."

"So they're, like, contract killers?" Doc sounded as appalled as she felt.

Bianca shook her head. "They're middlemen. For high-end, professional hits, they collect the fee plus their cut in advance from the commissioning party, hold it in an escrow account, post the contract, then pay the killer when the contract is fulfilled. The party who ordered the hit and the party who carried out the hit never meet. They never know each other's identities. It's all done through the Exterminators."

"*Marron!* What do we do?"

She wasn't sure what *marron* meant, but assumed it was Bronx-speak for something like *holy shit.*

"First off, I try not to die."

"Boss—" Ignoring her gallows humor, Doc wet his lips. "Can you pay them off?"

Bianca shook her head. Before she could say anything, he continued in a rush, "If you don't have a million dollars, we can get it. That payday loan company always has a ton of cash on hand. We can hit that. And the jewelry store chain—they—"

Bianca interrupted by holding up a hand. "I can't pay them off. The only way the contract is withdrawn is if the subject is killed or the commissioning party cancels it."

Doc stared at her. He was making no effort to hide his growing alarm. "We don't know who the commissioning party is."

"There's the rub." Only she did know. At least, she had a general idea. Whoever had killed Groton. No, whoever had ordered the killing of Groton. Whoever was in charge of eradicating all remaining traces of the Nomad Project.

Because that age-progressed picture of Nomad 44—of *her*—had eliminated all other possibilities as far as she was concerned.

The list of suspects had to be extremely small. The problem lay in identifying them.

Hard to cut off the head of the dog if you can't find the dog.

Doc said, "I'll figure it out. There has to be a way to figure it out." He turned and started typing furiously.

Bianca's mind was beginning to function again. "You get those pictures of me changed?"

Doc's fingers slowed. "All of them. Every last one."

"You think it was in time?"

Doc's fingers stilled altogether. "Think so. Hope so. I would've gotten that notification within minutes of that hit list thing being posted. I changed the last of the pictures maybe half an hour before." He huffed out a breath. "Talk about cutting it close."

"Yeah." Bianca thought for a minute. "Okay, they don't have the name Bianca St. Ives. You've changed all the pictures of Bianca St. Ives that were searchable online so that if someone runs facial recognition software on that picture—" she gestured at the age-progressed photo on the computer screen then remembered the possible forensic sketch that Mickey could come up with if pressed "—or anything else that shows *me*, nothing, in theory, should turn up. At least, I won't turn up."

Doc was breathing more heavily than usual. "That's right."

"So we've got a little while to figure this out." What Bianca didn't see any reason to tell him was that no hit that had ever been posted on the Exterminators' website had stayed there for longer than thirty days. Why not? Because no target had ever survived longer than thirty days.

Enlisting every professional and semiprofessional with a weapon in the world had proved to be a brutally efficient way to create a successful killing machine.

Could anybody say, dead super soldier walking?

Good thing panic wasn't something she did.

Doc said, "You think it's that prince? Al-collie something from Bahrain?"

Bianca knew it wasn't the prince. She didn't know how to explain to Doc how she knew that without telling him the rest, and coming up with complicated lies was temporarily beyond her. Right at the moment she seemed to be suffering from brain freeze. Her head kind of felt like she'd been gobbling down ice cream way too fast, only without the ice cream.

All the pain with none of the fun: was that the story of her life or what?

"I don't know." A thought forced its way through the throbbing in her head: once upon a time, her not-father had been involved with the Nomad Project—as an assassin tasked with killing her and her mother, but this wasn't the moment to quibble about details. He should know who was left alive who'd also been involved with it. He might know, or be able to guess or help her figure out, who had ordered this hit. Once she knew who to approach about fixing the problem, that's what she would do. If a polite request didn't do the trick— and she had a sad feeling that it might not—well, then, she was prepared to do what she had to do.

Snappin' necks beats killers cashin' checks. Oh, God, the stress was getting to her: she was channeling—well, mischanneling— Will Ferrell now.

The problem was, she had no way to contact her not-father. He was in the wind, hunkered down for his life just like she was. She had no phone number for him, no email address, no physical address. No idea where in the world he was—and he could be anywhere in the world. Mason Thayer was a pro at every nefarious thing he did, including hiding.

And if she probed around in some of the usual places to try to contact him, what she might succeed in doing was bringing the hounds down on both their heads.

Hmm.

Think, think, think. And try not to think that now you're channeling Winnie-the-Pooh.

Doc said, "Could we fake your death? I mean, Jennifer Ashley–Beth McAlister's death? From, like, before this was posted. We could say you died in a car accident. We could create an obituary with a picture and everything. We could—"

He broke off as Bianca shook her head. "They wouldn't fall for it. It's too pat. All it would do is intensify the hunt because they'd know for sure I was out here and aware of what was going on."

She took slight comfort in recalling that she had already faked her own death, pretty well if she did say so herself, and it was possible that whoever had put this hunt into motion wasn't sure if she was actually still alive. If she kept her head down and stayed quiet, maybe after a while the hunters would conclude that she really was dead and give up.

Yeah, and maybe tomorrow she'd sprout wings and be able to fly like a bird, too.

The chances of eluding a contract of this magnitude were slim to none.

"We can't just do nothing." Doc sounded anguished.

"You're right." An idea had occurred to her, which gave her one more thing to be thankful for: her brain was working again. "Can you set up a fake eBay seller account? One that could never be traced back to either of us, or Guardian Consulting, or Savannah, or anywhere close?"

Doc gave her a questioning look. "Sure, but...why?"

"Because I can use it to contact someone who can help fix this. I think."

"Who?"

"If I told you, I'd have to kill you. Just do it, please. How long will it take?"

"Not long. Half an hour? I need to boot up a virtual machine and then connect everything through the TOR network and bounce it off a couple of—"

She held up a hand to stop him. "You know I don't understand a word you're saying, right? You do you. I need to run home and get something. I'll be back."

Doc nodded and waved dismissal. He was already busy on his keyboard.

Bianca hitched her purse up higher on her shoulder, grabbed her briefcase from where it had somehow found its way to the floor and headed out.

She was so busy thinking through the ramifications of what she intended to do that she almost forgot about the Kill Bianca version of the Deadly Viper Assassination Squad that was out there combing the world for her—until she stepped out of the elevator at the lobby level and found herself knee-deep in people. Then her training kicked in.

Thanks to the combination of the Food and Wine Festival tents set up in the square across the street and the public restrooms in the lobby of their building, the ground floor was busy enough during what were still business hours to make an attack there unlikely. Heading for her car, Bianca scanned faces, read body language, kept on the move. The parking lot, too, was busy, and although the sun was setting in a fierce orange burst of protest against the dying of the light, there was still enough of it left to make it difficult for anyone to hide. She looked up, down, all around, checking for cars with tinted windows, for pickups with covered beds, or campers, or paneled vans—*the better to ambush you from, my dear.*

The back of her neck prickled as she considered the possibility of a sniper in a nearby building.

When she reached her car, she purposefully dropped her purse. As she knelt to retrieve it, she examined the Acura's undercarriage for bombs.

Just in case.

When she was in her car, she kept a careful eye out for following vehicles, checked cross streets, took extra care through intersections.

Because, as she well knew, T-boning happens.

By the time she pulled into her space in the underground parking garage at her condo, she was so tightly wound that she felt like one of those spring snakes stuffed as a joke into a nut can, ready to explode the moment the lid's unscrewed.

The sight of a woman hurrying toward her as she exited her car made Bianca instantly wary. The woman was carrying something in both hands, something weighty, substantial—a pot of some kind; maybe a pressure cooker bomb? Bianca shifted her weight to the balls of her feet in preparation.

She was short, plump, wearing a bright red, button-up-the-front coat over black pants. Flat shoes. Long black hair with a few gray strands done up in a bun.

An unlikely looking assassin, but—really, what assassin looked likely?

Bianca kept the car between them and curled her fingers around her throwing star.

"Hola," the woman called as she drew near. "Hello."

Bianca's brows drew together. Okay, assassins didn't usually say *hello.* Plus, this woman reminded her of someone—

"You are the one they call the guardian, *sí?*" the woman asked as she reached the Acura. Already beginning to see the light, Bianca let her hand drop away from her throwing star and walked forward to meet her. "I am Lila Nunez, Francisca's mother. My daughter told me what you did for her, last night. This is for you, to say thank you. *Muchas gracias.*"

She held the covered casserole dish she was carrying out to Bianca.

"Da nada." Bianca took the dish by the handles. It was heavy. Whatever was inside was hot and smelled spicy. She smiled at Senora Nunez, who looked exactly as she imagined Francisca would in about thirty years. "It was nothing. I was glad to be able to help."

"That is *pozole.* For your dinner. It also freezes very well. I was going to drop it off for that *maton* Sage—who is no longer permitted to see Francisca, *por cierto*—to take to you, but then I saw you pull in."

"It smells wonderful. Thank you."

Senora Nunez nodded. "My girl is precious to me. I will not forget what you did, ever."

"It was nothing," Bianca said again. She inclined her head at the pot she held. "Thank you for this. Actually, you'd be doing me a great favor if you *would* forget what I did, and that last night ever happened, and that I was involved. The gangs, you know..."

She let her voice trail off, hoping to imply that she was afraid of retaliation from the Bloods for what she had done.

Senora Nunez nodded vigorously. "I understand. No one will talk of this, ever. *Prometo.*"

"*Gracias.*"

Another car drove in. Bianca looked toward it with instinctive suspicion. Then she recognized it and relaxed. A neighbor.

Senora Nunez said, "I must go. Thank you again."

She patted Bianca's arm, Bianca nodded and smiled, and Senora Nunez walked away. Hoping like hell that the woman was right and no one would talk of last night ever, Bianca headed for her apartment.

Just as she had the night before, she took the stairs.

Only this time she was armed with a piping-hot casserole.

Assassins of the world, look out.

Bianca was back in Doc's office within the hour, but by then it was full dark outside. Except for a single security guard in the lobby and those who, for whatever reason, were still inside their offices, the building was deserted. The square across the street was lit up and bustling with activity as tourists and locals alike explored the offerings in the various tents. Music and laughter from the square could be heard even through the walls.

Bianca had arrived a moment before, and had ascertained

that Doc had the eBay account ready to go even as she closed the curtains over his pair of tall windows. She didn't think there was a sniper around, but no need to make things easy for one if she happened to be wrong.

"Put this on there," Bianca said. She handed Doc her phone, because she wasn't sure how to make certain that anything she emailed or texted him wasn't traceable, and she knew that he could render what she was giving him virtually invisible until it reached where he wanted it to go.

Showing on her phone's small screen was the photo she'd gone home to take: it was of a 1904 first edition of a small, red-bound book called *The Little Secrets*, by Frank Bonville. The book detailed the methods of a well-known cardsharp of the day, and was one of only two copies known to be still in existence.

She owned the book. She kept it in her bedroom. It had been given to her by Mason on her twelfth birthday with the admonition, *read this and learn everything in it*. She did, and she had.

And she'd kept it with her ever since, because it was one of the few personal-seeming gifts he'd ever given her, and she (had) treasured it. How she felt about it now that she knew he was *not* her father, that the complicated emotions she'd always felt for him were based on a false premise and the underlying love wasn't reciprocated, she hadn't figured out yet.

Not that it mattered right at the moment.

Now she was hoping to use the book to contact him.

He collected rare first editions on the subjects of card-sharping, sleight of hand, pickpocketry and other esoteric criminal arts. He'd found a number of them on eBay. When an auction featuring an author he knew, such as Bonville, appeared on eBay, he always received an alert.

Or at least, he'd always received an alert in the past. She couldn't be sure whether he still did. In his current circumstances, Bianca could not conceive of him buying a book from an online auction. A purchase might provide a link, a trail, something that possibly could be traced and used to find him.

But his interest in the topic would not have disappeared.

If he was still receiving alerts, he would recognize the book as soon as he saw it as the one he had given her all those years ago. He would realize that she had placed the post. He would look at it, read the listing.

That was how this should in theory work.

"You really gonna sell this?" Doc asked as whatever he had done to upload it succeeded and the photo of the book appeared on the screen.

Bianca took her phone back. "No. I'm using it to send a message." She thumbed over to the notes tab on her phone. "Put this in as the description. Exactly as I have it written here."

She handed her phone back to him. The words on the screen read: Mint edition exceptional text: master cardsharp explains secrets behind his skills. 1904 rare first printing. $18,000.00.

"You gonna tell me what the message is? 'Cause I'm not seeing it."

"No." Need to know, and Doc didn't. "And you're not supposed to."

"Fair enough." He was typing as he spoke.

The first four words represented a simple code that she and Mason had used since she was a little girl: first letter of every word until stopped by a colon, which represented the end of the message.

In this case, *m-e-e-t*: she was asking for a meeting.

If all worked as she hoped, he would get the message and reply. Communicating via eBay was not something they'd done before, but she had faith that he would figure out that he needed to use the "ask seller a question" link to give her a date, time and place.

Please God.

"I'm expecting the person I'm trying to contact to reply. Can you set up some kind of alert so we'll know if that happens?"

Doc nodded.

"This is actually, like, pure genius," Doc said as he finished typing in her message. "What kind of hit man's going to be monitoring eBay?"

"Exactly." Bianca watched as he submitted the item to the site, clicked "sell" and was done. "All right, get your Colonel Sanders outfit on. I'll wait out in the reception area."

"My what?" He swiveled away from his computer.

On her way to the door, Bianca nodded at the costume hanging from the file cabinet. "That. And hurry up. I have to go home again and change. I would have done it while I was there, but I didn't want to take the time, and besides, I have to go back to pick up Evie. Anyway, you're coming with me, so shake a leg. I'll change, we'll collect Evie and head out from there."

"We're still going to that historic thing? When you've got no telling how many contract killers after you?" Doc sounded aghast.

"Yep."

"That's just—wrong."

"Well, we could spend the night pacing the floor worrying instead, but I don't think that's going to do much good. And Evie's counting on us."

11

"Really, darling, don't you think it's time to put an end to your little sleepover with dear Bianca?" Rosalie, who was talking to Evie, sent a blinding smile Bianca's way; Bianca wasn't fooled. She'd never been Evie's mother's favorite person. Rosalie had always considered her, first, an *arriviste*, and, second and more important, a bad influence. Bianca had no doubt that Rosalie blamed her for what she considered Evie's current rebellion. "You need to go home and start decorating your nursery. I was thinking dark blue walls with white trim. So classic! Unless it's a girl. But still, if it is, you don't want to do anything as clichéd as pink, and dark blue could work for either. When *will* you find out what the sex is?"

Evie said, "I haven't scheduled an ultrasound yet, Mother."

Rosalie was just about the only person who could make Evie talk through her teeth, which was what Evie was doing now. Tall and as thin as a knife blade, with a long nose, square jaw, and dark brown eyes and hair, Rosalie was elegant rather than beautiful. She was also a perfect example of what could be accomplished by the best plastic surgeons: except for a couple of telltale creases on her neck, she looked ageless, although she would turn sixty a week before Christmas. In the shoulder-baring, flounced and beribboned lavender antebellum dress she was wearing, she could have passed for Evie's older sister.

Rosalie tut-tutted sympathetically. "Oh, I *know*. You've been so busy *working* that you haven't had time." She smiled at Bianca again. "It's so kind of you to give her a job. It must be quite an interesting office. Evangeline has *no* experience with paid employment, and you—well, dear, a *security* company? Although you do have that handsome police officer to run things for you. *He* should know what he's doing. He's accustomed to that type of work."

Bianca could feel Evie bristling beside her. It was ten minutes after eleven, supper was over and five hundred guests crowded the magnificent three-story mansion where the gala was in full swing. She and Evie were currently in the third-floor ballroom. The temperature had dropped into the low forties outside, the radiators that heated the pre–Civil War era house sighed and groaned as they cranked up, and to Bianca, in a long-sleeved, high-collared, snug-as-a-glove-to-the-waist taffeta dress, the room felt too warm. The exquisite long-leaf pine paneling that covered most of the walls in the house had, on this floor, been painted white at some much-lamented date before the Preservation Society had gotten involved. The ceiling was high and white, with a quartet of large and lovely crystal chandeliers that sparkled like diamonds hanging from it. Tiered displays of paperwhites and calla lilies and tall white candles were everywhere, in keeping with the all-white decor: their scent was the constant beneath whiffs of expensive perfume as women in their vintage gowns drifted by. White drapes were drawn across the tall, leaded glass windows, alleviating any concern Bianca might have harbored about a potential sniper. The floor was dark, polished wood, which, along with the black widow's weeds that she was wearing and the dark coats on some of the men, made a nice counterpoint to the butterfly garden effect of the rest of the ladies' dresses amid all that white.

That handsome police officer—Hay, looking, all right, *handsome* in a black cutaway coat and gray trousers—danced with Grace Cappy, a petite redhead in an apple green gown, some thirty feet away. There were maybe twenty other couples in the center of the room swaying to the lushly romantic strains of "I Only Have Eyes for You," which was being performed by a live band on a platform in the back of the room. Tables displaying some of the items up for auction lined the walls; more items were dispersed throughout the house. Dozens of partygoers browsed the offerings. Doc was among them, moving from table to table, tablet in hand as he tallied the bids: Colonel Sanders with a curly black man-bun and an iPad.

"Evie's doing a brilliant job for Guardian Consulting. And Hay is, too." Bianca's tone was mild. She'd been dealing with Rosalie's barbs for about fourteen years now, and she had long since mastered the fine art of not letting Evie's mother get to her. When she'd first started visiting Evie as a young teen, Rosalie's unstated but obvious conviction that her daughter had brought home a nobody opportunist had stung, especially because Bianca had been keenly aware of what her not-father actually did for a living, and that she herself was a part of it. As her high school years passed and the feeling didn't go away, she'd diagnosed herself as suffering from impostor syndrome because she secretly didn't feel like she belonged among the elite megarich kids who filled Le Rosey's halls. Then she'd realized that she suffered from impostor syndrome because she was, in fact, an impostor, which didn't make handling Rosalie's attitude toward her any easier. But she had persevered, and now she was able to deal with Rosalie with perfect equanimity. On more than one occasion, Evie had grimly pointed out that this was easy for Bianca as she didn't have any skin in the game.

"Hay's a great guy," Evie said to her mother. "And a good friend."

Evie was beginning to glower, which was never an attractive look for her and especially not tonight, when with her natural curls twisted into a headful of ringlets and her cheeks flushed and her red-lipsticked mouth pursed with annoyance she looked like a Kewpie doll. An angry, pregnant Kewpie doll. In a lemon yellow dress that fell straight from the twist of white ribbons that cinched it around the smallest part of her body—right under her breasts—to a flounce at her ankles. The look was more English Regency than Southern Antebellum, but as Evie had pointed out when she was trying on costumes, she would be wider than she was tall if she opted for a gown with a hoop skirt in her current condition.

Mary and Paul Bretton and Glenda Tandy joined them. All were Rosalie's contemporaries. Paul was the president of Georgia Sun Bank, and Mary and Glenda were partners in a decorating business. Mary and Paul had opted to age naturally. Both were a little plump, a little gray. Blond Glenda was as underfed and ageless looking as Rosalie. The mandatory hugs and air-kisses were rendered more awkward than usual because of the clashing hoops beneath the women's billowing skirts.

Mary said, "Evie, honey, you've done a simply wonderful job here tonight! People are bidding out the wazoo on some of those silent auction items." As Evie nodded her thanks, Mary looked at Rosalie. "Your little girl's doing you proud."

Rosalie smiled. "I know she is. She is the most accomplished thing! Did you know she's working for dear Bianca now? She did all this while she's actually holding down a *job*."

"That's amazing." Mary smiled at Bianca, while Glenda leaned in to ask Evie, in a confidential whisper, "How are you *doing*?"

Glenda was referring to the divorce rather than the pregnancy, as both her tone and her commiserating expression made clear.

"Just fine," Evie answered with a brittle smile.

Mary looked at Bianca. "I hear good things about that business of yours. You're really starting to make your mark in our little town."

Bianca responded with a polite murmur. The thing about Savannah was, if you weren't born there you were never really 100 percent one of them. But still, she loved the small city, and she was willing to work at being a part of it. It was the closest thing to home she'd ever known.

Paul said to her, "Les Harper's been singing your praises. Says you've got a guy who really knows his way around computer system security. Keep this strictly confidential, but our bank's been having some problems with that. Why don't you give me a call next week, and we can set up an appointment for you to talk to us about it?"

"I'll do that, Paul," Bianca replied with a smile.

"Did you see that condo in Aspen they're offering for Christmas week? I think it was Item Number 62," Mary said to Rosalie, pointing to a picture in the open catalog she was holding so Rosalie could check it out. "Glenda and I were thinking that we could get a few friends together and spend the holidays there this year."

"What a good idea." Rosalie looked up from the catalog. "Let's go see where the bidding is. Excuse us, darling." This she addressed to Evie.

Evie said, "Of course. You all have fun."

With murmured goodbyes, the quartet headed off.

"Thank goodness," Evie said, then nudged Bianca. "Sun Bank—see there? Networking pays off. And I'm still holding out for that bonus."

"You just keep on—" *holding*, was how Bianca was going to finish her reply, but Evie interrupted.

"Oh, no," she whispered. Her expression changed dramatically, going from teasing laughter to frozen rigidity in the space of about a second. She grabbed hold of Bianca's arm above the elbow. "Here comes Fourth."

Bianca looked in the direction that Evie was now carefully not looking.

Fourth was a hair short of six feet tall, with a runner's lean physique and a long, lantern-jawed face. His hair was dark gold, longish, brushed back. He was clean-shaven, with a long nose, long mouth and pale blue eyes. If Bianca hadn't known him so well, she might have thought he was handsome. But she did, and she didn't.

He was close, bearing down on them with a male friend. There was no time to avoid him, no place to go.

"It's okay. Just stand your ground," Bianca said for Evie's ears alone.

Evie nodded. Bianca could feel her nails digging in through the thin fabric of her sleeve. Her understanding of Evie's distress was such that she didn't even try to free herself.

Fourth was the reason Evie was hiding out, as she put it, on the third floor. She'd retreated to join Bianca there as soon as she'd come in out of the huge tent where supper had been served and discovered that Fourth was following her with the intent, presumably, of launching yet another attempt to persuade her to call off the divorce. Bianca was on the third floor because the mansion's wide front veranda was serving as an ad hoc red carpet. Klieg lights blazed bright among the classic Doric columns as the local print reporters vied with their sister TV stations to grab footage of folks attending the gala. The late-evening newscasts and presumably the morning talk shows and papers would be full of pictures of Savannah's elite looking ridiculous in hoop skirts and morning coats as they partied to raise money to preserve the city's treasured landmarks.

At least, Bianca felt like *she* looked ridiculous. She'd put in a last-minute call to the costume shop that had supplied her and Evie's dresses and requested a change. Instead of the blue-sprigged white gown she'd planned to wear, she was going with the full-blown widow's costume she'd seen on a mannequin when she and Evie had visited the store.

"Of course. The black will look lovely with your coloring," the proprietress had said, clearly not understanding Bianca's desire to wear widow's weeds to a gala but not wishing to argue with a customer.

Bianca could have explained that her change of costume was largely due to the hat with the gossamer veil that was the outfit's crowning—ha-ha; see what she'd done there? at least possible imminent death hadn't robbed her of her sense of humor—glory. But she didn't.

The veil was helping her get through the evening. It didn't completely cover her face, but the netting dipped low enough in front to mask the vital nose bridge area, and it also covered part of her cheekbones and the entirety of her ears besides obscuring the shape of her face.

Right now the game was all about defeating any facial recognition software.

The good news was that the chances of a contract killer being found among the costumed partygoers was practically zero, which meant that at least she probably wasn't going to die in a hoop skirt. Security was tight, no one was admitted without a ticket and everybody pretty much knew everybody else. The bad news was that everybody also had a camera with them in the form of their cell phones. Pictures were being taken by friends of friends, and Bianca had no doubt that Facebook and Snapchat and a whole host of other internet sites were already filling up with images of the gala.

She could avoid the cameras as long as she saw them coming. Her worst fear was that she would accidentally photobomb a Scarlett O'Hara wannabe's selfie.

All those cameras made the gala as hazardous for her as waltzing through a minefield.

Which was why she was playing defense to the max. Besides the veiled hat, and her garter belt, which would require some maneuvering to reach since her bell-shaped skirt was approximately as big around as a circus tent, she was carrying a *tessen*, also known as a Japanese war fan, that dangled from an antique-looking gold bracelet around her wrist. Disguised as an ordinary folding fan, it was made from paper-thin steel that was strong enough to deflect knives, blow-darts and arrows. It had a razor-sharp edge that made it ideal for use as a knife substitute or a throwing weapon. She was proficient in *tessenjutsu*, which was the use of the war fan in close combat.

And, unfurled and strategically positioned, it hid her features from errant cameras.

As a bonus, it was black with a delicate gold scroll design and made a beautiful accessory for her gown. She'd spent much of the evening fluttering it delicately in front of her face.

Kind of added a whole new dimension to that steel magnolia thing.

"There you are." Fourth and his friend were upon them. Fourth was looking at Evie, whose nails dug into Bianca's arm.

"Did you want something?" Evie responded. Bianca was proud of how composed she sounded. Evie's chin was up. Her eyes met Fourth's unflinchingly.

"I did," he said. "But it's something we should talk about in private. Bianca—" Fourth's eyes were cold with dislike as he directed his attention to her "—I don't think you know Chip Bridgewater. He's been pestering me to introduce you two, and he loves to dance."

Bridgewater was about Fourth's height and age, maybe a little more muscle, a good-looking guy with short dark hair and a nice smile. Like Fourth, he wore his old-fashioned costume like he was born to it. Which, like Fourth, he was. Bianca wasn't familiar with Chip, but she was familiar with the family name: they owned a shipping company that was worth a quarter of a billion.

"That wasn't exactly the lead-in I had in mind, but—" Bridgewater smiled at Bianca "—would you like to—"

Before he could finish, Hay joined them. He had Grace Cappy, who was looking flushed and radiant, on his arm.

"—such a good dancer." Grace finished what she'd been saying to Hay with a beaming smile. She looked around at the others. "Oh, hi."

"You all know Grace," Hay said. His eyes brushed Bianca's. From that brief glance, Bianca knew that Hay had spotted Fourth with her and Evie and had hurried over to lend his support.

"This will only take a few minutes," Fourth said to Evie, and nodded at a nearby alcove. "If you want to move over there out of the way—"

Grace had big hazel eyes, Bianca discovered as they fastened on Evie's face and sharpened with interest. Bianca could almost feel her storing away every word to be repeated later.

"I don't," Evie said. "Whatever it is, this isn't the place to talk about it."

Fourth's eyes narrowed. "It's time sensitive," he snapped. "And you won't return my calls."

With Fourth's arrival Evie had moved infinitesimally closer to Bianca. Bianca could feel the fine tremors coursing through her. Between her pregnancy and the divorce, Evie was currently hyperemotional. Bianca knew that right at the moment her greatest fear was that she would burst into tears in public and cause *talk*. Everybody was aware of the divorce and all the unsavory circumstances surrounding it, and Bianca could already see curious glances being cast their way. She could also see Grace soaking it all in and feel Evie's building distress.

"This feels like a good time to finish what I was saying earlier," Bridgewater said, smiling at Bianca. "Would you like to dance?"

Evie's nails dug into Bianca's arm like sharp little knives. Silent message: *don't you dare leave me.*

"I'd love to, but as you can see I'm wearing mourning." It

was the best excuse she could come up with given the short notice. Bianca used the fan to gesture at her dress and underline her point. "Back in the day ladies were forbidden to dance while they were wearing mourning, and I wouldn't want to break any rules." She smiled at Bridgewater, then looked at Grace. "Why don't you ask Grace instead?"

Only a quick flicker of his eyes revealed Bridgewater's lack of enthusiasm. But he was trapped, he knew it, and like any self-respecting Southern gentleman he gave in to the battering ram of good manners without a struggle.

He smiled at Grace. "I think they want to be rid of us. Would you like to dance?"

Grace shot a glance at Hay, who, as it happened, was looking at Bianca.

"Yes, thank you, I would," Grace said. Bridgewater offered his arm, and the two headed toward the floor.

"I've had an offer on the house," Fourth said to Evie. "It's a good one. I want to accept it."

"What?" Evie's eyes flew to his face. "It's not even for sale."

"You're not living there. You don't want us to be a family, to raise our baby there. You want a divorce. If that's really the way you feel, it's time to sell the house."

Evie's eyes filled with tears. "I don't—I can't—"

She broke off. Bianca knew that it was because she was too choked up to continue.

Fourth pressed on. "Or you can sign your share of the house over to me, and at least half the time our baby will have a home."

Evie's response was a strangled croak.

"You son of a bitch," Hay said, his voice too soft to be heard beyond their little group. "To come here and upset her—"

"She's my wife, so you can just back off," Fourth growled.

12

Evie's face turned tomato red. Her lips clamped into a straight line. She was clutching Bianca so tightly that Bianca knew she would have marks on her arm later. She also knew that Evie couldn't talk because she was barely holding in furious tears.

"Stop, both of you," Bianca hissed at the two men, then gave Fourth a look that made his eyes widen. "You. Go away. Right now, or first thing Monday she's talking to her lawyer about getting a restraining order." Fourth opened his mouth to say something. Conscious of the interested eyes that were turned their way, Bianca smiled and said, "I mean it."

The fact that she did must have shown in her eyes, because Fourth looked at Evie, said, "I'll be in touch," turned on his heel and walked away.

Evie leaned a little more heavily against Bianca's side. Her mouth was still clamped shut. She was breathing hard through her nose and blinking rapidly in an effort to hold back tears. Hay shifted position so that he blocked the sight of her from the rest of the room.

"You know he's just trying to get under your skin, right?" Bianca said to Evie. "Don't let him do it."

Evie nodded. Before anybody could say or do anything else, Bianca spotted Randall Wallace, president of the Chamber of Commerce, and Mark Graham, a wealthy real-estate developer, coming toward them. Wallace was short, portly and balding, Graham was tall, thin and balding. Both were in their early to midsixties.

What to do? Evie was in no shape to be seen by anybody outside their own little group.

"So what's up?" Doc appeared on Bianca's other side without warning and immediately frowned questioningly at Evie. To her chagrin Bianca realized that she had been so focused on the approaching businessmen that she hadn't even seen him skirting a cluster of would-be bidders crowding around a nearby table to join them.

"Shit from a shithead," Hay said. Doc looked confused, but there was no time to explain that "'shithead" was Hay's current favorite nickname for Fourth: Wallace and Graham were closing in.

"Here, take Evie and dance with her." Bianca thrust Evie toward Hay, who looked surprised but slipped a supportive arm around her. "We're about to have company, and nobody needs to see her like this. Keep her on the floor until she calms down. Then maybe we can all get out of here."

Evie made another strangled croak: words trying to force their way out.

"The auction doesn't end till twelve," Doc said, interpreting her thought, and Evie nodded. Translation: they couldn't leave before then.

"To hell with the auction." Hay was already turning away with Evie. Sheltering her from view as best he could with his body, he walked her onto the dance floor and pulled her against him so that her face was hidden in his shoulder.

"Bianca," Wallace greeted her. He and Graham stopped in front of her, blocking her view of Hay and Evie. She smiled at them, shook hands, introduced Doc.

"We have some good news," Wallace said, and Graham nodded. "It hasn't been officially announced yet, but I wanted you to know you've just been selected as one of six nominees for Savannah Businesswoman of the Year."

"Why, how nice." Bianca felt a warm little glow of pleasure. Until she remembered that there was a strong likelihood that she wouldn't be around or maybe even alive when the nominations were announced, much less when the award ceremony itself took place. She struggled to keep her smile in place. "I'm honored. And so proud of everyone at Guardian Consulting. They've all worked incredibly hard to make the company a success."

"We're just following your lead, boss," Doc said. Bianca's smile turned genuine as she glanced at him and reflected how far he'd come in the realm of putting a good corporate face on it.

"That's right—a good company results from a good leader," Graham said. Marshall nodded.

"Well, I wanted to give you a heads-up," Marshall said. "The official announcements will be made next Wednesday. Congratulations."

"Thank you," Bianca said. A few more pleasantries were exchanged, and they moved on.

"The good news train just keeps on chugging along," Doc said when they were gone. He cast a furtive glance around and held out his iPad to Bianca. "We got an answer. Here it is."

Bianca's pulse sped up as she looked at it.

She'd been right: Mason had figured out that he needed to reply through the "ask seller a question" link.

Marvelous acquisition can't afford unfortunately; what's your next number? Keep it low: M-A-C-A-U; W-Y-N-N? A question mark meant what followed were numbers: first letter in a word equaled the corresponding number—11-9-12.

Translation: Mason wanted to meet at the Wynn Hotel in Macau on November 9 at midnight.

Four days from now.

Bianca felt her stomach twist.

"That *is* your guy, right?" Doc sounded suddenly anxious.

"Yes."

Doc was frowning at her. She supposed her face must reflect the dread that was rising inside her like thick, deeply cold sap. She rarely allowed herself to feel anything too strongly. Not to do so had been drummed into her from an early age.

Keep emotion out of it: it was one of the rules.

But right now she was finding that impossible to do.

She could feel the life she had so painstakingly built for herself starting to evaporate around her. Her gaze slid from Doc to Evie, who no longer had her face buried in Hay's shoulder but was looking up at him and nodding to Hay as they danced. They were more than friends. They were her family: Evie and Hay, and now Doc, as well. There was Evie's baby: she didn't even know if it was a boy or a girl. Would she be around for the birth, to watch the child grow? She looked over the crowded ballroom: for better or worse, she knew almost everyone there. She thought of her condo, and Guardian Consulting, and the fact that the local business community thought enough of her to select her as a nominee for Savannah Businesswoman of the Year.

She thought of her clients, and the jobs Guardian Consulting currently had underway, and the prospects she still needed to pitch projects to and her plans to grow the business. She thought of the respect and the respectability she had worked hard to earn.

She thought of the Packs and Francisca and her mother and even Nora-with-the-bicycle who delivered the paper. She thought of the Starbucks on the corner near her office and the private gym she'd set up for herself in the basement of the ballet school she owned and all the little things, like the routes she liked to run and the places she liked to shop and the fact that the star-shaped leaves on the sweet gum trees in front of her office building were just starting to turn red.

It was a tapestry of people and places and things that meant something to her.

It was a *life. Her* life.

At the knowledge that she could lose it, her heart shivered and bled.

It was possible that once she left this place for Macau, she could never come back.

It was possible that she would die.

The thought of dying, of being killed, pop, bang, you're gone, scared her.

Duh, right? The thought of dying scared everyone.

Only she was suddenly so afraid of it that she felt as if her insides had turned to stone.

The reason? The reality that she was very likely to be killed within the next few weeks was beginning to hit home.

Plus, it had just occurred to her to wonder, given the circumstances surrounding her creation, if she even had a soul.

Heaven and hell, some kind of afterlife, had always been abstract concepts, fuzzy possible conclusions to one far distant, really bad day.

But the thought that *if* they existed she might not have a ticket to ride made her go weak at the knees.

To be blasted into nothingness—the idea made her mouth go dry. It made her want to pant with fear.

Yeah, well, cry me a river.

Time to cowboy up and deal with the situation as it stood.

Whether she liked it or not, she *was* a walking, talking, genetically enhanced test-tube experiment: nothing in the world she could do about that.

And there *were* a whole lot of people out there trying to kill her. Difference was, *that* she could possibly do something about.

So right now she was going to deal with the hard practicalities of continuing to stay alive, and let the existential stuff go.

Unless she was missing something, she had three choices:

(1) stay in Savannah, go about her business, and hope never

to be found; great choice, except—sooner or later, she would be found;

(2) go public. Call the national newspapers, the TV stations, the media outlets. Tell the world about the Frank-N-Furter gang that had created her. Tell the world about the murders of the forty-seven other Nomads and their gestational mothers. Tell the world what she was. That might take away the incentive to kill her. It would also shine a blindingly bright spotlight on her, blow up every aspect of her life, and let any would-be killers who were not deincentivized by publicity know exactly who and where she was. If she was a betting person—she wasn't; her not-father was the inveterate gambler—she would bet that she would be dead and disappeared before she could convince anybody that the fantastic story she was telling was the truth;

(3) find and kill the bastard—or bastards—who were trying to find and kill her. If she did that, if she was successful, if she could cut the head off the dog leading that vicious pack, she would live and get her life back.

It wasn't even really a choice: she was going with Door Number Three.

"Boss? You okay?" Doc's face was now a study in worry. His tone said that this wasn't the first time he'd asked.

"I'm fine," Bianca said. Not strictly true, but she was better. She could feel her body gearing up, her blood pumping, her muscles loosening, her senses sharpening. Preparing for a battle. "Send a reply—can't undersell."

Doc nodded, balanced the iPad in the crook of his arm and started to peck one-fingered at the virtual keyboard. "Can't undersell?"

"That's right." She saw a couple of Junior Leaguers and their husbands bearing down on them. "Got it?"

Doc nodded.

"Then get out of eBay and go back to adding up bids."

That's all she had time to say before the necessity of making small talk was once again upon her.

But the message had been sent: C-U. *See you.*

At the Wynn Macau, at midnight in four days.

13

The Direction Générale de la Sécurité Extérieure—DGSE—
was the French version of MI6 and the CIA. One year previously they had overseen the arrest in Paris of Phillippe
Bergere, a high-end fence with connections throughout Europe. Bergere was currently housed in Le Centre de Detention de Muret, a prison in the Auvergne region of France,
where he would be held for the next five years. The relative
brevity of his sentence was due to the fact that he had agreed
to cooperate with the DGSE and, by extension, other law-
enforcement entities, in certain highly sensitive investigations.

One of those investigations was into the whereabouts of the
notorious thief Traveler, who had subsequently been identified as Mason Thayer. Thieves, naturally, needed fences to
dispose of stolen goods. Thayer had made use of Bergere's
services in that regard on multiple occasions.

As Bergere put it, "You have a rare diamond, an old master-
piece, an *objet*, everyone knows I am the best."

Which was why Rogan, accompanied by DGSE agent
Henri Moreau, a dour-faced, fifty-something Parisian in a
tired brown suit, was at that moment seated in a folding metal
chair drawn up to a bolted-to-the-floor metal table, in a blue-
painted, concrete-walled room reserved for law enforcement
visits to prisoners, quizzing Bergere about known associates of
Thayer, as well as his possible whereabouts if he chose to lie
low. The room smelled of tobacco smoke and old piss. It was
cold. Heat cost money, and the French were very cost-con-

scious, especially in regards to their prisoners. A cheap fluorescent fixture overhead bathed the table in a squint-producing glare that reflected off the white paper in the notebook in which Moreau was jotting things down. The interrogation was being conducted in English, because Rogan, while passably conversant in French, didn't want to miss any nuances. The urgency was growing: with the CIA involved in the case, the race was on. Whoever got to Thayer first would have custody, and the CIA did not willingly share. The material Thayer had collected, some of it light-years beyond highly classified and gathered over years, could not be allowed to disappear into the black hole of the US intelligence services, to be used as they saw fit. It was sensitive enough to set the agendas of the white-hat countries of the world back decades. Not coincidentally, it also, or so Rogan had inferred from what he had seen and been obliquely told, contained enough dirt on various governments, world leaders, powerful institutions and people to sink more than a few ships.

Finding Thayer was also, in his estimation, the quickest route to locating Sylvia. He didn't know the reason behind the CIA's sudden interest in her, but the interest was definitely there. Thayer was a world-class bad guy. He was her boss. Which begged the question: what was she? There was something Rogan didn't know, obviously, but he wasn't ready to bring her to Durand's attention yet.

In any case, Hanes's interest in Sylvia meant that he was interested, too.

"He is everywhere, he is nowhere, that one," said Bergere, referring to Thayer. He was seventy years old, about five-eight and wiry, with thinning gray hair and wire-rimmed spectacles framing shrewd hazel eyes. His face was leathery from years spent in the sun, and he had the stained teeth of a longtime smoker. He wore a denim shirt over black belt-less pants, because in France prisoners wore their own clothing with the only restriction being in regard to items such as belts, which could pose a danger.

Rogan said, "When you met with Agee—" Adrian Agee was the name Bergere had known Thayer by "—tell me how it would happen."

Bergere took a long pull on the cigarette, which was one of a carton that Moreau, whose history with this informant was why he was there with Rogan, had brought him, and let the smoke curl out of his nose.

"He would come into my shop—" as a cover for his actual means of earning a living, Bergere had owned a bicycle repair shop in the Rue des Écoles in Paris "—and we would go into the back room. He would tell me what he wished to dispose of, the price he wanted and show me pictures. Then he would go away. When I had a buyer, I would notify him."

"How?" Rogan asked.

"A blue bicycle in my shop window. That directed him to take a certain course of action upon which we had previously agreed."

"Tell him," Moreau directed. Bergere looked wary. Moreau added, "You know Ghyslaine has already been brought on board."

"I do not like to inform on my friends," Bergere said with dignity. "And Ghyslaine—she is beautiful, *n'est ce pas*? I had hopes there, once."

"If you help us, you will be out before you know it," Moreau said. "Then you may once again pursue your hopes with *la belle* Ghyslaine." He shoved a foil ashtray toward Bergere as the ash trembling on the end of his cigarette grew dangerously long. "Tell him."

Bergere knocked the ash off his cigarette. "When he saw the bicycle, Agee would visit a certain street fair, purchase some paintings there, very low price, then have those paintings conveyed to Ghyslaine."

"Ghyslaine owns the Galerie d'or," Moreau put in.

Rogan knew it for one of the most respected art galleries in Paris. He nodded.

"Packed in with the paintings would be the items Agee wished to move," Bergere continued. "Ghyslaine would purchase the street paintings, worth very little, for the sum agreed upon for the items. She would issue a check, all proper, all—how you say?—aboveboard, to Agee for the paintings, you understand, with no one to raise an eyebrow because who are we, any of us, to put a value on art? Ghyslaine would then pass the items on to the buyer, and Agee would deposit his check in the bank, c'est ça."

Rogan spent no more than a couple of seconds admiring the efficiency of the money-laundering operation.

"What bank?" he asked.

Agee shrugged.

Moreau said, "Banque Martin Maurel. The money would disappear as soon as it hit the account. Tracing it has proved impossible so far."

Rogan knew exactly how impossible Thayer's finances were proving to trace. There was a whole team on it.

"What do you know about Agee? Family, things he liked to do, places he liked to visit, hobbies?" Rogan tried a different angle.

"I know nothing of that. I think maybe he is an American, because he once asked where he could get a decent hamburger, and, I ask you, who eats such things?"

Since Thayer's nationality was already established, that information was useless. Rogan gave Bergere a sudden sharp look. Was the Frenchman deliberately fulfilling his end of the agreement by revealing things investigators already knew? Because the only other thing he had revealed—the money-laundering scheme—had been known to Moreau and was useless to Rogan.

"If you were able to give me information that helped me find Agee, I could arrange for your release as soon as the information panned out," Rogan said.

Bergere looked at him steadily—*he knows something*, Rogan thought—then glanced at Moreau for confirmation.

Moreau shrugged and nodded. "It's true. He could."

"I want it in writing," Bergere said. "*Un contrat*. A contract."

"That can happen," Rogan said. "If the information is good."

"I want the contract first."

Rogan gave him a measuring look, then reached for the pad of paper Moreau was using and held out his hand for the loan of Moreau's pen. When Moreau passed it over, Rogan scribbled, *If information from Phillippe Bergere results in the discovery of the whereabouts of the man known as Adrian Agee, he will have discharged his obligation under his sentence and will be entitled to immediate release from detention.* He then signed his name with a flourish, tore the sheet of paper from the pad and slid it across the table to Bergere.

Bergere looked at it. "Is this *authentique*?"

Moreau shrugged. "Whether it is or not, you have my word that it will be so."

"Mine, too," Rogan said.

Bergere squinted at him suspiciously. "I do not know you."

Moreau said, "The matter is urgent. There is no time for *avocats*."

Rogan reached across the table to tap the piece of paper he'd just passed over. "This is the best you're going to do."

Bergere pursed his lips.

"Ah, bah. I will trust you, then." He looked from Moreau to Rogan. "There is one thing—Agee, he is a gambler. He goes to the big casinos, the best ones, two, three times a year. I have friends who have seen him, who have told me this. They said that he was lucky and usually won."

"What friends?" Moreau asked.

Bergere smiled and shook his head.

"Do you know which casinos?" Rogan asked. The news was of value: casinos had surveillance cameras, security staff, records of payouts. If what Bergere said was true, there would be a trail. A trail that could possibly be followed.

"That's all I know." Bergere sounded suddenly grumpy, like he feared he had said too much.

Rogan stayed for another half an hour, doing his best to pry any other nuggets of information from Bergere, but if the man knew anything else that might be of use he wasn't giving it up.

In the end Rogan walked out of the prison with Moreau, thanked him for his help, got in his car and drove away.

He then immediately got on his encrypted phone to place a call to Durand. He reported the tip he'd gotten from Bergere, and requested the activation of eyes on the ground—the network of local informers that spies cultivated in every major city in the world—in all the gambling meccas: Las Vegas, Reno, Atlantic City, Monaco, Singapore, and the big daddy of them all, Macau. He suggested that they go with something like a discreet sweep by, say, "tax authorities," to check the casinos' surveillance footage and payout books and get the names and personal information of winners over the last few years. Photos of Thayer should be passed around in those locales, and rewards offered for a sighting. Lesser gambling destinations would be targeted, too.

It was a broad net, but it was a net, which was more than they'd had before. The only thing to do was to wait to see if anything got caught in it.

In a white Audi parked in the visitors' lot of Le Centre de Detention de Muret, Brian Lesce observed Rogan exit the prison, shake hands with Moreau and drive off. The twenty-six-year-old American picked up his encrypted phone and placed a call.

"He's just left," Lesce said. He was a newly minted case officer, part of the CIA's human intelligence—HUMINT—sector: average height and weight, blue eyes, brown buzz cut, boyishly handsome face. For the past six months he'd been stationed in Lyon, and his usual job involved conducting routine espionage on designated French politicians. He'd been pulled from that task to form one of the surveillance teams that had been assigned to follow Rogan since shortly after his meeting with Interpol's Durand.

"Somebody picking him up?" Steve Hanes sounded impatient. Hanes was SOG, Special Operations Group. SOG was the most secretive special operations force in the United States. An offshoot of the CIA's Special Activities Division—SAD—it was almost unknown to the public. When the covert shit hit the really big fan, SOG was who they called. Lesce didn't know what Hanes's assignment was—the classification level was way above his pay grade—but he knew it had to be big. And for the purposes of said assignment, Hanes was his boss.

"Raney's waiting right outside the prison," Lesce replied.

Hanes didn't even acknowledge that. Instead he asked, "Who'd Rogan meet with?"

"Henri Moreau from DGSE—"

"I know that," Hanes interrupted. "Who did they talk to inside the prison?"

"Oh," Lesce said. He really hated what he had to say next. "I don't know."

"You—don't—know." Hanes's tone was scathing. "Well, get in there and find out. I want to know who they met with and what was said. *Now.*"

Thirty minutes later, Lesce was still shaken from the bawling out Hanes had given him over the length of time it had taken him to get the requested information, and Hanes, who was in Hamburg, Germany, following a lead, was on his encrypted phone to Greg Wafford, deputy director of the National Clandestine Service, which oversaw SOG.

"They're looking for Thayer hard," Hanes said. "In my opinion, finding Thayer's our best bet for finding *her.*"

"I agree." Wafford was speaking from his office in CIA headquarters in Langley, Virginia. "So find him. Question him. Use him to find her. Use whatever means you need to use to find her. She has to be liquidated. They both have to be liquidated. We've got to get this behind us."

"I understand," Hanes said. "I'm employing every available resource. I'll get it done."

14

Three days later, Bianca stepped off the jetfoil and walked into Macau's crowded Cotai Terminal. There was no sight line for a sniper inside the terminal, and it was doubtful that any seasoned operative would risk using a pistol where he would be sure to be caught, but another kind of attack—by, say, knife or even blow-dart—wasn't out of the question even with the amount of security present in the warehouse-like building. Shielded by oversize sunglasses, her eyes were constantly on the move, assessing possible threats. The tension in her shoulders from semiexpecting an attempt on her life at any moment was giving her a stiff neck. The chin-length brown wig she was wearing had long, uneven bangs and provided an acceptable degree of coverage from the overhead cameras, but it also gripped her head like a vise. She wasn't prone to headaches, but she was getting one.

Takeaway: trying to stay alive was no walk in the park.

She'd embarked from the Hong Kong–Macau Ferry Terminal, having landed at Hong Kong International Airport earlier in the day. The ride across the Pearl River Delta had taken about fifty-five minutes. It was a little blustery, but the temperature was a mild 63 degrees Fahrenheit and there was no rain. A thin golden haze hung over the Macau Peninsula, appropriate considering its status as the number one gambling destination in the world. That the haze was actually smog and the golden color was due to the setting sun hitting it only slightly diminished its dazzling effect.

The modern city with its skyline of many high-rises and the towering, needle-topped monolith that was Macau Tower felt familiar, if not precisely welcoming. She'd visited often over the years. This time she'd spent the better part of two days getting there. To be safe, she'd chosen to travel by a circuitous route, and in the process she'd lost a day. In Savannah it would be 7:19 p.m. on Monday. In Macau it was 7:19 a.m. on Tuesday. The meeting with Mason was scheduled for midnight the following day.

Doc was with her, but not by her choice. He'd been sitting in her hallway with his duffel bag when she'd left her condo at 4:00 a.m. Sunday, and flatly refused to let her go without him.

"You might need backup," he'd insisted after she'd ordered him to get lost as he followed her down the stairs to her car. "You know, in case you get—" his voice dropped to an ominous whisper "—attacked."

"What are you going to do, spam them to death?"

"Hey, I can do things—" he was starting to huff and puff as they reached the fourth floor, making his words come out in uneven bursts "—other things. Not just computer stuff." They reached the parking garage. He took a deep, wheezy breath and continued, "I can use a gun."

Bianca made a rude sound. "God help us both if our lives ever depend on that."

"Not...nice." He was still wheezing as they reached her car. Bianca was distracted, but not so distracted that she wasn't busy checking out the parking garage for possible assailants. Her roller bag was already in the trunk, carried down the night before so that she wouldn't have to make an ungodly racket on the stairs at four in the morning. "I can be a lookout, okay? Or maybe you'll need somebody to be the muscle."

She made another rude sound. "Right. Forget it."

Dropping to a prone position, she looked under the car. She wasn't expecting to find one, but—bombs happen.

"You doing push-ups *now*?" Doc asked in a surprised tone above her.

She rolled her eyes and got to her feet to frown at him. "I appreciate the thought, I really do," she told him. "Your loyalty means a lot. But these are serious people, and they're seriously out to kill me. If you're with me, they won't hesitate to kill you, too."

Doc shrugged. "Hey, we all have to die sometime, right? But maybe if I'm with you we can both hold it off a little longer, you know what I mean?"

"No," Bianca said, opening her car door. "You cannot go with me. End of discussion."

Doc looked at her across the roof of the car.

"I know where you're going," he said. "I broke the code. You don't take me with you, I'll just show up."

Bianca froze, staring at him.

He said, "You want me to say it? Ma—"

"Stop." There was no one around to hear, she was 99.9 percent certain. But it was that one-tenth of 1 percent that could get you killed. "Don't say another word."

"Hey, that's what computers are for." He sounded slightly uneasy. "I ran it through a program. Took about three minutes."

A whole host of unpleasant thoughts rushed through Bianca's head. The code was a seven-year-old's means of communicating in secret with her father when he wasn't around. It had never been designed to be unbreakable. The thought that Doc had done it was more annoying than frightening; his deed could only be accomplished by somebody more threatening than he was if they could find her eBay post, which hopefully they couldn't. The question now became what to do: she couldn't simply leave Doc behind, knowing what he knew...

"Is this one of those things where if I know what I know you're going to have to kill me?" His eyes met hers, alarmed.

Well, yeah.

"Get in the damned car," Bianca said through her teeth, and he did, tossing his duffel bag into the backseat.

"You have passports, driver's licenses, credit cards, *legends*? In multiples? That'll stand up to airport and border security?" She threw the questions at him as she drove through Savannah's darkened streets at a controlled speed, instead of flooring it as her state of mind urged her to do. She was already busy trying to figure out how, in explaining this to Evie and Hay, she was supposed to add Doc to an ostensible emergency trip to visit her suddenly acutely ill father. "We're going to be changing identities a lot."

"I've traveled with you before, remember?" he said. "And just so you know, creating legends is what us legends do."

That attempt at humor earned him a black look.

"Remember this when the bullets start flying," she said, settling on the story that her father's company needed a computer security check, and she was taking Doc with her because she'd decided to take care of that while she was there. "If you die, it's on you."

Bianca got her revenge for Doc's insistence over the course of two arduous days of travel. The jetfoil trip across the strait was the icing on the cake. The boat was fast, the water was choppy and the combination meant that the passengers were bouncing around like bunnies on speed. Finally Doc lost his cookies (literally—he'd unwisely fortified himself for the boat ride with a bag of Oreo Minis) over the side. Since they ostensibly weren't together, there wasn't much she could do to help him. They didn't speak until they'd passed through customs. By the time they walked—well, he tottered—out onto the open, paved pavilion that led to the street, she judged it safe enough to approach him.

"How you feeling?" she asked.

"Like I threw up all over the side of a multimillion-dollar boat."

"What can I say? Karma sucks."

But she bought him a Cherry Fizz—an icy combination of cherry juice and ginger ale—from a sidewalk vendor, and after a few sips he began to regain some of his color. As he leaned against a pillar and drank, she stood with her back against the wall in the shadow of a potted camphor tree and watched the new arrivals streaming out of the terminal. This was one of those rare situations when she would have given much to be carrying a gun. If ever there was a time when she needed to be packing heat this was it, when she was being ruthlessly hunted by no telling how many crackerjack government assassins and an equally unknown number of contract killers, and just about every computer-literate hit man in the civilized world would take her out if they spotted her. But guns and airline travel don't mix, and here in Macau she would be visiting the casinos with their metal detectors and security searches at key checkpoints. Being caught with a gun would instantly put her on the radar of way too many law-enforcement types, and the word would spread. That would bring the very killers she was doing her best to avoid down on her like ducks on a June bug. Better to keep to her current strategy of staying undercover and waiting until she knew the identity of the target she needed to take out to regain her life before making like Rambo and arming herself to the teeth.

In the meantime, keeping her eye out for trouble was the name of the game. But if she was being followed, she was having no luck spotting the tail. Altair the Assassin's Creed guy might be lurking among the tourists, but if so he could add master of disguise to his list of accomplishments.

The medicinal scent of the camphor joined with the sulfuric combination of smog and car exhaust to form a smell that was distinct to Macau. Half a dozen languages assaulted her ears at the same time—the native Cantonese, Mandarin, Hokkien, Portuguese, Tagalog, English. She caught a phrase here, a sentence there, but nothing stood out.

The problem was, assassins tended not to wear signs saying I'm an Assassin. All she could do was look for tells: a head swiveling as the would-be assailant tried to establish her whereabouts, a too-long glance cast her way, an alteration in someone's path or stride as they saw her, a hand reaching inside a coat or a bag—there were many, and most were subtle and easy to miss. Especially given the sheer number of people.

It didn't help that she'd been in an acute state of vigilance for so long now that she was afraid her senses might be beginning to dull.

She and Doc had traveled the last two legs of the journey, from Rome to Athens to Hong Kong for him, from Rome to Istanbul to Hong Kong for her, separately, then met up at the ferry terminal, as a matter of good tradecraft. For the sake of Doc's safety, she hadn't wanted to risk having them linked together as they arrived in Hong Kong in case something should go wrong and she should be recognized.

But Macau was safer. Macau was everything people expected clean, business-centric Hong Kong to be, but it wasn't. Macau was the Far Eastern version of the Wild West. As the new gambling capital of the world, it was bigger, louder, flashier, more over the top even than Las Vegas. A Portuguese territory until 1990 and now a Special Administrative Region of the People's Republic of China, Macau was a garish mix of clashing cultures. It teemed with people: tourists from everywhere in the world, high-rolling gamblers, hookers of all descriptions and in all price ranges, Triad gang members, workers from the Chinese mainland brought in to do the menial jobs that no one else wanted, and the western expatriates and Macau citizens who lived there year-round.

Small helicopters were as ubiquitous as mosquitoes in the sky. The streets were packed with everything from the latest, most expensive Rolls-Royces to battered Mini Coopers to overflowing buses to rattling trishaws, a tricycle-rickshaw combo, with drivers that thought nothing of weaving in and out of the frequently stopped traffic. Taxis crowded the terminal area. There were so many people, such a mix of nationalities, that her fear of being spotted declined even as the crowds swirled around her. Finally she pushed away from the wall, corralled Doc, pitched what was left of his drink and bundled him into a black and white taxi.

"The Grand Lisboa," she said to the driver in English. Her cover for the journey to Macau was Sarah Bowman, an accountant from Florida. Doc was Tony Gatti, a restaurant manager from the Bronx. They were casual acquaintances, having met in the ferry terminal in Hong Kong.

She'd chosen the Grand Lisboa because it was the tallest, most distinctive hotel-casino in Macau. The forty-seven-story building was shaped like a lotus blossom, and even among the extravagant follies of the other casino complexes it stood out. It was exactly the kind of place where wide-eyed tourists Sarah and Tony would stay.

The taxi honked and dodged its way onto the Cotai Strip, past the newest megacasinos and attractions, including the Venetian Macau, with its scaled-down version of the Piazza San Marco complete with a canal featuring real gondolas under a star-studded faux sky, and the Parisian, with its half-size Eiffel Tower. The taxi finally swerved off the Avenida do Aeroporto into the semicircular drive leading to the Grand Lisboa's lobby. Handing over the required amount of patacas, they got out, checked in and went to their rooms.

Two hours later, their appearances drastically changed along with their identities, they were checking into a different, more modest hotel, the MGM Cotai, without having checked out of the Grand Lisboa. For all intents and purposes, Sarah and Tony were still staying at the Grand Lisboa, and would spend two nights there. Ann Brabourne, a Canadian artist, and David Cohen, a car salesman from Detroit, were staying at the MGM. As Ann, Bianca artlessly admired the large, built-in aquariums that were part of the undersea theme of the lobby to the clerk at reception as she signed her (Ann's) name.

Again, it was a matter of good tradecraft. Switching hotels and identities made finding them that much harder.

For the same reason, as well as for ensuring Doc's safety and her own freedom of movement, they had separate rooms on separate floors. Before leaving Doc for the night, Bianca passed him a burner phone.

"You need me, hit speed dial one," she told him. They stood just inside his room, which was large and comfortable and looked out over the roof of One Central, a high-end shopping mall.

"What if you need me?" He juggled his key card, a large soda and a bag of burgers and fries from the McDonald's across the street. She'd made him buzz his head during their brief stop at the Grand Lisboa, because a three-hundred-pound American with a Bronx accent and shoulder-length black curly hair, whether man-bunned or ponytailed or loose, was just too distinctive.

"I look like a sumo wrestler," had been Doc's glum verdict after the deed was done.

He did, sort of, but it helped him blend in.

"Own it," was her advice.

He'd done his best, looking as badass as it was possible for a cherub-faced guy to look, even swaggering a little as he'd walked into the MGM. But now his shoulders slumped and he just looked tired. He made her think of a human Po, the sweet, clumsy main character in *Kung Fu Panda*. Not that she meant to tell him so.

She also didn't have the heart to burst his bubble: the chances that she would need him at this point were so negligible as to be practically nonexistent. His expertise was in computers, not combat or weaponry, and unless she happened to be carrying a laptop in front of a vital spot when the bullet with her name on it was fired, she didn't think computers could help her now. He was with her in Macau because he'd insisted on coming, and, truth be told, she was glad of his company. Having him with her was comforting, like holding on to a little piece of home. But after her meeting with Mason, she and Doc were going to go their separate ways, although he didn't know it yet. She meant to tell Doc that she'd accomplished what she'd come to Macau to accomplish, the kill contract was in the process of being withdrawn and now they could go back to Savannah. She would put him on a plane (well, a series of planes) bound for home, promise to meet him there, and then go do what she had to do to make this nightmare go away. She would live and return to Savannah and her life, or she would die. But she would send him home to safety either way.

If her heart clutched a little at the idea that after she put him on that plane for Savannah she might never again see him or any of the other people who made up home for her, well, too bad.

"If I need you, I hit speed dial one on my phone, too," she said.

She went to her room, two floors above, and immediately did a security sweep. First she checked the closet, the bathroom, behind the curtains—her window had a partial water view, very nice with all the neon reflecting off the smooth black surface of Lago Nam Van—and under the bed. Then she pressed a finger to the mirror above the credenza opposite the bed, looking for a miniscule gap between her fingertip and its reflection that might indicate the presence of a two-way mirror, and did the same to the bathroom mirror: nothing. She scanned for hidden cameras: nothing. Because modern TVs were notorious for being used to both watch and listen to people, she draped her clothes over the flat-screen on the credenza as she undressed instead of hanging them in the closet. Finally she secured the door with a door jammer portable lock and went to take a shower.

By that time she was so tired that she barely had the energy to eat the dried meat and fruit kabob she'd picked up from a vendor on the way into the hotel. Halfway through, she abandoned the effort.

What she needed most was sleep.

She took the extra pillows from the closet and made a human-shaped form in the bed, pulling the bedspread over it so that if someone should manage to breach her defenses and get inside the room, it would look like she was sleeping there.

Gathering up another pillow and a couple of blankets, she turned out the light.

Except for the faint glow from the open-all-night casinos that sifted in around the edges of the curtains—the room was now totally dark. One last quick scan of the room for a telltale pinprick of light that might indicate the presence of a hidden camera yielded nothing. Faint sounds of music and laughter, vehicular traffic and the occasional boom of fireworks—the Strip was big on fireworks—drifted through the walls.

Bianca went to the closet, opened it and made herself a pallet on the floor.

Then she stepped into the closet, closed the door and rolled up in the small bed she'd made.

The weapons she'd brought with her were close at hand.

Even a well-defended hotel room was subject to breach.

She was ready.

Two things she'd been trained in from birth were how to hide and how to survive.

15

"That's awesome." Doc watched the Chinese Dragon dance through the square across from the Wynn Macau with wide-eyed appreciation. It was nineteen minutes until midnight on Wednesday. The night was cool and overcast. The sky was a thick black soufflé of clouds. The square would have been as dark as pitch except for the brilliant neon colors of the casinos towering above it and the paper lanterns strung like dozens of miniature moons between the trees.

"Totally," Bianca replied, but Doc missed the teasing note—really, he'd sounded like a teenage girl, so she'd replied in kind—because he wasn't listening.

They were on their way inside the Wynn, and she'd paused across the street to case the entrance for possible trouble when a gong had sounded. The giant silk dragon had appeared to the accompaniment of clashing cymbals and singsong chants. It was a brilliant hot pink, with red, black and gold accents. Its fearsome head and snake-like body whirled and twirled through the obstacle course of food stalls, souvenir hawkers, fireworks carts, fortune tellers and tourists. Thin streams of smoke that smelled like incense belched at intervals from its nostrils. The dozen young men and women in red shirts and black shorts who gripped the sticks that worked it held them high overhead as they bobbed and dipped and ran in well-practiced unison, making the dragon appear alive. Keeping pace alongside, drummers beat out a rhythm that was a perfect accompaniment for the music that presaged the Wynn's famous dancing water show, which would commence in another four minutes and send fountains of water shooting skyward in front of the hotel's curved facade.

It had been more than a year since she'd visited Macau, and she'd been out earlier in the day to get the lay of the land. In case of emergency, knowing the terrain was important. Macau was a jumbled warren of one-way streets. If the need for a quick getaway should arise, relying on what you thought you knew was a good way to wind up dead. There were changes: a light rail system was under construction, blocking a couple of streets; a new hotel down by the lake blocked a few more. One dock had closed down. Selfie-stick wielding tourists everywhere were a menace, but she kept her head down, a big grin on her face, and a baseball cap pulled low over her forehead. As Ann, she wore sunglasses, a blue button-up camp shirt and black polyester pants: just one tourist among many. No one had noticed her, and she'd made it back to the hotel without incident.

Now, as Doc watched the dragon, Bianca was reminded that except for his abbreviated travels with her not-father's gang, he hadn't been outside the US. As far as providing cover went, his wonderstruck tourist reaction was perfect.

"Come on. We need to go." Bianca had to touch his arm to get his attention. She wasn't comfortable in the square. Since coming out tonight, she'd felt antsy, uneasy, as if she were being observed by unseen eyes, which really shouldn't have been a surprise, considering that any of the thousands of people thronging the Strip might have been there to hunt and kill her. But despite putting her best antisurveillance practices into play she'd seen no sign that she was actually being watched or followed, and that usually meant she *wasn't* being watched or followed.

Still, she couldn't shake the feeling, and it was getting to her. Ordinarily in times of crisis she grew cooler and steadier.

Tonight, though, her pulse was heightened and her skin prickled. She was anxious to get out of the open. There were too many people crowded into too small a space. Too many who were too physically near to her. The darkness helped to conceal her, true, and the dragon and its noise were a potent distraction that should serve to keep her from being noticed. But the darkness that concealed her could also conceal any sudden moves by an assassin, and the noise and distraction of the dragon could cover a quick knife thrust by an assailant, or the sound of a shot.

She'd protected herself against that to a certain extent, but Bianca fought back a shiver anyway: one thing she'd learned during the course of this debacle was that she really, truly didn't want to die.

"You got to find out—how did he *do* that? You and me, we both saw him burn." Doc frowned. He was referring to Mason, she knew. They were moving again, heading toward the Wynn. "Or at least, I thought we did. Guess not."

"Nope. But it did look real," Bianca agreed as, looking ahead, she watched the parade of people pushing through the revolving doors into the Wynn's lobby. Out of necessity—if he should spot Mason she didn't want him to be surprised into making some kind of outcry—she'd told Doc who she was meeting tonight. His reaction had been a rapid succession of surprise, disbelief, anger. Acceptance was the goal. Several hours later, he was obviously still processing and not quite there.

"Kinda harsh, abandoning his own daughter in Bahrain like that," Doc said as they crossed the street.

"He knows I can take care of myself." They dodged traffic and then pushed through the crowd gathered to watch the water show, which started up with a fanfare of music and an upward explosion of dozens of separate, brightly colored gushers a moment after they passed.

"Yeah, well, what about me?"

"I'm sure he trusted me to take care of you." Truth was, Mason probably hadn't spared a thought for Doc. He would have seen him as a hired hand, easily replaced, expendable, on his own when the job went south.

"I guess." His tone was neutral, which wasn't like Doc. Bianca shot a glance at him, but the darkness coupled with the kaleidoscope of colors from the water show that played over them made his face impossible to read.

He'd either get to the acceptance phase, or he wouldn't, she decided. Right now, her focus had to be on what lay before them.

Two red-coated doormen stood on either side of the large expanse of glass that included the brass-framed revolving door that she meant to enter through. Two more assisted new arrivals from their cars. She ignored them in favor of checking the shadows around the entrance for possible surveillance. The sheer number of people milling around made it impossible to be sure, but if anyone was watching she wasn't picking up on it.

"I'll meet you by the lion in the lobby," Bianca said, nodding at Doc to go in first. If there was a problem, she didn't want him with her, and inside the building was the safest place for him to be.

"Lion?" Doc gave her a doubtful look.

"It's a statue," she told him, and gave him a little push. "Big. Gold. You can't miss it."

He obediently headed across the cobbled drive toward the door. As he went, he squared his shoulders and got his fledgling macho on. He wore a black suit, custom-made over the course of three hours earlier in the day by the workers at Jin-the-Tailor because the gear he'd packed in his duffel didn't include anything suitable for the Wynn's casino, with a snappy black fedora pulled low. Watching him step up onto the walkway outside the Wynn's door, Bianca had to smile: *Kung Fu Panda* tries to go street.

It would have worked better without the oversize man-purse that he wore cross-body, but Doc insisted on keeping his laptop close.

She would have taken him to her own preferred Macau-based custom clothier, SiuSiu Tseng, for the suit, because SiuSiu was an old friend, a long-time collaborator and was holding an order for her that needed to be picked up besides, but a prime tenet of successfully avoiding being dead was, when you're the object of an international manhunt, never revisit any place you've been before. It's too easy for someone to discover your history and stake such places out.

SiuSiu was with her in spirit, however. SiuSiu had made the elegant smoke gray evening gown she wore. It was long-sleeved, high-necked, figure-hugging, reversible. Without actually being sheer, it gave the illusion of it—a filmy, se-quined column that was slit to the thigh on the right side. For ease of movement, of course. Also, ease of access to her garter belt with its handy-dandy switchblade. Its pièce de résistance, and the reason she was wearing it tonight, was that, from just below her neck to the top of the slit on her thigh, it was lined with a slip made from a military-grade material that was bulletproof.

Because going to a meeting—a fixed point at a fixed time where even one other person knew she was going to be—was dangerous. It was the perfect recipe for an ambush. Just in case someone besides Doc had managed to break her and Mason's code, or she'd been followed, or Mason had been followed, or any one of a thousand things that could go wrong actually did go wrong, she was covering her bases. Along with her assets.

As a final touch, because wearing gloves in the casino might attract too much attention and she clearly wasn't going to be able to wipe down everything she touched, she'd painted a thin, almost invisible layer of superglue over her fingertips to avoid leaving prints, and done the same for Doc.

Be prepared: those Girl Scouts were the bomb.

To complement her gown, she was wearing spike-heeled (literally) pumps. Her earrings were long, dangly crystal dazzlers with a central element that was actually *bo-shuriken*, or needle-like throwing darts. They were made, like the tools in her garter belt, of steel-strong plastic polymers that wouldn't trip a metal detector. Lethal if wielded by a skilled user, which she was. A bejeweled, reflective *bindi* between her eyebrows masked that nodal point. Draped loosely around her head, a sheer, sequined scarf could serve as a weapon as well as provide protection from cameras. Add in her sleek black Cleopatra-ish wig and she resembled an Indian maharani.

Which, under the circumstances, was way better than looking like Bianca St. Ives.

She'd left her hotel room as Ann, done a quick change in one of Jin-the-tailor's busy fitting rooms while Doc was picking up and changing into his suit, and voilà, she was now Kangana Bhatt. What was left of Ann was rolled up in a plastic shopping bag from Dress Shop, a boutique in Senado Square, and tucked inside her tote-size, fringed and spangled shoulder bag.

She entered the lobby and passed through the security checkpoint without incident. Two unsmiling guards ran her purse, with its secret, X-ray proof compartment large enough to carry the passports, other IDs, credit cards, and various other identity-confirming components of the legends she had brought with her, through an airport-style X-ray machine. She kept those sensitive items on her person because leaving them in an empty hotel room in Macau was just stupid. Even if nobody who was looking for her found her, the hotel rooms were vulnerable to random thieves, curious hotel security guards, dishonest housekeeping staff and the like.

To be on the safe side, she also routinely wiped down her room to eliminate fingerprints before leaving it. She did the same for the outside of her suitcase, which she made sure was securely locked. If someone besides herself tried to unlock it, pick the lock or otherwise open it, she'd concocted a small explosive out of Magician's Fire Paper, gunpowder from the ubiquitous fireworks and alcohol that would ignite instantly and burn in a quick, brilliant flash, reducing the suitcase and everything inside it to ash in minutes. As a fail-safe, in case she should be captured, she'd added a detonating device that set off the explosive if it wasn't reprogrammed every twelve hours. She'd done the same for Doc's room and his duffel bag. His various IDs were in custom-made pockets in his suit jacket. And, of course, his laptop was in his murse.

Her not-father had avoided being arrested or killed over years of being on the world's Most Wanted lists, and making sure that nothing traceable was left behind in hotel rooms or other places he stayed was one of the reasons why.

It was a matter of tradecraft, and as ambivalent as she was feeling toward Mason Thayer right now, she had no doubt that she had learned from the best.

Looking uneasy, Doc stood by the lion statue in the lobby waiting for her, and she picked him up with a flick of her eyes as she walked past him.

Without speaking and with Doc trailing a couple of yards behind, they crossed the lavish red and gold lobby and headed for the casino. The thing about casinos was, they had surveillance everywhere. Cameras, two-way mirrors, security staff. Bianca had already gone over the plan with Doc: once they were inside, he was to go up to the open gallery above the main gaming floor and act as a lookout from there. An important job that had the secret, added advantage of keeping him out of the way.

Bianca would meet with Mason alone.

She entered through what she recognized as an intention-ally designed choke point—a hallway that served as a narrow funnel through which new arrivals were subjected to extra, covert scrutiny, with another metal detector at the end of it. As she passed on out onto the central gaming floor, she was met by a smiling woman in a scarlet cheongsam who offered her a glass of champagne and the greeting, "Have a glamor-ous night!"

Declining the drink with a smile—she never drank on a job, and keeping her hands free was important in case of attack—she stood for a moment, looking out over a palatial chamber that was almost as big as a football field, with hundreds of ta-bles and thousands of patrons milling around inside.

It was abuzz with the electronic chirping of rows of slot machines, the rattle of roulette wheels, the slap and clink of cards and dice, and the drone of dealers calling out to pa-trons to *place your bets*. Laughter, chatter and the tinkle of ice in glasses rose and fell in waves. The baccarat tables and the blackjack tables operated in separate, roped-off areas. Know-ing Mason as she did, Bianca headed for the blackjack tables. He liked playing blackjack at the Wynn because he liked to win, and the house edge was just 0.09 percent. The lighting was warm and intimate, emanating from wall sconces as well as massive chandeliers that reminded her of nothing so much as inverted blooming onions dripping gold and crystal beads from the high, curved ceiling. Enormous artworks adorned the walls. Gold statues in recessed niches and deep red car-peting added to the air of opulence.

Security was everywhere, discreet but, for someone who knew what to look for, unmistakable. To guard against theft, cheating, undesirable behavior, acts of vandalism or violence, or anything else that might go wrong when dealing with the kind of fluid population that passed through one of the world's most profitable casinos, the Wynn employed a small army of trained security personnel.

Red velvet ropes on two sides partially cordoned off the high-end blackjack tables from the main floor. Bianca stepped inside them, waved away a waiter who offered her a choice from a tray full of drinks and scanned the area for Mason.

An electric tension hung in the air as scores of serious gamblers tried their luck. Various numbers of players were seated around a dealer at semicircular green-felt-covered tables that could accommodate eight. There were dozens of such tables. Only a few were empty. On the tables stacks of chips were positioned between the dealer and players, and swiftly moving cards were the focus of attention. Plush gold upholstered chairs were placed around the curved side of tables for the players. The dealers sat alone on the straight side. Male and female dealers alike wore tuxes, while players were mostly clad in cocktail or formal wear. Red-and-black-clad waiters and waitresses carried trays of complimentary drinks.

Doc had gone up the marble staircase to the right when he had emerged through the choke point behind her, and was now following her progress from the second-floor-level gallery that circled the room. One of many who had chosen to watch from that vantage point, he stood with both hands gripping the wrought-iron railing as he looked down at her.

Despite the distance between them, she could feel the weight of his gaze. Clearly he was determined not to miss a thing.

He was, Bianca thought, about as inconspicuous as the raven above Poe's chamber door in the eponymous poem, but there was nothing she could do about that at this point. She did her best to ignore him.

It took her two sweeps of the tables before, with a spark of surprise, she spotted her not-father. Mason's disguise was even more thorough than hers. If she hadn't known him well and been specifically looking for him, she never would have recognized him. The bespectacled, wrinkled, balding old codger in the motorized wheelchair that had been pulled up to one of the closed tables bore almost no resemblance to the man he was in real life. The ancient-looking gray suit jacket and limp white shirt he wore, the dark blanket tucked in around his legs—he might as well have been wearing an invisibility cloak for all the impression he made. And, normally, Mason Thayer made quite an impression. At sixty-four, he stood six foot one with a slim, elegant build. The term silver fox could have been coined with him in mind. He had thick hair that was, yes, silver, high cheekbones, a long, straight nose, well-cut lips and a square chin. The crow's-feet and creases around his mouth merely served to add gravitas to his extraordinary good looks.

What caught her eye was the motion with which he flipped one of the thousand-dollar casino chips in the air and caught it. The movement was practiced, graceful—and familiar. She'd seen him do that with various small objects a million times over the years. She had to consciously keep her eyes from widening. He was at the last seat at the last table, facing the room with his back to the wall—yes, that was familiar, too—and he had a good-sized pile of chips in front of him, which he appeared to be sorting into random piles. He was alone at the table.

Her heart gave an unexpected little pump of joy. She felt an inner warmth, a burst of happiness, an instant sense of belonging, of being safe and secure in the presence of the one person who by the very nature of their father-daughter relationship loved and had always protected her.

Only he didn't, and he hadn't.

Cold reality did its best to douse her instinctive, conditioned reaction to this man whom she'd always thought was her parent. He was not, either biologically or in his mind and heart. He was the man who'd saved her life as a child and had raised her as his daughter, yes. But she strongly suspected now that he had done it for his own ends, because it suited him to have the kind of partner in crime that he and a bunch of mad scientists somewhere had made her.

She was as certain as it was possible to be that if she hadn't found out the truth in that horrific encounter in Heiligenblut he never would have told her.

Instead, he would have kept on using her.

Her lips compressed.

What was it they said? *Fool me once, shame on you. Fool me twice...*

But for better or worse, right now, for her, he was looking like the only game in town.

She walked toward him.

He looked up. Through the spectacle lenses his eyes met hers. They were a bright denim blue.

She would know those eyes anywhere. Her own eye color was a little lighter, a little icier—more of a crystalline blue. Still, the shades were close enough so that she'd always thought that she'd inherited her eye color from him.

Mark that down as one more thing she'd spent her life being wrong about.

He knocked some casino chips to the floor as she drew near.

It was done on purpose, to provide her with an excuse to strike up a conversation with him in case anyone was watching.

"Oh, dear." Affecting a plummy British accent, he looked down at the chips on the carpet, a poor, befuddled old man who couldn't quite reach.

"I'll get them," she said, crouching to pick them up.

"That's very kind." When she placed them on the table in front of him he added, "Would you happen to know what one of these is worth?"

"One thousand dollars US." Bianca pointed to the amount stamped in the middle of the chip. "See?"

"That's the problem. I can't." He gave her a rueful smile. "Old age, you know. I can't tell the colors apart, either."

He was good, all right. It was the perfect opening. She pulled out a chair and sat down beside him.

"Let me help you sort them out," she said.

16

"I'd appreciate that." Mason smiled at her. Bianca didn't smile back. Her emotions where he was concerned were too raw, too complicated. One thing she knew for sure was that there was no going back to what they had been.

So move on already.

A quick, comprehensive glance around told her that no one was paying any attention to them. In the next row over, another empty table filled up and another dealer sat down and opened the bank. Dealers and players were focused on the action at their own tables. The steady hum of talk was punctuated by the dealers' patter and the sounds of the game. Sinatra's "The Lady Is a Tramp" played over the sound system. The noise level was such that it should preclude someone being able to overhear any individual conversations. A scan of the table and their immediate surroundings confirmed that, unless the area was bugged, which she was relatively certain it wasn't, they could speak privately.

"A wheelchair?" Cocking a questioning eyebrow at him, she started sorting his pile of chips into denominations as she spoke.

"After our last adventure, I had to have surgery. Lost my spleen. Pin in my hip." His voice was his own again, its volume lowered for her ears only.

"I'm surprised you're up and around."

"Duty calls." He shrugged. "I won't be going on any long

walks for a while, but I can get up and move if I have to. Only thing I can't do at all is stairs."

A passing waiter paused to lower a champagne-flute-laden tray in their direction. "May I offer you a drink?" Mason waved him away.

"How are Marin and Margery?" Bianca asked when they were alone again. A small twinge of pain as she mentioned his seven-year-old daughter and his wife was all she allowed herself. For years she'd thought of them almost hungrily, imagining they were her family, indulging in secret fantasies that she didn't even like to remember, centered on the hope that they would one day get to know each other, that maybe she and Marin, as half sisters, would grow close. All in ashes now, of course: they were no more kin to her than was the man sitting beside her.

Ah, well. Life sucks and then you try not to die.

"Alive. In hiding. I'm doing what I can to get them settled and keep them safe."

"Yeah." With the thousand-dollar chips now in four neat columns in front of him, she started in on the five-hundred-dollar chips. There was no telling how much or how little private time they had, so she abandoned the less important matters to get to the point. "Darjeeling Brothers have a hit posted on me. A million dollars."

"I saw."

She glanced at him quickly.

He said, "I follow the news."

She took that to mean the underground network of information that was always being traded among criminals and their associates. Well, she'd known that virtual Wanted Dead or Alive (okay, scrap the Alive part) poster would get wide dissemination.

"I need to find out who placed the contract."

"So you can get it called off?" He shook his head. "Don't

even try. That's exactly the move they'll be expecting you to make. They'll have people watching. You go near whoever it is, they'll take you out."

Bianca's fingers stilled on the chips. The icy knot of fear that had been lodged in her chest since she'd seen her own face on that computer screen made like the Grinch's heart and grew three sizes. The possibility of a waiting ambush had occurred to her, but having him put it into words made it seem even more horribly real. The problem was, she didn't have a lot of other options.

"So maybe I won't go near them." She was thinking aloud. "Maybe I can find a way to bargain with them from a distance. You know as well as I do that getting that contract canceled is my only chance, and if I'm going to do that I first need to know who placed it. I'm sure it has to do with—" she almost said *what I am*, but thinking of herself as different, other, possibly even less than human, was not, she felt, conducive to good mental health; not that good mental health was her number one priority at the moment "—the Nomad Project. You were there. Who else is left who was there? Who was in charge of it?"

"Kemp was around. He's dead. Groton was around." He lowered his head, peering at her through his spectacles. "Did you take him out, by the way?"

Still stacking chips—the black and magenta hundred-dollar ones now—she shook her head. No need to tell him that she would've if she could've. "I was going to ask you the same thing."

He shook his head: *no*. Even so, Bianca couldn't be 100 percent sure he was telling the truth. Although she supposed his physical condition precluded his involvement. Unless he was lying about that.

The thing about liars is, they lie.

Bianca said, "I think whoever's behind the contract on

me is out to have everyone who was involved in the Nomad Project killed. That means you, too, you know."

Reminding him that he had skin in the game might get him probing more deeply into his memory. Although he had to have thought of that. Mason rarely missed anything.

He said, "I only came into play toward the end. After the powers that be got cold feet and decided to terminate the project. There were some scientists still around, some medical types, plus the women and babies, who were being kept confined in a hospital-like setting. Most of those were euthanized pharmaceutically right after I came on board. I doubt they ever knew what happened. I was sent after the runner. That was Issa. With you. God, she was a fighter." A faint, reminiscent smile touched his mouth. Bianca felt a stab of pain so sharp that it was all she could do not to grimace. He said *Issa*, she thought, however erroneously, *my mother*. "Groton was there from the beginning. His boss at the time would be aware, I'm sure. I don't know who that was right off the top of my head, but it shouldn't be too hard to find out. Probably there was a whole chain of command. The project would have had political backing. Somebody high up. My guess is that somebody is now trying to cover his ass by burying the evidence. That would be you. And anybody who knows about you."

"You have a name?" She tried to keep the tension out of her voice.

He shook his head, and she felt disappointment and anxiety combine to make her stomach twist.

"I have something better," he said. She looked at him wordlessly. The latex wrinkles, the semibald hairpiece, all faded away as she met the keen eyes she knew so well. "I didn't come here empty-handed. I know how to get the Darjeeling contract canceled. I have a way to make this whole thing go away, to keep you and me and my family safe. To call off the dogs and keep them called off so we can all get on with it and have a life."

Her fingers stilled on the chips. She was so intent on hearing the rest that his reference to *my family* barely even hurt. "What is it?"

"I know people at the BND," he said, referring to the Bundesnachrichtendienstes, the German equivalent of the CIA, "who've spent years collecting information on the Americans. They're not happy with what they see as the increasing subservience of the BND to the CIA and the other American intelligence services. The material they possess includes information, physical objects and video and audio recordings explosive enough to take down the current administration and possibly a number of other extremely powerful political leaders, as well. The Germans can't use it. It was obtained in the most clandestine ways possible. If anyone knew they had it, let alone leaked it, it would cost them their lives. But they're willing to trade it to me, to let me leak it for them. In fact, I've already made a deal with them for it that unfortunately I can't fulfill now due to—" he made a gesture encompassing his body in the wheelchair "—this." He looked at her. "But you can. As soon as you got in touch with me, as soon as I saw that contract on you, I knew this was the way to go for both of us."

Her eyes narrowed. "What kind of deal?"

"They'll give me the material in return for King Priam's Treasure."

"What?" She knew what King Priam's Treasure was: priceless artifacts including magnificent jewelry that was fabled to have once belonged to Helen of Troy. Unearthed in Turkey by a German archaeologist, it was kept in storage in a Berlin museum during World War II. When that museum was looted by the Red Army during the fall of Nazi Germany, King Priam's Treasure was whisked away to the USSR, where it was

secretly held in an off-site storage building that belonged to the Pushkin Museum of Art. While the Germans searched the world for it, the Russians spent almost fifty years denying that they had it or knew anything about its disappearance. Then, in 1993, the Russian Minister of Culture said to hell with it, thumbed his nose at the Germans, pulled the collection out of storage and eventually placed it on display at the Pushkin Museum. The Germans were up in arms, demanding the treasure's return on the grounds that it had been stolen. Russia refused, declaring that the treasure would only be returned in exchange for the artifacts, such as the long-missing Amber Room, that the Germans had supposedly looted from the USSR.

In a word, stalemate.

"Your sources at the BND want you to steal *King Priam's Treasure*?" Bianca had to ask, if only to make sure she had that right. He gave a nod. She knew her Greek mythology: Priam was the King of Troy and father to Paris, who ran off with Helen of the-face-that-launched-a-thousand-ships fame. No stranger to Moscow, Bianca had visited the Pushkin, seen the intricately wrought solid gold diadem that Helen of Troy had supposedly once worn as a headdress, seen the other jewelry, the plateware, the weapons, the tools. She thought of the tightly controlled state, of the urban environment, of the ubiquitous Russian intelligence service the SVR and its FBI-equivalent sister the FSB, of the abundant police presence in Moscow, of the Pushkin itself, its location, its security… "That's impossible."

He made a face. "Difficult, rather. I could do it. So can you."

Bianca stared at him. "So the deal is that you, no, I steal this priceless treasure and turn it over to Germany, and in return they give you this blackmail file and you leak it for them? Because I see a flaw in the plan. If you leak it, then it loses its value as blackmail, and it won't keep anyone from killing me. Or you."

"I'm not going to leak it. I'm going to use it, for me and for you, to keep us safe. But my contact doesn't have to know that. At least until I get my hands on that file."

She stared at him. "You're going to double-cross him."

"I'm going to do what I need to do. Don't tell me you object."

Slowly she shook her head. "No. Whatever works."

A smile just touched his mouth. "I've always admired that practical streak of yours." Her brows twitched together. "Speaking of my practical streak, since you didn't burn up in that garbage truck, I'm presuming the two hundred million dollars from Bahrain didn't burn up, either. I want my share of that money."

His smile widened. His eyes twinkled at her. A familiar expression employed most often when he'd been caught with his hand in the cookie jar. "No, it didn't burn. But there's not that much left. After we got out of Austria, I had to bribe a lot of people to find a safe place to stash Marin and Margery. And getting the kind of medical care I needed under the radar isn't cheap, either."

She gave him a skeptical look. "You can tell me all about it later. When we talk about how you're going to pay me my cut. But to stay on topic, why don't we just steal the file? Seems easier than robbing the Pushkin."

"It's not. The material's been split up, and it's kept in different, highly secure locations. Guarded by elite operatives of the BND, who will kill to protect it. Plus, if we steal it, the BND won't have much trouble figuring out exactly who did it, and they'll be coming after us with everything they've got. While if the Pushkin robbery is done right, the Russian intelligence services will be too busy wreaking vengeance on the Germans to worry about us."

Bianca knew it was a lost cause, but still she tried. "You couldn't bribe some venal agent to hand the material over?"

He shook his head. "These people are patriots, in this for their country. The German chancellor has let it be known that she wants King Priam's Treasure back in Germany. This is personal for her. Several years ago, she made an official visit to Russia which included a tour of the Hermitage Museum in St. Petersburg in the company of the Russian president. King Priam's Treasure was on display there at the time. The chancellor took this flaunting of Germany's rightful property under her nose as a slap in the face to her, and to Germany. She demanded of the president, in person, that the treasure be repatriated. He refused. The visit got tense. The chancellor went home mad, gave certain orders, and since then the intelligence services have been looking for a way to avenge her honor and Germany's by regaining possession of King Priam's Treasure. Stealing it back is the obvious solution, as well as being a huge middle finger stuck up in the air from Germany to Russia, but to begin with the BND isn't quite sure they can pull it off, and if they tried and failed, or even if they tried and succeeded, the consequences of having German agents involved in stealing priceless artifacts from inside the sovereign state of Russia would cause an international incident at the very least. They've been casting around for a solution for some time, and eventually my contacts thought of me. If a professional thief manages to steal it and they buy it from him—well, that's more an embarrassing reflection on the state of security at Russian museums than an incitement for war. I wasn't interested, not for the money—there are all kinds of easier ways to earn the twenty million bounty they were offering that don't involve possibly ending up being tortured and killed in a basement in SVR headquarters—but then I heard through the grapevine about this material they'd been collecting. So we struck a deal. I'd steal the treasure, they'd give me the material. My intention was to use it to put the fear of God in the CIA and have them do the same to every other bloody agency and operative who might be looking for us. I was just getting down to work on it when I was so rudely interrupted by the recent emergency in Heiligenblut. As you can see, I'm not quite up to par again, but now with the Darjeeling Brothers contract your problem is urgent so we're out of time."

Bianca frowned. "You really think this file is enough to get the contract on me canceled and call off the CIA and keep us both safe? What if your contacts are lying about what's in it?"

"Think I'd make a deal like this without checking out the merchandise first? I insisted on being given a look at the material in the file. I wasn't shown everything, or even most things, but I was shown enough to be convinced that this is the poison pill we need." His expression grew intent. "Plus, there's still the twenty million. Fifty-fifty split. You in?"

Bianca met his gaze. Trying to steal King Priam's Treasure out from under the nose of the Russians came as close to being a suicide mission as anything she'd ever attempted. If Germany's intelligence services were humming with the chancellor's desire to recover the artifacts, one thing that was certain was that Russia's intelligence services were aware.

Forget Beauty and the Beast: spies spying on spies was the real tale as old as time.

The Russians would be taking extreme precautions; their president wasn't a man to be crossed.

On the other hand, she took Mason's word for it that trying to steal the material from the Germans would be potentially even deadlier.

Also, finding whoever had placed the contract on her and threatening them with death to cancel the contract might work, especially if she killed the individual afterward. (People never liked being threatened; once they were in a position to do so, they inevitably came after the threatener with both barrels. Best to get what you need, take them out and have done.) But that did nothing to stop anyone else who might be coming after her. It did nothing to stave off possible future contracts. Unless she killed everyone who knew that she was—oh, God, might as well own it—a genetically enhanced super soldier, getting rid of whoever had placed that contract would be like cutting off one head of a many-headed hydra. There were lots more where that one came from, and sooner or later another one of those heads would be coming after her. Probably sooner.

All righty, then.

"I want four-fifths," she said. "Sixteen million, because I'm the one doing the work, and I'm the one taking the risks."

"Done," Mason said.

"Then yes, I'm in."

He smiled. "Excellent. It's the best solution for all of us, believe me. There's a flash drive in my pocket with all the research I've done to get ready for the job on it. As well as information that will give you access to a fund to cover operational expenses, and how to contact me once the job is done so I can make the trade with my BND friends. I'm going to drop it, so you'd best drop something to cover picking it up. It's encrypted. You can get that computer geek I hired to decrypt it for you. Oh, yes, I see him." He shot a glance toward Doc, who was casually leaning against the railing now while glancing at his burner phone and pretending not to watch them. "He's not exactly inconspicuous, is he?"

Mason's hand moved to his pocket as he spoke. A small object hit the carpet. Bianca struck a couple of chips with her elbow—"Oops!"—then bent to pick them up. Along with the chips she scooped up the elegant silver cigarette lighter in which the flash drive was undoubtedly hidden. The lighter went in her bag. The chips she restored to the table.

Mason said, "I can't believe you brought him with you, by the way. I can't believe you're still in touch with him at all. You should have left him in Bahrain. You know the rule about crossing channels."

Yes, she did. It was a simple one: *never cross channels.* That meant never let anyone brought in to help with a job know the real identity of anyone else. Well, so much for that. If she'd left Doc in Bahrain, he'd be dead now. After being captured and tortured until he sang like a bird. Not that at the time he'd known very much to sing about.

Mason was a stickler for never crossing channels.

She gave him a hard look. "He's part of my team now. Leave him alone." That carried a note of clear warning, in case Mason was having any big ideas about taking Doc out and thus uncrossing the channels she had crossed.

"Like I said, he can help you out by decrypting that flash drive." His tone added a subtext that she had no trouble deciphering: *lucky for him.*

"Leave him alone," Bianca repeated, with more menace this time. Their eyes locked. It was the first time she'd ever really stood up to him about an operational matter, but on this, on Doc, she wasn't backing down.

He gave a grunt that could have meant anything. "Don't worry, he's safe from me."

"Damn right, he is." Bianca let that sink in for a minute, then added, "You going to tell me how that whole you-didn't-die-in-Bahrain thing went down?"

"The cab of the garbage truck had a false bottom panel. It was part of plan B, just like having a guy stationed at a third-floor window above that suq to fire on my signal was part of plan B. In case things went wrong and we had the military after us, which as you know is what happened. When the missile hit the back of the truck, which we'd larded with explosives tucked in with the counterfeit money, I gave it a strategic minute in which I pretended to be burning alive, then triggered the false bottom, dropped out and rolled into the bay."

"You didn't think to *tell me* about plan B?"

"Strictly need to know. And you didn't."

Bianca fought the urge to grind her teeth. That constant refrain of his was getting old.

"Were you going to tell me that you were alive?"

"When the opportunity presented itself, certainly."

"There was no opportunity in almost six months?" The approximate length of time she'd thought he was dead and grieved for him, before stumbling across him, alive and well and apparently unconcerned about her or what he'd put her through, in Heiligenblut.

"I needed to be careful."

"What about Grangier and Findley?" The men who'd been with him in the cab of the truck.

"What do you think? They got out, too. No idea where they are now."

A waiter was offering drinks to a nearby table. Mason signaled him. To cut short the conversation that he no longer felt like having, she knew.

"So who burned? There had to have been bodies in the truck."

"There was a special on unclaimed corpses at the local morgue. I acquired some."

There was something beneath the flipness of his tone that made her certain that she wasn't being told the whole story. Probably, she decided, she didn't want to know. At least not right now.

"And the real money? How'd you work that? And where is it?"

He smiled.

The waiter arrived, right on (from Mason's perspective, she was sure) cue. With a word of thanks, Mason removed a champagne flute from the tray, saluted her with it and took an appreciative sip. Maybe half of that glass would be all he'd allow himself. Any more would be bad tradecraft.

As for Bianca, he didn't bother getting her a glass because he knew she wouldn't touch it.

The whole episode had been a delaying tactic as, she guessed, he calculated exactly how much he wanted to tell her.

"Yes?" Bianca prompted as the waiter moved on. Before Mason could resume explaining exactly how he'd been able to get away with the money and where he was keeping what was left of it, two middle-aged couples sat down at the other end of their table. They wore formal wear, but of the rent-a-tux variety. Both women had bouffant updos, one streaked blond, one black, and their long dresses were black chiffon. The difference was that one had kimono sleeves and the other a halter neck and matching stole. One of the men, a burly gray-haired forty-something, Australian from the accent, immediately called for a dealer, with an aside to Mason.

"The tables are chockers, mate. You here to play?"

A dealer was already on the way over.

Mason made a sweeping gesture welcoming them to the table. "I am." The plummy accent was back.

Bianca's reply was a thin smile. For the sake of her and Mason's cover, she would play. But she had no intention of letting the conversation about the money drop; in a little while she would signal him that she was ready to leave the table—their code for we need to talk privately had always been *I'm getting hungry*—and then they would continue.

The floor boss came over to unlock the lid—the cover over the chips that kept them safe—and the dealer sat down, signed the tally sheet and picked up the shoe.

"My name is Delia," she said. "Are you enjoying your evening?"

She nodded and smiled at their answers, and then the game

was on. Five decks, HK five hundred dollars or US one hundred dollars per hand.

The Australians, for so they indeed proved to be, talked (loudly) among themselves. The dealer focused on the game. Bianca exchanged a few desultory, topic neutral, suitable for public consumption remarks with Mason and, to a lesser extent, the Australians. Cards were dealt, bets placed. Neat stacks of chips waxed and waned in front of each player. The dealer, a thirty-something Macanese woman, did her job with businesslike efficiency. The spicy scent of her perfume, her bright red nails as she dealt the cards, the dark flash of her eyes as she darted looks at each of them in turn, formed the backdrop of the game.

Blackjack was a favorite of Mason's, and like everything else Bianca had learned at his behest, he'd drummed the rules into her.

"Hit me," she said, tapping the felt on a soft seventeen, which consisted of an ace and a six. The next card she was dealt was a three, giving her a twenty. Mason got twenty-one and won.

"Stand," with a negative head shake was her response a few hands later to a hard seventeen, a queen and a seven. The dealer took that round, raking in the chips.

Those were the rules for seventeen: hit on a soft, stand on a hard. She knew all the rules. Always split—which meant separate into two bets—aces and eights. Never split fives or tens. Never stand on twelve through sixteen. Insurance is a sucker's bet. Followed consistently, you'd win more than you lost. Probably, although she'd never played enough blackjack to be 100 percent sure.

Bianca was doubling down on an eleven when a soft chiming sound from inside her purse caused her to blink with surprise.

It was her burner phone, signaling that she'd received a text message.

The only person in the world with the ability to contact her on that phone was Doc. She shot a quick look up at the gallery, where she'd last seen him leaning against the rail.

He was nowhere in sight.

She frowned.

Most casinos forbade cell phones at the table, under the theory that they could be used to help patrons cheat. She had no idea if the Wynn adhered to that rule. At the moment, she didn't particularly care.

If Doc was texting her, something was up.

Bianca's purse was in her lap. As the dealer won again and raked in the chips she snuck a hand inside, grabbed the phone, flipped the flimsy, cheap thing open and looked.

Adrenaline flooded her veins. She was instantly juiced, wired, aquiver with alarm.

"Ma'am, I apologize, no cell phones at the table," the dealer chided. Her English was flawless. Her accent, a soft mix of Cantonese and Portuguese.

"Sorry." Bianca closed her phone and pulled her hand back out of her purse, her game face—she hoped—firmly in place.

She'd seen everything she needed to see.

The message was from Doc, all right. It said, Cop from San Jose on your nine.

17

The cop from San Jose—it couldn't be. It was *almost* impossible. Maybe—*please God*—Doc was mistaken. After all, he'd seen him only once.

Bianca's chest felt tight, making it harder to breathe. She turned her head to her left, directing a sweeping gaze over the players at the blackjack tables and the five-card-stud tables beyond them, over the people milling around the tables, over—

The dealer flipped her an ace to go with her eight.

"Stand," Bianca said, her attention of necessity recalled to the table. One thing about the rules: they made it possible for her to continue playing while (fatally? She really hoped not) distracted.

She looked again toward her nine o'clock. Carefully, casually, she scanned the Pai Gow area and the wide, crowded aisle that ran through it, looked toward the eastern entrance and over the busy casino floor on the other side of the aisle.

It wasn't a mistake, she realized a moment later: there he was, standing over by the cashier window.

The cop from San Jose: *Mickey.*

Not his real name, but it was the best name Bianca had for him.

As it turned out, he *was* on her nine, much closer than she'd expected. He was less than a hundred feet away.

Her heart leaped. Her pulse shot into overdrive. She barely managed to stay in her seat as the impact of his presence hit her.

And that would be because her first impulse was to run.

No way was the fact that he was here a coincidence.

Be cool. You're Kangana, remember? He won't recognize you.

Groans all around as the dealer took the hand. Bianca forced her gaze back to the table as the chips were raked in and the cards collected.

All the while she was battling the urge to stand up, to walk away from the table. To slowly, casually, unobtrusively flee.

She couldn't leave Mason. Or Doc. And any such move might attract the very attention she was trying to avoid.

Keep your game face on. She placed her bet, was dealt a nine.

The dealer continued on around the table. Unable to control the urge, Bianca snuck another look at Mickey.

He stood with his hands in his pockets, a still figure in a classic black tux amid the colorful ebb and flow of tourists moving past him. His eyes were on the players around the roulette wheels, moving from face-to-face. He was a good-looking guy, tall, broad-shouldered, leanly muscular, with wavy raven hair that could use a trim and a deep tan that spoke of quite a bit of time spent in a really hot (no, probably not that one) place. His forehead was wide, his cheekbones broad, his chin square and clean-shaven. His nose was aquiline, a small bump on the bridge. His mouth was long, a little thin, a little cruel looking. She happened to know that he was a really good kisser.

He worked for Mason's nemesis, Laurent Durand of Interpol, and there was absolutely no doubt in her mind that he was there in his official capacity as some kind of international cop. (She was still a little hazy on precisely what kind of international cop that would be. Their previous meetings hadn't exactly included heart-to-hearts.)

He was there because he was looking for someone, she knew. She didn't think it was her. In fact, the last time he'd seen her she'd been falling to her death into a Grand Canyon–

like abyss just outside Heiligenblut, so it was likely that he thought she was dead.

He had to be there for Mason.

She recognized the probability of that with an icy little thrill of dismay.

Somehow he must have known that Mason would be here tonight.

It was the only thing that made sense.

How? She had no answer.

Didn't mean that he wouldn't detain her too if he recognized her.

Or, *oh, God*, was it possible that he knew the truth? About the whole super-soldier thing? The dreadful thought shook her. The last time they'd spoken, he'd had no clue, although to be fair neither had she.

What a difference a day (or a couple of weeks) makes.

He'd been there at the black site in Heiligenblut. He might know—there was no other less dehumanizing way to put it, or if there was she couldn't think of it at the moment—what she was.

He might know about the contract.

Her stomach clenched. Her heart thumped. Her mouth went dry.

Had the contract *brought him? Was it possible that he was there for* her? *To kill her?*

No. She instantly, instinctively, rejected the idea. He might detain her, might have her arrested, but that was it.

He wouldn't kill her. She was almost sure.

It was that *almost* that sent cold prickles slithering down her spine.

She'd kissed him twice, fought with him, successfully bested and eluded him. Truth was, she kind of liked him.

Didn't mean she knew him.

It was entirely possible to be handsome, charming, likable—and a stone-cold killer.

Mason being a case in point.

She remembered the sensation she'd had earlier of being watched. But even if there had been surveillance out there in the square, it couldn't have brought Mickey to Macau. There hadn't been time.

He must already have been in the city. He'd tracked her, or Mason, or both of them, some other way.

Not that the how of it mattered, not right now. What mattered was that she and Mason were in acute danger.

We have to get out of here.

The thing was, Mason had no idea who Mickey was. If Doc hadn't spotted Mickey, if she hadn't had previous run-ins with him so that she and consequently Doc recognized him, he could have taken Mason unaware.

She wrenched her eyes away from Mickey, afraid that he would look her way, attracted by the force of her gaze. If he saw her, recognized her—

Whatever his purpose in being there, it wouldn't end well.

We're screwed, was the thought that flashed like a neon sign through her head. Because Mickey wouldn't be in the casino alone. He had to have a team—

"Ma'am. What do you want to do?" the dealer asked. With an inner start Bianca realized that the dealer was speaking to her and that she'd been holding up play. She glanced at the cards in front of her. Without her even registering it, a three had been added to her facedown ace.

She tapped the table.

"Hit me," she said. As the dealer complied and moved on Bianca's eyes met Mason's. He was looking at her, frowning a little, clearly aware that something was wrong.

She never lost concentration in the middle of a game.

"Headache," she said, their code word for trouble, and

looked back toward Mickey with the intention of having Mason follow her gaze.

Mickey wasn't there. Nowhere in sight. Alarm shot through her veins.

She looked quickly back at Mason, her glance skimming everyone else at the table on the way. No one was paying the least attention to her.

Cop, she mouthed, and indicated with a gesture that she didn't know where he'd gone.

Mason's expression never changed. His posture never changed. But she could feel the change in his energy, the sharpening of his senses, the readying of his body.

Which was currently broken and confined to a wheelchair.

At the moment, Bruce Lee he wasn't.

"House wins," the dealer said, to the accompaniment of groans from the Australians, and scooped up cards and chips.

As another hand started, Bianca searched the crowd for any sight of Mickey. She couldn't find him. Her chest felt tight. Her heart felt like it was trying to beat while caught in a vice.

There were half a dozen legitimate places he could have gone.

Or he could have spotted them and gone to direct his men to surround them. He could even now be springing the trap. Once she was in custody, what were the chances that word would leak out and somebody would come along and kill her for the reward?

She was guessing about 99 percent.

A card landed facedown in front of her. Distracted, Bianca spared a second to check: a queen.

Then she immediately went back to searching for Mickey.

The irony was, even if Mickey walked right past them, he might very well not spot Mason in his current disguise. He'd never met Mason, never spoken to him, had had no real-life interaction with him. It was remotely possible that he'd seen him in Heiligenblut, but if so it could have been no more than a glimpse at a distance, when Mason had been all bundled up against the cold, dodging bullets, and then escaping. At best, all Mickey had to recognize him by were a few pictures, and the wheelchair-bound old man next to her would bear no resemblance to any of them.

"Hit me," she said when the dealer came around to her again. An eight. "Hold."

Despite her excellent disguise, Mickey was far more likely to recognize *her*.

She knew him, he knew her, and that wasn't good. This whole situation was a catastrophe in the making. The only thing to do was disappear, fast. But would attempting to leave at this point draw the very attention she was hoping to avoid?

Should she just sit tight and hope?

A roar went up from the Australians, refocusing her attention on the table. The man—Bix, his name was—who'd first summoned the dealer had won.

"Good on ya, Bix!"

"There's a quick quid for you! Better than a scratchie!"

The Australians were jubilant as Bix gathered in the chips, his friend high-fiving him in congratulations, his wife hugging his arm and his friend's wife beaming at him.

Under the cover of the general hubbub, Bianca whispered to Mason, "One of Durand's men is here. We need to go."

Mason had an impeccable poker face, but the flicker in his eyes gave him away. He knew as well as she did that this wasn't a coincidence, that the hunt was closing in.

The casino was probably crawling with law enforcement. *Stay calm. Think the problem through before you make a move.*

She cast an assessing glance around. Mickey's team shouldn't be that hard to spot. To begin with, they were almost certain to be standing—

"Ah!" Mason bumped his champagne flute with a careless

gesture. It went sailing off the table, hitting the carpet between him and Bianca with a dull thud.

"Dash it!" he said, looking down.

They both leaned over at the same time, supposedly to retrieve the glass.

"Roof of the parking garage next door. There's a helicopter on standby," Mason murmured as he picked up the unbroken glass.

"You go first. I'll follow after a couple of hands."

"I'll wait for you. Don't be long."

"Take this." Unwilling to lose contact, Bianca grabbed her burner phone from her purse and thrust it at him. He stowed it away under the blanket covering his legs even as he straightened with the now empty flute, which he placed on the table.

"Frightfully sorry about that," he said to the dealer, who nodded acknowledgment. He then passed some folded bills to the waiter who was already blotting up the spill.

Bianca placed her bet, shoving two stacks of chips into the betting circle.

The dealer distributed the first round of cards. Bianca checked hers—an ace. To her right, Mason did the same thing. At the other end of the table, so did the Australians.

She guessed that Mason would excuse himself and make his way out of the casino after one or two more hands.

Furtive glances around located casino security—at least six men within easy reach of their table. Coincidence? Who knew? Those same glances also turned up at least two others who might be part of Mickey's team—something about the way they moved through the crowd put them on her radar. Like they knew how to handle themselves. Like they were expecting trouble. Like they were looking for someone—

Swish. Her second card landed in front of her.

She looked down at it—a seven. Which gave her an eighteen.

"Hold," she said.

A tingly sensation made her look up.

Mickey had just emerged from between rows of flashing, chattering slot machines. He was much farther away than he had been before—maybe a quarter of the way across the casino. There was a sea of people between them, moving in all kinds of different directions, intent on all kinds of different things.

He was looking straight at her.

That tingly sensation had been the weight of his gaze.

Bianca's blood froze. Her breathing suspended. Her eyes held his for one horrible, pregnant instant.

Across a crowded room. Like no one else was even there.

Even as her pulse slammed into triple time, she recollected herself enough to break eye contact and glance casually away.

No way he could recognize her at that distance, she told herself.

But her deepest instincts shouted that he did.

"You little beauty!" Bix slapped his hand on the table.

Which meant, she discovered as the Australians once more erupted, that he had won again.

As they hugged and fist-bumped and otherwise congratulated their hero, Bianca dared a quick glance back in Mickey's direction to find that he was moving toward her. Purposefully.

Her stomach knotted.

"I smell strawberries," she said to Mason under the cover of the Australians' noisy celebration. It was their code for *extreme emergency, get ready to move.*

She could feel the instant uptick in his energy.

No time now for an orderly exit. Forget sitting out another hand or two.

Oh, God, the two men she'd identified as possibly being members of Mickey's team—they were moving her way, too.

The dealer was sweeping in the chips. Next she would collect the cards.

Bianca already knew what she had to do. It was called hand mucking, and she'd been taught how to do it by one of the best card mechanics in the business. It was a minor talent, occasionally useful. She was good at it.

The difference was, this time she meant to get caught.

She palmed her ace before the dealer could take it, holding the tiniest sliver of an edge pinched between her thumb and forefinger with the rest of the card concealed in her hand. In a normal game, she would hide it in her lap or somewhere similar until the next hand was dealt, then swap out whatever card she chose to replace for the ace. It was an easy cheat, and if done well allowed a player to rack up an impressive pile of chips.

No one noticed. No one spotted the cheat.

A furtive look toward Mickey revealed that he was still coming. The other two men were even closer.

The next hand was already being dealt. A card—she didn't even bother to check to see what it was—landed in front of her. A harried glance confirmed that Mickey had cut the previous distance between them by half. He strode through the milling crowd like Moses through the Red Sea.

She tilted her hand, flashing the ace she was holding toward the dealer, *who didn't notice.*

Quick, quick, quick. Holy crap, what does it take to get hauled off by security around here?

In desperation, she fumbled with the card she'd been dealt, pretending to check it while flashing her concealed ace at Bix.

Whose eyes widened.

"What ho!" Bix grabbed her wrist.

"Let me go!" Bianca pretended to try to yank free. His hand was thick, meaty, sweaty. She suspected he thought his grip was iron. "What do you think you're doing?"

"Bix!" his wife gasped.

"Sir!"

As if forced to it by the strength of Bix's grip, Bianca released her hold on the card she held. The ace fluttered to the table. Everybody stared at it as it lay, in damning evidence of her guilt, on the green felt.

"Bit of a bludger," Bix said.

"She was *cheating*!" one of the women cried.

The dealer said, "Sir, let her go. Ma'am—"

Bianca really hoped that the reason the dealer was reaching under the table was to press the button that summoned security.

"Cooee! Cooee!" Bix stood up, waving his free hand, the subtleties of attracting security by concealed button apparently lost on him.

Mickey's attention was now riveted on their table. His strides lengthened as he dodged through shifting groups of oblivious casino patrons. He was close—maybe 150 feet away. His minions were closer still, and closing in—

Bianca yanked her hand free of Bix's hold, grabbed the rack that held the dealer's neatly stacked rows of tens of thousands of dollars' worth of chips and flung it—and them—up in the air in Mickey's general direction in hopes that the swarms of people that immediately squealed and dived for them would slow him down.

Then she grabbed her purse and ran.

18

Straight into the arms of the quartet of security guards that had rushed from another part of the casino to head her off.

"Stop it! No! I didn't do anything," Bianca protested, struggling feebly as two of them grabbed an upper arm each and practically lifted her off her feet.

The half-dozen security guards who had been chasing her fell back in response to a sharp, Cantonese *"Faan faan"* (go back) from one of her captors as they changed course and, with two of them half carrying, half dragging her between them and the other two providing backup, hauled her away.

Which is exactly what she wanted them to do. As far as distractions went, this one got the job—which was allow Mason to escape while keeping her out of Mickey's hands long enough for her to do the same—done. Casino security in Macau being what it was, however, she suspected she would be in for a bad time as soon as they got her far enough off the floor that no one could hear her scream.

Forget the civilized summoning of the police that might await a found-out cheater in Vegas. Here in Macau, ripping off or attempting to rip off a casino merited a far more old school response. Scamming a million or more would get you permanently disappeared. A couple of hundred thousand, tortured and beaten and finally, as long as they got the money back, tossed barely alive into the street. Palming a card, as she had done? She wasn't sure, but having a sledgehammer crush the offending hand sounded about right.

Add in throwing tens of thousands of chips to the crowd, and she had no idea what punishment the security staff might come up with. She did know that she didn't want to know.

Good thing she wasn't planning to hang around to find out.

From the corner of her eye, she saw Mason in his wheelchair whirring his way toward the east entrance. A quick glance over her shoulder found Mickey struggling to get through the tangle of people fighting over the chips she'd thrown. His minions had faded from sight, which told her that whoever they were, they weren't working with security. She couldn't see Doc anywhere. Her only hope was that, wherever he was lurking, he could see her and would stay close. Otherwise, when the time came to run for real, searching the casino for him was going to prove problematic. The only thing to do would be to join Mason on that rooftop, take her phone back from him and call Doc from there.

"Where are you taking me?" Her faux-fearful question was in English, which was widely spoken in India, where Kangana was supposedly from. It came as they dragged her through a door in one of the golden walls into a long, dimly lit interior corridor. There was no answer. She had no idea if they spoke English, and speaking to them in Cantonese would raise too many questions about her in their minds. As soon as the door closed behind them and they were safely cut off from the view of the casino, their attitude changed. Their grip on her arms tightened. They hustled her along, conversing among themselves in Cantonese, which they clearly had no idea she understood.

"She's pretty." That was a rough translation of what was said with a suggestive leer by the man holding her left arm. He was about eight inches taller than she was, which given the heels she was wearing meant he was around six foot six. He was built like the Hulk, all gorilla arms and bulging muscles. Like the others, he appeared to be a local. He wore the tux that was apparently required for all the casino workers. It strained across his back and shoulders.

"What do we do with her?" This came from one of the men trailing behind.

"I can think of some things," said Left Arm Guy. Bianca was really beginning to dislike him. His fingers dug painfully into her upper arm; she was going to have bruises. The way he was looking at her—well, she knew that look. If she'd been as helpless as she was pretending to be, she'd be in real trouble. As they hurried her along, she was supremely conscious of the ticking clock: Mickey wouldn't just give up and go away. Whether he could get to her while casino security had her in custody she didn't know, but she wasn't about to chance it.

She had to *go*, and keeping that in mind, she evaluated her surroundings with an eye to escape. There had been a single security camera facing the door they'd entered through, but she didn't see any others. The floor was marble, the walls painted the same shade of yellow-gold as those in the casino. The lighting came from widely placed sconces up near the ceiling. Niches in the wall held bronze statues. It was cold from the air-conditioning, and smelled faintly dank, like a cave. No windows, and so far she'd only seen the one door.

Going back out it was not ideal, but it might be the best she could do.

"We take her to the office and leave it up to Novo." The man holding her right arm seemed to be in charge. He was older, fiftyish, about six foot one. She was guessing he weighed around two hundred pounds to the other man's 350-plus. "You two go back to the floor. Paulo is all the help I need."

The men walking behind bowed their heads in acknowledgment and left.

"Novo does not like cheaters. He will say she needs to be taught a lesson." Left Arm Guy—Paulo?—stroked her arm with his free hand suggestively. Fortunately her dress had sleeves. Their long strides meant that her leg in its sheer black stocking flashed in and out of the slit in her dress as she was forced to hurry to keep up. Paulo openly ogled the display. "We could take care of that ourselves and save him the trouble."

"We will leave it to Novo," Right Arm Guy said. They made a sharp left into an intersecting corridor and almost immediately came to a short flight of four steps heading down. About sixty feet beyond the steps, at the end of the hallway, were three doors. All were closed. Bianca presumed that they led to offices. A security camera mounted near the ceiling was trained on those doors. Its range did not extend as far as the stairs.

The problem lay in the people who might be inside the offices. She was being taken to Novo, who was almost certainly inside one of those doors. There were likely others in there, as well.

Paulo released her arm as they reached the stairs, which weren't wide enough for three to descend abreast, especially when one of the three was the approximate size of a building. Right Arm Guy hung on, staying beside her as he walked her down.

This is it.

"Oh!" Pretending to stumble, she fell down the last two steps. It was a simple matter to pull him down with her. They both hit the floor—and Bianca rolled and knocked him unconscious with a single hard chop to the side of his neck that landed right on target in a highly sensitive place between the bottom of his ear and the top of his spine.

She liked to think of it as the G-spot. As in, *gotcha.*

"Hey!" Paulo was on the second step on his way down as he apparently registered what was happening. Before he could even so much as finish processing what he'd seen, Bianca shot to her feet, launched herself at him and used on him the same blow that had felled his coworker.

The lightning-fast strike didn't even hurt her hand.

"*Ahh.*" Paulo's eyes rolled back in his head. He collapsed like a sack of potatoes.

Unfortunately, he collapsed like a sack of potatoes right on top of her. All 350 some odd tank-like pounds of him slammed into her. She staggered backward, lost her footing on the steps and crashed to the floor. She hit hard, on her back, cracking her head on the marble as she landed. If she hadn't had the wig for cushioning, she probably would have been knocked out. But the pain of that was nothing compared to the agony, a split-second later, of having the solid mountain of deadweight that was Paulo drop on her.

"*Ooph.*" That was the sound of the breath exploding from her lungs as he landed. Instantly she was being crushed, flattened, suffocated, by his bulk. He lay facedown at a slight angle across her, and with her hands trapped between them there was absolutely nothing she could do about it.

For a stunned moment she simply lay where she had fallen. Stars revolved in front of her eyes, and her compressed lungs ached with emptiness. Then her mouth opened, and she gasped like a landed fish as she fought to suck in air. Her lungs wouldn't fully inflate, but she managed a couple of shallow, wheezing breaths. Paulo, unconscious, lay sprawled on top of her like a roofied gorilla. She tried to squirm free, tried to push him off her, tried to find some anchorage for her feet and use that and her body to heave him to one side, but the floor was too slick to provide purchase for her shoes, her hands were trapped and there was no way to get enough leverage with the rest of her body to shove the leviathan off her.

Final verdict on the takedown: epic fail.

Somebody could come along at any time. Paulo and Right Arm Guy could regain consciousness at any time.

This is bad. Move your ass.

She'd regained enough of her senses to start trying to pull together a workable plan to extricate herself that didn't involve just lying there waiting for Paulo to wake up when someone stepped into her line of vision (which because she had Paulo's side-of-beef-like shoulder wedged beneath her chin was pretty much limited to straight up) and smiled down at her.

"Hello, beautiful," Mickey said. "Or Sylvia. Or Cara. Or whatever name you're going by tonight."

Bianca's heart would have leaped like a goosed rabbit if her chest wasn't currently being pancaked. As it was, it just gave an alarmed flutter and got back to the business of trying to keep her circulation going under such adverse conditions.

No use pretending she didn't know him. It had been clear from the moment they'd first locked eyes in the casino that he recognized her.

The question was, why was he here? To capture Mason? Or to kill her?

Looked like she was about to find out.

If he wanted to kill her, fate wasn't going to present him with a better chance.

You gotta ask yourself, do you feel lucky?

Unfortunately, she didn't.

"Drop dead," she said. Or, rather, gasped, breath being in short supply. She wriggled in an attempt to remedy that and managed to shift enough so that Paulo's rib cage wasn't pressing directly on her diaphragm and she could actually almost breathe.

Mickey said, "Speaking of dead, I'm glad you're not." His caramel brown eyes twinkled at her. Okay, so she was in a ridiculous position. No need to rub it in.

"Oh, that makes me feel all warm inside." Talking halfway

normally was an effort, but for him she made it. The citrusy smell of Paulo's hair pomade filled her nostrils. She turned her head as far to the side as she could to get away from it.

"What are you doing in Macau?" Hands in his pockets, Mickey walked around her and Paulo, pretending to examine the predicament in which she found herself from all angles.

"Vacation." Except for her eyes, which followed his every move, she lay perfectly still now: squirming like a worm on a hook was downright undignified. Useless, too. "What are you doing in Macau?"

"Same thing."

"Enjoying yourself?"

"The good part's just started. Once again, loving the garter belt." The smirk he assumed as he eyeballed her legs, which she was pretty sure were exposed all the way up to the toned, tanned and bare tops of her thighs, affording him a view of lacy black stocking tops attached to the satiny black straps of her garter belt, annoyed her. She remembered that in the course of a previous encounter she'd deliberately removed her escape cord dispenser from her garter belt in front of him just to blow his mind, and gave herself a mental kick. Showing off never ended well. "No one would ever guess you use it as a holster. That's genius. Mind if I check it out?"

"Touch it and die," she said. "Pervert."

He grinned. "Careful, you're going to hurt my feelings." Without making a move to touch her garter belt—*okay, so maybe not a pervert*—he strolled around to where she could look up at him without straining her neck. "Not that I'm complaining, mind you, but you seem to spend a lot of time flat on your back when I'm around."

"Oh, ha-ha." Her voice was stronger now. Watching him warily, she worked on getting her hands into the right position to give Moby Dick the mother of all shoves. Unfortunately, to do that she first had to get her hands out from between them: not that easy.

"What are you going to do when Big Boy here wakes up, I wonder? Because it doesn't look like you're going anywhere until he moves."

She finally succeeded in jerking her hands free. Summoning all her strength while simultaneously giving Mickey an eat-dirt look, she got both hands beneath the behemoth's shoulder and shoved.

Paulo's shoulder lifted maybe six inches. Then it fell back to exactly where it had been before. Once again, the problem was no leverage.

Epic fail, the sequel.

"Nice try," Mickey said. "You've got to ask yourself, what does it take to get that big? A diet of raw meat and steroids?"

Inwardly Bianca sizzled. Outwardly, she hoped, she remained cool. Well, as cool as it was possible to remain while being squashed like a bug by a hot, sweaty, NFL-linebacker-sized mound of human flesh.

"Want to help me out here?" she asked, doing her best to keep the poisonous out of her sweet.

"Depends." He smiled down at her, his eyes crinkling at the corners, his teeth a flash of white against the bronze of his skin. "Are you going to attack me if I do?"

He'd seen her in action. Actually, he'd experienced her in action. He knew what kind of fighter she was.

"No," she said. And tried to sound like she meant it.

He laughed, and she felt some of the edginess that had kept her watching him like a hawk fade. The fact that he was really kind of gorgeous did not weigh with her. The fact that she possibly sort of liked him and that her inner antenna wasn't pinging with all sorts of alarm messages did. She'd learned over the years to trust that inner antenna. Bottom line, she really didn't think he was there to kill her. If he was, he did the best fake good-guy act in history, plus he was taking his sweet time getting on with it.

So he was either a total sociopath, or her origins and/or the contract on her life had no bearing on his presence in Macau.

He said, "You know I know you're lying, right?"

Her brows twitched together. "Are you going to help get this monster off me or not?"

"Sure." His eyes twinkled at her. "Just as soon as we've finished our chat. This is better than having you in handcuffs, or a jail cell. My guess is that you could escape from either of those. This, not so much."

"I'm suffocating here."

"I'm betting you can hold out a little longer." His face changed, grew serious. "Thayer's here in the casino, isn't he? If he is, if he's anywhere in Macau, we're going to catch him. This is your chance to make a deal before we do. Tell me where I can find him, give me a statement detailing what you know about the things he's done, and you walk. Absolutely free. With immunity. No charges brought. Trust me, it doesn't get any better than that."

So he *hadn't* recognized Mason as the old guy sitting next to her. Well, she'd barely recognized him herself, and she'd known him all her life.

"You know what you can do with your offer, right?"

His lips tightened. "If you refuse, the flip side is I have you arrested and you spend the next couple of decades in some shitty jail. Believe me, Thayer wouldn't turn down a deal like that for you."

"Well, gee, now that you put it that way…" She let her voice trail off tantalizingly. Then she added, "The answer's still no."

His lips tightened even more. If she'd *thought* his mouth could look cruel, now she was sure of it.

"To earn that kind of loyalty, he's got to be more to you

than a boss. What, is he your lover or something? Because you should know those May-December things almost never work out."

"Bite me."

He bent to pick up something from the floor. When he straightened she saw to her horror that he had her purse in his hands. It had fallen to the floor beside her when she'd landed.

"That's private. Put that down," she snapped. Too late: he was already unzipping it. "I have personal things in there!"

"I'm counting on it." As he rifled through the contents, she got a glimpse of her Ann wig, the clothes she'd worn earlier and her small makeup kit, which he unzipped and looked inside. Then he came up with her passport. Or, rather Kangana's passport. He flipped it open. "Kangana Bhatt, huh?" He looked at her skeptically and said, "Just so you know, your wig's crooked, Kangana."

Then he shoved the passport back in her purse and continued rummaging.

Any minute now he would find the secret panel beneath the lining that concealed her other IDs.

She said, "Look, anybody could come out of those offices back there. Anybody could come in from the casino. These two goons could wake up. I'd really rather not be here when that happens. If what you want is to talk, could we please do it someplace else?"

"Think I don't know that the minute I let you up you're going to try to take me out and run away?" He fished the cigarette lighter Mason had given her out of her purse and looked at it. Bianca held her breath, but he dropped it back in her purse without seeming to notice anything amiss.

"You can't keep me trapped here forever." Even to her own ears she sounded cross. "Did I mention that Paulo here weighs a ton and I'm having trouble breathing?"

"I can keep you here—or somewhere—as long as I need

to. You don't seem to have grasped it yet, but I currently have you in custody. All I have to do is make one phone call, and it gets official. The people I have searching the casino for Thayer will show up here and put you in handcuffs and leg shackles or a straitjacket or whatever it takes to keep the lid on. Then you'll be loaded on a private plane to be flown to an interrogation site, where, believe me, you won't be able to escape. Once all that starts to happen, by the way, the deal I offered you is off the table. Right here, right now, is your one chance."

As he spoke, he felt the outside of her purse, ran his hands over the bottom and the straps, plucked at the clasp, while she watched with bated breath. Well, the thing was supposed to be pat-down proof. Hello, extreme field test.

Time to change tactics. Stop being so in your face. Make him think he had a chance of persuading her to turn on Mason. All she had to do was persuade him to help her get out from under Shamu. Then they'd have a whole different conversation.

"Say I decide to accept your deal. What then?"

"First you have to convince me you mean it. You can start by telling me where Thayer is. If your information checks out, we're good to go."

"How do I know you'll keep your promise about giving me immunity?"

"You have my word."

Batting her eyes at him was probably too much, she decided. Especially since she was flat on her back with the human equivalent of a Mack truck parked on top of her. Instead she gave him her best, big-eyed, Bambi-who'd-just-lost-his-mother look and said, "I want to trust you."

"You can. As long as you're straight with me. Let's start with, where's Thayer?"

She closed her eyes. Her lips trembled briefly. Then she

firmed her lips, opened her eyes, and, with the air of one who's just come to a momentous decision, said, "He's supposed to meet me at the blackjack tables in the casino. He hadn't shown up yet when I saw you. He should be out there looking for me as we speak."

Her hope was that he would decide to haul her to her feet and march her out to the casino floor to lure and/or identify Mason.

Crossing his arms over his chest, he studied her face. Her purse, thank God, now dangled unmolested from his wrist.

"Try again, beautiful. Think I don't know when I'm being played?"

"I am not playing you. You say you want me to trust you. How about you try trusting me?" Angry, frustrated, she gave Paulo another abortive shove. His shoulder rose, fell. Then to her alarm he snorted and moved a little.

"He's waking up," she ground out. "For God's sake, get him *off* me."

Mickey grimaced and leaned over Paulo. Bianca thought— *thank you, God!*—that he was finally going to help heave him off her and got her hands in position to push one more time.

Then a big, blurry streak of gold sliced down through the air toward Mickey's head. Before Bianca could do anything more than watch its lightning-fast descent in wide-eyed surprise, it slammed into the back of his skull with a resounding *thunk.*

Mickey dropped without a sound.

19

"Oh, Jesus, is he dead?" Bouncing up and down on the balls of his feet with agitation, Doc looked at Mickey's crumpled figure. He held the gilded, baseball-bat-sized statue of—was it Bacchus? Yes, she thought it was—that he'd used to fell Mickey by its neck. Bianca recognized it from one of the niches in the hallway. "I can't believe I just killed a cop. Do they have the death penalty in Macau?"

"No, and he's not dead," Bianca said. She was almost sure, but no need to share that niggle of doubt with Doc. Paulo groaned and stirred again, distracting her. "Quick, hit this one. *Not too hard*."

That last she added as a squeaked-out rider as Doc, muttering, "Oh shit oh shit oh shit," his face screwed up with terrible resolve, arced the statue over his head like Lizzie Borden with her ax with the clear intention of bringing it down on Paulo's skull with all his might.

Despite her warning, it still landed with a solid thud. Paulo went as limp as a corpse.

Okay, not a good comparison. Fortunately, it took only a moment to ascertain that he was still breathing: she could feel the rise and fall of his chest.

"Oh shit," Doc said. "Oh shit oh shit."

"Help get him off me. Quick," she said.

Doc set the statue down and complied. Working together, the two of them managed to shift Paulo enough so that Bianca could roll out from under him.

"Thank God." She staggered to her feet. She felt dizzy and achy and limp from her ordeal, worried (she hated to admit it) about Mickey, even more worried about her and Doc's prospects for escape.

"He's, like, a Colossus." Doc stared down at Paulo while Bianca yanked her purse from Mickey's limp arm. Then, unable to help herself, she did a fast check of Mickey's pulse. His skin felt warm beneath her fingers. She could feel a reassuringly steady beat beneath. His tall body sprawled beside Paulo's on the marble. He was slack-faced and pale. The good news was, she didn't see any blood.

Of course, Doc had clobbered him in the back of the head, and his hair was thick and black, so in the absence of a scarlet fountain there was really no way to tell.

Think good thoughts.

"It was the only thing I could think of to do." Doc had to be in some kind of mild shock. He was sweating buckets, as white as paper, babbling. Not a surprise: she'd already figured out that violence wasn't in his nature.

"You did good. Are you kidding? You saved me." Mickey and Paulo were out for the count, no question about it. But she gave Right Arm Guy a second chop in the G-spot just to be sure.

"I saw these two yo-yos drag you back here. Then what happened?" Doc's teeth were chattering. His hat had fallen off during his assault. Bianca spotted it, grabbed it and handed it to him.

"Tell you later. Come on."

She grabbed the statue he'd set down. No point in leaving what amounted to a smoking gun behind. On the way back down the hall, she gave Bacchus a hasty wipe down and restored him to his temporarily empty niche. She knew for sure that Mickey had never seen what, or who, had felled him. With luck, no one would ever think to check the statues in the hall for any kind of forensic evidence. It was the best she could do. The statue was too big, and too noticeable, to carry with them.

The only way out that she knew of was the door she'd been dragged in through. The cameras were a problem, but a glance at them told her that the images were not stored in the cameras themselves, which meant that they were being kept in some remote site that she didn't have time to search for. Mickey, for one, already knew what she looked like, but for Doc's sake she would have taken a minute to destroy the cameras if it would have made a difference.

At least Doc was once again wearing his hat. With luck, that might shield his face.

"Keep your head down and walk to the east entrance. You go first. I'll be close behind you. In case we get separated, we're heading for the top of the parking garage next door."

He rolled his eyes in her direction. Beneath the pulled-low brim of his hat, she could see the whites. "You got a plan? Please tell me you got a plan."

"Always," she said.

He nodded, and then he was out the door.

Bianca spent a second contemplating reversing her dress—SiuSiu's designs were always reversible—or changing back to Ann again. But the cameras had already recorded her going in, and they had recorded Doc going in and out. If she changed clothes, she would simply give whoever was monitoring the cameras a look at her new identity. Remembering Mickey's crack about her wig, she gave it a tug, redraped the scarf around her head and walked out onto the casino floor.

Ten minutes later, she and Doc emerged onto the fifteenth-floor roof of the adjacent parking garage. The roof was essentially a helipad, and just as Mason had said, a small white and silver helicopter, its rotor stilled, waited at the far end. It was nearly 1:00 a.m. No moon, no stars. The heavy black blanket of clouds was so close that she felt like she could almost reach up and touch it. The stiff wind blowing in off the water was cool and heavy with the promise of rain. It ruffled her wig, caught the ends of her scarf, the edge of her dress. As she looked around, then rushed to check the helicopter—only the pilot, with whom she exchanged a few brief words, was aboard—she was thankful for her long sleeves. Dim halogen lights on tall metal poles were set into the waist-high concrete wall that formed the edge. Supplementing their frosty glow, the strobescent neon of the Cotai Strip painted the rooftop with a kaleidoscope of ever-changing pattern and color. The color of the moment was blue, and even as she looked around more carefully, probing the corners and the shadows at the base of the light poles and the freestanding generator, the hue changed to red.

"So where is he?" Doc was still bent over, hands on his thighs, gasping from the rushed climb up fourteen flights of stairs it had required to reach the roof, when she rejoined him. He'd accepted the explanation for taking the stairs that she'd tossed over her shoulder—elevators are death traps—without argument, but that hadn't made getting up to the roof any easier on him. On the way, she'd given him the abbreviated version of what he'd missed, ending with the fact that Mason had a helicopter waiting on the roof to whisk them all away.

"Don't know," Bianca said. Mason should have been there. He'd had ample time, way more than they'd had, to make it. The pilot, who spoke only Mandarin, had seen no one, he'd told her in response to her question. Was she ready to go? he'd asked. No, she'd replied in the same language, and turned away. Not until Mason came.

Something, clearly, had gone wrong. Her pulse was already heightened from the escape. Now she could feel it racing. She was tense, on edge with the knowledge that by now the pursuit had to be under way. They couldn't wait around for long—but she couldn't leave Mason. Had he been captured? Or worse?

Walking over to the half wall, she leaned over it, looking down. If anything terrible had happened, she would expect to see police cars, or ambulances, or some kind of obvious official presence, on the street below.

The street was packed. Cars crawled along, bumper-to-bumper, their lights spearing the pedestrians streaming along the sidewalks in front of the casinos. The Wynn's water show was at its height: vividly colored plumes of water danced in the wind, watched by a large, amorphous crowd. Across the street, the square was a hotbed of activity. The paper lanterns strung between the trees looked like stars at that distance.

The glittering, glitzy Cotai Strip seemed very much business as usual.

Closer at hand, the floors of the parking garage below emitted a faint, whitish glow. They were configured like the tiers of a wedding cake. The fifteenth through the eleventh floors were the same size, and the smallest. The tenth through the fifth floors were about twelve feet wider all around. The extra twelve feet on the tenth floor formed an open observation platform that at the moment held only a few people, most of whom were standing at the rail observing the water show below. The fifth through the second floors were about twelve feet wider still. The bottom floor was the widest of all.

Because, Bianca suspected, of the casinos, suicide was not an infrequent occurrence in Macau. The owners had built that parking garage with an eye to making sure that anyone leaping from it wouldn't end up going splat in the street.

Except for the fifteenth and tenth floors, the floors were entirely under roof.

"What do we do?" Doc joined her at the wall. He had his breathing mostly under control now. "You know the cop and those other guys have regained consciousness by now. Or someone's found them. They'll be looking for us hard."

"I know." Hands curling around the rounded edge of the wall, Bianca stared sightlessly out into the night. Then she remembered something and felt a spurt of excitement. "Quick, give me your phone."

Doc looked at her in surprise, but fumbled in his pocket and handed it over. "Why?"

"Because I gave Mason mine." She was already punching in the number, which she'd memorized.

When it started to ring, her eyes widened. She could hear it. Not through the phone. From somewhere outside.

"Where are you?" she asked without preamble when Mason answered. She was already looking over the edge, looking down, because the ringing had seemed to be coming from below.

"Tenth floor of the parking garage. We've got a problem. They're working on the elevators. Until they get finished, this is as high as they go."

"Oh, no." Bianca thought of him in the wheelchair. This was bad. Also, something he should have known. "So how did you get down to the casino when you got here?" Her voice was tinged with exasperation.

"I came by limo, not helicopter. Never leave the same way you go in, remember?"

She did. It was one of the rules. Not that it mattered now.

"Any way you can get up the stairs?"

"No." His tone made it definite.

"Holy hell. All right, we'll come down and help you up."

"Five flights? I don't think so. I put any weight at all on this leg, I'll bust a hundred different things open. I'm going back down to the street."

"And do what? Catch a taxi in your wheelchair?"

All of a sudden Bianca saw him. He'd come out into the

tenth-floor observation area and was rolling along in his wheelchair as he talked on the phone. The tourists who'd been watching the water show had turned away from the rail—a glance told her that the show had ended—and he fell in behind them, heading, presumably, for the elevator.

"Stop," she told him. "Stay where you are. Look up and you'll see me. I have an idea."

Mason looked up. The small, flip-open phone was held to his ear. His face was a pale oval in the multicolored darkness.

Bianca didn't wave. There was no point: he clearly saw her, although he didn't wave, either. What he needed was an elevator. She was going to provide him with one. Well, the field version of one.

"I'm going to drop my escape cord down to you," she said into the phone. "Tie yourself into it. Securely. We're going to make an elevator for you."

Unclipping the cord dispenser from her garter belt as she spoke, she tossed it over the edge to him, making sure to keep hold of the loose end of the dental-floss-thin cord. She'd used it as an emergency means of escape many times and was confident in its steely strength.

Whirring forward, Mason caught the dispenser in one hand. "How?"

"The pulley system. Weight, wheel, counterweight." She patted the steel-embedded-in-concrete light pole near her. It was round and smooth, cool to the touch, and sturdy. Obviously very sturdy. The glow the light itself emitted was faint enough that the more vivid colors flashing across the Strip swallowed it up, but it still enabled Mason to see her. "We'll use this for the wheel. Pull you right up."

"If I'm the weight, and that's the wheel, what are you going to use for a counterweight?"

"I'll call you right back. Tie into the cord." Disconnecting, she looked at Doc, who was standing beside her. His expression was already mistrustful. She had to assume he'd overheard both ends of the conversation and had drawn the obvious conclusion.

Holding up both hands, he took a step back from her. "Whoa. Is this where you, like, tell me I have to jump off the building?"

Clearly he'd recognized his role as the counterweight. She would have done it, but her body weight wasn't enough to pull Mason up. If she tried, Mason wouldn't budge, and she'd end up dangling fifteen stories in the air.

"You don't have to," Bianca said. "But it's safe, I promise. You go down, he comes up. Then you grab the wheelchair, carry it up the stairs and we're all out of here."

"That's five stories down. That rope—" he took a look at the circumference of the cord she was holding in her hand, and his eyes widened "—that *thread* breaks, I could die. And did I mention I don't like heights?"

"Your call." Bianca held up the filament-thin cord so that he could see the silvery trail of it snaking over the concrete wall. "Otherwise we're going to have to go down there and carry Mason up five flights of stairs. If he'll let us. And even if he does, it's going to take longer than we probably have."

"He said he'd take a taxi," Doc replied with a groan. But his tone, and the gesture that accompanied it, made the words a capitulation.

"I said that. Anyway, are you really prepared to fly away to safety in the helicopter he ordered and let him fend for himself? In a wheelchair?" She was fashioning him a rudimentary harness out of the cord as she spoke. It was long enough to enable her to descend nineteen stories. Between Mason and Doc, they would be covering a distance of approximately ten stories so she allowed for that, then still had plenty to work with. Finishing, she showed him how to extricate himself from it when he landed by pulling on the clip at the end.

"He left us behind in Bahrain." The plaintive tone of that made no difference: Bianca had him trussed up like a chicken and was pushing him toward the wall.

"Water under the bridge." She checked to make sure the cord was tucked smoothly around the light pole. Then as Doc leaned over the wall to look dubiously down, she phoned Mason.

"Doc's the counterweight and he's ready," she said.

"Let's do it." Mason pushed himself out of the wheelchair to lean unsteadily against the guardrail beside it.

Disconnecting, Bianca tucked her phone in Doc's pocket, because when he got down to the tenth floor Mason, who had the other phone, would have taken his place on the fifteenth and it was always good to have a means of communication.

"I think I'm gonna barf," Doc said as she checked his harness one last time. He handed her his hat. She put it on the ground beside them.

"You'll be fine. It'll all be over in a flash."

"That's what I'm afraid of."

"Look at Mason. He's not nervous." She helped Doc, who was grimacing, clamber over the wall so that his stomach was resting on it and he was facing her. His legs hung over the five-story drop.

"He doesn't weigh three hundred pounds," Doc said.

"Doesn't matter. If the cord breaks, you're both dead."

"Oh, wow. Great bedside manner you got there, boss."

"All you have to do is push off. Hang on to the cord for balance as you go and bend your knees when you land. Then unhitch yourself and get back up here as fast as you can."

"Oh shit," Doc said.

"Go," Bianca said, then had a thought. "And don't scream. Or kick. Or do anything except hang on to the cord."

"Hail Mary, full of grace…" Muttering, Doc closed his

eyes and screwed up his face. "Cowabunga, dude," he said in conclusion, and pushed off.

He dropped, not quite like a stone because he was spinning but almost that fast. At least, Bianca thought as she leaned over the wall to watch, he remembered not to scream, not to kick and to hang on to the cord. Mason shot up toward Bianca, his ascent far more graceful than Doc's descent. The zipping sound of the cord against the light pole set Bianca's teeth on edge: she hadn't been kidding about what would happen if it broke. But they made it, both of them, Doc collapsing to his knees as he hit and Mason shooting up so that all she had to do was grab him and help him over the wall.

"I'm getting too old for this," Mason said as he freed himself from the cord. Doc's end of the cord came flying back into the dispenser when she pressed the button, so she knew he'd managed to get his harness off, too. Expecting Doc to join them momentarily, she wrapped an arm around Mason's waist and helped him hop, one-footed, toward the helicopter, which at a signal from him had already started to rotate its blades.

His arm wrapped tight around her shoulders. He leaned heavily on her as he tried to cover the distance to the helicopter as fast as he could. She felt a weird pang in her heart at the feel of his arm around her. He'd never been one for hugs or any kind of physical affection. As a young girl, she'd sometimes watched other fathers and daughters meet up, watched them hug or kiss or even bump fists, and thought, that would be nice. Now she realized that he'd always treated her as a protégé. Which was exactly what she'd been to him. She'd loved him, he'd taught her. The bone-deep hurt she felt would heal, but the lessons would never leave her. When enough time had passed, she might even consider it a reasonable trade.

"As I was leaving the casino, I spotted a man I think I recognized," Mason said. He was breathing heavily. His voice was labored, and he was in obvious pain. In front of them, the helicopter blades were picking up speed. She could feel the wind of it on her face. The steady *whomp-whomp-whomp* made her lean closer to him to hear. "If I'm right, he's part of a CIA kill team, and I think I'm right. Those guys are their best, crack assassins, and if they're here—"

The sound of a ringing phone interrupted. It could only be Doc, on her burner phone. Already experiencing a cramp in her stomach at the idea of a CIA kill team in the vicinity, she frowned as Mason fished the phone out of his pocket and, with an irony-tinged "I think this is for you," handed it over.

Why would Doc be calling? By now, he should have joined them.

Bianca never even had a chance to say *where are you* into the phone.

Talking so fast the words practically tripped over themselves, Doc said, "There's guys coming up the stairs at you *right now*. We're talking some badass dudes. Get out of there."

"What?"

"They just searched this floor. I managed to hide. They found the wheelchair, checked it out. They're probably going floor by floor. I think they're looking for Mason—and you. I can't get to you. You got to *go*."

Despite the shock of it, Bianca managed to stay cool enough to assimilate the news.

"Got it," she said, her mind racing to explore the various ramifications. "You go too. I'll call you." Bianca had to disconnect as she and Mason reached the helicopter. It was small, a four-seater, and the pilot leaned over to open the passenger door from the inside.

Mason had clearly heard every word. "That'll be the kill team." His face was hard and set. "Get in. We're heading to Hong Kong, and we need to haul ass. They'll be armed to the teeth, and I don't even have a damned gun on me."

She helped Mason get up into the passenger seat. The pilot put his headphones on and said something into the radio.

"I'm not coming with you." She had to raise her voice to be heard over the rotors. "I can't abandon Doc."

Doc would have no clue how to hide from a kill team or the security from the Wynn or anyone else. Without her, and with his image almost certain to be recoverable from the security cameras in the casino hallway, he'd be a sitting duck.

"Leave him. They're here to kill you and me, not him."

"I can't. I'll be careful." She started backing away from the helicopter.

Mason leaned out the door. "Bianca—between the CIA kill team and the Darjeeling Brothers contract, you don't have much time. Acquire that thing we talked about as fast as you can and get it to me. Before it's too late for both of us."

Nodding, she held up a hand in farewell. He turned away, slammed the door. He didn't look her way again.

Her throat tightened.

Never look back: it was one of the rules.

Which meant it shouldn't hurt.

But it did.

She turned and ran for the wall as the helicopter lifted off.

20

An escape-cord-assisted leap over the wall, a hair-raising elevator ride down, a switch-up of her dress and a quick phone
call later, Bianca caught up to Doc in the square opposite the
Wynn.

It wasn't the rendezvous point she would have chosen.

Never leave the way you go in.

But the square was where Doc had fled, so that was where
they were. It was thin of company now, because a few fat
drops of rain had fallen minutes earlier. The rain had stopped
for now, but from the heaviness in the air it was obvious that
it could start up again at any time. The dragon was gone. The
street cart vendors were beginning to close up shop. A few
diehards made last-minute purchases of paper parasols and
fireworks and Macau's favorite dessert, the creamy, delicious
egg tarts. The paper lanterns threw shadows everywhere as
intermittent gusts of wind rocked them.

"You should've gone with him," Doc greeted her.

"Where's the fun in that? We're a team, remember." Bianca looked him over critically. Buzzed head, black suit and
all, Doc still looked like Doc: way too recognizable. "You
did good back there, by the way."

"That was like extreme sports, only for criminals," Doc
said. "Extreme criminaling. Could we not do any more of it?"

"No promises. Hold still." She took advantage of the deep
shadow beside a potted cherry tree to plop her Kangana wig
on his head. At this point, disguise was good. Even if, in it,

she decided as she straightened it for him, he did look kind of like Sonny from the seventies *Sonny and Cher Show*. She was wearing her Ann wig and the reverse side of her SiuSiu Special gown, which was a deep cranberry red, shortened to knee-length by a hidden zipper in the skirt. She'd considered putting on Doc's hat, which she'd grabbed before exiting the fifteenth floor, but had decided against it and tucked the crushable into her purse. The Ann wig was a better disguise anyway. She'd even altered her shoes, because nobody ever did and shoes were a dead giveaway. A trained operative always looked at shoes. Her four-inch spike heels were now flats. The spikes were in her purse.

She'd even reversed her purse, which was now gold, smooth and worn cross-body over her dress.

"He able to help out with the contract?" Doc asked.

"Yes. Tell you later. Let's go." After casting a sweeping look around, Bianca started off across the square.

"This is embarrassing," Doc said as he caught a glimpse of his reflection in the window of a now-closed tea shop as they passed it.

"Better embarrassed than dead." Every instinct she possessed shouted that they needed to get out of there. She couldn't get the uneasiness she'd felt in the square earlier out of her head. Was this where Mickey had picked up their trail? Or, worse, the CIA kill team?

Was there surveillance here that she wasn't able to detect?

The thought made her heart beat faster.

"True that." Doc hurried to catch up.

"Stay back a few feet," Bianca said. If something went wrong, she was the target. In case of attack, he would have a better chance of escaping if he could simply fade away without anyone realizing he was with her. "If anything happens, you run one way and I'll run the other. I'll call you when we get clear, and we'll meet up again."

"Yeah, okay," Doc said.

She was busy evaluating their surroundings. Rooftops, open windows, balconies: all held potential danger. So did trees, trash cans, the wheeled vendor carts—anywhere an assailant could lurk. The tourists milling around buying souvenirs looked harmless, but that didn't mean they were. Like the Wynn, the nearby Macau Dome and the even closer tennis center overlooked the square: any would offer multiple vantage points for a sniper.

She could almost feel her skin crawl.

And then there was the fact that Mickey wouldn't stay unconscious forever. Once he was awake again, he would be coming after her full bore.

"Umbrella, lady?" An enterprising local with a basket of umbrellas over her arm popped up out of nowhere, brandishing a pocket-size (probably fake) tote. She addressed Bianca in English; Bianca remembered the Ann wig. Clearly it made her look like English was her native language.

"No, thanks," Bianca replied, waving her off and lengthening her stride.

"Only fifteen patacas," the woman persisted, scurrying to keep up. She was middle-aged, plump. Macanese from her appearance and accent. Dressed in a loose black top, black pants and the local version of flip-flops. Bianca imagined her with a family at home, seeing the rain, scurrying out to make a few extra patacas. Under better circumstances, she would have bought an umbrella.

"No, thank you," Bianca said again, shaking her head, and kept walking.

Her immediate goal was the busy Avenida de Cotai that ran between the Parisian and Studio City. With luck, they should be able to grab a taxi there. The Lotus Bridge wasn't far away.

Goal number one: get off the Strip.

"Uh, boss, the hotel's the other way."

"We're not going back to the hotel." The hotel—either hotel—was too dangerous. It made for a fixed spot, a place where someone might assume she would come, an ideal arena to set up an ambush.

"We're not? Like, ever?"

"No. We—" She turned her head to explain and bumped smack into something that hadn't been in her path a few seconds previously.

"It is soon to rain," Umbrella Woman said. She waved the tote at Bianca, who, looking around even as she recoiled from the sturdy form she'd collided with, staggered back a pace. Bianca understood that the woman had planted herself in her path in a more determined bid to make a sale and was just opening her mouth to firm up her *No* when the woman's chest imploded, blossoming scarlet in an instant before collapsing into a geyser of blood and shredded matter that blasted out through her back.

Crack.

Silencers didn't work well on many sniper rifles; quite often the suppressor simply muted what would have been a high decibel explosion to the volume of a pistol's bark. But it didn't take the sharp sound for Bianca to realize what had happened.

The woman had been shot. By a sniper with a high-powered rifle.

She was standing right where Bianca would have been if seconds ago she hadn't put herself in Bianca's path.

Her heart leaped into her throat. Her pulse skyrocketed. That bullet had been meant for her, she had absolutely no doubt.

The kill team? Or someone else?

Under Bianca's horrified eyes, Umbrella Woman crumpled bonelessly to the cobblestones, her eyes already glazing over in death. Her blood gushed from the wound to form a rapidly growing puddle on the ground. The smell of it—raw meat—rose sharp and hideous to Bianca's nostrils.

A burst of adrenaline blasted her out of her shock-induced immobility.

"*Get down.*" Bianca dived for the protection of a nearby vendor cart even as she yelled the warning to Doc.

She hadn't yet hit the ground when something that felt like a bunched fist punched her hard in between her shoulder blades and smacked her out of the air.

Crack.

She slammed down on the bumpy cobblestones with her arms extended and her legs stretched out and found herself staring, stunned, at a worm's-eye view of what was happening all around her. She was light-headed and breathless with pain. Nothing seemed quite real.

In those few seconds, the square had transformed into a scene of utter chaos. Everywhere people screamed and ran, taking cover, doing their best to get out of the line of fire. A few lay bleeding on the ground.

I've been shot.

Her heart thundered wildly. She tried to breathe, couldn't. The burning sensation between her shoulder blades, the difficulty she was having drawing in air, this feeling of being hot and cold at the same time, terrified her.

I don't want to die.

"*Boss.*"

Doc landed beside her, his eyes shiny with terror. Flat on the cobblestones, he reached for her outflung hand—

Crack.

That round splintered a cobblestone inches from her face. Instinctively she flinched and rolled away. Her blood felt like ice water in her veins. Her mouth went sour with fear—but she could move.

Crack.

A couple of feet beyond where she lay, a fleeing man screamed and fell to the ground. Blood poured from his back.

You can move. So move.

"Come on." She could see the relief in Doc's eyes as she spoke. Despite the pain in her back, she rolled to a crouch and scrambled for the shelter of the nearest vendor cart. Doc scuttled after her on all fours.

The fact that she was hurt, not dead, was, she realized as the initial trauma of being hit faded, entirely due to the bullet-proof garment she wore under her dress. The impact of the bullet had been stunning, but she didn't think she'd suffered more than a superficial injury.

Thank God for SiuSiu.

Crack. Crack. Crack.

Rounds fired in quick succession splintered the cart's wooden front even as she and Doc huddled behind it. A shower of leaves from the potted cherry tree behind them rained down on their heads. They weren't alone: a petrified-looking man crouched behind the cart, too. He spoke frantically to them in Mandarin, but for once Bianca was unable to translate: she was too rattled. Her back ached like someone had stabbed an ice pick into it, and her heart pounded and her mind raced as she tried to come up with a plan.

"Are you hit? I thought for sure you were hit." Doc's voice was shaky with anxiety. His hand ran over her back. Lifting it away, he looked at his palm as though expecting to find it covered with blood.

"I'm okay." Time enough to explain the ins and outs of it when they weren't facing imminent death.

The Wynn's water show with its accompanying music was in full swing. The sound and the spectacle were enough to keep anyone outside the square from immediately realizing what was happening. The crowded street and the busy hotels and casinos were keeping on keeping on: show business as usual. They could have been a world away.

She looked around desperately. Establishing a safe exit route was priority number one. Simply making a run for it would be suicidal. There was little cover. The night was dark, but the paper lanterns and the neon glow from the nearby hotels illuminated the square. A sniper with a decent scope would have no trouble taking out anyone he pleased. Terrified people crouched behind whatever they could find that might serve as a shield. Some screamed, some wept and a few were on their cell phones. Help would be coming soon: security, police.

Probably not soon enough.

A few intrepid souls took advantage of the cessation of fire to bolt for safety. A group of hand-holding women dashed past the cart.

Crack. Crack.

Another scream. One of the women went down. Another cried out and dropped to her knees beside the victim while the rest fled.

Following the angle of the shot, Bianca looked up in the direction from which it had come. She could see nothing: the distance was too great, and between the flashing neon and the darkness, the lighting was too erratic. But by calculating the angles she was able to pinpoint the sniper's general location. It was the top of the parking garage next to the Wynn.

"They're shooting at us, aren't they? At you. Think it's those dudes from the parking garage?" Hunched over behind the cart so that he was as small as he could make himself, Doc looked at her with eyes so wide she could see the whites all the way around the irises.

"Maybe."

"We're not going to die here tonight, right?"

"Hope not," she replied, more honestly than she probably

should have. Doc groaned while the man on her other side once again chattered at her in Mandarin.

"*Shui zai zuo zhege?*" he said. *Who is doing this?*

Now the translation came to her automatically. Her back might ache but least her mind was fully functional again.

There was no way she was telling him what she suspected. That answer could not help, and it opened up a whole 'nother can of worms. Her reply was a universal gesture: she shrugged.

Oh, God, she needed a *plan*.

In her heart, she knew this couldn't be a result of the Darjeeling Brothers' contract—it had to be the CIA. Despite the fact that a well-trained sniper wouldn't be firing indiscriminately, which was what this one seemed to be doing. He wasn't waiting for his target (her, she was almost positive) to show herself. Snipers were almost surgically precise: they took out their target and were done, and a CIA kill team had some of the best snipers in the world. This one was shooting at everyone and everything. Five people that she could see from her vantage point lay dead or wounded on the cobblestones. Bullets had torn up the square. But the most damage had been done to the cart she was sheltering behind, the tree above her, and the tall ceramic jars that held the brightly colored paper parasols that were this cart's merchandise and now lay scattered over the ground in blue and white shards.

The only way any of that made sense was if the sniper's object was to make her killing look like part of a random mass shooting.

While maybe pinning her down as the rest of the kill team closed in to make sure she was dead.

Her insides curdled. Her mouth went dry.

In a word, *bingo*.

All these people murdered for no other reason than to eliminate her. The ferocity and ruthlessness of it horrified her. The inhumanity of it infuriated her.

"What do we do?" Doc's voice was an octave higher than usual.

"Stay put." *She had a plan.* It had burst upon her as she'd looked one more time for the best possible exit route. Charting a path from cart to cart, she'd seen something that might actually be the answer to her prayers. To all their prayers. "I'll be back."

She hoped. If she didn't die.

Taking off like a champion sprinter, she darted for the next cart over.

Crack. Crack. Crack.

There was no mistake: the rounds targeted her, taking a chunk out of the cobblestones a slit second before her feet hit that spot, shattering a large, ornamental ceramic planter a split second after she crossed in front of it, zipping so close to her head that she felt the breeze of it blow past her forehead.

Heart thundering, galvanized by the nearness of the miss, she abandoned running to dive for cover.

Crack. Crack.

The front of the cart she rolled behind exploded in a shower of splinters as bullets raked it.

Two women crouching there, a local woman and a teenage girl who from the look of them had been working the cart, screamed.

"Puk gai." The woman used a common Cantonese curse as the girl's first scream degenerated into an outburst of ear-splitting hysteria. Wrapping her arms around the girl, rocking and patting her, the woman—Bianca thought she might be the girl's mother—pulled the teenager's head down to her shoulder and crooned soothingly to her while rolling terrified eyes at Bianca.

Crack. Crack. Crack.

The cart shook under the onslaught.

"Dak laa," Bianca said to them in Cantonese as she reached

up, snagged a large, clear plastic bowl from the top of the cart and plopped it down on the cobblestones near her knees. The rough translation was, *it's going to be okay*, and the thing was, she thought as she dug through her purse for the lighter Mason had given her, she was pretty sure she was telling the truth.

If the damned lighter actually worked.

It did. Bianca grabbed a handful of the many small smoke bombs that filled the bowl, lit the wicks and tossed them out into the square. Their thick smoke instantly shot skyward in mushrooming clouds of vivid blue, red and purple. She was already lighting and throwing more. Yellow, green, pink, garish and beautiful, the smoke clouds created a shifting, billowing wall between victims and sniper. Seeing what she was doing, the woman let go of the still-keening girl, pulled a lighter from her pocket and began lighting smoke bombs too and throwing them out into the square with swift efficiency.

She and Bianca exchanged looks: emergency comrades in arms.

Crack. Crack. Crack.

The sniper was still shooting, but he was shooting blind now. He couldn't see anyone to target them. The malodorous smoke was denser than London's thickest pea-soup fog. It filled the square, blanketed it, providing the best cover imaginable.

"Run. Go," she told the woman and girl in Cantonese as the bowl emptied.

The woman looked at her, nodded. The girl, who was maybe fourteen, shook and sobbed but no longer screamed.

"*Mhgoi,*" the woman said, thanking her as she grabbed the girl's hand and pulled her to her feet. Together they bolted.

"*Mang.*" Bianca shouted *run* in Cantonese to everyone else in the square as she lit the last of the bombs. Throwing them, she catapulted from behind the cart and flew to collect Doc. There was an immediate mass exodus as everyone who'd been hunkered down jumped up and stampeded through the billowing, suffocating smoke toward safety.

She reached Doc and together they bolted.

Crack. Crack. Crack.

The rounds pinged off cobblestones, slammed into tree trunks and ceramic pots, smashed windows across the square. The sound of shattering glass was sharp and startling.

Crack. Crack.

No one screamed. No one coughed, although the smoke was thick enough now to clog the lungs. Everyone seemed to instinctively realize that sound was the enemy, that it was the one thing that would allow the sniper to pinpoint them. Except for the muffled thunder of feet, the survivors fled as silently and invisibly as ghosts.

Crack.

A scream. A random bullet had found its mark. Wincing at the sound, gripping Doc's hand to guard against losing him in the smoke and dragging him after her like a speedboat with a trailing anchor, Bianca sprinted toward the alley she had earlier chosen as the most promising exit. She didn't bother to zig or zag, for the simple reason that, with the shooter blind, she was as likely to zig into the path of a bullet as zag away from one.

Crack. Crack.

Scrunching up her eyes against the burning smoke, she ran. And prayed.

Crack.

She and Doc charged into the alley, pounded down it. Other survivors ran through the alley, as well. The headlong panic of their flight reminded her of something she'd seen once at the running of the bulls. It was impossible to identify anyone: glimpses of dark shadows flitting into view and out again as they all ran for their lives. The alley was narrow and smoke filled as the cloud blanketing the square was pulled through it as if drawn by a chimney.

If a kill team was on its way in to make sure the sniper's job was done, the members would be rushing toward the scene at that moment, possibly from different ingress points. Bianca's worst fear was that she and Doc would run smack into one or more of them.

They burst out into the street without incident. It was busy even at nearly 2:00 a.m., because the pleasure near-island that was Macau was another of those cities that never sleep. Some people were already turning to look curiously at the drifts of smoke coming out of the alley as the survivors rushed from it. The survivors shouted, screamed, pointed back toward the square, alerting passersby to the atrocity that had just occurred.

With Doc in tow, Bianca melted into the crowd. Doc was coughing now, in deep, spasmodic bursts that he tried to muffle behind his hand. Bianca shushed him under her breath.

"Whoa." *Cough.* "We almost died back there."

"I warned you." She cast a quick look behind them: no pursuit that she could see. All the activity was concentrated around the mouth of the alley. "Next time I tell you to stay home, maybe you'll listen."

"Live and learn." *Cough.*

"Give me your phone." Bianca forced herself to maintain a steady pace because running headlong as her every instinct screamed at her to do would attract the very attention she was desperate to avoid. The people who were out to kill her could be anywhere. Right now, the best, safest thing she and Doc could do was keep a low profile while putting as much distance between themselves and the square as possible.

The harrowing truth was, the hunt was on and she was the prey.

Doc handed over his phone. He knew as well as she did that the phones were liabilities now: they were too easily tracked.

Bianca dumped them down the nearest storm drain.

Shouts coming from the direction of the square told her that help in some form or another was arriving for the victims. In the distance, sirens wailed.

"So where are we going?" Five minutes later, Doc still coughed spasmodically from the smoke. Bianca had just finished acquainting him with the fact that they wouldn't be returning to their hotel rooms and that the items left behind in them would soon self-destruct. They had reached Old Town. The gaudy lights of the big new casinos were left behind. The centuries-old brick streets were dark and thin of company. The only light was provided by an occasional street lamp, or the spill of an interior light through a curtained window. Favored by bargain hunters, this part of Macau was considered dangerous for visitors at night, so the few people about were locals, most of whom were probably up to no good. There were no sidewalks now, only narrow streets and tall, side-by-side buildings that formed canyons on either side of them. If a kill team came upon them here, they were toast. But at this point all the exits out of Macau were being watched, Bianca was sure. To show up at one was to court instant death.

The only thing to do was to go to ground.

"Somewhere safe," she said, while silently adding *Please God* as they emerged into the too-large, too-open space of Senado Square.

21

The small shop was located just around the corner from the ruins of St. Paul's, a tourist favorite. Its arched door was painted bright red and outfitted with black iron fittings. The stucco facade of the shop itself was painted ocher yellow. The colors had been selected, Bianca knew, to provide an eye-catching contrast with the black and white mosaic tiles of the square itself.

In the dead of the night, though, as this was, it was all shades of gray.

From the outside, no lights could be seen through the small square windows on either side of the door. Given that business hours were long over, it might have been expected that the shop was empty.

Bianca knew it wasn't. The question was, would whoever was inside pretend like it was?

She was breathing too hard. Her heart was beating too fast. Once out of the busy streets surrounding the Strip, she and Doc had kept close to walls, staying in the shadows, moving as fast as they dared. Now, as they paused opposite the shop, she carefully probed the darkness around the door and looked up and down the nearly deserted street before climbing the four shallow steps that led to the door.

Coming here was a gamble. This was a place that she had been to before. That made it dangerous to come back. The problem was, not coming here was probably more dangerous still.

She calculated that she could expect to survive about six hours if she stayed at large in Macau, which was small. It was contained. There were too many eyes to see, people to be bribed. She would be spotted. She would be killed.

On the other hand, she was supremely conscious that if she'd made the wrong call in coming to the little shop, she—and Doc—could die in the next few minutes.

Place your bets. Take your chances.

She spared a wistful thought for Mason's helicopter.

"Frieda's Fancy Clothing?" Doc read the sign that hung above the door in a hushed voice as Bianca pressed the bell. Three short rings, three long, then three short again: the universal SOS signal.

"I talk, you don't." Bianca reminded him of the instruction she'd given him before they'd reached the shop. The people inside didn't like strangers at the best of times. These were not the best of times.

Even if there wasn't an ambush waiting for them, they could still be killed just because the person beyond that door didn't like the way they looked.

A tiny, round peephole in the heavy wood door opened as its old-fashioned cover was swung to one side.

Bianca had been expecting it. She gave a little three-fingered wave at the dark, glinting eyeball that peered out at her.

"*Pang yau,*" she said. It was the code, the signal that she was one of the fraternity that patronized the alternate business that was conducted at this shop. Roughly translated from the Cantonese she used, it meant *friend*.

The door opened. A compact, muscular man in a loose white shirt and trousers looked them over, then peered past them up and down the street. Apparently satisfied, he gestured at them to enter.

They stepped inside a dark, low-ceilinged hallway that smelled of sandalwood.

"SiuSiu?" Bianca asked as he closed and locked the door behind them. Except for the faint glow emanating from what, she saw, was the cloth-covered, battery-powered lantern he carried, the establishment was dark as pitch.

He grunted, turned away and started walking.

Bianca felt a measure of relief that apparently she and Doc had passed muster. This man, the gatekeeper as he was known among the community that was familiar with this place, could instantly have had them killed. She was aware of the heavily armed men waiting silently in the shadows on either side of the hall for a word from him.

The word didn't come.

With a gesture that told Doc to stay with her, Bianca walked the gauntlet. As they passed beyond the entry hall, the gatekeeper pulled off the cloth he'd draped over the lantern. The purpose of the cloth, presumably, was to prevent any trace of light from being seen by anyone outside and thus alerting any chance observer to the after-hours business conducted in the shop.

The lantern's meager light allowed them glimpses of things Bianca already knew were there. He led them through a mirrored showroom with racks of garments lining the walls and mannequins in custom-made dresses and suits occupying the prime real estate in the center of the floor, another large room outfitted with at least a dozen sewing machines and other accoutrements of a tailor's trade, a storage room packed floor to ceiling with bolts of cloth, and then another storage room with bins on the shelves lining it.

Their guide paused at the end of this room to press the heel of his palm against the wall between two shelves.

The wall swung outward.

A warm yellow glow, the sound of voices, and an earthy, basementy scent announced the presence of a lower level. Behind her, Bianca heard Doc's indrawn breath.

They followed their guide downstairs to the vast, underground Aladdin's cave that was filled with everything from custom "spy clothes" as SiuSiu called them—Bianca's bulletproof dress was an example—to specially designed gadgets and equipment to truck-size stacks of (counterfeit) bills from practically every currency in the world to weapons.

There was nothing counterfeit about the weapons.

Workers labored at various tasks. Armed guards lurked in corners. A few looked at Bianca and Doc as they followed in the gatekeeper's wake. Most did not.

A glance back at Doc's face as they were led through the treasure trove of illicit goods showed Bianca that he was doing his best not to gape.

A woman emerged from a side chamber to pick her way through mounds of ordinary-looking umbrellas, musical instruments and power tools, all of which, Bianca knew, had multiple concealed functions.

SiuSiu.

She was around forty but looked younger due to amazing, creamy skin and a petite build. Her features were even, her eyes dark. Her long black hair was worn up, secured in a luxurious bun on top of her head by a pair of what looked like golden chopsticks. She wore a black silk top, a pair of tight, western-style jeans and platform pumps that added inches to her height.

For a moment she stared hard at Bianca. Then she smiled.

"Julie T! Is that you?" She spoke in excellent, American-accented English, because Julie Taberski, which was the name she knew Bianca by, was American. The double air-kiss she presently bestowed on Bianca was a rare mark of esteem from the hard-nosed businesswoman, and was indicative of the length of time they'd known each other, which was a little less than twenty years. They'd first met when Mason had brought Bianca to the shop. He'd had dealings with SiuSiu's grandfather, who at that time had been the shop's proprietor. SiuSiu had been his apprentice. The then twenty-year-old had been assigned by her grandfather to look after the six-year-old daughter that Mason, whom they knew as Peter Taberski, had brought with him.

"This is not Peter." There was the faintest of condemning undertones to SiuSiu's statement as she gave Doc a frowning once-over.

Knowing that bringing in strangers was generally verboten, Bianca said, "This is my associate. I vouch for him."

To vouch for someone to SiuSiu came with serious consequences. As in, get it wrong and die. SiuSiu was serious about the preservation of her organization. Although she and SiuSiu were longtime friendly acquaintances, Bianca never made the mistake of thinking that if something she did threatened that organization SiuSiu wouldn't have her killed without batting an eye.

SiuSiu gave Doc another long look, nodded and turned her attention back to Bianca.

"You have come for your order?"

"That and—I need your help."

Rogan stood in the Wynn's small Security Office, leaning over a cluttered metal desk as he grimly rewatched the video that showed a chubby guy in a black suit and a hat that obscured his face entering the interior hallway after him, and that same guy exiting just ahead of Sylvia some minutes later.

The bastard had snuck up behind him and clubbed him over the head with something. There was no other explanation for how he'd wound up unconscious on the floor.

Chubs had then escaped with Sylvia.

Whoever he was, he was definitely not Mason Thayer, who Rogan had just identified on another video as the wheelchair-bound old man seated next to Sylvia at the blackjack table where he'd first spotted her. Rogan was kicking himself for not having seen through that disguise instantly. After all, Thayer was the reason that he'd traveled to Macau, and he'd been right beside Sylvia, the first place any competent investigator should've known to look. His only excuse, and it was a piss-poor one, was that once he'd set eyes on Sylvia, she was the only thing he saw.

That wasn't an explanation he planned to share with anyone.

Other than that, Rogan had no idea who the guy who'd hit him was.

To say that Rogan wanted to get his hands on him—on him and Sylvia both—was putting it mildly. Almost as much as he wanted to get his hands on Thayer.

Thayer was his primary target and he'd apparently gotten away clean. According to Rogan's intel, a chopper had flown him from the roof of the adjacent parking garage to Hong Kong, where he'd vanished. Watching the video of Thayer zipping in his wheelchair out through the east entrance in the teeth of Rogan and his team who were right there in the same room was one of the more chagrin-making experiences of his life.

All in all, it hadn't been the best night's work he'd ever put in.

The knot on the back of his skull was the approximate size of a golf ball. Rogan held in one hand a cold soda can from the vending machine in the nearby employee break room that he kept applying to the bump. So far it hadn't helped. His head hurt like hell.

His pride hurt worse. In hindsight, it didn't take a genius to figure out that Sylvia getting herself collared by security had been a distraction designed to give Thayer time to escape. And in the case of Chubs, it been a long time since anyone had managed to get the drop on Rogan.

At least he'd managed to get to Sylvia first, even if he hadn't been able to talk her into turning on Thayer. But if things worked out the way he hoped, maybe—

Shouting in the hallway outside interrupted his thoughts, made him look up. The language was Cantonese, so he had no idea what all the excitement was about. But the security guard who'd been deputed to assist him in reviewing the surveillance videos and who'd been sitting in a plastic chair against the wall leaped to his feet. From the look on his face something major was up.

Before Rogan could react in any more substantial way, one of his own men, Fergus Benchley, burst through the door. Benchley was his age, thirty-two, blond, brawny and loyal. When the tip had come in that Thayer had been spotted in Macau, Rogan had tapped him along with three other Cambridge Solutions employees, all former British SAS, to fly into the gambling mecca with him because capturing Thayer was not something that he trusted the Public Security Police Force of Macau to be able to help him with.

Benchley looked at him and said, "There's been a shooting in the square across the street. That fit bird you were keen to nab? Word is she was there when it started."

Rogan's gut clenched. He really didn't like the fact that it did. "Was she hit?"

"The local police are in the square ID'ing the dead and wounded now."

Rogan strode from the office without another word.

Ten minutes later he'd determined that Sylvia was not among the victims. Neither was Chubs. Witness accounts of what had happened were garbled, but they'd almost universally included salvation via a massive cloud of multicolored smoke as well as a woman who'd created the cloud by means of lighting and throwing smoke bombs. Several reports of said woman's flight to safety hand in hand with a fat man sealed the deal: Sylvia.

He had no trouble at all picturing her in the role of heroine.

Rogan had determined something else, too, by examining the locations of the victims, the angle of their wounds and the spent rounds. The killings had been perpetrated by a single sniper firing from atop the parking garage adjacent to the Wynn. From the markings on the recovered bullets, he was fairly certain that the weapon was an MK12, which was a favorite of the US Special Forces.

Combine that with an unexpected and unwelcome image he'd seen while reviewing the casino videos, and he wasn't especially surprised to see Steve Hanes walking toward him across the square.

Rogan was growing more certain by the minute that, for whatever reason, the CIA wasn't only after Thayer. They were after Sylvia, too, and they wanted her dead. The question was, why?

"Murdering civilians now?" was how Rogan greeted Hanes as the man reached him. The harshness of the klieg lights the police had set up in the square made Hanes's hair look redder than Rogan remembered, and his face look unnaturally pale. In the CIA uniform of a dark suit and white shirt, he looked exactly like what he was: a US federal agent. No attempt at subterfuge at all.

They didn't shake hands.

"I don't know what you're talking about." Hanes's tone wasn't friendly. Which was fine. Rogan wasn't feeling friendly, either. Antagonistic was more like it. He was doing his best to keep a lid on it. "I'm here to apprehend Thayer. Who, from everything I've heard, you let get away."

Rogan held up a recovered round. "I'm willing to bet that this came from an MK12. A favorite of your special forces."

Hanes's eyes narrowed at him. "Are you trying to imply something?"

"Not at all. I'm *saying* that I think you set one of your men up there on top of that parking garage to shoot up the square. I'm saying I think you're responsible for the deaths of these civilians."

Hanes's face didn't change. "And why would I do that?"

"To take out Thayer's female associate."

Hanes gave a scornful laugh. "You can't prove that round came from a MK12. Anyway, plenty of people have access to one. Shooter could have been anybody. For my money, it was totally random—one of those terrorist things. But *if* the target of this shooting *was* Thayer's female associate—by the way, we've learned that she goes by any number of names, but the one she's been using the longest is Beth McAlister—anybody could have done it. She's got a contract out on her—one million dollars for the hit. You ever hear of Darjeeling Brothers?"

Rogan had.

Hanes continued, "She's on there, big as Ike."

In rapid succession, Rogan felt surprise, consternation, and out and out fear, all on Sylvia's behalf. Darjeeling Brothers was the dark web's answer to Murder, Inc. Get listed on there, and you didn't live long.

Much as Rogan hated to admit it, if that was true it broadened the list of suspects who could've shot up the square. Half the hit men in the world would be gunning for Sylvia. Or Beth. Whatever her name was.

He felt as antsy as hell, on edge with the urgent need to find her before anyone else did. All it would take was one wrong decision, one wrong move, one bit of bad luck on her part, and she would be dead.

He asked, "Why would one of Thayer's flunkies rate a million-dollar contract by Darjeeling Brothers?"

Hanes shrugged. "She must've been a real bad girl."

In the interest of not alerting Hanes to the fact that he seemed to be developing a really inconvenient soft spot for Sylvia, Rogan swallowed the choice words that crowded the tip of his tongue. Hanes must've been able to read something of what he didn't say in his face, because his expression turned ugly.

"You contractor types, you're all alike," Hanes said, his voice laced with contempt. "You collect your paycheck and walk away. You don't have any idea about the big picture. I thought we had an agreement. You were going to keep me in the loop on what was going on in your investigation. Yet here you are in Macau, which means you obviously got a tip that Thayer was going to be here, and I didn't hear squat from you. Why is that?"

Forget swallowing.

"Piss off," Rogan said. "I don't work for you."

"You work for Interpol, which cooperates with us upon request. So fucking cooperate. Next time you get a bead on Thayer or this Beth, you let me know."

"I'll be sure to do that," Rogan said.

Hanes said, "I'm right now officially requesting your cooperation. That girl—Beth—couldn't have gotten far. I want to sweep the area, bring her in, see what she can tell us about where to find Thayer, before some freelancer puts a bullet in her brain. Combine your men with mine, and we can get the job done."

Rogan realized he had a choice: he could do what he wanted to do, which was tell Hanes to go fuck himself, launch his own hunt for Sylvia and hope to find her before Hanes or someone else did. Or he could go along with Hanes, join in the search for Sylvia and do his best to protect her if she was found.

"Let's do it," he said.

22

Five days later Bianca and Doc stepped off the train in Budapest, Hungary, and trudged out of Nyugati station into the
gathering twilight. Planes, trains and automobiles had nothing on their odyssey: add in bicycles, buses and boats, and
you were in the ballpark. They bore little resemblance to
the travelers who had boarded in Bucharest, after a series of
journeys that had begun with SiuSiu smuggling them out of
Macau on a freighter along with a gun shipment destined for
the Philippines. Bianca had abandoned the freighter as soon
as possible, because as fond as she was of SiuSiu, placing too
much trust in anyone under these conditions was a good way
to wind up dead.

Knowing that the hunt for her was in full cry, Bianca had
called on every bit of tradecraft she'd ever learned to get them
safely to this point. Call her paranoid, but she saw potential
killers everywhere: in the homeless man who came up to them
begging for money in Yerevan, in the police officer directing traffic in Istanbul, in the train ticket agent who looked
at her a little too closely in Bucharest. The thing was, all it
took was one keen-eyed individual with access to the dark
web and she was in trouble.

You're not paranoid if they're really after you.

"There's a KFC down the street. How about we grab some
food?" Doc looked with real longing at the iconic red and
white bucket on a sign near the closest intersection. The lure
of the fast-food staple was strong. Bianca knew, because she

felt it, too. They hadn't eaten since breakfast. But the danger, she judged, was too great. It wasn't a stretch to imagine that, knowing that she was an American, places like KFCs that might be expected to appeal to an American palate were being watched: the CIA had eyes on the ground everywhere, and then there were random bounty hunters to consider. And a restaurant like that would have security cameras, counter clerks—no, it was best to steer clear.

"Food truck." Bianca pointed to a blue van pulled up to the curb. It was doing a brisk business with the locals. Doc grimaced, but once he bit into his pulled pork sandwich he was clearly resigned. The food was good. Bianca ate her sandwich and drank a Hungarian cola, Doc did the same and, refreshed, they moved on down the street to find a taxi.

It was a cold, clear evening. The moon was nearly full, a pale ghost in a deepening blue sky that showed more and more tiny twinkling stars with every passing minute. Bianca was glad of her dark gray, fleece-lined jacket, which she wore over a long-sleeved fisherman's sweater in an indeterminate oatmeal shade with jeans and hiking boots. A long, dark brown wig confined in a single plait and a pair of tortoiseshell glasses completed her outfit. Doc wore jeans and a heavy flannel shirt under an olive military-style jacket. A gray knit watch cap was pulled down over his head, and he sported a thick black faux mustache that made Bianca want to laugh every time she looked at it.

The clothes and accessories had been provided by SiuSiu, along with a selection from her specialized weapons arsenal. A cylindrical silver rape whistle that Bianca wore as a pendant was in actuality a one-shot gun that she fired by pushing down on the mouthpiece with her thumb. (She never carried a gun; the fact that she now did meant that the situation was beyond serious.) The smaller matching earrings held additional bullets. Her old-fashioned-looking watch contained a knockout spray that she dispensed by hitting the small windup mechanism.

In addition, SiuSiu had given her a large amount of cash in various currencies. (Bianca's fervent hope was that it was real—not counterfeit—cash; SiuSiu had included the amount in the bill Bianca had paid by wire transfer from a special account she kept for just that purpose, but with SiuSiu one never knew. In any event, Bianca had had no trouble spending it during the journey, so whether it was real or not it got the job done.)

Bottom line, she and Doc looked like tourists, which was the point.

As one of the largest cities in the European Union, Budapest hosted over four million tourists a year. English was widely spoken. With their gear stowed in backpacks, Bianca was confident that they blended right in.

She flagged down a taxi at the corner near the KFC and directed it to Szabadkai Way. Budapest taxi drivers were notorious for preying on travelers, but she was familiar with how they worked and after a sharp word when the driver would have gone the wrong way (twice) she was able to sit back and admire the deep sapphire waters of the Danube River, which cut through the heart of the city, and the Chain Bridge, which connected the rolling hills of the Buda District with the flat Pest District. The Gresham Palace and St. Stephen's Basilica were as magnificent as she remembered. The city itself looked beautiful, lit up as it was against the evening sky. She'd last visited it with Mason, years ago.

Remembering, she felt sad, and immediately banished the recollections. If she'd learned nothing else in her life, she'd learned that feeling sad was a waste of time.

Beside her, Doc stayed silent. He was tired, she knew, as was she. Homesick too, probably, although he wouldn't admit it. But she guessed, because she was feeling a little homesick herself. She kept in touch with Evie and Hay by email: she knew they'd worry if they didn't hear from her. She'd even ducked into a hospital to call Evie from a pay phone in the lobby—European hospitals still had pay phones—just to keep the fiction going that she was at the bedside of her sick father.

Hearing Evie's voice had brought her life—her real life in Savannah—back to her in vivid detail.

More than she had ever wanted anything, she wished she was back there. She wanted to get out from under this nightmare and *go home*.

Where were magical red ruby slippers when you needed them?

Nowhere, that's where.

Time to cowboy up.

After they'd gotten out of Macau, she'd offered to send Doc back to Savannah—no one would be shooting at him if he wasn't with her, as she'd pointed out—but she was secretly glad that he'd refused. He'd become more than a useful subordinate for whom she felt responsible. He was a companion, a friend, an ally. A source of the occasional bit of mood-lightening amusement, his mustache being a case in point. A reason to make doubly sure her tradecraft *i*'s were dotted and *t*'s were crossed.

Plus, she needed his expertise if she hoped to succeed in liberating King Priam's Treasure from the Pushkin Museum. Defeating the security system required expertise she didn't possess. Once she'd been sure she couldn't persuade Doc to return to Savannah without her, she'd filled him in on the deal Mason had struck to get the Darjeeling Brothers' contract canceled and to make sure they were left alone in future.

"Can you do it?" Doc asked, referring to the theft.

She'd been brought up to be a thief. She was excellent at it. And this was life or death: *her* life or death. Could she do it? "Yes."

"Then I'm in."

Over the course of their travels she'd made use of Doc's laptop to pore over the information Mason had left for her. It had included everything from detailed photos of each piece of the treasure, photos of the room in the Pushkin where it was kept, details of the security arrangements, including the location of surveillance cameras, the number and schedule of the security guards, and floor plans. It had also included access information for a bank account with more than enough money—eight million, which she assumed was part of the still-to-be-divvied-up haul from Bahrain—to do whatever she needed to do to get the job done.

After examining everything Mason had put together, and thinking things through, and mentally running through a million scenarios, Bianca had come up with the broad strokes of a plan.

Which was why she and Doc were in Budapest.

If her plan was going to work, she needed help. And the help she needed was (she hoped) currently located just a few miles away.

She wanted to reach their destination before it was full-on night. They were headed to a bad section of the city, and after exiting the taxi they would need to walk across several deserted fields to reach it. Actually, as far as the fields were concerned, deserted would be best-case scenario. Druggies, hookers and the homeless had been known to congregate in those fields in large numbers. Fortunately, she thought the night might be too cold.

She and Doc left the taxi at a corner near a run-down apartment building and a gas station, walked behind the gas station and started tramping across acres of trash-strewn, scraggly brown grass. It was cold enough so that the grass was crisp with frost and crackled beneath their feet. When they exhaled, their breath made small white clouds.

"So the last time you talked to these people was ten years ago?" Doc looked nervously around at the abandoned railroad track, the denuded trees and the rusted, broken wire fence that ran along one side of the field. On the other side of the field was a creek. A hill rose directly in front of them, and on the other side of that, unless things had changed, was their destination.

Washed in pale moonlight, alive with shadows, the way forward looked eerie and unwelcoming.

"More or less." Doc had no idea of the type and extent of the training Mason had put her through while she was growing up, and she didn't mean to enlighten him. Some things were just too personal.

"What if they're not here?"

"We go to plan B," Bianca replied. She tried not to sound as grim as she felt. Coming up with plan A had been hard enough. At this stage, plan B was the equivalent of flying on a wing and a prayer. "Anyway, they're always here from the first of November through the end of February. At least, they always used to be."

"You're friends with an itinerant gang of Hungarian thieves." He sounded uneasy. Bianca put that down to the darkness, the isolation, the desolate, seedy landscape, the howling of wolves in the distant hills—okay, so maybe that was a train whistle but the effect was the same. In any event, their surroundings were enough to daunt a hardier soul than Doc.

"And con artists. And smugglers. And forgers. Basically, anything you need." She'd given Doc only a limited amount of information about what to expect at their destination, mainly because she didn't want to have to answer a lot of questions about her past. Like, what do you mean you first met these people when Mason left you with the total strangers they had been at the time for a whole summer when you were nine years old? "They're also more of a family than a gang."

"We're getting ready to do a cold call on a crime family that you haven't seen in ten years. Super. What could go wrong?" Doc huffed and puffed as the hill grew steeper.

"Welcome to the dark side," Bianca said. They were almost at the top of the hill, and she could smell it: the campfire. It brought back memories. The last time she'd been here, she'd been sixteen, it had been Christmas break, and she'd let Mason make arrangements for her because she'd been too embarrassed to accept Evie's standing invitation to Christmas at her house. And that would be because, when she'd visited at Thanksgiving, Rosalie had asked her pointedly if she didn't have a home of her own.

The answer, of course, was no, but she hadn't said that.

Bianca reached the top of the hill a few steps before Doc and looked down to find that everything was just as she remembered: a central campfire in a flat, weedy field, with trucks and campers circled around it like a wagon train in a Western. A couple of people sat in lawn chairs near the campfire. A few more were seated at a picnic table nearby. There was a grill, which from the smell of roasted meat in the air had recently been put to good use. A generator hummed. Its presence accounted for the lights that were on in some of the campers.

"Come on." Conscious of a slight lightening of the heavy burden of dread that had been weighing on her, Bianca started down the hill.

Doc followed. "Shouldn't we give them a shout-out or something? I'd hate to be shot on sight."

"No need." As if to prove her point, as they neared the bottom of the hill, a huge, menacing shape got to its four feet in the darkness at the edge of the campfire, shook itself, looked in their direction and let out an earthshaking roar.

"What the hell?" Doc, who'd just caught up with her, fell back. "That's a—*lion*."

"His name's Zoltan." Bianca smiled as a pack of six wildly barking small dogs streaked past the outer line of vehicles toward them. Thus properly alerted, the people around the campfire got to their feet now and turned to look in their direction. Almost certainly drawn by the commotion, a white-haired woman came to stand in the door of one of the campers. She was tiny, stooped and looked to be about a hundred years old. She lifted a hand as if to shade her eyes as she peered out.

"Who's that?" a tall, hulking man called out in challenge as he squinted through the darkness at them, while a plump platinum blonde came tearing after the dogs, who had reached them and leaped around them barking in a fierce, concerted warning that would have been terrifying if it hadn't been so shrill and the dogs hadn't been miniature poodles.

"Uletka! Hunor! Magor! Levedia! Emese! Baba! *Abba most!*" Calling the dogs sby name, the blonde ordered them to stop right now.

The dogs paid no attention, yapping vociferously and jumping around the newcomers as Bianca, with Doc staying cautiously close, approached the camp.

"*Szia, es* Maggy." *Hello, it's Maggy*, Bianca called back, because when she'd stayed with them they'd known her as Maggy Chance. "Dorottya, *te vagy az?*" *Is that you?* "*Szia*, Lazlo." *Hello, Lazlo*, she greeted the hulking man, who was Dorottya's husband.

"Maggy? Maggy, is it really you?" Switching to English, which she knew was Maggy's native language, Dorottya came bustling up, snapping her fingers at the dogs and scolding them in an aside that did no good at all while she stared hard at Bianca's face. "It *is* you! Look, Lazlo, it's Maggy! Oh, you are all grown up!"

Dorottya embraced her, kisses to both cheeks, then handed her off to Lazlo, who did the same. By then the dogs had trotted off to search for scraps beneath the picnic table and Bianca had been pulled into the circle of firelight. The old woman—Dedi—came out of her camper, followed by an equally old-looking, shrunken and grizzled man with a small brown monkey perched on his shoulder.

"Oskar!" Bianca greeted the old man, then to the monkey added, *"Szia,* Griff!"

"Maggy!" Oskar kissed both her cheeks. Griff, displeased at the close contact, chattered and scrambled around to cling to Oskar's back and from there pulled Bianca's hair—or wig, rather.

"Oh!" Bianca drew back, laughing, and more formally greeted the rest of the group that had gathered around, most of whom she didn't recognize. Among themselves they might speak Hungarian, but they were fluent in English, as were most Hungarians, and they switched to it as a courtesy now, as they had years ago, whenever "Maggy" had stayed with them.

"You remember Kristof. And Franz." Now that Dorottya brought the two strapping young men to Bianca's attention, she did remember them. They were Dorottya and Lazlo's sons, and when Bianca had last seen them they'd been fourteen and twelve years old.

"I do." Bianca smiled at them. They'd been scrawny little boys, younger than she and too bashful of the unknown American girl parked in their midst to do more than throw an occasional mutter her way. Now they were both over six feet tall and, from what she could tell through their coats and jeans, extremely muscular. "And—" she peered at the slender, black-haired teenage girl who hung shyly back "—is it Bela?"

Dorottya's and Lazlo's youngest, who would be—Bianca did a quick calculation—about sixteen, gave a quick nod, while Dorottya crowed, "It is! You have a good memory, Maggy."

"This is Bruce." Bianca introduced Doc by his newest fake name. Eyes narrowed with trepidation, Doc was eyeing Zoltan, who had lain back down on the grass just outside the circle of firelight but was watching the proceedings with interest. Since Zoltan was the size of a small pony, had a massive tawny mane, glinting golden eyes and was a full-grown male African *lion*, she could understand Doc's fascination. With a sweeping gesture that encompassed the group, which was twelve strong not including the animals, she added, "Bruce, meet the Circus Nagy."

23

Circus? The startled look Doc shot Bianca asked the question, but all he said was a feeble, "Nice to meet you," addressed to the group at large.

"Since 1891," Oskar told him proudly. "I am the sixth generation. My mother—" he nodded at Dedi "—is the fifth. My son—" he nodded at Lazlo "—is the seventh. His sons and daughter will be the eighth."

"Though possibly the first to starve, *nagyapa*," Kristof said.

His grandfather gave him a dark look. "We have weathered bad times before. The audiences will come back."

"This is not to be talked of now. We have guests." Dorottya turned to Bianca. "You don't know Kristof's wife, Maria, and Franz's wife, Elena. They do the trapeze and the silks." She gestured to a slim redhead and a slim blonde in turn, both of whom were pretty women in their early twenties, before turning to a tall, muscular man who bore a strong resemblance to Lazlo. "Or Lazlo's brother, Sandor, or his sons, Bence and Adam. They also perform with us now."

"When we perform." Kristof's comment was half under his breath, but still his grandfather scowled at him.

"Sandor is the human cannonball, and also does the snakes. Bence and Adam do the high-wire act with Kristof and Franz." Hurrying into speech in an obvious effort to prevent Oskar from saying something unpleasant to her son, Dorottya took Bianca's arm, urging her toward the lawn chairs. "Have you eaten? There is still, I think, some food."

"We've eaten." Bianca allowed herself to be drawn forward, but said, "Could we go inside instead? And catch up? I have so much to tell you and Lazlo, and Dedi and Oskar."

Dorottya had operated on the wrong side of the law far more than she had on the right side over the years, and she immediately picked up on Bianca's unspoken meaning: she wanted to have private speech with those of the elders that she knew.

"Naturally you will want to tell us all that you have been doing." Dorottya smoothly ran with Bianca's pretense. Angling away from the lawn chairs, she steered Bianca toward the camper where Bianca had first seen Dedi standing in the doorway. Reaching out a hand for Doc, Bianca pulled him along with her. She knew that he would be uncomfortable with being left outside with strangers—and Zoltan. And no telling how the younger Nagys would tease him. "Lazlo! Oskar! Dedi! We will go and talk to Maggy now." She cast a look back at the others. "You lot, get this cleaned up out here. If we leave garbage out, the wild pigs will come."

"We call that a meal delivery for Zoltan." Franz's tone made it clear that he was joking, but his mother pointed a finger at him.

"You know Zoltan does not like the wild pigs. He is old, and they are fierce. So you will pick up the trash, scrub the table, clean the grill, make sure the campsite has nothing to attract them. And put Zoltan in his house before you come inside."

"Yes, Mama," Franz replied, sounding chastened.

Dorottya ushered Bianca, with Doc following, inside the camper. A faint smell of what she thought must be goulash soup reached Bianca's nostrils as they climbed the rickety metal steps that led to a door in the back and stepped into a small living area lined with cheap imitation wood paneling. It contained a two-seater couch, an easy chair, a dining booth with benches, and, at the far end of what was approximately an eight-by-twenty-foot space, a sleeping area—open curtains and what looked to be a queen-size mattress—that was tucked above the truck's cab.

Appliances, including a stove top with, indeed, a pot of soup simmering on it, were built into the wall opposite the dining booth. A boombox-size TV rested on a counter.

It was warm inside; a steady hum meant the heat was on.

The camper was suddenly very full as Lazlo, Dedi and Oskar with Griff filed in behind them. All six dogs rushed past their feet to bound through the small interior space. They ended up lying in a panting row on the loft bed, their white curly coats standing out against the blue comforter, their dark eyes bright as they looked down on the humans in the living area.

"*Rohadt kutyak,*" Dedi muttered, which meant *damn dogs.* To Dorottya she added, "Do they have to go with you *everywhere* you go?"

"Yes," Dorottya replied, with the air of one making a simple statement of fact. Besides being Lazlo's wife, the mother of Kristof, Franz and Bela, and a sometime thief and pickpocket, Dorottya was a professional dog trainer. The Amazing All-Star Dog Acrobats had been a staple of the Circus Nagy since long before Bianca had first come to stay with them. The dogs were different now, but the act clearly lived on.

"Sit down, sit down." Oskar gestured to the couch. While Bianca sat down with Doc beside her and Dedi took the chair, the others remained standing, surrounding them in a semicircle. Griff, chattering, hopped off Oskar's shoulder, ran along the counter and leaped to the top of the bed curtains, where he hung by one small hand from the rod, swinging gently just above the dogs.

Beside her, Doc watched Griff wide-eyed.

"And what of your father, Maggy? Is he well?" Dorottya

asked. She had her arms crossed over her chest, a stance that Maggy had learned during her time living with them denoted anxiety. Dorottya's frown deepened the wrinkles in her forehead. Worry narrowed her blue eyes. Both she and Lazlo would be in their late forties now. They looked older, and that would be because, Bianca knew, the circus life was a hard one. Under the harsh light of the single overhead fixture, Dorottya's blond hair was brassy with dye, and her makeup—lots of bright blue eye shadow, too much blush and scarlet lips—had settled into dozens of tiny lines around her eyes and mouth that were new since Bianca had last seen her.

"Yes, he's very well, thanks," Bianca lied. As well as contributing to certain aspects of her education, various members of the Circus Nagy had worked jobs with Mason. They had known him for many years as a supremely successful thief, but that aspect of his life, and hers, was all they knew.

"We heard a few months ago that he was killed. A rumor only?" Bald and heavily tattooed, Lazlo was a talented juggler as well as being the circus strongman. He looked menacing but was actually totally under Dorottya's thumb. His act included lifting a small car, which, to be honest, had been stripped down so that all he was really lifting was the shell. Still, it brought down the house every time. It was he who had masterminded the art of smuggling—people, contraband, currency—by using the animals in their specially modified traveling vehicles as a guard against a too-close inspection at checkpoints. This was an important reason why Bianca had zeroed in on the Circus Nagy: stealing the treasure would be hard. Getting it out of the country afterward would be harder.

"A rumor only," Bianca confirmed.

"There have been many rumors lately, about old friends being arrested or simply vanishing." Oskar, who was around seventy, had always been small and wiry, but over the years he had shrunken to the size of a jockey. But his gray hair was still thick, and his nearly black eyes were keen with intelligence. He'd once been a jewel thief. He'd also once been an acrobat, but a fall from a roof a dozen years ago while stealing a diamond necklace had left him with a back injury and a limp that made it impossible for him to continue in either activity. When Bianca had last seen him, he'd been reduced, as he called it, to performing in a comedy routine with Griff and Zoltan that, to his disgust, was far more popular than his old acrobatic act had been.

"There are always rumors. It is the price of growing old. Enough of this small talk. Why have you come to see us, Maggy?" Dedi got to the point with an impatient gesture. With her chopped-short white hair, crinkly olive-toned skin, hawk nose and deeply hooded dark eyes, Dedi had always seemed ancient to Bianca. A quick calculation confirmed that she had to be in her early nineties now. A former trapeze artist, she had reworked herself into a Gypsy fortune-teller in her old age, with a booth that was a primary source of extra income everywhere the circus set up. Within the family, it was an open secret that she had no gift for it and simply made stuff up, but she looked the part and income was income. She was also a first-class forger of, among other things, relics, artifacts and various historically significant objects, which was another of the reasons Bianca had chosen to approach the Circus Nagy with her plan.

Bianca said, "I came to tell you about an opportunity that has come my way. A robbery, a big one. It's high-profile, and if and when the theft is discovered, the search for the thieves will be massive. But I have a plan to carry it out, and the payday for you, if you should choose to help me and we succeed, would be four million dollars."

Four pairs of eyes were suddenly riveted on her. Lazlo sucked in his breath. Dorottya licked her lips. Oskar made a whistling sound under his breath.

Dorottya said, "This is you and your father together?"

Bianca shook her head. "Not my father. It's only me." She patted Doc's knee. "And Bruce."

Doc dredged up a weak smile. Dorottya's frown deepened.

"He is your young man?"

"No." Bianca shook her head. "He's my associate."

Dedi said, "Four million US?"

"Yes," Bianca said. "Four million US dollars."

The family exchanged looks. Their faces said everything: the hard times they'd been experiencing, the uncertain future for the circus and themselves, the enormous sum four million dollars represented and the difference it would make in their lives.

"That would be like winning the lottery," Lazlo said.

"Tell us about this robbery," Dedi said.

Bianca did. Judiciously. She left out the part about the Darjeeling Brothers' contract, because exposing even long-time friends to the temptation the reward presented would just be stupid, in her estimation. As far as her listeners were concerned, her motivation for the theft she proposed was purely profit. She told them she'd been hired to steal King Priam's Treasure from the Pushkin Museum, which was all they needed to know. Anyway, what concerned them was the nature of the job itself, the difficulty of pulling it off, the likelihood of getting caught and their share of the paycheck.

After a little more discussion, they seemed to reach a consensus that their share of the paycheck made every other detail something that could be worked out.

"Moscow," Lazlo said in a meditative way. "Russia is difficult. So many *rendorseg*—police. They are like cockroaches: everywhere."

"My cousin works in Nikulin's Circus." Oskar pursed his lips thoughtfully. "Perhaps we could visit. We could say we are seeking positions there."

"We could say we are bringing the children to audition." Dorottya looked at her husband. "They want young ones to train. And Kristof and Franz's high-wire act—"

"Needs work," Dedi said. "But that might serve."

"What if they are accepted? Whatever happens, I am not leaving the children behind in Russia." Dorottya's voice was sharp.

"They won't be accepted," Dedi said. "Don't concern yourself. The Nikulin only takes the best of the best."

Dorottya bristled at her grandmother-in-law.

"We won't leave them behind," Oskar promised before she could say anything. "But they are a way in."

"We are in agreement, then?" Lazlo looked at each of his family members in turn.

Oskar nodded, followed by Dedi and Dorottya.

"We are in agreement," Lazlo told Bianca. Then, to Oskar, "Break out the pálinka. Tonight we celebrate. Tomorrow we go to work."

24

Moscow is a city of some twelve million inhabitants. One out of every fifteen Russians lives there. It is huge, ancient and mysterious. At first glance it looks European, but its spirit is unmistakably Russian. Babushkas existing on tiny pensions share the broad boulevards with more billionaires than reside in any other city on the planet. Petty criminals are as common as rats, preying on rich and poor alike. Contract killers haunt the shadows, their existence an accepted price of success. Vodka is the drink of choice, and many citizens choose it. Bathhouses, tea shops, nightclubs, casinos, theaters, operas, high-end shopping—the capital has it all: every vice, every pleasure, every danger. Its architecture is a dazzling mix of a little bit of everything, ranging from the colorful onion domes of sixteenth-century Byzantine cathedrals to the ugly shoeboxes of fifties-era Stalinesque modernism to the tall and elegant skyscrapers of the twenty-first century.

To understand the city, it helps to think of it in terms of the ever-popular Russian nesting dolls: the Kremlin and Red Square, including Lenin's Mausoleum and St. Basil's Cathedral and the Armory Museum and GUM's department store, are the tiny doll in the center, and the rest spreads outward in concentric circles, with the last one encompassing one-time monasteries and former country estates of nobles and the tsars. The whole vast, unruly sprawl is circled by Moscow Ring Road. The Moskva River winds through it all.

There were, Bianca thought as they crept along with the

traffic into the heart of the city, two things to keep in mind about Moscow: (1) nowhere worth going to was more than a fifteen-minute walk from a Metro station, and (2) Big Brother is always watching, and his eyes are blue.

She rode in the cab of the big rig, the largest of the vehicles, a semitrailer truck that held the big top tent, stadium seating, pieces of the ring and other necessary equipment, with Lazlo behind the wheel. Six days had passed since she and Doc had combined forces with the Circus Nagy. The big rig was in the middle of the convoy of campers, animal wagons and support vehicles. It had been an arduous three-day journey over bad roads and through checkpoints where the guards had for the most part waved them on with no more than a cursory glance at their papers. Only at the Russian border had they been ordered to stop while the vehicles were searched. Six-foot-high razor wire spirals ran along either side of the narrow, pitted road. An elevated guard tower complete with Kalashnikov-wielding guards and a powerful searchlight overlooked the proceedings. This was in addition to the more ordinary barrier gate and armed guards from the Border Guard Service. The effect was intimidating.

After looking inside the big rig and several of the campers, the guards reached Zoltan's truck. When the back garage-style door was rolled up to reveal the big cat, tail slashing, glaring at them from behind iron bars, and he greeted them with a mighty roar, they backed off and let the convoy proceed.

Which was a good thing, because Bianca, who didn't want to endure the scrutiny of the border guards for fear that her forged papers might not pass muster, or a guard might recognize her as the subject of a Darjeeling Brothers' contract or even remember her in case anyone came hunting for her later, was concealed in a hidden compartment in the front of Zoltan's cage. It was also a way to test the effectiveness of her exit strategy: next time the convoy passed through that checkpoint, a portion of King Priam's Treasure would be, if all went well, concealed in that compartment.

Doc passed through the checkpoint inside another hidden compartment. That one was at the back of the cage housing two twenty-foot-long Burmese pythons named Zsa and Atila that Sandor used in his act. Like Zoltan, the giant snakes served as a slithering disincentive for further inspection of the vehicle.

Shortly after passing through the checkpoint the whole convoy pulled over, and Oskar rewarded Zoltan for his robust greeting to the guards—a greeting that Oskar had painstakingly trained him to perform whenever the metal door covering the back of his cage was rolled up—with a hunk of raw beef.

Also at that time, Bianca transferred to the cab of the big rig, and Doc was invited to choose between riding with Dorottya and her dogs or Oskar and Griff.

Doc chose Oskar and Griff (the choice boiling down, Bianca could only assume, to a truck cab stuffed with six dogs or presided over by a single monkey). When the convoy pulled away again, a glance in the big rig's rearview mirror showed Bianca that the monkey was perched on the seat back between Doc and Oskar, triumphantly holding the knit cap that he'd obviously just pulled from Doc's head.

Imagining Doc's subsequent dealings with Griff kept Bianca smiling for quite some time.

It was snowing, a light drifting of fat white flakes that looked like powdered sugar being sifted over the ground, and sunny and cold when the convoy reached Tsvetnoi Boulevard and the building that housed the Circus Nikulin came into sight. It was late afternoon, a Monday, and there would be a performance that night. The circus was dark on Tuesday and Wednesday, and then on Thursday started up again. For now, there was already a growing line in front of the ticket office hoping to score seats for the 7:00 p.m. performance. A smattering of tourists walked up and down the long flight of wide stone steps leading to the multiple glass-paned doors of the entrance. More tourists took pictures of themselves posing out front with the life-size bronze statue of the late beloved clown Yuri Vladimirovich Nikulin, from whom the circus took its name.

Russians loved circuses, as they did nearly all forms of live entertainment. There were two circuses in permanent residence in Moscow alone, and both played to near capacity crowds every night. The Circus Nikulin was the older of these, and had been performing at the same address since 1880. Bianca had visited before, but she still got a thrill of pleasure from the sight of the large white and yellow stone building with the two illuminated prancing horses bracketing the sign bearing the Nikulin's name.

"I'm impressed that Oskar's cousin was able to arrange accommodation for all of us," Bianca said as Lazlo drove the truck around back, to the alley that led to the circus's loading dock and barn area. It also led to the side entrance for the large, Soviet-era apartment complex next door that housed, among hundreds of other tenants, a number of circus employees and visiting performers. "I was expecting that we'd be staying in the campers."

"Patrik has done well for us, yes? We have been given the use of two apartments." Lazlo said that as though so much space was a luxury to be marveled at, which indeed it was: housing in Moscow was at a premium, with upward of a dozen people sometimes crammed into a single small unit. He started braking as he spoke. Bianca saw that they were nearing the side door to the apartment complex. "You should go inside. Dedi will be waiting with the girls to take you up to the apartment you will share. The rest of us are needed to get the animals settled in. Your Bruce will wish to go up with the men."

Bianca imagined that by now "Bruce" was heartily wishing that he'd stayed behind in Savannah, but she nodded agreement as she reached for her things.

She said, "You anticipate no trouble locating a fire truck?"

Lazlo shook his head. "I will have all day tomorrow, and Wednesday too if necessary, to acquire one. It should not take longer. If necessary, with the amount of money available to us for expenses, I can buy an old one and say it is for use as a circus prop. Or we can steal one."

"As long as it runs reliably," Bianca said as the truck stopped. "I'm leaving the acquisition of that very crucial piece of equipment up to you. Just let me know when you've found one."

"I will." He hesitated. "Ah—there is one more thing. An addition to the timeline."

Bianca looked at him inquiringly.

"You know that the children will be rehearsing over the next couple of days, and their audition is set for Thursday afternoon, which leaves the rest of us free to prepare. I had thought to have nothing to do Friday except make sure all is ready, but Tibor Alexandrovich—" he was the Nikulin's manager, Bianca knew "—has invited us to do a guest performance on Friday night. He wants us to open the show. Tibor Alexandrovich said that they will be honored to feature the Circus Nagy." The pride in Lazlo's voice told Bianca how much the invitation meant to him. "He requests a shortened set, 7:00 to 8:00 p.m., which I think will work for our larger purpose. No one will realize, but it will be the Circus Nagy's final performance. Then, later that night, we will get rich."

By that, he meant that the robbery was scheduled for Friday night, when the Pushkin would be hosting a gala to celebrate the opening of a newly arrived traveling exhibit featuring the Savitsky State Art Museum's avant-garde paintings. Banned in

Stalin-era Russia, which had required art to be both support-ive of the state and comprehensible to the average worker, the bold-colored representations of shapes and images and scenes that did not fit the Soviet narrative had been hidden away in the dust-bowl city of Nukus for decades. In this more per-missive era they had been rediscovered and were touring the country to much acclaim.

The timing was perfect. As soon as she'd learned of the gala, Bianca had realized that it could be turned to her advan-tage. The Pushkin's security had been ramped up from barely adequate to state-of-the-art within the last year. (Why, Bianca could only speculate.) King Priam's Treasure was located in the main building, which was, therefore, the one Bianca was concerned with. Its security included surveillance cameras, motion detectors and infrared systems inside the building and multiple alarms attached to the building's outer shell, includ-ing all doors, even upper-level windows and skylights. Armed security guards roamed the building after closing hours. Metal gates at the entrances to the most important rooms, includ-ing Room Three where the treasure was located, were closed and locked when the museum was shut down for the night. Closed-circuitTV cameras kept watch outside the building.

Figuring out a way to navigate through all that security had presented Bianca with a puzzle that she'd been working hard to solve ever since she'd first been confronted with it while going over the information Mason had left for her. When she'd learned of the gala, it had hit her that she didn't have to. Instead of defeating the layers of security that kicked in when the museum was closed, the best thing to do was sim-ply avoid it. The time to strike would be while the building was open and filled with guests.

The plan she was going with was a modified snatch-and-run. The rudimentary outline went like this: she would set up a distraction in the form of explosions timed to go off fifteen minutes before the commencement of the theft in two of Moscow's major tunnels, the Lefortovo and the Northwestern. Those would serve to draw the attention of a large portion of Moscow's police and fire personnel. When the explosions went off, she would be inside the Pushkin attending the gala under the pretext of being an invited guest. While there, she would pick the locks of the nineteen display cases in which the treasure was kept. Then she would set a still-to-be-determined number of charges that would trigger several small fires, which, with a little help from her, would immediately begin to fill the building with dense smoke. Alarms would sound. The guests would be evacuated. The fire department would be called.

Meanwhile, Doc would have gained access to the museum's computer and phone systems. He would have disabled the display case alarms before Bianca unlocked the cases. When the fire alarms went off and the fire department was summoned, Doc and whatever wizardry he had used to take over the system would be the only ones receiving the emergency calls. He would then cue Lazlo and the others, who would come roaring to the rescue in the newly acquired fire truck. In firefighter gear complete with helmets and oxygen masks (talk about a perfect disguise!), they would storm the building carrying several large trunks with them that onlookers might suppose to contain such equipment as was needed to fight the fire. While Kristof and Franz ran around putting out the fires, the rest of the gang would empty the display cases Bianca had unlocked, removing the treasure and replacing it with the replica artifacts that Dedi was still in the process of creating. Those replicas were, of course, what actually would be carried in in the trunks. The real treasure would go into the trunks in place of the replicas, Bianca would relock the display cases and don a spare firefighter's uniform and the whole group of them would dash out and skedaddle in the fire truck. The fire truck would carry them to a secluded location near the river where the circus campers would be waiting along with the animals and those of the party who were not in on the main job. The fire truck would be driven into the river, to, hopefully, never be found, and they would load the treasure and themselves into the circus campers and head out of Moscow and out of Russia, trusting in Zoltan and the snakes to get them across the border again with the treasure on board.

With luck, they would have at least twenty-four hours and possibly far longer to disappear. The point of the replicas was to give them time to get safely out of Russia: a theft wouldn't be suspected if nothing appeared to be missing. Bianca didn't expect the replicas to remain undiscovered forever: to begin with, there wasn't time to make them to a standard where, upon close examination, the substitution wouldn't be detected. What Bianca had asked Dedi to aim for was something that wouldn't be immediately spotted if someone was looking at it through a glass display case. If the theft of King Priam's Treasure from the Pushkin Museum was found out before they made it across the border, escape became infinitely harder. The country would go into lockdown. All of Russia's considerable stops would be pulled out to catch the thieves and recover what had been stolen.

The Kremlin's response would be roughly equivalent to, *let loose the kraken.*

"If you think it would be better, I can turn Tibor Alexandrovich down," Lazlo said. Bianca could tell from the lack of inflection in his voice how much he would regret having to do that.

"No, you should accept." Bianca curled a hand around the door handle as she spoke. "The gala starts at eight, which is about the time your part of the show should finish. I'm guessing you won't need to be at the museum until around nine.

I'll give you a more precise time after I measure the distances and check out a few more details."

"I was thinking the performance could be like an alibi for us, if questions are ever asked about where we were during the robbery," Lazlo said.

"It would," Bianca agreed. "But let's hope those questions are never asked."

"From your lips to God's ears," Lazlo said.

Through the window Bianca saw Dedi, who'd been standing inside the apartment building out of the cold as she apparently waited for Bianca to arrive, step outside and gesture impatiently at her. With a quick smile for Lazlo, Bianca slid out of the truck. The blast of cold air that greeted her made her shiver.

The apartment was a third-floor walk-up. The stairway was cold and grungy. The smell of borscht was strong. The stairs and hall were uncarpeted linoleum with greasy walls. Sound from the two dozen apartments that opened off the hall ranged from babies crying to a couple arguing to several loud TVs blaring. If there was insulation, you couldn't tell it.

The number of the apartment that Dedi took Bianca, Bela, Elena and Maria to was 318, identified by cheap metal numbers nailed on the cheap hollow-core door. Inside, the apartment consisted of a small living room with a couch, two armchairs and a dining table with four chairs, and a galley kitchen opening off one end. A single bedroom with two sets of triple bunk beds that, placed against the walls, left just enough open floor space for someone to walk between them and a bathroom completed the apartment. The walls were avocado green; the two windows were covered with grimy lace curtains.

Bianca reflexively chose a top bunk to make it harder for anyone to sneak up on her as she slept.

After Dorottya had arrived with her dogs, and the men

along with Griff had gone up to their fourth-floor apartment, the whole gang, minus the animals, got together and went down to have dinner at the Burger King around the corner. Bianca was wary of patronizing an American franchise, but she was still in the long brown wig and glasses she wore as Maggy and she was one of a troupe of circus performers, groups of whom often frequented the restaurant, which should provide additional cover. She figured that she was safe enough for the brief time it took them to order food and eat.

But the homey smells of burgers and fries notwithstanding, she was uncomfortable the entire time she was inside. The bright lights of the restaurant coupled with the darkness of the night outside made it possible for anyone on the street or in passing vehicles or nearby buildings to see everyone in line at the counter, or seated at the tables and booths. She enjoyed the ketchup-dipped fries in particular, but she didn't like the idea that someone could be watching her while it was too dark outside for her to see them. And she couldn't shake the crawly feeling at the back of her neck.

The ubiquitousness of the FSB was a concern, as were the professional killers who made the capital their home. The CIA kill team wouldn't have given up: she had no doubt that they were still hunting her and Mason. And then there was Mickey, who she was sure was still searching for her and Mason, as well.

Nobody had any reason to suspect that she was in Moscow. As crowded and busy as the city was, Maggy Chance was just one more grain of sand on the beach.

On the other hand, they'd tracked her to Macau.

That was the worry she couldn't get out of her head.

25

After they ate, the entire troupe went over to the Nikulin and met Tibor Alexandrovich. A short, burly man of around fifty, he had thinning dark hair and a bristling salt-and-pepper mustache. He was dressed like a seventies-era John Travolta, in a white suit with a red silk shirt open halfway down his chest, which was festooned with gold chains. He greeted them warmly, welcoming them to his circus and telling them how much he was looking forward to seeing the Circus Nagy perform on Friday night. He then passed them on to Oskar's cousin Patrik Szabo.

Patrik was sixty-two. He resembled Oskar, with the same nearly black eyes and wiry build, but his face was far less lined and weathered and, all in all, he gave the impression of a man who was enjoying a good life. Like Oskar, he had once been an acrobat. He had retired from performing fifteen years previously and now worked as the circus's assistant manager.

"Vy gordites nashey semyey," he said to Oskar—*You do your family proud*—as he released him from an embrace, then looked at Oskar's four grandsons. "So these are our hopefuls."

He still spoke Russian, but Bianca's ear had adjusted and she now translated without having to think about it.

As the young men rather shyly agreed that they were, indeed, the hopefuls, and Dorottya proudly extolled their virtues as performers, Patrik showed the entire group around the building. It looked more like a luxuriously appointed theater than a typical circus. In the lobby, which was full of people there for the evening performance, guests could buy popcorn, cotton candy, ice cream, cookies, soda—and also get their photos taken with two of the night's animal stars, a tiger and a leopard, both of whom seemed to regard the commotion with bored tolerance. Inside the arena, the venue was breathtaking, with frescoes and gilt embellishments surrounding the high-domed ceiling, an elaborate staircase down which the principal performers entered and a stage for the live orchestra that played every show. Tiered, red-plush seating for two thousand surrounded a single well-groomed ring. Four more performers' entrances—two beneath the staircase and two on opposite sides of the ring—caught Bianca's eye as the lights went down and a troupe of clowns poured into the ring through them.

As Patrik introduced them to those of the acts that they came across and showed them around the labyrinthian backstage area, Bianca's attention kept being drawn to the ongoing performances in the ring.

Jugglers juggled. Dancers danced. Magicians pulled rabbits out of hats. Trapeze artists flew overhead. Tightrope walkers played leapfrog thirty feet above the ground. Dazzling white horses cantered around the ring while their riders leaped through hoops of fire. Two enormous brown bears lumbered into the ring, climbed into two clown cars and drove away, to the comic dismay of the clowns.

All to the tune of the audience's wild applause.

Catching a glimpse of Lazlo's face as he, too, watched the action in the ring, Bianca was reminded that this was the life that he and all of his family had been born into and loved. Even with the lure of a four-million-dollar payday, she thought that they would find leaving it behind bittersweet.

Before she returned to the apartment, Bianca went to check on Dedi, who since the family had come on board about the theft had been working tirelessly to make copies of all 101 objects that made up the main part of the treasure. This was the part that was on display in Room Three of the Pushkin, and this was what she was planning to steal. Other, less famous pieces were in storage elsewhere or on display at various other museums, but she wasn't going to worry about them.

One of the camper trucks contained Dedi's small workshop, which included a workbench and tools, a small kiln and, among other things, loads of faux gold stamping blanks, which were penny-size and used with metal stamps for jewelry making. Bottles of different solutions and powders for antiquing the finished product, refining the color and producing an authentic-looking period piece were housed in spice-bottle-like racks. A potter's wheel was set up in a corner.

To anyone who didn't know what Dedi was really doing, it looked like she was making ordinary costume jewelry for sale. Which, as she caustically told Bianca when Bela, who was helping Dedi and who she was training to one day take her place, admitted her to the truck, was what she told anyone who was nosy enough to ask.

"How's it coming?" Bianca approached the workbench with interest. The truck was parked in the open area behind the barns, and the generator was running. The interior was warm and well-lit. Dedi had been pounding away with a rubber mallet when Bianca entered. Now, as Bela resumed her place on the bench beside Dedi and picked up a metal stamp to press a design into one of a string of penny-size gold discs, Dedi upended a plastic bottle over her creation, which was a small, basket-shaped gold earring.

Bianca recognized it instantly as a replica of one the earrings in the treasure. Looking past Dedi, she saw that a detailed picture of the original piece along with its size and weight specifications was pinned to the corkboard affixed to the wall. Also on the corkboard was the picture of the smaller of the two gold diadems—headdresses—that supposedly had once been worn by Helen of Troy. The strand of golden discs Bela was working on clearly belonged to it.

"The job will be finished in time," Dedi replied as a few drops of a milky fluid were squeezed out of the bottle onto the earring. She set down the bottle and used a brush to work the solution into the earring. Almost immediately the gold started to take on an antique patina. A strongly astringent smell that made Bianca think of rubbing alcohol had her wrinkling her nose. "Most of the pieces are very simple." With a nod she indicated a quartet of finished bracelets set off to one side of the work bench that were nothing more than spirals of gold wire. "These we are working on now are the more complicated ones."

A *ping* in the background caused Bela to put down the metal stamp and get up.

"The kiln," Dedi explained as Bela opened what looked almost like a microwave and, by means of a long-handled platter, removed the item inside. It was, Bianca saw, the two-handled sauceboat that was unusual enough to rate its own small display case. The only problem was, this sauceboat was made of clay and was a dull terra cotta in color, while the real sauceboat was made of solid gold and was colored, uh, gold.

"Do not worry, it will be spray painted later," Dedi reassured her, Bianca's expression clearly having betrayed her surprise. "Put it with the others," she directed Bela, who nodded and carefully carried the pottery sauceboat from the truck.

Dedi's expression softened as she watched her great-granddaughter go.

"She is a good child, that one," she said to Bianca after the door closed behind Bela. "She is why I will make sure that these pieces are *good*. Our life, the circus, always the worry about money—it is too hard. I want her to have *more*."

Bianca nodded. "She is lucky to have you," she said, and meant it.

"I am lucky to have her," Dedi replied. "I am old now, and I know—family is the most important thing."

Before anything more could be said Bela returned, and Bianca left them to it.

"You mean to tell me they're *fake*?" Doc was whispering, but his voice was still loud enough with outrage to make Bianca shush him under her breath. The few people around them were clearly tourists, but speaking English would attract attention in and of itself and, anyway, one couldn't be too careful.

"Yes." Her voice was scarcely louder than a hiss. She was fluent in Russian. At the moment it did her no good whatsoever: Doc couldn't speak the language.

He quieted down. "All of them?"

"Yes. Here's a tip-off—that's Michelangelo's *David*." Bianca nodded to a supersized piece of sculpture on a pedestal in the middle of the room. "The original's in Florence, remember? And it's smaller. And marble. That's a plaster cast reproduction."

Doc gave the sculpture a squinty-eyed once-over. "I totally knew that."

"Moscow University used to use this building as a teaching aid, so they made copies of a lot of valuable art that they don't actually possess," Bianca said.

"Ain't nothing like the real thing, huh?" Doc looked at the towering statues around them with fresh eyes. "Only, I guess not so much."

It was the following day, just after lunchtime. They were inside the Pushkin Museum's main building passing through what Bianca thought of as the Hall of Statues. It had massive Greek columns and oversize replicas of famous statues, along with mosaics, vases, and a pulpit against one wall.

The gala would be held on the first floor, according to her information. If she were a betting person, she would bet that any catering tables would be set up in this very hall. It was long and wide, centrally located—and drafty enough to draw smoke like a flue.

Be still my heart.

They were making their way toward Room Three, which was dedicated solely to King Priam's Treasure, or, as it was billed in the museum literature, The Treasure of Troy. They'd started out walking from the apartment building, then after about a mile had caught a taxi. (Almost any private citizen could turn their car into a taxi; the key was to be cautious and it helped that Bianca spoke the language.) They'd ridden around in the taxi for a bit and then set out on foot again, all through a lightly falling snow. There was as yet no accumulation on the ground. That would come later in the month, and certainly by Christmas. Bundled up in coats and hats and scarves against the cold, they blended easily with the throngs of pedestrians on the busy streets.

A three-mile trip that, walking the entire way, should have taken forty-five minutes, had required an hour and a half.

And that would be because she was operating under Moscow Rules.

Being identified was now a perpetual concern of hers, but between her layers of outerwear and the sheer number of people out and about, she thought that the chances of a would-be assassin spotting her were remote. Nevertheless, tradecraft had been invented for a reason, and that reason was to keep those who practiced it alive. Moscow Rules had been developed during the cold war specifically for agents who were conducting clandestine operations in that city because it was said to be the most hostile environment in which to work.

The rules were:

Assume nothing.

Never go against your gut.

Everyone is potentially under opposition control.

You are never completely alone.

Go with the flow; blend in.

Vary your pattern and stay within your cover.

Lull them into a sense of complacency.

Do not harass the opposition.

Pick the time and place for action.

Keep your options open.

Bianca had extended the list to include the most extreme form of antisurveillance tactics. The CliffsNotes version was: a straight line might be the shortest distance between two points, but never take it if you're traveling somewhere. Start left if you mean to go right. Double back frequently. Walk around the block in the middle of a route. If you start out walking, switch to a vehicle and then switch back. Ducking into a store is a good way to uncover surveillance. Window-shopping, because windows could be used as a mirror to spot tails, is your friend. Do not take the Metro, because (1) the Metro is full of surveillance cameras, and (2) everybody takes it, including agents of the FSB and SVR.

Her purpose in visiting the museum, of course, was to see the treasure and the cases containing it, check out the locks she would need to pick and any encumbrances, such as surveillance cameras and alarms, they might encounter, and evaluate the size, probable weight and appearance of what they would be stealing.

It was always important to see the site of an upcoming job in person, to measure distances and obstacles so that she could come up with a precise timeline, to identify entrances and exits and get a true visual handle on the space. The trick lay in only visiting once, if at all possible. Multiple visits were problematic in that they might arouse suspicion. "Casing the joint" was a concept as well-known in Moscow as anywhere. Even if it wasn't noticed by the museum staff at the time, such suspicious activity would be glaringly obvious if a theft was discovered and surveillance footage was reviewed by, say, the FSB. For that reason, she didn't want the Nagys to visit the museum prior to the robbery. For their own safety, they would have to learn everything they needed to know from pictures and diagrams. That precaution, coupled with the fire-fighters' uniforms they would be wearing when they did the job, should keep them from being identified even after the theft was discovered, as sooner or later it would be.

Doc was with her because he needed to probe the computerized portion of the Pushkin's security system with an eye to hacking into it on the night in question. For that purpose, he had his laptop with him, concealed in a slit in the lining of his coat because the Pushkin required all bags, backpacks, etcetera to be checked into lockers at the door. In a few minutes, he would go to the men's room, find a stall, sit down, get out his laptop and run his tests. After that they would be ready to leave.

In the meantime, here they were checking out the museum.

The design of the building itself, which dated from 1912, was based on the model of a Greek temple. Its classical facade was fronted by a row of Ionic columns. Inside, it was ornate and old-fashioned and beautiful, with soaring domed ceilings punctuated by large, mullioned skylights (or, as they were known in the trade, means of ingress). The walls were a combination of white with pastels—eggshell blue, mint green, soft yellow. Paintings, statues and artifacts were displayed on walls, on pedestals, in corners and in dedicated display cases. The display cases and pedestals were old, the benches and woodwork showed wear, and the overall impression was one of magnificence that had been allowed to grow shabby.

The place smelled just a little musty.

"Kind of reminds me of the Met," Doc said.

Knowing that Doc, a Bronx native, was referring to the

Metropolitan Museum of Art, Bianca glanced at him in surprise. "Did you go there a lot?"

"All the time. Best free Wi-Fi in the city."

That explained much. "Oh."

They did a quick walk-through of rooms One and Two, which contained the Ancient Civilization Exhibit from Greece, Rome and Egypt, including art, weapons, jewelry, and, as a pièce de résistance, two really cool mummies. Other rooms in the two-story building housed other exhibits, including Dutch masterpieces from such artists as Rembrandt in rooms Nine through Eleven.

The second floor was largely devoted to the seventeenth and eighteenth centuries, although Room Twenty-Nine was dedicated exclusively to more reproductions from Michelangelo. The *David* statue in the vast downstairs hall was obviously an escapee.

So as not to make their interest in Room Three obvious, Bianca was determined to walk through the whole place.

An office housing the computers controlling the surveillance cameras and other security systems was located in a covered two-story courtyard just beyond Room Three. The courtyard was full of statues and busts on pedestals, and had a skylight overhead and a gently bubbling fountain in the center. Bianca had known the office was there from the floor plans, and she eyed it with (veiled, she hoped) interest. It was a small space compared to the size of the courtyard, perhaps twelve-by-sixteen feet. The walls were made of wood up to a height of about four feet, at which point thick glass took over and soared the rest of the way to the ceiling, undoubtedly to allow light from the skylight into the office. Four wooden desks were in the room, with computer monitors on each desk. Two uniformed security officers sat behind two of those desks.

Bianca gave Doc a nudge. "There's the security office."

He was already looking at it. "Wonder what kind of signal strength they have?"

Since Bianca had no idea, she pulled him with her into Room Three.

The walls were painted a dull gold. The lighting was dim. The exhibit had clearly been in place for many years and looked tired, despite the fact that the artifacts themselves were magnificent.

King Priam's Treasure was displayed in old-fashioned glass cases with black bases. Gold jewelry including rings, brace-lets, necklaces and earrings had been simply laid out on what looked like white shelf paper on glass shelves. A number was handwritten on the paper beside each piece, and a card that backed the shelf had printed descriptions to match the num-bers. The large and small diadems, each of which consisted of a fringe of small gold discs that covered the wearer's fore-head and cascaded down either side of the face like a shoulder-length wig with bangs, were displayed on black wig stands in their own cases in the middle of the room. The so-called Tro-jan sauceboat of the terra-cotta replica fame, which was one of the prize pieces of the exhibit because of its size and two handles, sat on a clear pedestal inside its own case. Milky rock crystal lenses the size of quarters, a pencil-thin orange-red cylinder of carnelian, amber beads and a thumb-size bronze figurine of what looked like a bear cub were arrayed on glass fronted shelves along the wall. Golden goblets, silver vessels, bronze plates, and four axes, one of which had a lapis lazuli blade, filled more glass-fronted shelves.

One hundred one objects in nineteen cases. None appeared to be secured to the display in any way. The only barriers were the locked door of the display cases and the alarms attached to them. If each piece was carefully replaced in its numbered spot by its replica and the cases were locked again, it might be longer than Bianca had first thought before the theft was discovered.

Unless Germany wanted to brag about the treasure's recovery, which it probably would. Then the shit would hit the fan. Fortunately, by that time they would all be out of Russia.

Looking around, Bianca felt good about the job. Most of the items were small and should easily fit in, say, three trunks. None of them looked heavy. Whispering to Doc to go ahead and do his thing, which he did, moving away to the bathroom for privacy to check out the computer system by exploring it with a program launched from his laptop, she got busy taking surreptitious photos of the exhibits with the handy-dandy pen camera she'd stowed in her pocket for just that purpose, and examining the display cases without seeming to do so. The locks securing them were laughable. Time needed to pick one? Maybe thirty seconds each. Still, there were nineteen cases, so that was nine and a half minutes. Add to that the time required to move between cases—

She was discreetly measuring the distances when Doc came back into the room.

"Boss."

She held up a finger as she finished counting. Twenty paces between the large diadem and the sauceboat. That translated to ten seconds.

"*Boss.*"

Doc had followed her. The urgency of his tone communicated itself to her, and she looked at him inquiringly.

"We've got a problem," he said.

26

Of course they had a problem. She should have known from the moment she'd spotted those unsecured items in those barely locked cases that the job was coming together too easily: her luck was never that good.

Bianca stopped measuring distances to frown at Doc. "What is it?"

"The entire system is air-gapped."

"What?"

"It's a secure LAN—local area network—system. No Wi-Fi. No Bluetooth. No outside connection to the internet. It's a self-contained system." His tone was stark. "I can't take it over. It can't be hacked. Not remotely. I'm going to have to get physical access to the computers themselves to do anything."

"Are you serious?" Bianca asked, visions floating through her head of having to break into the security office during the gala, silently knock out whatever guards were inside at the time, and keep everybody from noticing that anything was amiss in the glass-walled room while a not-exactly-inconspicuous Doc hunched over the computers hacking away.

"'Fraid so."

A whole string of swear words crowded her tongue. She didn't say them.

"We'll figure something out," she said, going back to her measurements while Doc stood frowning into space. What that something would be she wasn't quite sure, but never say die (literally) was her new mantra. Going all karate kid on the guards in a glass-walled room in the middle of a gala was probably out: pretty sure somebody was going to notice. Knockout gas pumped in through a vent? A ruse to draw the guards out? A fake delivery to get Doc inside?

She might be able to do something like leap out of a giant, celebratory cake delivered to the security office in the midst of the gala, but Doc probably wasn't going to be able to pull that off.

Hmm.

They were nearly back to the apartment building, moving through a thick area, which meant one that was so heavily traveled that surveillance was hard to spot. As they shouldered their way through a crush of workers all apparently heading for the nearby Metro station—a glance at her watch told Bianca that it was just after five o'clock, which meant rush hour was under way—Doc said, out of nowhere, "What I need is a raspberry pie."

Bianca looked at him. "We're not in Kansas anymore, Toto. There is no River Street Sweets around here."

"It's not a dessert." Doc shot her an impatient look. "*P-I*, not *P-I-E*. It's something I can use to fix our problem."

They'd reached the Burger King next door to the circus. Bianca pulled him across the street and into the pharmacy on the corner to reconnoiter from the candy aisle, from which vantage point she could watch the passersby through the window.

Always check for a tail before returning to the place you're staying in.

"So what is this thing?" Bianca asked.

Doc explained. Most of the technical jargon he used was incomprehensible to her, but the bottom line was that a Raspberry Pi was a credit-card-size device that he could configure and preprogram with instructions on everything they needed the Pushkin's computer-controlled systems to do. Once plugged into the actual computer, it would download those instructions into the operating system, which would then automatically follow its instructions, doing things like deactivating the alarm systems and rerouting any emergency signals and phone calls to wherever they chose.

Finishing up with his description as they left the pharmacy and headed toward the circus, Doc said, "Once I'm within reach of their computer system, it'll take five seconds to install." He made a jabbing gesture with his hand. "Plug it in and *boom*, we're good to go."

Bianca grimaced. "Five seconds is better than, say, fifteen minutes, but we still have to figure out how to get you in and the guards out for long enough to do it."

"It doesn't have to be me. Anybody can do it. Like I said, all you do is plug it in. Easy as pie." Grinning at his own joke, he looked at Bianca. "You could do it."

He said that in very much the tone in which he might've said, *any idiot can do it.*

"Thanks a lot." She was already turning over in her mind various scenarios by which she might gain access to the security office. The glass walls coupled with the number of people sure to be milling around in the near vicinity of the office made the whole thing difficult. On the plus side, she'd picked up a brochure advertising the gala, and it showed very dim lighting in the rooms where the Savitsky paintings were not being displayed. She suspected the atrium would be one of those dimly lit rooms. On a side note, Room Three would probably be another, which was a plus. "Is there any means of access besides the door?"

The door to the security office was front and center, opening right off the atrium. It would be in full view of anybody in the atrium, and of many guests in the Hall of Statues or near the entrance to Room Three or—no telling where. Probably all kinds of places. She would have to check.

It was safe to say that if she went in by the door, lots of people would see her.

"You mean like coming down through the skylight? I don't know. Let's look."

They were inside the circus building by that time, cutting through the stands surrounding the arena because that was the shortest path to the back door of the apartment building. The circus was dark that day, so only a few people were in the seats. In the ring, Lazlo, Kristof, Franz, Adam and Bence were rehearsing their separate acts. Lazlo was on the ground juggling, while high overhead his sons and their cousins practiced traversing the high wire in a giant four-wheeled X-shaped machine in which each young man walked in a wheel to propel the contraption along the wire.

Bianca observed all that in a single, distracted glance as she sat down beside Doc, who'd dropped into one of the red plush stadium seats.

Extracting his laptop from his coat, not without some difficulty, Doc called up the floor plans of the Pushkin's main building.

"Skylight's out," he said, as he and Bianca peered at the diagram. "It's not over the office. There's a chimney—"

Bianca could see it. Sporting a vented metal cap, it ran down from the roof and opened into the very back corner of the office's two-story-high ceiling. Besides being high—people rarely looked up—the opening was well behind the desks, which meant that the backs of any guards present would be turned to anything emerging from it. It was a workable point of ingress except for one problem—it was about as big around as a large Maxwell House coffee can.

She said, "It's a ventilation shaft, and I don't think I'm going to fit."

"No," Doc agreed regretfully.

The other problem with going in through the door was that the guards would certainly notice and remember her. That was bad, but what was worse was the unsettling worry that one of them might have seen the Darjeeling Brothers' contract. Of course, she would be in disguise but, still, she didn't like to be so exposed.

Bianca was just thinking, *I could have Doc take them a pizza*, when her eye was caught by a tiny figure descending a rope that dangled from the aerialists' rig up near the ceiling. It was Griff, and he came down furry brown paw over furry brown paw, passing Kristof and the others on the high wire, then flipping upside down so that he was sliding headfirst by his feet before launching himself into the air like a flying squirrel when he was still some twenty feet above the ground. He wore a red vest–type harness, and she saw that far from falling, he was being lowered, spread-eagled, tail arched over his back in a tight curl, to the ring by a red rope clipped to the harness.

Once he touched the ground, Griff unclipped the rope and scampered to Oskar, who'd just run into the ring with Zoltan. Griff sat and offered Oskar a banana that he pulled from his vest. When Oskar leaned down to accept the banana, Griff snatched the black bowler hat from Oskar's head, leaped on Zoltan's back, and, clutching the hat, rode the loping lion around the ring with a comically angry Oskar in hot pursuit.

As an act, it was mildly amusing. But what riveted Bianca's attention was Griff.

She felt Doc's eyes on her and glanced his way.

"Are you thinking what I'm thinking?" he asked.

"Depends. I'm thinking that maybe Griff could do it."

"Great minds," Doc said. "'Cause that's what I was thinking, too."

Bianca waited until Oskar had finished his rehearsal, then went down to the ring to talk to him.

By 9:00 p.m. Thursday, everything was on track for the job the next night. Lazlo had acquired a used fire truck along with the necessary number of uniforms and equipment trunks to carry the fake treasure in and the real treasure out. Dedi and Bela were almost finished with the replicas, and Dedi vowed that everything would be completed and ready to pack up by noon the next day. Doc had visited a number of computer and hardware stores in the vicinity and had found the needed components for a Raspberry Pi. He was busy assembling and programming it to the exact timeline and specifications provided by Bianca, who had planned out the job to the minute. She always did so, but the fact that the Raspberry Pi meant that the Pushkin's computer system would be completely pre-programmed with the instructions Doc fed it meant that she had to be especially careful to be accurate. If an emergency call went out to the police, for example, before Doc was able to intercept it, they would be screwed.

Oskar had greeted Bianca's question about whether his pet could perform the needed action with scorn. Of course he could! Griff would require only the smallest amount of practice, his own act only the smallest of additions so that the needed practice could be acquired during rehearsals in the ring, which would allow them to work from the necessary height.

Watching Oskar's addition to his act, Bianca had been impressed with both the old man's ingenuity and Griff's ability to learn. Now, after Griff descended the rope, flew into space and touched down in the ring, he unhooked himself and scampered over to a computer Doc had provided that was as nearly identical to the one used by the Pushkin security system as he'd been able to find. The computer was placed on a desk in the middle of the ring. Oskar sat behind the desk working on something. Griff crept up to it, looking cagily at Oskar who pretended to be unaware, and in a lightning movement plugged in a card designed to mimic the Raspberry Pi. That triggered a light show, and while Griff hooked himself back onto the rope and was whisked toward the ceiling, Oskar jumped up and clapped his hands to his cheeks in surprise as brightly colored polka dots and stars and figures made of light began to revolve crazily around the arena. Oskar ran out of the ring in mock fear, the light show finished and stagehands rolled the desk away. Oskar then reemerged with Zoltan, seemingly for protection, looking warily around the ring before Griff descended the rope again and they went into the original act.

As entertainment, it actually kind of worked.

Bianca, for her part, had determined that the invitations to the gala had been sent by e-vite and had obtained one by the simple expedient of having Doc hack into the event planner's file and print one for her. She had also assembled the explosives she needed for both the tunnels and the gala. Two old cars, purchased for cash on the black market that was so prevalent in Moscow, had their trunks loaded with the kind of charge that would produce a lot of noise, a lot of smoke, but very little danger to anyone. Elena would drive one and Maria would be in the other. Feigning car trouble, they would leave the vehicles on the shoulder inside the tunnels and return to the rendezvous spot in a vehicle driven by Dorottya. Dedi and Bela would be there with the caravan and the animals. There the five of them would wait for the rest of the group to join them postrobbery. At the same time, the explosives in the cars, which were on a timer, would go off as scheduled.

The circus's 7:00 p.m. show was under way and the rest of the group was fully occupied with either completing their tasks for the robbery or watching the show or, in the case of Kristof, Franz, Adam and Bence, fretting about the result of their audition, which had taken place that afternoon. (For pride's sake they wanted to be awarded a place, and Dorottya and Lazlo wanted them to be awarded a place. But given what was to come, they all agreed that it would be for the best if they were rejected.)

Tibor Alexandrovich had promised to tell them the verdict of the committee that made those decisions after the evening's performance.

Bianca, meanwhile, was engaged in walking the first leg of the journey back to the circus from the Pushkin. She was alone, and in a mood to appreciate both privacy and anonymity. Usually right before a job she was amped up and laser focused. Tonight she just felt tired, and even a little down. Being constantly on the run was getting old, but since the alternative was dying, the only thing to do was buck up and get on with things.

She'd come out to get a look at the museum during the time the robbery would take place. Tonight the museum had closed at eight, but she'd lingered to check out such details as outside lighting and any exit closings that might trip them up. Roof access for Oskar and Griff was another concern, but a particularly dark and sheltered area around back would work well for an expandable ladder, which Oskar would then draw up behind him until it was time to come down.

Her observations had confirmed her opinion that if the Raspberry Pi worked as Doc swore it would, it should be a relatively simple job. The museum complex was spread out over a number of buildings, there was road access from all sides of the complex, and, although there were two outside guards patrolling the parking lots, the museum relied extensively on each building's internal security plus the local police for protection.

The night was as dark as pitch and bitterly cold. Snow fell at a steady clip and was starting to accumulate in grassy areas such as the small park across the street. She strode along the wide avenue that was Ulitsa Kremlevskaya, her head down, taking care to blend with the rest of the foot traffic on the sidewalk. On her left was Taynitskaya Tower and coming up on her right was one of the two bridges that crossed the

Moskva River in this area. The river glinted inky black beneath the streetlights. The Seven Sisters—Stalin-era skyscrapers that formed an arc around the city center—loomed in the distance like monstrous bats with dozens of golden eyes. There was no moon, no stars; the cloud cover was too dense. But the city itself, as it always was at night, was alight. Bars and shops and restaurants were open, drawing people in, disgorging others. The sounds of traffic, muted laughter and voices, doors opening and closing, footsteps, combined to create a steady drone in her ears. The air smelled of snow.

Bundled up in a hooded brown puffy coat that covered her from the top of her head to her knees, with a dark green knit scarf wound around her neck and the lower half of her face for both protection from the cold and concealment, Bianca could still feel the bite of the wind. She had on dark green knit gloves, medium-heeled boots, jeans, a sweater. She'd had to tuck her tortoiseshell glasses into her pocket: the cold made them fog up. But she wore her brown wig, the length of it twisted into a messy bun and tucked inside her hood, and she was confident that the most eagle-eyed observer would not be able to identify her.

Which was why the prickly feeling that was starting to creep across the back of her neck was so disturbing.

Until now, even in the midst of so many people, she'd felt alone.

She no longer did.

It was as if she could feel the weight of invisible eyes on her back. The idea that she was being watched, followed, took possession of her mind, making her heart beat faster, her breathing quicken. In the windows she passed, in the shiny surfaces of the cars driving by, she checked for a tail. She couldn't spot one.

She kept her pace steady.

There were pedestrians behind her. Men in tall Russian

hats, heavy overcoats. Women wrapped up in fur. Groups and singles. Going into restaurants and bars. Hurrying home.

No one looked suspicious. No one seemed to be paying her any attention.

Never look back.

She didn't. She looked for a taxi instead.

The creeping sensation intensified.

Her shoulder muscles tensed. Her stomach fluttered.

It was possible that she was being paranoid. That the gaze she was sensing belonged to a lusty Russian with an eye for a pretty woman. The ticktock urgency of the Darjeeling Brothers' contract was always at the back of her mind. Add to that what had happened in Macau, and it was understandable if she saw assassins around every corner.

She walked downhill, past a photo gallery with a few people inside and large pictures of beautiful Russian women in the window. Next up was a gift shop, and she was just thinking that her best bet might be to go inside and watch for a tail through the window when she spotted, at the red light getting ready to drive through the next intersection, what she sought: a taxi.

It was an official one with the taxi lights on top, not a private car, and it was only about two hundred yards away. She picked up her pace, striding toward it, hoping to leave whoever was watching her, or her imagination plus the heebie-jeebies, behind.

There were fewer pedestrians in front of her now as the little shops and cafés gave way to a closed department store. A glance in its darkened window revealed that there were no longer as many people behind her.

Wait, stop—that tall man in the *ushanka*, fur earflap hat, with the scarf wound round his lower face—had he been behind her before?

Before she could decide, the light changed. The first cars in line started to move through the intersection, and she knew she had to hurry or lose the chance.

She started to run.

"*Taksi!*" she cried, holding up a hand as the taxi moved into the intersection. "*Taksi!*"

It hesitated. She thought the driver saw her—

A blur of movement to her left. Multiple screeching brakes. Horns blaring. A thump.

A dark blue Lada sedan hurtled across two lanes of traffic to explode onto the sidewalk in front of her, cutting her off, making her jump backward with a cry.

27

People on the sidewalk screamed and dived out of the way as the Lada slammed to a stop. Still recovering her balance, still getting oriented as to what was happening, Bianca gaped as its doors opened and two men jumped out.

They had guns.

They aimed at her.

A hit. The realization burst upon her in all its icy horror as another car—a white panel van—screeched to a stop at the curb. A sliding door in its side opened. More men armed with more guns jumped out.

More screams as bystanders scattered.

Bianca's heart gave a great leap. She could stand and fight with the best of them, but the odds were not in her favor. She turned to run—

She didn't even have time for a single bound in the opposite direction before a third vehicle plowed onto the sidewalk behind her. Two more men, two more guns, leaped out.

Trapped.

Oh, God, they had her penned in. Looking desperately around, she confirmed that there was no way out. She was armed herself, with multiple weapons, including a switchblade in her pocket. Her own gun pendant was zipped inside her coat. Even if she could get it out in time, it held a single shot. There were seven, no, eight, of them now, to her one.

"Beth McAlister," one of the men who'd been in the first car yelled. In English. Her last remaining doubt was thus erased: they knew—kinda, sorta—who she was. Although if they were calling out her name, they must be checking for a reaction, which meant they must have at least a sliver of doubt.

"*Nyet,*" she cried, whipping back around to face the man who had spoken, telling him in her next breath that he had the wrong person. "*U tebya nepravil'nyy chelovek!*"

Fat chance that was going to work.

"It's her all right," one of the others shouted. Their voices were American. CIA kill team? No time to speculate. The man who'd yelled her name was already in firing stance.

His weapon was a Glock 22 with a suppressor. The suppressor told her that he was a pro, and that he didn't want obvious gunfire that must immediately bring the Russians, the police, the FSB, hotfooting it to the scene.

He aimed at her chest. Her widening eyes zeroed in on his gloved finger as it tightened on the trigger.

In a microsecond of comprehension, she understood that they meant to kill her and whisk her body away in the van.

She went cold, professional, fearless. Her goal was to survive, to escape.

Her hand shot for her pocket, for her knife.

He pulled the trigger. The mouth of the pistol jerked.

She did the only thing she could do: leaped toward him as he fired, diving low, flying under the bullet. Her single thought was to take him out, run away.

Pfft: a deadly whisper more galvanizing than the loudest scream passed over her back.

Jarring impact: her shoulder with his knees. He yelled as she hit him, took him to the ground.

Pfft. Pfft. Pfft. Pfft. Pfft.

An explosion of bullets, of men yelling, of screams and the sounds of people fleeing as she scrambled up his stunned-inert body.

The man beneath her recovered before she could incapacitate him, cursed, bucked, fought.

She drove her knife into his shooting arm even as he tried to get his gun between them, sliced savagely sideways, took out his biceps.

He screamed. His gun somersaulted away.

Pfft. Pfft. Pfft. Pfft. Pfft.

Cringing in expectation of taking a bullet to the back at any second, she chopped her would-be murderer in the throat with the side of her hand. In her peripheral vision, she saw her attackers either fall bleeding to the ground or take cover, saw their weapons turning not on her but on—

"Sylvia."

Oh, God, she knew that voice: *Mickey.*

Snatching her knife out of the now-unconscious man she straddled, Bianca swiped the blade across his coat to clean it and leaped to her feet. Instantly she found her wrist being grabbed and her person being hauled along behind Mickey, in a long gray overcoat and, yes, the Russian earflap hat she'd seen reflected in the window, as he bolted past the Lada.

"*Come on,*" he barked as she registered his presence with a shocked glance, as people scattered screaming around them, as she instinctively looked back.

Tradecraft had her registering five attackers down, three unaccounted for.

Three too many.

"*Move your ass.*" He snapped shots off behind them as she got with the program and they ran for their lives.

Pfft. Pfft. Pfft. Pfft.

His weapon was sound suppressed, too.

Pfft. Pfft. Smack. Smack. Smack.

Ah, there the survivors were: the smacks were return fire hitting the Lada.

"What are you doing here?" Bianca gasped it out as she

raced beside him to the intersection where she'd seen the taxi, closing her knife and dropping it back into her pocket as she went.

"Vacation."

Despite everything, that response almost made her smile.

He also pocketed his gun, the better to blend in, she knew. Dozens of others fled the violence as well so that the two of them were absorbed into the midst of the panicking crowd. At the intersection she let him steer her to the right past a few more startled pedestrians and ran with him down a block that was less trafficked than the busy thoroughfare they'd left behind.

Sirens sounded in the distance. A few people started to run toward, rather than away, from the scene.

Mickey pulled her after him into a cobblestoned alley. Snow fell heavily now, hitting her face like wet, cold kisses, limiting her vision as well as, hopefully, the vision of anyone who might be giving chase. The ancient stones were slick beneath her feet. She slipped and slid in shoes that were never meant for a race over such a surface as they dashed down the alley. His grip shifted so that he was holding her hand, glove to glove, steadying her as they went. Their pace didn't slacken as they turned down a second alley and then a third. He seemed to know where he was going: the alleys grew more deserted and narrower and darker with every turn.

Until headlights appeared at the mouth of the alley they were in, she'd been thinking they'd shaken off any possible pursuit. But the headlights moving slowly toward them, bright in the darkness, raking the cobblestones and the uneven brick walls of the buildings on either side, got her heart thundering again: were these her attackers, or at least what was left of them, on the move and hunting for them?

The possibility made her stomach knot and her mouth go dry.

She tugged urgently on their joined hands. "Car's coming. We need to get off the street."

"I see it."

He whisked her around a corner and then jerked her into a recessed doorway so that whoever was in the car wouldn't see them if they should look down this passage as they drove past. As she came up against him, chest to chest, he drew his gun and held it down to his side in readiness.

Until then, she hadn't even questioned her blind trust in going with him. But huddled close to him in that small space, leaning against him as her heart pounded and she worked to catch her breath, she started to think. Forget that he had a gun in his hand and wasn't pointing it at her. Forget the comfort of his arm around her and the solid strength of him against her. Forget the fact that she was attracted to him and that the electrical charge between them was strong enough to generate heat even in this icy weather. Forget too that she liked him, and that, for a few brief moments once, she'd thought she'd felt even more.

Remember that this was the second time that he'd shown up where she was and she'd wound up nearly getting shot.

"That was a CIA kill team," she said. She was still wired from all the adrenaline, still breathing raggedly from their run, and her voice was fierce. "What, did you bring them? Are they with you?"

He looked down at her. His face was lean and handsome, his mouth hard. It was so dark that she could barely read his expression, but she was ready to swear that the surprise in his eyes was genuine.

"No." It was a forceful denial. His arm that was around her dropped away. She got the impression that he'd only then realized where it was. "I just saved your life back there, in case you missed that."

"Thanks, but I had it handled." Maybe. Good as she was, the numbers had been eight on one. And she wasn't bulletproof. She might not have survived.

He snorted. "Like hell you did."

"I took that guy down. I had a decent chance."

"You would have been shot."

They both shut up as the headlights reached the entrance to the alley they were in. As the car drove slowly past, Bianca saw that it was a white van. *The* white van? It seemed likely.

"Shit," he said, confirming her opinion.

"You have to be with them. It's too much of a coincidence otherwise. They were there in Macau, too." She started to step down, out of the doorway, with getting away from him the next item on her agenda. Now that the van was gone, she could. *I'm out of here* was on the tip of her tongue when she saw headlights at the very far end of the alley they were in: another car, coming slowly but surely toward them.

"Damn it," she said, shrinking back.

"Damn it's not good." He looked out, saw what she'd seen, drew back.

"They're searching for us," she said.

"Looks like it. The good news is, there can't be many of them left. If it is the CIA, they'll search in a grid. It's what they do. We need to stay where we are until they've passed. They're not likely to spot us here. As long as they don't, we'll be fine."

"Oh, as long as." Her tone was caustic, but she stayed put: he was right.

"Just to test your theory, if I was with them, what's stopping me from flagging them down right now and handing you over?"

"Besides the fact that I'd kill you before you could? I guess not much."

"Beautiful, I've been watching you in action. A killer you're not."

Her gaze collided with his. "Try me."

"That guy back there tried to blow you away. You slit his arm, not his throat."

"Maybe I'm just choosy about who I'm willing to risk a murder rap for."

"Yeah." His tone was dry. "Which brings us to the question, what the hell did you do to get a CIA kill team after you?"

He didn't deny that there was a CIA kill team hunting her, didn't even question it, which spoke volumes. Bottom line: he knew it was true. His gun was out; her pitiful excuse for one was buried deep in zipped-up goose down. Reaching for the knife in her pocket, she took a step back from him and found herself up against the unyielding stone of the embrasure. He was right: she would have a hard time making herself kill him. But she could cut him in places that would definitely slow him down.

She said, "You're with them. You have to be."

"I fucking *shot* them. How with them could I be?"

"You work for Durand. For Interpol."

"That's not the CIA."

"They cooperate."

"I don't."

"How do I know that?"

"For starters, because I'm hiding in this doorway with you."

Good point. Given that, she couldn't quite figure out what his angle was.

She took a shot in the dark. "Think I don't know a good cop, bad cop routine when I see one?"

He snorted. As a response, it was spontaneous, genuine, reassuring. "Think about it. I've had lots of chances. Have I tried to kill you yet?"

Hmm. Okay, then. Maybe she accepted that.

"You've tried to arrest me. Multiple times. Case in point, you handcuffed me to a rail."

"Are you still harping on that? You threw me overboard. Did you know that those waters are notorious for being shark-infested? And, just to refresh your memory, you hit me over the head with something and knocked me out last time we met."

"I didn't."

"Oh, I'm sorry, your friend did. Not very nice, that."

"I hope you woke up with the mother of all headaches."

"I did."

"Good."

"Just to set your mind at rest, I'm willing to let bygones be bygones."

"Big of you."

"At this point, I'd say we're pretty much even. How about we agree to call a truce until we get you out of this?"

She made a scoffing sound. "Is that supposed to make me think you're on my side now?"

"I am on your side, beautiful. My job is to bring in Thayer, not you. You just keep getting in my way. You I'd actually like to keep alive. So why don't you try trusting me? Given all this—" his gesture encompassed their surroundings "—you could do worse."

Her eyes narrowed at him. Darkness obscured the subtle nuances of his expression, but he *sounded* sincere.

Her chest grew tight. Her pulse took on a frantic rhythm.

She was at a crossroads. One that was literally life or death.

She could abandon the robbery, throw in her lot with him and trust him to help keep her safe.

Which maybe she would be—for now.

But not forever.

They—whichever *they* got to her first—would come for her.

Even if they didn't, even if he was as good as his word and as good as he seemed to think he was and managed to help keep her safe, if she chose him her life as she knew it would be over.

She thought of Savannah, of Evie and Hay, of her *life*.

And then she thought, *no. I'm not going to just give up.*

I've come too far. I'm too close.

If she could get rid of him, nothing had to change. She could do what she'd come there to do, get out and *go home*.

The thing was, there was no way he could know about the Pushkin, about the robbery she had planned. If he was telling the truth and he wasn't working with the CIA, he actually knew nothing that mattered about her. He didn't know what she was. And even the CIA didn't know who she was. And she was going to do her best to make sure it stayed that way.

She was going all in, shooting the moon.

Keeping her secrets was the only way she not only survived, but got her life back.

First order of business: ditch him. Only she had to do it carefully and with sufficient planning, because if things were going to work out the way she hoped he needed to stay ditched.

He'd found her twice now. She needed to make sure it didn't happen again.

In his classic *Art of War*, Sun Tzu had said it best: *All warfare is based on deception. Hence, when we are able to attack, we must seem unable; when using our forces, we must appear inactive; when we are near, we must make the enemy believe we are far away; when far away, we must make him believe we are near.*

This was war.

28

"How about this?" Bianca was careful to make her response sound ever so slightly grudging. "I'll try trusting you, and we'll see how it goes."

"Fair enough. You want to impress me with your commitment to our new alliance, you could start by putting the knife away."

She hadn't realized that he was aware she was holding it. It was megadark, and she pretty much had the thing palmed.

"Fine." She pocketed it, held up her empty hand, wiggled her fingers at him. It was a silent, *see?*

"I'd reciprocate with my gun just to demonstrate goodwill, but I'm thinking I might need it to shoot somebody with in case our friends spot us."

She grimaced agreement. Then, because the thought made her uneasy, she leaned a little sideways and peered out. The headlights were still coming. Slow and sure, still some distance away.

She shivered. Her heart beat faster. Which, given her recent near-death experience, was only to be expected. Probably she'd been traumatized.

She said, "Maybe we should make a run for it. While we can."

"They're not likely to see us in here. We're out of the alley, in the dark. They'll be looking ahead, into the light." He frowned down at her. "You weren't hurt back there, were you?"

"No." He was right, she decided. Running for it posed the

greater risk. Now that the die was cast and her decision was made, she was beginning to get her act together, to plan. First things first: taking a deep breath, she unwound her scarf and unzipped her coat.

"You were following me," she said. There was accusation in her tone. What she wanted was to gather as much information about what he knew as she could.

"I was," he agreed, watching with interest as she slid out of her coat and thrust her arms into the sleeves, yanking them wrong side out. The brown coat reversed to blue. "Good God, do all your clothes do that?"

"Not all of them." If he read something suggestive into her words, whose fault was that? She slipped into her now-blue coat, zipped it up, stuffed her scarf into the pocket. "The question is, how did you know I was in Moscow? Were you looking for Mason?"

"Finding people is part of what I do."

He was being evasive. She knew it when she heard it.

"What's the other part?"

"Different things." He smiled at her, a quick smile with a dazzling amount of charm that she strongly suspected was calculated to, um, dazzle her. With what end game? Cajoling her into giving up Mason, if she were to hazard a guess. "I'm not trying to be obtuse. I don't actually work for Interpol, you know. I'm a contractor. I work for whoever will pay me, government agencies mostly."

"Like the CIA?"

"Not lately."

"That's reassuring." Her voice was dry.

"I'm trying to build trust here. I could have just said *no*, you know." That smile again, a flash of white teeth in the darkness. "Your turn. Tell me something about you."

She wanted to tell him many things, chief among which was that she was never, ever, ever going to help him catch

Mason, so he might as well give it up, but headlights shining past the doorway distracted her, made her stiffen and catch her breath.

"Ah," he said. "Here they come."

He pulled her against him, wrapped an arm around her and pushed her back into the corner. His back was turned to the alley. He held his gun down at his side. Bianca grabbed on to the front of his coat and ducked her head against his chest. His coat was dark gray. His hat was black. From the alley he should look like just one more shadow among many. What they had to guard against was having their faces reflect the light as the car passed.

He was tall enough and wide enough to make a really effective wall, as she had discovered before.

He smelled of soap and snow.

They were in the far corner closest to the direction from which the car was coming. She could see the light as it hit the embrasure's opposite wall. For a moment the light grew brighter, covered more of the wall, and she tensed.

Then the light was gone. As darkness enshrouded them once more, she heard the slushy sound of wheels rolling over wet pavement.

They waited. One minute. Two.

"Let's get out of here," he said.

That's when she knew for sure the car was gone.

She lifted her head, let out a breath and let him pull her out into the alley.

His hand was wrapped around hers. She didn't resist, holding his hand as they walked quickly back the way they had come, because the van and the car were going the other way.

"Where to?" she asked, trying not to sound as wary as she felt. She was almost 100 percent sure he wasn't delivering her to the CIA, but suspicion had been drummed into her from an early age and, anyway, there were other unpleasant things he could have in mind, like locking her up somewhere and throwing away the key until she told him what he wanted to know, as he'd threatened to do before.

You pays your money and you takes your chances.

"My hotel is right around the corner," he said. "I suggest we go there, unless you have a better idea. It'll get us off the street, give us a chance to figure some things out."

"All right," she said, as inspiration dawned.

Careful of the slippery stones, wanting to bend her head against the cold and swirling snow but afraid to look down lest she miss another vehicle on the hunt, or a search party on foot, or danger of any description heading their way, she kept pace with him.

The hotel he took her to was in an old brick building near the river. They went in a side door, and, by silent, mutual, agreement, took the stairs to the fourth floor. The purpose, of course, was to avoid surveillance cameras in the elevators. They kept their heads ducked for the same purpose when they emerged into the fourth-floor hallway. When they reached his room, she noted the bit of thread that fell to the carpet when the door opened—positioned between jamb and door, it was a tell that would alert him if anyone had entered the room while he was gone—the clothes draped over the mirror to thwart any camera that might be filming through it, the fact that the first thing he did was turn on the TV to drown out their conversation in case the room was bugged.

Classic tradecraft, and she approved of it.

He'd left the lights on, the better, she guessed, to make any observers on the street who might be interested think he was inside the room when he was not.

"Who *are* you?" she asked when he came back to her after turning on the TV. The room was warm, and her cheeks tingled slightly as they thawed. She had little doubt that they, and the tip of her nose, were rosy red. A sweeping glance to ensure that they were alone had reassured her that they were. Also, that the room was clean, a little threadbare, nothing special. Earth tones everywhere. Double bed, sloppily made. A pair of tub chairs with a small round table between them in front of closed, patterned drapes. A console table against the wall she'd entered through that served as a mini-kitchen with coffee maker, foam cups, packets of mixes that, added to water, equaled beverages, and a small refrigerator. A door led to a private bathroom. The door was open and she could see inside: ordinary and empty.

"My name's Colin Rogan. Coat?" He gestured at hers. She slipped out of it and handed it to him, reluctantly removing her gloves and tucking them in the pocket before she did so. She hated the idea of having bare hands and leaving fingerprints, but then she could always be careful and wipe the room down before she left. She kept her purse.

His gaze swept her, touching on her sure-to-be-disheveled wig, her cream-colored crewneck sweater, her jeans. As she did what she could to tidy her faux hair, he took off his hat and coat and stowed the garments in the small closet. Instead of having hat head, as one might have expected given the close confines of the *ushanka*, his black hair had succumbed to what was apparently a tendency to curl. He was wearing jeans and an untucked blue button-up shirt, and he looked hot.

She wouldn't have been human if she hadn't noticed. Not that it made a particle of difference to anything.

"And you are?" he prompted as he turned back to her. "Real name now, mind."

"Beth," she said. The man who'd tried to shoot her had yelled Beth McAlister at her in the street, and she was fairly certain that Colin—whether or not that was his real name, it suited him much better than Mickey—had heard him. Therefore, in the interests of truth and trust and all that good stuff, Beth she was. "Beth McAlister."

The flicker in his eyes told her that he had, indeed, heard that her name was Beth. She'd scored a point. Yay, team truth and trust.

"Sit down. Can I get you something to drink?" He moved over to the mini-kitchen and rifled through the packets as she sat down in one of the tub chairs. They were gold, with a nubby texture. "I've got coffee, tea, hot chocolate—or booze. Lots of booze. The minibar is surprisingly well-stocked."

"Coffee, please." She watched him put the coffee on. "When I asked who you are, I wasn't asking about your name, although that was going to come up. What I meant was, what alphabet agency? If you're really not CIA."

He shot her a glance over his shoulder. "None."

"I know spooks. And you're a spook."

"Former." He finished with the coffee maker, came to stand over her. He was tall, broad-shouldered, leanly muscular, very fit. She knew firsthand how good he was at martial arts. A worthy opponent—almost. "MI6. I left it a while back to start my own company. What about you? Spook? Former spook?"

She gave a little shrug. "Nope."

"You're better than well-trained. You're a pro, one of the best I've seen."

"Thank you."

"So—Thayer?"

"Among others."

"Is he here in Moscow?"

She gave him a long look. "If this is some kind of quid pro quo, where I give you Mason in return for your protection, you can forget it."

"I didn't say that."

"Good. Because I'm not talking about him."

"Fine. Let's circle back around to an earlier topic of conversation. What the hell did you do to get an agency kill team on your tail?"

Well, see, I was born. "I guess they don't like the company I keep."

He folded his arms over his chest. "They wouldn't be coming after you only because you work for Thayer. And that doesn't explain the Darjeeling Brothers' contract. I assume you know there's a million-dollar price tag on your head."

Her instinct was to deny it. But he obviously knew.

"I can see you do," he said. The smell of coffee was strong now. He turned away to pour them both a cup. When he came back and handed her hers, she accepted it, wrapped her fingers around the foam and took a sip. The brew was on the bitter side, but it was steaming hot, strong and black, which was how she drank her coffee: no sugar, no milk.

"Could I get some sugar?" she said. "Just one packet will do."

"Sure." Setting his cup on the table, he turned away to get the sweetener.

Quick as a cat, Bianca stretched her wrist over his cup. Prying up her watch face with a fingernail, being careful not to depress the windup mechanism so as not to release the contents as an aerosol, she poured the small pool of clear liquid contained in the watch case into his coffee. She gave the steaming brew a quick stir with her pinkie, wincing at how hot it was. Then she closed the watch face and wiped her pinkie on her jeans.

"Sweet 'n Low do?" He turned back around with a pink packet dangling from his fingers.

"Perfect," Bianca said. It was clear he'd seen nothing. He brought the packet to her, she poured it into her coffee, stirred it with the little plastic stir stick he also brought her and went back to sipping the now repulsively sweet liquid. "Thank you."

Colin picked up his cup, stood in front of her again and drank. He, too, seemed to prefer his coffee black. He didn't appear to notice anything wrong with the taste, and she heaved an inner sigh of relief: SiuSiu had assured her no one would. The liquid was a custom-mixed, souped-up form of Special K, ketamine, a knockout drug that in its unaltered iteration was known as a date rape drug. He was a big guy, and he was ingesting it a little at a time, but, working off the specifications that SiuSiu had given her, her best guess was that he had something less than fifteen minutes to remain standing upright. After that, he would sleep like a baby for up to twenty-four hours.

And she would go rob the Pushkin, hand off the booty to Mason and go home.

He said, "When I found out that both the CIA and somebody willing to pay a million dollars to make it happen wanted you dead, my first thought was that Thayer must have turned you into an assassin like himself. But clearly that's not it. To my knowledge there's only a short list of things that anybody can do to get those kind of people that pissed off—traitor, drug kingpin, human trafficker—so I repeat, what did you do?"

"You wouldn't believe me if I told you," Bianca said. She was deriving considerably more enjoyment from the exchange than she had been a few minutes ago. She wondered when the realization would hit him that he'd been drugged—or if it would.

"Try me."

She sipped her coffee, smiling at him over the rim as he followed suit. "I have no clue."

His brows snapped together. He lowered his cup. "Bullshit. You know."

Keep him engaged—and drinking. "If I had to guess, I'd say it had something to do with the two hundred million we tried to steal from Prince al Khalifa in Bahrain, because as far as I know nobody ever wanted to kill me before then, but that's just a guess."

His lips compressed. "What do you mean, tried to? You got away with it. At least, I assume that if Thayer faked burning up with the money, the money survived too."

Same conclusion she'd reached. Not that that was anything she wanted to share.

"What I want to know is how you found me," she said. "In Macau. And here."

He gave a slight shrug. His coffee, she saw, was considerably reduced. But if he was feeling the drug, he gave no sign of it.

"Intelligence," he said. "Eyes on the street. A sixth sense. Lots of things go into it."

She frowned. That was too vague to be of any help at all. And vagueness, as she knew from experience, was usually employed as a means of masking the truth. In Macau, she could maybe see it. After all, she and Doc had flown in to Hong Kong, and international airports are seething nests of intelligence assets. But she'd sneaked into Russia, and in Moscow she'd kept to a limited area, and employed her very best antisurveillance tactics, which if she had to say so herself were pretty damned good.

"What's more surprising is that the CIA found you," he said. His tone and expression were suddenly thoughtful. He drank more coffee. There couldn't be much left in his cup.

"Maybe they followed you," she said. "Maybe somebody somewhere tagged you with some kind of tracking device."

She said it flippantly, because she thought it was unlikely and because she wanted to keep him talking and finishing his coffee until he started to exhibit signs of, say, collapsing in a heap.

For the briefest of moments, his gaze dropped. She realized that he was looking at her purse, which was in her lap.

"Stranger things have happened," he said, his eyes back on her face, and she thought from his tone that that was him keeping it light. Not something that in her experience of him he was known to do. "I'm more inclined to think they got a tip that you're here."

But by then a thought had hit her, and she frowned down at her purse, which, its appearance altered once again, was the same one she'd carried in Macau.

As a general rule, men did not notice women's purses. The way he'd focused on it, however briefly, struck her as being just slightly odd.

Then she remembered how he'd picked it up off the floor and searched it in Macau.

She remembered him running his hands all over it. He'd paid particular attention to the straps—

He was saying something, but she didn't even register the words. As a hideous thought blossomed like a mushroom cloud in her brain, she slid her hands along the straps, feeling for bumps or anything that didn't belong.

She found it inside the opening where one of the doubled straps was stitched around a metal hoop, which joined it to the body of the purse.

"What are you doing?" He broke off whatever he'd been talking about to say, as she picked up the little plastic stir stick from the table beside her and stuck it into the small tunnel created by the stitched together, doubled strap.

Bingo: a tiny metal tablet popped out of said tunnel into the palm of her hand.

She looked at it. She knew what it was. She looked up at him.

Consternation, alarm, guilt—for that single unguarded moment all those emotions played across his face.

They added up to a single damning word: caught.

Her fist clenched around the capsule.

"Intelligence, my ass." Shaking her clenched fist at him, she came out of the chair to get right up in his face. "You planted a tracking device on my purse."

29

"Now, hold on. You should be thanking me." Colin's hands clamped onto her shoulders, holding her away from him as, she was sure, the outrage exploding inside her blazed from her eyes. "Without it I wouldn't have been walking behind you in Moscow tonight, and I wouldn't have been able to save your ass back there."

Then he made the fatal mistake: he grinned.

Bianca never lost her temper. Never, under any circumstances.

Keep emotion out of it. It was one of the rules.

So consider this the proverbial exception:. her temper had just officially gone *boom*.

She should have known. She should have guessed. Checking for tracking devices was elemental tradecraft, and she'd never even thought of it when it came to her and him. He'd put one over on her, big-time, and he was *grinning*.

"You no good dirty rotten son of a bitch." She slugged him in the stomach, and when he gasped and fell back and bent over, she grabbed her purse and charged past him. "You tricked me. You *lied* to me. What else are you lying about, hmm? Is the CIA going to—" *come charging through the door at any minute*, was what she was going to say—but he grabbed the tail end of her sweater as she rushed toward the closet and her coat and the door and yanked her back so that she slammed into him.

"Hang on a minute, I—" was as far as he got before she

turned on him, slamming both hands into his chest, knocking him backward. "Hey!"

His legs hit the edge of the bed. He fell backward onto it.

And grabbed her arm and took her with him.

The minute she hit, he rolled on top of her, using his superior weight, doing his best to pin her down.

"Get off me!" Bristling with fury, she aimed a chop at his throat, a head butt at his nose.

He dodged both, grabbed her wrists, bent his head—and kissed her.

His lips were warm, and firm, and—there it was, the flare of heat, the surge of electricity, the attraction that she'd found it impossible to shake.

She was still mad as hell.

But color her distracted.

His kiss was hot, and slow, and deep. She kissed him back, opening her mouth to his, pulling her wrists free of his grip so that she could wrap her arms around his neck.

She kissed him and kissed him. Hungrily.

"Beth," he whispered—which should have been a wake-up call, for sure. But his hand was on her breast and his hard weight was pressing her into the mattress and he was kissing her with endless, drugging kisses that made her dizzy, that made her shivery, that made her—

"I feel weird," he said, and lifted his head and looked down at her.

Her arms were looped around his neck. Her lips were parted, she was breathing hard, and her body was making sexy little moves under his.

Their eyes met. Hers widened: she'd almost forgotten—

His eyes were black with passion, but as she watched something else came into them: a dawning realization.

"You drugged me," he said.

She didn't even have time to reply before his eyes rolled back in his head and he collapsed.

Five minutes later, after a thorough search of his room that turned up nothing of interest except ID verifying his name and giving the name of the company he worked for as Cambridge Solutions, Ltd.—something to have Doc check out when they got the chance—and a quick wipe down to take care of fingerprints and other possible evidence, she was on her way out the door. With his gun. Because you never knew when you might encounter some CIA-type really bad guys.

One last look back showed him passed out on the bed in the middle of the scene she had set: half a dozen empty minibar booze bottles on the night table and aromatic vodka splashed liberally all over him and the bed to give him that bender vibe, in case he had any confederates who might drop by to check on him before he woke up.

By the time he was coherent enough to tell anybody about their little adventure, or to come looking for her, she meant to be long gone.

Screw truth and trust. The game they were really playing was, may the best man win.

And she'd just kicked his ass.

By 8:05 the following night—Friday—Bianca was so antsy she could barely stand still. She was still at the Circus Nikulin, already five minutes behind schedule, and given that the Raspberry Pi was programmed to precise times, that was not good. The thought that Colin might wake up sooner than expected had preyed on her nerves all day. The fear that what was left of the CIA kill team—or a whole new kill team—might find her before she could vamoose was making her sweat. She needed to leave for the Pushkin—it was, after all, Robbery Night at the Museum—but she couldn't go until she had all her co-conspirators safely dispatched.

Doc and Oskar were on their way with the Raspberry Pi and Griff.

Elena and Maria were on their way with the exploding cars.

Dorottya and her dogs were about ten minutes behind them, on track to pick them up.

Sandor had done his thing with Zsa and Atila, and the snakes were loaded in their truck.

Zoltan was in his truck.

All the vehicles except the ones containing the animals had been driven to the rendezvous point by the river, where they were currently parked.

Dedi and Bela were waiting to drop her off at the museum before proceeding to the rendezvous point, where they would stay with the caravan to watch out for the animals.

Lazlo had taken his final bow and left the ring. He and Sandor were waiting with Bianca in the wings. They would be driving the animal trucks to the rendezvous point and then, when Dedi and Bela arrived, heading for the fire truck, which was stored in a rented garage, just as soon as they could get going.

So what was the hold up?

Kristof, Franz, Adam and Bence, who were supposed to ride with Lazlo and Sandor to the fire truck. The six of them, plus Dorottya, Elena and Maria, were the fake firefighters who would participate in the actual robbery. But the four young men were still in the center of the ring along with Tibor Alexandrovich. They were taking bows right and left under multiple spotlights and to thunderous applause as Tibor Alexandrovich held up each of their hands in turn like he was introducing the winner in a prizefight. Moments before they had completed their Wheel of Death tightrope act and been publicly announced as the newest act to win a place at the Circus Nikulin.

Yeah. It was shaping up to be that kind of night.

The rest of the family, who'd been informed of the audition results right before the start of the show, were almost as thrilled as the four young men. For a moment when the news broke, Bianca had feared that the lure of the circus might prove stronger than the enticement of one last, lucrative job.

"Can you believe it? Our boys," Dorottya said rapturously, and Lazlo wiped away a tear.

"They did it." Sandor hugged his brother and Dorottya.

"It is tradition," Oskar said, beaming.

Dedi said, "Ah, bah, we will talk about tradition after we get four million dollars. Tradition is fine, but it is nothing you can eat."

Fortunately for the sake of the plan, that seemed to be the family consensus.

The job was on.

By 8:47 p.m.—now seventeen minutes behind schedule—Bianca was dropped off at the museum. The Raspberry Pi was programmed to shut down the alarms connected to the display cases at precisely 9:00 and start collecting and rerouting calls at precisely 9:25. That was designed to give her half an hour to unlock the nineteen cases and set the incendiaries, with a five-minute overlap on call collection to ensure that there were no gaps in coverage. It was impossible to precisely time the emergency calls that would go out. The official ones would be instigated automatically by the security system once the fires were detected. Those automatic calls would also, almost certainly, be supplemented by calls placed by the guards and possibly even some guests on their cell phones. Bianca's best guess was that they would begin to occur at around 9:30. The fire truck would show up within three minutes of the official call being placed—it would already be nearby—and the firefighters, carrying the trunks that were now labeled "equipment" and contained the replicas, would storm the museum about two minutes after that. By then the guests would have been evacuated and the actual theft could commence. With Adam and Bence busy putting out the fire, that left eight of them to replace the treasure with the replicas. The trunks contained precise diagrams of where each piece should go. Ten minutes after arriving, they should be out of there with the treasure.

For the gala, Bianca was Shura Federov, an art critic for the online magazine *Krasivaya*. Her goal was to be extremely *un*memorable. To that end she wore her Ann wig, which was a plain brown bob, her Maggy tortoiseshell glasses, and a gray suit with a white blouse and low-heeled black shoes. Underneath the nondescript clothing was a flesh-colored, custom-made bodysuit that made her look pleasantly plump and had the advantage of allowing her easy access to what it contained. That would be the explosives and smoke grenades she would need to achieve a quick and thorough evacuation of the building.

"Dobryy vecher." She said good evening upon arriving at the door.

A woman—not a security guard—at the door nodded while barely glancing at her or her invitation before waving her in. A security guard stood nearby as she dropped her coat—a gray cloth one, not the puffer—off in the cloakroom.

The gala was in full swing, with the exhibit spread throughout the two large, hall-like rooms that opened off either side of the entryway at the front of the building. Those were rooms One and Eight. They featured The Art of Ancient Egypt and The Art of Germany and the Netherlands, respectively, so between them there was plenty of art to go around. With the entry hall, they took up the entire front of the building and formed what Bianca thought of as the Hall of Statues. The Savitsky paintings were arranged on gilded easels amid the permanent displays. The rooms were bathed in a dim golden glow from the overhead fixtures. Small spotlights highlighted the featured paintings. The buzz of conversation underlay haunting music from a violinist playing her instrument in the entry hall.

Looking both ways, Bianca estimated that about 140 guests were present of the two hundred that she knew, from Doc's hack of the event planner's files, had been invited. From what she could see, most of the guests were Russian. She recognized none of them, which was a relief because she'd harbored a terrible fear that someone—Colin, any associates that might be with him, the CIA and/or their associates—could have gotten wind of her plans and would be there, at this fixed time and place where she would show up, to take her out. But these all seemed to be ordinary people doing ordinary things. They mostly wore business attire, although here and there a cocktail dress stood out, and sipped cocktails and talked among themselves. The guests seemed to be spaced out fairly evenly among the paintings on display, with knots of people progressing from one to another in a route designed to take them from the door, down to the buffet at the far end of Room One where a line of guests filled their plates, back through the entry hall to Room Eight and out to the entry hall again.

"Khotite li vy broshurou?" One of the docents approached her to ask if she would like a brochure. The docent had about two dozen in a basket draped over her arm. Bianca accepted one.

"Spasibo." She expressed her thanks.

Moving quickly through Room One without, she hoped, seeming to do so, Bianca made a show of consulting the brochure, which listed the Savitsky paintings in the order in which they were displayed and gave their provenance. She paused several times to look at one because, after all, they were supposed to be the reason for her presence. Most of them were not precisely her cup of tea. An evil looking cubist cow made her devoutly thankful that she'd had chicken rather than beef for lunch. As she reached the three long catering tables that had been placed together at the far end of the room, she noted the floor-length white tablecloths covering each and cast a cursory glance over the platters of smoked salmon and blini and bowls of red caviar to focus on the chafing dishes full of beef Stroganoff and shashlik. Those were located on the middle table, and were kept warm by means of gas heating elements with tiny, flickering blue flames beneath the dishes. Dropping her brochure, she contrived to look beneath the tablecloth as she retrieved it. Extra Sterno fuel canisters for the chafing dishes were stored beneath the table.

When the table went up, the chafing dishes and their fuel would undoubtedly be blamed. And they would add to the fire.

For safety's sake, she'd made the explosives herself. What she wanted was a quickly flaring fire, a lot of smoke and mass evacuation. What she didn't want was anyone hurt or priceless artifacts destroyed. Place what were essentially Baggies full of gunpowder in thermoses half full of kerosene, add some wicks, light them up and, once they went off, add some smoke grenades to the subsequent confusion, and the thing was done. Later, it would be thought that a mishap with the catering tables had caused the fire.

"*Ya mogu vam pomoch?*" One of the two servers behind the buffet tables asked if she could help her, picked up a plate and indicated the food.

"*Blini, pozhaluysta,*" she said, politely requesting the blini.

The woman put two of the thin, sour-cream-and-strawberry-jam-garnished pancakes on the plate and handed it to her.

"*Spasibo,*" Bianca said, and passed on.

To the right of the long hall that was Room One, Room Two had been set up with small tables and chairs for guests who wished to sit and eat. About half the tables were occupied when Bianca entered. Room Three opened off the back of it. As she had expected, Room Three was dark except for the very minimal security lighting. With a polite smile for the single seated guest who happened to glance her way, she headed for the table closest to Room Three. She meant to sit, eat, then wander off, supposedly (if anyone should ask) in search of the ladies' room, which was an excellent catchall excuse for being caught almost anywhere you weren't supposed to be.

A glance at her watch told her that it was already 8:56. The Raspberry Pi should be in place. In case of glitches, she meant to leave it until 9:05 before moving into Room Three and starting in on the display cases.

Bianca smiled at the elderly couple occupying the table next to the one she was heading for as she moved toward them, and then glanced casually over their heads in the direction of the atrium, which had been decked out with twinkly white Christmas lights for the occasion. Her purpose was to check out the security office. If it seemed to be business as usual, she would consider that the Raspberry Pi was in place and they were all systems go.

Between the Christmas lights and the blue glow that emanated from the computer monitors, the security office was well lit enough to allow Bianca to see that there were two guards present, both seated at their desks and both apparently absorbed in whatever was happening on the monitors in front of them.

While Griff descended like Tom Cruise in *Mission Impossible* above their heads.

Suspended from his harness and the rope, the little monkey was coming down fast, flat on his stomach with his legs stretched out in front and behind and his tail curled over his back.

Dun dun dada dun dun dada—she could almost hear the *Mission Impossible* theme song playing in her head.

Bianca was in laser-focused, cool, calm professional mode, but her heart jumped when she spotted him. It was all she could do to keep from stopping dead in her tracks. If her eyes didn't widen, it wasn't because they didn't want to.

The guards never looked up. They never looked around as Griff disappeared behind them.

Staring at the security office in fear of seeing the guards leap to their feet, or cringing in anticipation of shouts erupting from them, was probably a mistake. Bianca found her table, put her plate down and cast a quick glance around to see if anyone else was looking toward the atrium. No one was.

Over the years, she'd participated in so many robberies she'd lost count. She had developed nerves of steel.

Didn't matter. The thought of Griff scuttling through that small office with two fully awake and aware security guards in it was enough to give her butterflies.

She'd timed it: it was supposed to take Griff exactly fifty-four seconds from the time he hit the security office floor to reach the computer, pull the Raspberry Pi out of the pocket Dedi had created in his vest, plug the thing into the port and hook himself up to the rope again.

It had been one minute since he'd disappeared from her view.

She couldn't stand it. She glanced toward the atrium again.

Hooked to the rope, Griff was ascending skyward like a missile in flight.

The guards still sat in front of their monitors. If they'd moved, she couldn't tell it.

Griff reached the hole in the ceiling, disappeared inside.

Deep breath.

Okay. She had to assume that the Raspberry Pi was in place. She had to assume that the guards were as oblivious as they seemed.

She had to assume they were good to go.

30

Bianca held her breath while unlocking the first display case. If anything had gone wrong with the Raspberry Pi, or Griff's installation of it, this was the moment of truth: an alarm would screech.

It didn't. There wasn't a lot of visibility in Room Three because only a quartet of low-level security lights were on, two on either side of each door. But then she didn't need much light, and actually the gloom worked to her advantage in that it kept her from being easily seen by any chance passerby. Keeping a wary eye on the open doorway, she wielded her lock pick with practiced ease. Fourteen minutes later, she had all nineteen display cases unlocked.

Restoring the lock pick to its sheath in her garter belt, she left the treasure room and slipped back into Room Two.

There were more guests at the tables than before. None of them paid attention to her reentry into the room. A glance toward the atrium at the security office confirmed that the guards still sat in front of their monitors, seemingly unaware of any problem.

It was 9:19. She had eleven minutes to set the place on fire and smoke everybody out.

As she walked back toward the buffet tables, she heard the wail of multiple sirens, faint and fading because they came from outside the museum and were heading away.

Bianca ticked another item off her mental checklist: that should be the response to the tunnel explosions.

The bodysuit had pockets that secured everything in place until it was time to put the items to use. All she had to do was wait until no one was looking, reach inside the artful draping of her blouse and grab what she needed. First up was a bag of the gunpowder mixture. Palming it, she let the contents spill out in a thin trail that led from the tablecloth of the table nearest the buffet in Room Two to the buffet itself. She kept her body between what she was doing and the rest of the assembly, and her actions remained unremarked as she walked from one room to the next.

With the bag empty, she put it in her pocket.

Her next step was placing the explosives and setting the wicks alight. It would take approximately one minute for the wicks to burn down.

She needed a distraction so that she could set the charges without being observed. She also wanted to make sure that the women behind the tables serving the food were out of the way, and that the fire spread in the direction she intended. She accomplished all three goals by the simple expedient of "accidentally" tripping a man who was approaching the dessert table—that would be the third table, the one closest to Room Two—and supplementing that with an artfully disguised shove that sent him reeling into the table with a cry of dismay.

"*Ty che blyad!*"

The far end of the table collapsed under his weight, sending man and desserts crashing to the floor.

"*Oj!*"

"*Bychit!*"

Exclaiming, the servers rushed to his aid—or to try to save the desserts. It was impossible to be sure. The four other people cruising the buffet either jumped back or gathered around the fallen.

In any case, no one was watching her.

Bianca thrust one explosive each beneath the chafing dishes, making sure the wicks came into contact with the flame. She didn't fear shrapnel, because she had specifically chosen to pack the charges in thermoses that were made of heavy Styrofoam to avoid it.

Then she hurried over to help with the downed man, who struggled to sit up amid a welter of curses and apologies.

She'd no sooner crouched beside him than the explosives went off, one right after the other.

Boom! Boom!

The table erupted in a sheet of flame that instantly stretched from one end to the other and soared toward the ceiling. It raced across the collapsed dessert table, found the trail of explosive powder, burned wildly toward Room Two and set the first table in that room alight. Those nearest the blaze—the fallen man, the servers, everyone who'd gathered to help or gawk, the diners in Room Two—screamed, jumped up, ran. Screaming herself and skittering backward just for the look of it, Bianca surreptitiously rolled two smoke grenades into the conflagration.

Dense black smoke began to billow up and out, filling the rooms, creating total panic. A crescendo of screams filled the air as people dashed for the exit.

The building's fire alarm went off. The deafening clang of it hurt Bianca's ears.

Then the Sterno fuel canisters blew: *Bang! Bang! Bang! Bang! Bang! Bang!*

The sharp, loud explosions coming in rapid succession sounded like gunfire. The blaze crackled and roared. The smoke was intense.

Two security guards rushing toward the blaze with fire extinguishers did a quick one-eighty when the canisters went off and headed away from the fire, shooing patrons out before them.

"Vsekh! Vsekh!" They urged everyone out.

Bianca fell back toward Room Three and the clearer air there while everyone else disappeared into the smoke as they bolted for the door. She coughed a little—the smoke was thick—but she wasn't worried about it or about getting trapped in a burning building: the explosives were designed to cause an intense, fiery eruption, create a lot of smoke and then quickly burn out.

The shriek of a close-at-hand siren pierced the screams of the fleeing patrons and the rush and pop of the fire.

A moment later, shouts from men heading in her direction told her that the cavalry had arrived.

"Ochistit zdaniye!"

"Ustupat dorogu!"

Orders came to clear the building and to make way. Bianca knew those voices: Lazlo and Sandor.

A double line of helmeted, masked firefighters in their red and black uniforms thundered toward her. One line pulled a big hose with them. The other bore three equipment trunks.

Two of the hose bearers stopped and prepared to douse the fire.

The rooms were empty of everyone except their gang. Bianca joined the others who ran toward Room Three, and quickly donned the uniform Lazlo tossed to her. She left her mask hanging around her neck for the moment; she would need it for only cover on the way out. The others had lowered their masks as well, to make it easier to work.

"Hurry, hurry!" Dorottya's voice was sharp with anxiety.

Her urgency reflected the reality that they all knew: if they got caught, years in a Russian prison was the least of what they faced.

They worked in teams: Lazlo and Dorottya; Kristof and Maria; Franz and Elena; Bianca and Sandor.

One removed the treasure, storing it the trunk, while the

other replaced each item with its replica. Exchanging all 101 pieces took precisely eight minutes, thirty-nine seconds. Bianca timed it with quick glances at her watch.

The moment the last artifact had been replaced, as the rest of the team closed up the trunks, Bianca locked the display cases.

It was then, as she reached the last display case, that she saw it: the Trojan sauceboat, which was so important that it merited its own individual display case in the center of the room, had toppled from its pedestal. It lay on its side on the bottom of the case.

One of its gold-painted handles had broken off, clearly revealing its plebian terra-cotta soul.

Bianca's stomach dropped to her toes.

"Oh, no!" Her dismayed reaction had everyone looking around.

"What is it?"

"Oh my God!"

"Franz, that was yours to do! You clumsy—"

Doing her best to tune out the peanut gallery, Bianca reached inside the case and picked up the two pieces. There was no doing anything about it: the handle was no longer attached. And, yes, someone was going to notice. If not the minute they walked back into the museum, soon afterward. They needed ten hours to get out of Russia. The chances that they were going to get them just plummeted.

"What can we do?"

"Glue it."

"We have no glue!"

"And no time! Leave it! We must go."

Bianca had an epiphany: they did have glue—kind of. Carefully setting the two pieces inside the display case, she reached up under her Ann wig, tore two pieces of double-sided wig tape used to secure the thing from the net base and applied them to the sauceboat. Then, praying hard, she stuck the handle back on.

Miracle of miracles, it held.

Not forever. Probably not for long. But hopefully for long enough.

Oh, so carefully, she set the sauceboat back on its pedestal and locked the case.

"Let's go," she told the others, who were watching wide-eyed.

They did, pelting toward the entrance, picking up Adam and Bence on the way. The fire was out. The black burned remnants of the buffet and the one small dining table made a soggy, stinking mess. Smoke still filled the building, rolling out the door in a thick gray cloud.

They burst out through that cloud into the cold, crisp night to discover that quite a crowd had gathered.

"Vam nuzhno, chtoby dym byl chistym!" Lazlo lifted his mask slightly to yell to the crowd that they needed to let the smoke clear as the "firefighters" dashed down the stairs.

The fire truck, boxy and red, waited at the foot of the stairs.

They loaded the trunks, piled on and were away.

Ten nail-biting hours later, they were at a small, under-the-radar airfield in a remote part of northern Belarus. The terrain was hilly, which served to hide the airport because it was nestled in a depression circled by the low hills. Unless someone was specifically looking for it, they were unlikely to find it. Unless they knew what it was, what they would see was a long, low corrugated metal warehouse with a narrow road running beside it. The circus caravan was parked inside the warehouse: it would be dismantled, sold off, disposed of.

Two planes idled on that road, which was actually a single, snow-dusted runway. The planes were discards from the Russian military. Now they were used by smugglers, primarily of guns but also of people and other things. The pilots, like-wise, had formerly been Russian military. But the military had been downsized, they had lost their jobs and they had families to feed. They hired out themselves and their planes to anyone who could pay them. With Mason, Bianca had used them before, and she'd made the arrangements for them to be waiting for them today.

It was 8:00 a.m. Saturday, a cold gray morning that threat-ened imminent snow. The smell of airplane fuel hung in the air. Standing beside the first plane in line, Dorottya grabbed Bianca and hugged her goodbye. She, Lazlo, and Dedi were the last to board the plane. The rest of the family, plus the dogs, Zoltan and Griff, were already inside. Their desti-nation was Spain: they were headed to a remote ranch in Andalucia where the plane could touch down without having to bother with inconveniences such as customs. They would stay there as long as they liked while they figured out how best to spend the four million dollars that Bianca had wired to their new, numbered bank account.

"Ah, Maggy, we will miss you!" Dorottya said, letting Bi-anca go. She wiped tears from her eyes. "Just like we will miss the circus. This is to say goodbye to all of our old friends, all of our old life."

"I have been thinking," Lazlo said. "That we do not have to say goodbye. Not forever. The boys and I have been talk-ing. Why cannot we have the money and the circus, too? If, in the spring, there is no word that anyone is connecting us with the robbery, we can perhaps come back. Tibor Alex-androvich told the boys he would hold their place, and—"

"Ah, bah, bite your tongue and get on the plane," Dedi in-terrupted, shoving him toward the stairs that led to the plane's open door. "Men are fools, all of them." She looked at Bianca as Lazlo, with Dorottya behind him, started up the stairs, and pointed an admonishing finger at her. "You remember that, you." Then her expression softened. "The money means a great deal. Now my great-granddaughter has a chance at a decent life, and I can go to my Maker with an easy heart."

"Not too soon, I hope," Bianca said.

Dedi, no hugger, smiled and patted Bianca's shoulder. "Another ninety years, God willing."

Bianca, no hugger herself, clasped her hand. "God willing," she echoed. "Goodbye, Dedi."

Dedi nodded, then turned and headed up the stairs.

Oskar was looking out a window. Bianca lifted a hand at him in farewell, then, as the plane's door closed behind Dedi, hurried to board the second plane that was to take her and Doc on the first stage of the journey to Berlin.

31

The sun set early in Berlin in November, and by a quarter to six that same Saturday the purple of twilight had passed on to full night. The city was ablaze with light. Its bold, avant-garde architecture created an arresting skyline against the starry black sky. Traffic was heavy as Bianca drove the rented Mercedes-Benz G-Class past the iconic Brandenburg Gate toward the Tiergarten, which was Berlin's answer to New York's Central Park. Located in the center of the city, its massive green space encompassed restaurants and playgrounds and walking trails and a zoo. It was toward the zoo that Bianca was heading: she was to meet Mason there.

She'd contacted him earlier, and he'd set the meeting for 6:15 p.m. in the parking lot next to the zoo. It would be a simple exchange. She would get out of the boxy SUV, which had the three treasure-filled trunks in the back, and Mason would get in, drive the treasure away and turn it over to whoever he needed to turn it over to. Meanwhile, she would get into the car he arrived in and drive back to Frankfurt, where she had put Doc on a commercial flight to Toronto earlier, Toronto being the first leg of his roundabout journey back to Savannah.

Bianca would board a commercial flight to Copenhagen the next morning, and from there would make her way to Savannah in the same surveillance-defeating stages.

Both she and Doc would be home on Monday.

And if Mason delivered on his promise, she would be able

to put the whole CIA kill team and Darjeeling Brothers' contract nightmare behind her and get on with her life.

She'd been on the move for nearly forty-eight hours, with only a few snatched hours of sleep. She was bone-tired and a little punchy from what she thought must be adrenaline withdrawal. But she felt good. Almost happy.

She'd done it. She'd succeeded.

The relief was indescribable.

Reaching the Tiergarten, she drove along the dark roads that wound through the forest to the zoo. In November, the zoo closed at 4:30 p.m., so only a few yellowish security lights illuminated the parking lot. It was nearly empty, maybe six cars scattered throughout, which she guessed belonged to employees of the zoo. The exchange was to take place at the elephant gate entrance. As she cruised past, she took a moment to admire its green tile roofs and stone arches. Then she proceeded, as directed, to the far left side of the parking lot and pulled into the last space.

She'd barely shoved the transmission into park before another vehicle, an older Volkswagen Passat, pulled up next to her and stopped. She looked—yes, that was Mason getting out of it. She would recognize his profile and his tall body even in silhouette, which was all she could really see of him, anywhere. He left the Passat's lights on and the engine running. She did the same with the Mercedes. The headlights stabbed into the dark swath of trees beyond the parking lot.

Getting out, she walked around the back of the car. The area was full of shadows. As Mason came toward her, she saw that, while he was walking now, he had a pronounced limp.

They met behind the Mercedes, stopped. He wore a black overcoat against the cold, but no disguise. Bianca, who was once again in her Maggy wig with a short red car coat she had acquired in Frankfurt, felt overdressed.

It was good to see him, but she didn't say that.

"You did it," he said. He wasn't smiling, didn't sound proud. Didn't sound anything. It was a simple statement of fact.

She looked at him. "Yes."

"Is it in the car?"

"In the back."

He nodded, started to walk around her, business concluded. She felt—what did she feel? Let down? Hurt? If so, she needed to get over that STAT.

"Bianca." He stopped, put a heavy hand on her shoulder, gripped it hard. That was an unusual thing for him to do. She frowned and looked around inquiringly—and was just in time to catch a glimpse of his other hand flying toward her in a quick blur of movement.

She didn't even have time to process, much less react, before she felt the sting of something—a hypodermic needle, she'd caught a glimpse of it, *my God, what's he doing?*—being plunged into her neck.

"What—" She grabbed his arm. It was too late. She felt the hot spurt of liquid into her vein and knew that he'd depressed the plunger, that he'd injected her with something. Across the parking lot she saw lights flash on in the cars she'd thought were empty, heard the thrum of engines and saw the cars come barreling her way. But the drug was fast acting. From the moment she became aware of what was happening, she could barely move. Everything started to blur. All she could see, leaning over her as he caught her collapsing body and kept her from hitting the ground, was his face. She frowned and shook her head, rejecting what she knew was true. This couldn't be happening—

"Dad?" she said. Her voice was unsteady, a squeak. Pitiful. The pain of betrayal was almost as acute as her fear.

"I had to trade you to them along with the treasure," he said, speaking rapidly. Her muscles were no longer working.

She was dizzy and knew she would soon pass out. "For Marin and Margery's safety, not just mine."

The bitter anguish she felt then was like a knife stabbing her through the heart.

Skewered by the headlights of the cars that now slammed to a halt in front of them, her ears ringing with screeching brakes and slamming doors, her terrified gaze full of dark shapes running toward her, she heard him saying something else—a quote from the Bible; she recognized it, but it made no sense.

She let it go.

Then she passed out.

The hiss sounded mechanical. The smell was some kind of strong chemical. The steady burbling sound had to be a liquid. Cold air blew over her skin.

It was the cold that woke Bianca.

Her eyelids felt heavy, like they had weights attached. Bianca forced them open.

Immediately she wished she'd kept them shut.

Through thick glass walls, she looked out into what appeared to be a laboratory. The light was whitish fluorescent, from ceiling fixtures. The walls were white, the floor black tile. Immediately in front of her were what appeared to be tall glass sculptures. Beyond them, black-topped tables held microscopes, Bunsen burners, racks of test tubes and other lab equipment, plus a microwave and small refrigerator. A CAT scan machine, a couple of long tables, two full-size upright freezers and a large centrifuge took up the far wall. A window at one end of it had the blinds drawn, but the blinds were crooked. Around the edges she could see that it was night.

Where am I?

She remembered her father, no, *Mason*, and her heart began to pound.

The glass wall she was looking through wasn't the only one. A second glass wall stood between her and the laboratory she was looking into. That glass wall separated the section of the room she was in from the laboratory.

Her head ached like someone had taken a hammer to it. It hurt to move it, but she did. The glass wall around her was curved, she saw as her head turned. She blinked stupidly through it for a moment before the true horror of her situation hit her.

I'm in a tube.

A human-size test tube, to be exact. She was being kept upright by sturdy cloth straps looped around her shoulders that held her suspended from the ceiling. Or, rather, from the lid of the tube, she discovered as she looked up. It was clear, too, and above it was a glass tank slowly filling with a cloudy liquid that bubbled and gave off vapor.

Not good.

Alarm washed over her in a wave.

Her mind was clearing. She tried to make sense of what was happening. She was in a tube, suspended upright by cloth straps beneath a tank filling with an ominous-looking liquid. Her feet—they were bare; a downward flick of her eyes told her that she was wearing only her bra and underpants—touched the ground, which was a black raised platform completely enclosed by the tube.

Bianca sucked in air, glanced quickly around.

There was no one present that she could see. She was alone in a room about the size of a basketball court. The only sounds were mechanical and liquid—and the now harsh rasp of her own breathing.

The sculptures she had looked past before weren't sculptures at all, she discovered as she examined them more closely. They were tubes just like the one she was in.

Two neat rows of human-size tubes that took up half of the room.

The other tubes were not empty.

They were full of a bubbling liquid that reminded her of clear lava lamps.

Except floating in the midst of the liquid were small shapes. *Babies.*

Bianca's heart clutched.

Dead, preserved babies with numbers affixed to the tops of the tubes they were in. The one across from her was marked with number 22. Sick with dread, Bianca looked up and down the row. There were twenty-four tubes, according to the number 24 on the last one. Twenty-four on the side she was on, too, because they were evenly matched.

Forty-eight in all.

From the position of her tube, she knew she had to be in number 44.

Bianca felt as if all the blood was draining from her head.

The Nomad Project. She was Nomad 44.

Mason had given her over to them.

Sheer terror kicked the last, enervating effects of whatever drug Mason had used on her from her system. The tank of liquid over her head suddenly took on galvanizing significance.

Her best guess was that when it was full it was going to be emptied into the tank she was in. She was going to be drowned in it, preserved.

She began to fight against the straps holding her in place.

"You shouldn't be awake." The mildly annoyed voice made her jump. It was male, it was coming to her over an intercom and the speaker was nowhere in sight. The language was American-accented English. She broke out in a cold sweat. "You weren't supposed to wake up."

"Well, I am awake. Let me out of here." Inside she might be a shaking glob of gelatin, but her voice was strong and firm. Maybe she could convince whoever this was to release her. More likely, she was going to have to break herself out. She got her arms out of the straps, which, since they had clearly been designed to hold her unconscious body in place while the liquid poured in over her rather than to restrain her conscious, fighting self as she was murdered, required no more than her grabbing on to each one in turn, pulling herself up so that she was no longer suspended from them by her body weight, and yanking her arms through. From the way the straps were affixed to the top of the tube, she thought that they were designed to be removed from the tube once she was dead, preserved and floating like the others in bubbling liquid.

The horror of it made her blood congeal. She pushed on the walls of the tube.

There was no give.

"I can't do that." He sounded genuinely apologetic. "I have my orders."

"To hell with your orders. I'm a living, breathing human being. *Let me out.*" There was a barely visible crack in the glass of her tube: a straight line, a door, she saw as she followed it down. Of course, they'd had to have some way to get her in. She would use it to get out.

She threw herself against the crack, then when nothing happened did it again and again.

"Stop that!" He sounded alarmed. "You'll bruise yourself. *There's no way out.* It won't hurt. I promise, it won't hurt."

"Fuck that! Open this door! You know you can." She pounded at the crack with her fists, honed into weapons by years of martial arts training. She kicked at it, threw her shoulder against it. The glass barely shook, showed no sign of breaking. Panic was starting to set in. A glance up told her that the tank was over halfway full and filling fast. When it was deep enough to drown her, she had no doubt that he would release it into the tube she was in. Then she was dead, she knew.

"There's no way out, I tell you. It's a voice-activated lock, and once it's activated the whole sequence is automatic. You have to know the code to open the door, and to stop the sequence, and you have to say it into the microphone in here."

She saw him then, in an elevated office at the far side of the room opposite the window. A scientist in a white lab coat, peering out at her through the long window that overlooked the lab. He had both hands pressed against the window, and his expression was one of dismay. Behind him were banks of what looked like computers and other equipment.

"So say it! Say the code into the microphone!" She attacked the tube with fresh vigor even as she screamed it at him. "Otherwise, what you're doing is murder. You're not a murderer. You don't want to be a murderer! Say the damned code!"

"I don't know it," he said. "I'm so sorry—it'll be over soon."

Glancing up, Bianca saw that the tank overhead was almost full. Fresh terror sent adrenaline torpedoing through her veins, and she threw herself against the walls of the tube, using every trick she knew to break through.

I can't believe you did this to me: she sent the pain- and rage-filled thought winging toward Mason as the knowledge that he had traded her life for his *family* burned like acid through her soul.

Then she remembered the quote from the Bible he'd whispered to her right before she'd lost consciousness.

And she knew: he'd set her up, but he'd also given her the key.

"The truth shall set you free," she screamed, as loud as she could so that it would go over the intercom and be picked up by the microphone in the office. *"The truth shall set you free."*

The tube door opened, and she leaped out.

Immediately alarms started to sound.

"Oh, no, oh, no!" the scientist cried. Then he was summoning help. "Emergency, emergency, fourth-floor lab. *Hurry.*"

Bianca didn't know what was coming, but she was pretty sure it wasn't good. From the fact that the Nomad Project was being kept inside it, she had to assume that the facility was controlled by the CIA. She had to expect a military-quality response.

Escaping by the door was out. Whatever security force they had would be coming through that.

She was unarmed. Totally weaponless.

Luckily, she was good at making do.

With alarms wailing and the scientist still yelling for help over whatever communication system he had and what she had to assume was some kind of armed response team on the way, she darted to the window, shoved the blind aside, looked out.

Four stories up. Hard ground down. A chain-link fence. A road. What looked like a river on the other side of the road.

Unfortunately, she couldn't fly. If she leaped from that window, she wasn't going to make it to the river. She was going to go splat on the ground.

Unless she slid along the power line that ran from just above the window to the pole on the other side of the fence.

The window cranked open. She tried the crank. It worked.

"Hurry, hurry, hurry," the scientist screamed. "She's trying to get away!"

Running back into the lab, Bianca yanked loose both the rubber hoses that fed gas into the Bunsen burners. They were a good length, about three feet each. Rubber was strong—and insulating. She would throw them over the power line, grab the ends, slide to the pole, climb down.

The smell of natural gas was strong as it spewed out into the room.

She could have blown the lab up easily. Spewing gas plus a piece of metal in a microwave equals big bad *boom*.

But she didn't. She just wanted to get away.

Plus there was the thought, fleeting but inexorable, that everything she wanted to know about herself might be contained in this lab. How the Nomad Project came into being, who was responsible, the identity of her biological parents—

No time to speculate. The best she could do was not destroy what was present, and make a silent promise to herself and her fellow Nomads, the babies in the tubes: *I'll be back*.

She ran for the window, cranked it open enough to get out.

She was up on the sill, balancing precariously on her toes as she hooked the doubled sections of hose over the wire, when a squad of soldiers burst into the room.

"She's there at the window! Get her, get her!" the scientist screamed.

"Stop or we'll shoot!" a soldier yelled.

Bianca's one thought was, *they won't take me again*.

Grabbing the ends of the hose, she flung herself out into the night.

The soldiers opened fire en masse.

Bullets smacked into the wall, whizzed into the darkness, passed through the spewing cloud of natural gas.

And the lab blew up with an earthshaking roar.

32

It was almost Christmas. Bianca and Doc had been back in Savannah for nearly a month. Reaching safety had involved hiding in the back of a vehicle being evacuated from the explosion and resulting raging fire at the black site in Stare Kiejkuty, Poland, where as it turned out the lab was located, then running for her life along a highway while barefoot and in her underwear until she was able (probably with the underwear's help) to flag down a man in a car. When, acting under a wrong assumption about her attitude toward casual sex that she might have helped put in his head, he stopped at a roadside hotel, she accompanied him inside, knocked him out and stole his clothes and car. After that, it was merely a matter of plugging into her contacts to acquire money and a passport and, voila, she was on her way home. If the Russians had discovered that King Priam's Treasure was missing, they were keeping it quiet. So far, Germany—assuming the treasure had ended up in Germany; her trust in Mason had taken a major dip—was keeping quiet, too. The Darjeeling Brothers' contract was no longer posted. Bianca wanted to think that it had been withdrawn, possibly as a result of the deal Mason had struck. Or maybe whoever had posted it thought she was dead, killed in the lab explosion.

Yeah, she doubted it, too.

Truly, her luck was never that good.

As far as she knew, the CIA kill team had been called off, as well. Of course, that was one of those things that she might very well only learn she was wrong about when she suddenly got shot. She was wary, afraid that she was still a huge target, that the hunt for her hadn't been called off but, rather, had gone underground.

Which would make it all the more dangerous.

But until she knew more, there wasn't a whole lot she could do. Except keep an eye out, and her fingers and toes crossed.

And live her life unless and until she couldn't anymore.

Today was a happy one. Guardian Consulting had signed a new client that morning. And she'd done some Christmas shopping over lunch.

Laden with packages, she was on her way back up to the office. Tonight they were taking some of their biggest clients to dinner at The Olde Pink House, one of Savannah's nicest restaurants, for an early Christmas celebration. In honor of that, she was wearing a red knit long-sleeved dress with a narrow black belt around the waist, black stockings and black heels. Her blond hair was brushed back from her face and tucked behind one ear.

Bottom line, she was looking *and* feeling good.

Her phone dinged to announce the arrival of a text as she stepped off the elevator. As she approached the office, it dinged again, then again, in quick succession. Bianca frowned, but her hands were too full to allow her to check her phone for messages.

She would do that as soon as her hands were free.

Shouldering through Guardian Consulting's door, she was greeted by Evie.

"You have a walk-in," Evie said, low-voiced.

Bianca looked around the reception room: no walk-in in sight.

"In your office," Evie said, and Bianca's eyebrows went up. Evie never let people inside her office when she wasn't there.

"I told him to go on in," Doc popped out of his office to

say. He waggled his eyebrows and grimaced speakingly at her behind Evie's back, but stopped as Evie turned around. "I just sent you a text. Or three."

That explained the *dings from her phone*.

Bianca felt the first niggle of concern.

"So who is it?" she asked Evie as she headed for her office.

Doc was making faces again behind Evie's back. He drew his hand across his throat in a universal kill gesture. Bianca frowned at him.

"Tower Consulting," Evie answered, opening the door to Bianca's office for her.

Smiling her thanks, Bianca walked in.

A tall man in a dark suit stood in front of the window. He turned to face her as she entered.

Bianca stopped dead. She nearly dropped every package she held.

The man smiled at her.

"Hello, Bianca," Colin said.

★ ★ ★ ★ ★

ORDER THE NEXT BOOK IN THE SERIES,
***THE FIFTH DOCTRINE*, NOW**

ACKNOWLEDGMENTS

It takes a team to publish a book, and I'm fortunate enough to have a fabulous one.

Thank you to my wonderful editor, Emily Ohanjanians, for her discerning eye and unfailing support.

Thank you to Meredith Barnes, who does such a great job with publicity.

Thank you to Margaret Marbury, who oversees an enormous operation and does it with style and grace.

Thank you to MIRA Books for all their efforts to get my stories in front of as many readers as possible.

Thank you to my agent, Robert Gottlieb, and everyone at Trident Media Group for working tirelessly on my behalf.

And finally, thank you to my readers. Where would I be without you?